Sidney Sheldon is the author of *The Other Side of Midnight, A Stranger in the Mirror, Bloodline, Rage of Angels, Master of the Game, If Tomorrow Comes, Windmills of the Gods, The Sands of Time, Memories of Midnight, The Doomsday Conspiracy, The Stars Shine Down, Nothing Lasts Forever, Morning, Noon and Night, The Best Laid Plans and Tell Me Your Dreams*, all number one international bestsellers. His first book, *The Naked Face*, was acclaimed by the *New York Times* as 'the best first mystery novel of the year'. Mr Sheldon has won a Tony Award for Broadway's *Redhead* and an Academy Award for *The Bachelor and the Bobby Soxer. Rage of Angels, Master of the Game, Windmills of the Gods* and *Memories of Midnight* have been made into highly successful television mini-series.

He has written the screenplays for twenty-three motion pictures including *Easter Parade* (with Judy Garland) and *Annie Get Your Gun*. He also created four long-running television series, including *Hart to Hart* and *I Dream of Jeannie*, which he produced. He was awarded the 1993 Prix Littéraire de Deauville, from the deauville Film Festival, and is now included in the *Guinness Book of Records* as 'The Most Translated Author'. Mr Sheldon and his wife live in Southern California and London.

For more about Sidney Sheldon, see his website at http://www.sidneysheldon.com.

SIDNEY SHELDON

THE STARS SHINE DOWN

THE
BEST LAID
PLANS

HarperCollins*Publishers*

This omnibus edition published in 2001 by
HarperCollins*Publishers*

HarperCollins*Publishers*
77-85 Fulham Palace Road,
Hammersmith, London W6 8JB

www.fireandwater.com

ISBN 0 00 764577 5

Printed and bound in Great Britain by
Mackays of Chatham plc, Chatham, Kent

The Stars Shine Down

The stars shine down
And watch us live
Our little lives
And weep for us.

MONET NODLEHS

Acknowledgements

I owe a debt of gratitude to those who were so generous with their time and expertise:

Larry Russo who led me through the arcane maze of the biggest gamblers of all – the real estate developers.

The musical mavens who invited me inside their private world – Mona Gollabeck, John Lill, Zubin Mehta, Dudley Moore, André Previn, and the Trustees of The Leonard Bernstein Estate.

I wish also to express my appreciation to the citizens of Glace Bay for their warm hospitality. I hope they will forgive me for the few dramatic licences I felt it necessary to take.

The expertise in the book belongs to those listed above. Any errors are mine.

THE AUTHOR

This one is for Morton Janklow,
A Man for All Seasons

Book One

1

Thursday, September 10, 1992
8:00 p.m.

The 727 was lost in a sea of cumulus clouds that tossed the plane around like a giant silver feather. The pilot's worried voice came over the speaker.

'Is your seat belt fastened, Miss Cameron?'

There was no response.

'Miss Cameron . . . Miss Cameron . . .'

She was shaken out of a deep reverie. 'Yes.' Her thoughts had been drifting to happier times, happier places.

'Are you all right? We should be out of this storm soon.'

'I'm fine, Roger.'

Maybe we'll get lucky and crash, Lara Cameron thought. It would be a fitting end. Somewhere, somehow, it had all gone wrong. *It's the Fates*, Lara thought. *You can't fight the Fates*. In the past year her life had spun wildly out of control. She was in danger of losing everything. *At least nothing else can go wrong*, she thought wryly. *There is nothing else*.

The door of the cockpit opened and the pilot came into the cabin. He paused for a moment to admire his passenger. The woman was beautiful, with shiny black hair swept up in a crown, a flawless complexion, intelligent eyes, cat-grey. She had changed clothes after they had taken off from Reno, and she was wearing a white, off-the-shoulder Scaasi evening gown that accented a slender, seductive figure. Around her throat was a diamond and ruby necklace. *How can she look so damn calm with her world collapsing around her?* he wondered. The newspapers had been mercilessly attacking her for the past month.

'Is the phone working yet, Roger?'

'I'm afraid not, Miss Cameron. There's a lot of interference because of the storm. We're going to be about an hour late getting into La Guardia. I'm sorry.'

I'm going to be late for my birthday party, Lara thought. *Everyone is going to be there. Two hundred guests, including the Vice President of the United States, the Governor of New York, the Mayor, Hollywood celebrities, famous athletes, and financiers from half a dozen countries.* She had approved the guest list herself.

She could visualize the Grand Ballroom of the Cameron Plaza, where the party was being held. Baccarat crystal chandeliers would hang from the ceiling, prisms of light reflecting a dazzling diamond-like brilliance. There would be place settings for two hundred guests, at twenty tables. The finest linens, china, silver and stemware would adorn each place setting, and in the centre of each table would be a floral display of white orchids mixed with white freesias.

Bar service would have been set up at both ends of the large reception hall outside. In the middle of the hall would be a long buffet with an ice carving of a swan, and surrounding it, Beluga caviar, gravlax, shrimps, lobster and crab, while buckets of champagne were being iced. A ten-tier birthday cake would be in the kitchen waiting. Waiters, maître d's and security guards would all be in position by now.

In the ballroom, a society orchestra would be on the bandstand, ready to tempt the guests to dance the night away in celebration of her fortieth birthday. Everything would be in readiness.

The dinner was going to be delicious. She had chosen the menu herself. Foie gras to begin with, followed by a cream of mushroom soup under a delicate crust, fillets of John Dory, and then the main course: Lamb with rosemary and pommes soufflées with French beans and a mesclun salad with hazelnut oil. Cheese and grapes would be next, followed by the birthday cake and coffee.

It was going to be a spectacular party. She would hold her head high, and face her guests as though nothing were wrong. She was Lara Cameron.

When the private jet finally landed at La Guardia, it was an hour and a half late.

Lara turned to the pilot. 'We'll be flying back to Reno later tonight, Roger.'

'I'll be here, Miss Cameron.'

Her limousine and driver were waiting for her at the ramp.

'I was getting worried about you, Miss Cameron.'

'We ran into some weather, Max. Let's get to the Plaza as fast as possible.'

'Yes, ma'am.'

Lara reached for the car phone and dialled Jerry Townsend's number. He had made all the arrangements for the party. Lara wanted to make sure that her guests were being looked after. There was no answer. *He's probably in the ballroom*, Lara thought.

'Hurry, Max.'

'Yes, Miss Cameron.'

The sight of the huge Cameron Plaza Hotel never failed to give Lara a glow of satisfaction at what she had created, but on this evening, she was in too much of a hurry to think about it. Everyone would be waiting for her in the Grand Ballroom.

She pushed through the revolving door and hurried across the large spectacular lobby. Carlos, the assistant manager, saw her and came running to her side.

'Miss Cameron . . .'

'Later,' Lara said. She kept walking. She reached the closed door of the Grand Ballroom and stopped to take a deep breath. *I'm ready to face them*, Lara thought. She flung open the door, a smile on her face, and stopped in shock. The room was in total darkness. Were they planning some kind of surprise? She reached for the switch behind the door and flicked it up. The huge room was flooded with incandescent light. There was no one there. Not one single person. Lara stood there, stunned.

What in the world could have happened to two hundred guests? The invitations had read eight o'clock. It was now almost ten o'clock. How could that many people disappear into thin air? It was eerie. She looked around the enormous empty ballroom and shivered. Last year, at her birthday party, this same room had been filled with her friends, filled with music and laughter. She remembered that day so well . . .

2

One year earlier, Lara Cameron's appointment schedule for the day had been routine.

September 10, 1991

 5:00 a.m. Workout with trainer

 7:00 a.m. Appearance on 'Good Morning America'

 7:45 a.m. Meeting with Japanese bankers

 9:30 a.m. Jerry Townsend

 10:30 a.m. Executive Planning Committee

 11:00 a.m. Faxes, overseas calls, mail

 11:30 a.m. Construction meeting

 12:30 p.m. S & L meeting

 1:00 p.m. Lunch – *Fortune* Magazine Interview – Hugh Thompson

 2:30 p.m. Metropolitan Union bankers

 4:00 p.m. Zoning Commission

5:00 p.m.	Meeting with Mayor – Gracie Mansion
6:15 p.m.	Architects meeting
6:30 p.m.	Housing Commission
7:30 p.m.	Cocktails with Dallas Investment Group
8:00 p.m.	Birthday party at Grand Ballroom – Cameron Plaza

She had been in her workout clothes impatiently waiting when Ken, her trainer, arrived.

'You're late.'

'Sorry, Miss Cameron. My alarm didn't go off and . . .'

'I have a busy day. Let's get started.'

'Right.'

They did stretches for half an hour and then switched to energetic aerobics.

She's got the body of a twenty-one year old, Ken thought. *I'd sure love to get that into my bed*. He enjoyed coming here every morning just to look at her, to be near her. People constantly asked him what Lara Cameron was like. He would answer, 'The lady's a ten.'

Lara went through the strenuous routine easily, but her mind was not on it this morning.

When the session was finally over, Ken said, 'I'm going to watch you on "Good Morning America".'

'What?' For a moment Lara had forgotten about it. She had been thinking about the meeting with the Japanese bankers.

'See you tomorrow, Miss Cameron.'

'Don't be late again, Ken.'

Lara showered and changed and had breakfast alone on the terrace of the penthouse, a breakfast of grapefruit, cereal, and green tea. When she had finished, she went into her study.

Lara buzzed her secretary. 'I'll do the overseas calls from the office,' Lara said. 'I have to be at ABC at seven. Have Max bring the car around.'

The segment on 'Good Morning America' went well. Joan Lunden did the interview and was gracious, as always.

'The last time you were on this programme,' Joan Lunden said, 'you had just broken ground for the tallest skyscraper in the world. That was almost four years ago.'

Lara nodded. 'That's right. Cameron Towers will be finished next year.'

'How does it feel to be in your position – to have accomplished all the incredible things you've done, and to still be so young and beautiful? You're a role model for so many women.'

'You're very flattering,' Lara laughed. 'I don't have time to think about myself as a role model. I'm much too busy.'

'You're one of the most successful real estate developers in a business that's usually considered a man's domain. How do you operate? How do you decide, for instance, where to put up a building?'

'I don't choose the site,' Lara said. 'The site chooses me. I'll be driving along and I'll pass a vacant field – but that's not what I see. I see a beautiful office building or a lovely apartment building filled with people living comfortably in a nice atmosphere. I dream.'

'And you make those dreams come true. We'll be right back after this commercial.'

The Japanese bankers were due at 7:45. They had arrived from Tokyo the evening before and Lara had arranged the meeting at that early morning hour so that they would still be jetlagged after their twelve hour and ten minute flight. When they had protested, Lara had said, 'I'm so sorry, gentlemen, but I'm afraid it's the only time I have. I'm leaving for South America immediately after our meeting.'

And they had reluctantly agreed. There were four of them, diminutive and polite, with minds as sharp as the edges of Samurai swords. In an earlier decade, the financial community had wildly underestimated the Japanese. It no longer made that mistake.

The meeting was held at Cameron Center on Sixth Avenue. The men were there to invest a hundred million dollars in a new hotel complex Lara was developing. They were ushered into the large conference room. Each of the men carried a gift. Lara thanked them and in turn gave each of them a gift. She had instructed her secretary to make certain the presents were wrapped in plain brown or grey paper. White, to the Japanese, represented death, and gaudy wrapping paper was unacceptable.

Lara's assistant, Tricia, brought in tea for the Japanese and coffee for Lara. The Japanese would have preferred coffee, but they were too polite to say so.

When they had finished their tea, Lara made sure their cups were replenished.

Howard Keller, Lara's associate, came into the room. He was in his fifties, pale and thin, with sandy hair, wearing a rumpled suit, and managing to look as though he had just got out of bed. Lara made the introductions. Keller passed around copies of the investment proposal.

'As you can see, gentlemen,' Lara said, 'we already have a first mortgage commitment. The complex will contain seven hundred and twenty guest units, approximately thirty thousand square feet of meeting space, and a one-thousand car parking garage . . .'

Lara's voice was charged with energy. The Japanese bankers were studying the investment proposal, fighting to stay awake.

The meeting was over in less than two hours and it was a complete success. Lara had learned long ago that it was easier to make a hundred-million-dollar deal than it was to try to borrow fifty thousand dollars.

As soon as the Japanese delegation left, Lara had her meeting with Jerry Townsend. The tall, hyper, ex-Hollywood publicity man was in charge of public relations for Cameron Enterprises.

'That was a great interview on "Good Morning America" this morning. I've been getting a lot of calls.'

'What about *Forbes*?'

'All set. *People* has you on the cover next week. Did you see the *New Yorker* article on you? Wasn't it great?'

Lara walked over to her desk. 'Not bad.'

'The *Fortune* interview is set for this afternoon.'

'I changed it.'

22

He looked surprised. 'Why?'

'I'm having their reporter here for lunch.'

'Soften him up a little?'

Lara pressed down the intercom button. 'Come in, Kathy.'

A disembodied voice said, 'Yes, Miss Cameron.'

Lara Cameron looked up. 'That's all, Jerry. I want you and your staff to concentrate on Cameron Towers.'

'We're already doing . . .'

'Let's do more. I want it written about in every newspaper and magazine there is. For God's sake, it's going to be the tallest building in the world. *In the world!* I want people talking about it. By the time we open, I want people to be *begging* to get into those apartments and shops.'

Jerry Townsend got to his feet. 'Right.'

Kathy, Lara's executive assistant, came into the office. She was an attractive, neatly dressed black woman in her early thirties.

'Did you find out what he likes to eat?'

'The man's a gourmet. He likes French food. I called Le Cirque and asked Sirio to cater a lunch here for two.'

'Good. We'll eat in my private dining room.'

'Do you know how long the interview will take? You have a two thirty with the Metropolitan bankers downtown.'

'Push it to three o'clock, and have them come here.'

Kathy made a note. 'Do you want me to read you your messages?'

'Go ahead.'

'The Children's Foundation wants you to be their guest of honour on the twenty-eighth.'

23

'No. Tell them I'm flattered. Send them a cheque.'

'Your meeting has been arranged in Tulsa for Tuesday at . . .'

'Cancel it.'

'You're invited to a luncheon next Friday for a Manhattan Women's Group.'

'No. If they're asking for money, send them a cheque.'

'The Coalition for Literacy would like you to speak at a luncheon on the fourth.'

'See if we can work it out.'

'There's an invitation to be guest of honour at a fund-raiser for muscular dystrophy, but there's a conflict in dates. You'll be in San Francisco.'

'Send them a cheque.'

'The Srbs are giving a dinner party next Saturday.'

'I'll try to make that,' Lara said. Kristian and Deborah Srb were amusing, and good friends, and she enjoyed being with them.

'Kathy, how many of me do you see?'

'What?'

'Take a good look.'

Kathy looked at her. 'One of you, Miss Cameron.'

'That's right. There's only one of me. How did you expect me to meet with the bankers from Metropolitan at two thirty today, the Zoning Commission at four, then meet with the mayor at five, the architects at six fifteen, the housing commission at six thirty, have a cocktail party at seven thirty and my birthday dinner at eight? The next time you make up a schedule, try using your brain.'

'I'm sorry. You wanted me to . . .'

'I wanted you to *think*. I don't need stupid people

24

around me. Reschedule the appointments with the architects and the housing commission.'

'Right,' Kathy said stiffly.

'How's the baby?'

The question caught the secretary by surprise. 'David? He's . . . he's fine.'

'He must be getting big by now.'

'He's almost two.'

'Have you thought about a school for him?'

'Not yet. It's too early to . . .'

'You're wrong. If you want to get him into a decent school in New York, you start before he's born.'

Lara made a note on a desk pad. 'I know the principal at Dalton. I'll arrange to have David registered there.'

'I . . . thank you.'

Lara did not bother to look up. 'That's all.'

'Yes, ma'am.' Kathy walked out of the office not knowing whether to love her boss or hate her. When Kathy had first come to work at Cameron Enterprises, she had been warned about Lara Cameron. 'The Iron Butterfly is a bitch on wheels,' she had been told. 'Her secretaries don't figure their employment there by the calendar – they use stopwatches. She'll eat you alive.'

Kathy remembered her first interview with her. She had seen pictures of Lara Cameron in half a dozen magazines, but none of them had done her justice. In person, the woman was breathtakingly beautiful.

Lara Cameron had been reading Kathy's résumé. She looked up and said, 'Sit down, Kathy.' Her voice was husky and vibrant. There was an energy about her that was almost overpowering.

'This is quite a résumé.'

'Thank you.'

'How much of it is real?'

'I'm sorry?'

'Most of the ones that come across my desk are fiction. Are you good at what you do?'

'I'm very good at what I do, Miss Cameron.'

'Two of my secretaries just quit. Everything's snowballing around here. Can you handle pressure?'

'I think so.'

'This isn't a guessing contest. Can you handle pressure or can't you?'

At that moment Kathy was not sure she wanted the job. 'Yes, I can.'

'Good. You're on a one-week trial. You'll have to sign a form saying that at no time will you discuss me or your work here at Cameron Enterprises. That means no interviews, no books, nothing. Everything that happens here is confidential.'

'I understand.'

'Fine.'

That was how it had begun five years earlier. During that time Kathy had learned to love, hate, admire and despise her boss. In the beginning Kathy's husband had asked, 'What is the legend like?'

It was a difficult question. 'She's larger than life,' Kathy had said. 'She's drop-dead beautiful. She works harder than anyone I've ever known. God only knows when she sleeps. She's a perfectionist, so she makes everyone around her miserable. In her own way, she's a genius. She can be petty and vengeful and incredibly generous.'

Her husband had smiled. 'In other words, she's a woman.'

Kathy had looked at him and said, unsmiling, 'I don't know what she is. Sometimes she scares me.'

'Come on, honey, you're exaggerating.'

'No. I honestly believe that if someone stood in Lara Cameron's way . . . she would kill.'

When Lara finished with the faxes and overseas calls, she buzzed Charlie Hunter, the ambitious young man in charge of accounting. 'Come in, Charlie.'

'Yes, Miss Cameron.'

A minute later, he entered her office.

'Yes, Miss Cameron?'

'I read the interview you gave in the *New York Times* this morning,' Lara said.

He brightened. 'I haven't seen it yet. How was it?'

'You talked about Cameron Enterprises and about some of the problems we're having.'

He frowned. 'Well, you know, that reporter fellow probably misquoted some of my . . .'

'You're fired.'

'What? Why? I . . .'

'When you were hired, you signed a paper agreeing not to give any interviews. I'll expect you out of here this morning.'

'I . . . you can't do that. Who would take my place?'

'I've already arranged that,' Lara told him.

The luncheon was almost over. The *Fortune* reporter, Hugh Thompson, was an intense, intellectual-looking man with sharp brown eyes behind black horn-rimmed glasses.

'It was a great lunch,' he said. 'All my favourite dishes. Thanks.'

'I'm glad you enjoyed it.'

'You really didn't have to go to all that trouble for me.'

'No trouble at all,' Lara smiled. 'My father always told me that the way to a man's heart was through his stomach.'

'And you wanted to get to my heart before we started the interview?'

Lara smiled. 'Exactly.'

'How much trouble is your company really in?'

Lara's smile faded. 'I beg your pardon?'

'Come on. You can't keep a thing like that quiet. The word on the street is that some of your properties are on the verge of collapse because of the principal payments due on your junk bonds. You've done a lot of leveraging, and with the market down, Cameron Enterprises has to be pretty over-extended.'

Lara laughed. 'Is that what the street says? Believe me, Mr Thompson, you'd be wise not to listen to silly rumours. I'll tell you what I'll do. I'll send you a copy of my financials to set the record straight. Fair enough?'

'Fair enough. By the way, I didn't see your husband at the opening of the new hotel.'

Lara sighed. 'Philip wanted so much to be there, but unfortunately he had to be away on a concert tour.'

'I went to one of his recitals once about three years ago. He's brilliant. You have been married a year now, haven't you?'

'Yes – the happiest year of my life. I'm a very

28

lucky woman. I travel a lot, and so does Philip, but when I'm away from him, I can listen to his recordings wherever I am.'

Thompson smiled. 'And he can see your buildings wherever he is.'

Lara laughed. 'You flatter me.'

'It's pretty true, isn't it? You've put up buildings all over this fair country of ours. You own apartment buildings, office buildings, a hotel chain . . . How do you do it?'

She smiled. 'With mirrors.'

'You're a puzzle.'

'Am I? Why?'

'At this moment, you're arguably the most successful builder in New York. Your name is plastered on half the real estate in this town. You're putting up the world's tallest skyscraper. Your competitors call you the Iron Butterfly. You've made it big in a business traditionally dominated by men.'

'Does that bother you, Mr Thompson?'

'No. What bothers me, Miss Cameron, is that I can't figure out who you are. When I ask two people about you, I get three opinions. Everyone grants that you're a brilliant businesswoman. I mean . . . you didn't fall off a hay wagon and become a success. I know a lot about construction crews – they're a rough, tough bunch of men. How does a woman like you keep them in line?'

She smiled. 'There *are* no women like me. Seriously, I simply hire the best people for the job, and I pay them well.'

Too simplistic, Thompson thought. *Much too simplistic. The real story is what she's not telling me.* He decided to change the direction of the interview.

29

'Every magazine on the stands has written about how successful you are. I'd like to do a more personal story. There's been very little printed about your background.'

'I'm very proud of my background.'

'Good. Let's talk about that. How did you get started in the real estate business?'

Lara smiled and he could see that her smile was genuine. She suddenly looked like a little girl.

'Genes.'

'Your genes?'

'My father's.' She pointed to a portrait on a wall behind her. It showed a handsome-looking man with a leonine head of silver hair. 'That's my father – James Hugh Cameron.' Her voice was soft. 'He's responsible for my success. I'm an only child. My mother died when I was very young, and my father brought me up. My family left Scotland a long time ago, Mr Thompson, and emigrated to Nova Scotia – New Scotland, Glace Bay.'

'Glace Bay?'

'It's a fishing village in the north-east part of Cape Breton, on the Atlantic shore. It was named by early French explorers. It means ice bay. More coffee?'

'No, thanks.'

'My grandfather owned a great deal of land in Scotland and my father acquired more. He was a very wealthy man. We still have our castle there near Loch Morlich. When I was eight years old, I had my own horse, my dresses were bought in London, we lived in an enormous house with a lot of servants. It was a fairytale life for a little girl.' Her voice was alive with echoes of long-ago memories.

'We would go ice skating in the winter, and watch

30

hockey games, and go swimming at Big Glace Bay Lake in the summer. And there were dances at the Forum and the Venetian Gardens.'

The reporter was busily making notes.

'My father put up buildings in Edmonton, and Calgary, and Ontario. Real estate was like a game to him, and he loved it. When I was very young, he taught me the game, and I learned to love it, too.'

Her voice was filled with passion. 'You must understand something, Mr Thompson. What I do has nothing to do with the money or the bricks and steel that make a building. It's the people who matter. I'm able to give them a comfortable place to work or to live, a place where they can raise families and have decent lives. That's what was important to my father, and it became important to me.'

Hugh Thompson looked up. 'Do you remember your first real estate venture?'

Lara leaned forward. 'Of course. On my eighteenth birthday, my father asked me what I would like as a gift. A lot of newcomers were arriving in Glace Bay and it was getting crowded. I felt the town needed more places for them to live. I told my father I wanted to build a small apartment house. He gave me the money as a present, but two years later, I was able to pay him back. Then I borrowed money from a bank to put up a second building. By the time I was twenty-one, I owned three buildings, and they were all successful.'

'Your father must have been very proud of you.'

There was that warm smile again. 'He was. He named me Lara. It's an old Scottish name that comes from the Latin. It means "well known" or "famous". From the time I was a little girl, my father always told

31

me I would be famous one day.' Her smile faded. 'He died of a heart attack, much too young.' She paused. 'I go to Scotland to visit his grave every year. I . . . I found it very difficult to stay on in the house without him. I decided to move to Chicago. I had an idea for small boutique hotels, and I persuaded a banker there to finance me. The hotels were a success.' She shrugged. 'And the rest, as the cliché goes, is history. I suppose that a psychiatrist would say that I haven't created this empire just for myself. In a way, it's a tribute to my father. James Cameron was the most wonderful man I've ever known.'

'You must have loved him a lot.'

'I did. And he loved me a lot.' A smile touched her lips. 'I've heard that on the day I was born, my father bought every man in Glace Bay a drink.'

'So, really,' Thompson said, 'everything started in Glace Bay.'

'That's right,' Lara said softly, 'everything started in Glace Bay. That's where it all began, almost forty years ago . . .'

Glace Bay, Nova Scotia
September 10, 1952

James Cameron was in a whorehouse, drunk, the night his daughter and son were born. He was in bed, sandwiched between the Scandinavian twins, when Kirstie, the madam of the brothel, pounded on the door.

'James!' she called out. She pushed open the door and walked in.

'*Och, ye auld hen*!' James yelled out indignantly. 'Can't a mon have any privacy even here?'

'Sorry to interrupt your pleasure, James. It's about your wife.'

'Fuck my wife,' Cameron roared.

'You did,' Kirstie retorted, 'and she's having your baby.'

'So? Let her have it. That's what you women are guid for, nae?'

'The doctor just called. He's been trying desperately to find you. Your wife is bad off. You'd better hurry.'

James Cameron sat up and slid to the edge of the bed, bleary-eyed, trying to clear his head. 'Damned woman. She niver leaves me in peace.' He looked up at the madam. 'All right, I'll go.' He glanced at the naked girls in the bed. 'But I'll nae pay for these two.'

'Never mind that now. You'd just better get back to the boarding house.' She turned to the girls. 'You two come along with me.'

James Cameron was a once-handsome man whose face reflected fulfilled sins. He appeared to be in his early fifties. He was thirty years old and the manager of one of the boarding houses owned by Sean MacAllister, the town banker. For the past five years, James Cameron and his wife Peggy had divided the chores: Peggy did the cleaning and cooking for the two dozen boarders, and James did the drinking. Every Friday it was his responsibility to collect the rents from the four other boarding houses in Glace Bay owned by MacAllister. It was another reason, if he needed one, to go out and get drunk.

James Cameron was a bitter man, who revelled in his bitterness. He was a failure, and he was convinced that everyone else was to blame. Over the years he had come to enjoy his failure. It made him feel like a martyr. When James was a year old, his family had emigrated to Glace Bay from Scotland with nothing but the few possessions they could carry, and they had struggled to survive. His father had put James to work in the coal mines when the boy was fourteen. James had suffered a slight back injury in a mining accident when he was sixteen, and had promptly quit the mine. One year later his parents were killed in a train disaster. So it was that James Cameron had decided that he was not responsible for his adversity – it was the Fates that were against him. But he had two great assets: He was

34

extraordinarily handsome and, when he wished to, he could be charming. One weekend in Sydney, a town near Glace Bay, he met an impressionable young American girl named Peggy Maxwell, who was there on vacation with her family. She was not attractive, but the Maxwells were very wealthy, and James Cameron was very poor. He swept Peggy Maxwell off her feet, and against the advice of her father, she married him.

'I'm giving Peggy a dowry of five thousand dollars,' her father told James. 'The money will give you a chance to make something of yourself. You can invest it in real estate, and in five years it will double. I'll help you.'

But James was not interested in waiting five years. Without consulting anyone, he invested the money in a wildcat oil venture with a friend, and sixty days later, he was broke. His father-in-law, furious, refused to help him any further. 'You're a fool, James, and I will not throw good money after bad.'

The marriage that was going to be James Cameron's salvation turned out to be a disaster, for he now had a wife to support, and no job.

It was Sean MacAllister who had come to his rescue. The town banker was a man in his mid fifties, a stumpy, pompous man, a pound short of being obese, given to wearing vests adorned with a heavy gold watch chain. He had come to Glace Bay twenty years earlier, and had immediately seen the possibilities there. Miners and lumbermen were pouring into the town, and were unable to find adequate housing. MacAllister could have financed homes for them, but he had a better plan. He decided it would be cheaper to herd the men together in boarding houses. Within two years, he had built a hotel and five boarding houses, and they were always full.

Finding managers was a difficult task because the work was exhausting. The manager's job was to keep all the rooms rented, supervise the cooking, handle the meals, and see that the premises were kept reasonably clean. As far as salaries were concerned, Sean MacAllister was not a man to throw away his money.

The manager of one of his boarding houses had just quit, and MacAllister decided that James Cameron was a likely candidate. Cameron had borrowed small amounts of money from the bank from time to time, and payment on a loan was overdue. MacAllister sent for the young man.

'I have a job for you,' MacAllister said.

'You have?'

'You're in luck. I have a splendid position that's just opened up.'

'Working at the bank, is it?' James Cameron asked. The idea of working in a bank appealed to him. Where there was a lot of money, there was always a possibility of having some stick to one's fingers.

'Not at the bank,' MacAllister told him. 'You're a very personable young man, James, and I think you would be very good at dealing with people. I'd like you to run my boarding house on Cablehead Avenue.'

'A *boarding* house, you say?' There was contempt in the young man's voice.

'You need a roof over your head,' MacAllister pointed out. 'You and your wife will have free room and board, and a small salary.'

'How sma'?'

'I'll be generous with you. James. Twenty-five dollars a week.'

'Twenty-fi . . . ?'

'Take it or leave it. I have others waiting.'

In the end, James Cameron had no choice. 'I'll tak' it.'

'Good. By the way, every Friday I'll also expect you to collect the rents from my other boarding houses, and deliver the money to me on Saturday.'

When James Cameron broke the news to Peggy, she was dismayed. 'We don't know anything about running a boarding house, James.'

'We'll learn. We'll share the work.'

And she had believed him. 'All right. We'll manage,' she said.

And, in their own fashion, they had managed.

Over the years, several opportunities had come along for James Cameron to get better jobs, employment that would give him dignity and more money, but he was enjoying his failure too much to leave it.

'Why bother?' he would grumble. 'When Fate's agin you, naething guid can happen.'

And on this September night, he thought to himself, *they won't even let me enjoy my whores in peace. Goddamn my wife.*

When he stepped out of Madame Kirstie's establishment, a chilly September wind was blowing.

I'd best fortify myself for the troubles aheid, James Cameron decided. He stopped in at the Ancient Mariner.

One hour later, he wandered toward the boarding house in New Aberdeen, the poorest section of Glace Bay.

When he finally arrived, half a dozen boarders were anxiously waiting for him.

'The doctor is in wi' Peggy,' one of the men said. 'You'd better hurry, mon.'

James staggered into the tiny, dreary back bedroom he and his wife shared. From another room, he could hear the whimpering of a newborn baby. Peggy lay on the bed, motionless. Dr Patrick Duncan was leaning over her. He turned as he heard James enter.

'Wa's goin' on here?' James asked.

The doctor straightened up and looked at James with distaste. 'You should have had your wife come to see me,' he said.

'And throw guid money away? She's only havin' a baby. Wa's the big . . . ?'

'Peggy's dead. I did everything I could. She had twins. I couldn't save the boy.'

'Oh, Jesus,' James Cameron whimpered. 'It's the Fates agin.'

'What?'

'The Fates. They've always been agin me. Now they've taine my bairn frae me. I dinna . . .'

A nurse walked in, carrying a tiny baby wrapped in a blanket. 'This is your daughter, Mr Cameron.'

'A *daughter*? Wha' the hell will I dae wi' a daughter?' His speech was becoming more slurred.

'You disgust me, mon,' Dr Duncan said.

The nurse turned to James. 'I'll stay until tomorrow, and show you how to take care of her.'

James Cameron looked at the tiny wrinkled bundle

38

in the blanket and thought, hopefully: *Maybe she'll die, too*.

For the first three weeks, no one was sure whether the baby would live or not. A wetnurse came in to tend to her. And finally, the day came when the doctor was able to say, 'Your daughter is going to live.'

And he looked at James Cameron and said under his breath, 'God have mercy on the poor child.'

The wetnurse said, 'Mr Cameron, you must give the child a name.'

'I dinna care wha' the hell ye call it. *Ye* gie her a name.'

'Why don't we name her Lara? That's such a pretty . . .'

'Suit your bloody self.'

And so she was christened Lara.

There was no one in Lara's life to care for her or nurture her. The boarding house was filled with men too busy with their own lives to pay attention to the baby. The only woman around was Bertha, the huge Swede who was hired to do the cooking and handle the chores.

James Cameron was determined to have nothing to do with his daughter. The damned Fates had betrayed him once again by letting her live. At night he would sit in the living room with his bottle of whiskey and complain. 'The bairn murdered my wife and my son.'

'You shouldn't say that, James.'

'Weel, it's sae. My son would hae grown up to be a big strapping mon. He would hae been smart and rich, and taine good care of his father in his auld age.'

And the boarders let him ramble on.

James Cameron tried several times to get in touch with Maxwell, his father-in-law, hoping he would take the child off his hands, but the old man had disappeared. *It would be just my luck the auld fool's daid*, he thought.

Glace Bay was a town of transients who moved in and out of the boarding houses. They came from France and China and the Ukraine. They were Italian and Irish and Greek, carpenters and tailors and plumbers and shoemakers. They swarmed into lower Main Street, Bell Street, North Street and Water Street, near the waterfront area. They came to work the mines and cut timber and fish the seas. Glace Bay was a frontier town, primitive and rugged. The weather was an abomination. The winters were harsh with heavy snowfalls that lasted until April, and because of the heavy ice in the harbour, even April and May were cold and windy, and from July to October it rained.

There were eighteen boarding houses in town, some of them accommodating as many as seventy-two guests. At the boarding house managed by James Cameron, there were twenty-four boarders, most of them Scotsmen.

Lara was hungry for affection, without knowing what the hunger was. She had no toys or dolls to cherish nor any playmates. She had no one except her father. She made childish little gifts for him, desperate to please him, but he either ignored or ridiculed them.

When Lara was five years old, she overheard her father say to one of the boarders, 'The wrong child died, ye ken. My son is the one who should hae lived.'

That night Lara cried herself to sleep. She loved her father so much. And she hated him so much.

When Lara was six, she resembled a Keane painting, enormous eyes in a pale, thin face. That year, a new boarder moved in. His name was Mungo McSween, and he was a huge bear of a man. He felt an instant affection for the little girl.

'What's your name, wee lassie?'

'Lara.'

'Ah. 'Tis a braw name for a braw bairn. Dae ye gan to school, then?'

'School? No.'

'And why not?'

'I don't know.'

'Weel, we maun find out.'

And he went to find James Cameron. 'I'm tauld your bairn does nae gae to school.'

'And why should she? She's only a girl. She dinna need nae school.'

'You're wrong, mon. She maun have an education. She maun be gien a chance in life.'

'Forget it,' James said. 'It wad be a waste.'

But McSween was insistent, and finally, to shut

41

him up, James Cameron agreed. It would keep the brat out of his sight for a few hours.

Lara was terrified by the idea of going to school. She had lived in a world of adults all her short life, and had had almost no contact with other children.

The following Monday, Big Bertha dropped her off at St Anne's Grammar School, and Lara was taken to the principal's office.

'This is Lara Cameron.'

The principal, Mrs Cummings, was a middle-aged grey-haired widow with three children of her own. She studied the shabbily dressed little girl standing before her. 'Lara. What a pretty name,' she said smiling. 'How old are you, dear?'

'Six.' She was fighting back tears.

The child is terrified, Mrs Cummings thought. 'Well, we're very glad to have you here, Lara. You'll have a good time, and you're going to learn a lot.'

'I can't stay,' Lara blurted out.

'Oh? Why not?'

'My papa misses me too much.' She was fiercely determined not to cry.

'Well, we'll only keep you here for a few hours a day.'

Lara allowed herself to be taken into a classroom filled with children, and she was shown to a seat near the back of the room.

Miss Terkel, the teacher, was busily writing letters on a blackboard.

'*A* is for apple,' she said. '*B* is for boy. Does anyone know what *C* is for?'

A tiny hand was raised. 'Candy.'

42

'Very good! And *D*?'

'Dog.'

'And *E*?'

'Eat.'

'Excellent. Can anyone think of a word beginning with *F*?'

Lara spoke up. 'Fuck.'

Lara was the youngest one in her class, but it seemed to Miss Terkel that in many ways she was the oldest. There was a disquieting maturity about her.

'She's a small adult, waiting to grow taller,' her teacher told Mrs Cummings.

The first day at lunch, the other children took out their colourful little lunch pails and pulled out apples and cookies, and sandwiches wrapped in wax paper.

No one had thought to pack a lunch for Lara.

'Where is your lunch, Lara?' Miss Terkel asked.

'I'm not hungry,' Lara said stubbornly. 'I had a big breakfast.'

Most of the girls at school were nicely dressed in clean skirts and blouses. Lara had outgrown her few faded plaid dresses and threadbare blouses. She had gone to her father.

'I need some clothes for school,' Lara said.

'Dae ye now? Weel, I'm nae made of money. Get yourself something frae the Salvation Army Citadel.'

'That's charity, Papa.'

And her father had slapped her hard across the face.

*

The children at school were familiar with games Lara had never even heard of. The girls had dolls and toys, and some of them were willing to share them with Lara, but she was painfully aware that nothing belonged to her. And there was something more. Over the next few years, Lara got a glimpse of a different world, a world where children had mothers and fathers who gave them presents and birthday parties and loved them and held them and kissed them. And for the first time, Lara began to realize how much was missing in her life. It only made her feel lonelier.

The boarding house was a different kind of school. It was an international microcosm. Lara learned to tell where the boarders came from by their names. Mac was from Scotland . . . Hodder and Pyke were from Newfoundland . . . Chiasson and Aucoin were from France . . . Dudash and Kosick from Poland. The boarders were lumbermen, fishermen, miners and tradesmen. They would gather in the large dining room in the morning for breakfast and in the evening for supper, and their talk was fascinating to Lara. Each group seemed to have its own mysterious language.

There were thousands of lumbermen in Nova Scotia, scattered around the peninsula. The lumbermen at the boarding house smelled of sawdust and burnt bark, and they spoke of arcane things like chippers and edging and trim.

'We should get out almost two hundred million board feet this year,' one of them announced at supper.

'How can feet be bored?' Lara asked.

There was a roar of laughter. 'Child, board foot is a piece of lumber a foot square by an inch thick. When you grow up and get married, if you want to build a five-room, all wood house, it will take twelve thousand board feet.'

'I'm not going to get married,' Lara swore.

The fishermen were another breed. They returned to the boarding house stinking of the sea, and they talked about the new experiment of growing oysters on the Bras d'Or lake, and bragged to one another of their catches of cod and herring and mackerel and haddock.

But the boarders who fascinated Lara the most were the miners. There were 3,500 miners in Cape Breton, working the collieries at Lingan and Prince and Phalen. Lara loved the names of the mines. There was the Jubilee and the Last Chance and the Black Diamond and the Lucky Lady.

She was fascinated by their discussion of the day's work.

'What's this I hear about Mike?'

'It's true. The poor bastard was travelling inbye in a man-rake, and a box jumped the track and crushed his leg. The sonofabitch of a foreman said it was Mike's fault for not gettin' out of the way fast enough, and he's having his lamp stopped.'

Lara was baffled. 'What does that mean?'

One of the miners explained. 'It means Mike was on his way to work – going inbye – in a man-rake – that's a car that takes you down to your working level. A box – that's a coal train – jumped the track and hit him.'

'And stopped his lamp?' Lara asked.

The miner laughed. 'When you've had your lamp stopped, it means you've been suspended.'

When Lara was fifteen, she entered St Michael's High School. She was gangly and awkward, with long legs, stringy black hair, and intelligent grey eyes still too large for her pale, thin face. No one quite knew how she was going to turn out. She was on the verge of womanhood, and her looks were in a stage of metamorphosis. She could have become ugly or beautiful.

To James Cameron, his daughter was ugly. 'Ye hae best marry the first mon fool enough to ask ye,' he told her. 'Ye'll nae hae the looks to make a guid bargain.'

Lara stood there, saying nothing.

'And tell the poor mon nae to expect a dowry frae me.'

Mungo McSween had walked into the room. He stood there listening, furious.

'That's all, girl,' James Cameron said. 'Gae back to the kitchen.'

Lara fled.

'Why dae ye dae that to yeer daughter?' McSween demanded.

James Cameron looked up, his eyes bleary. 'Nane of your business.'

'You're drunk.'

'Aye. And what else is there? If it isn't women, it's the whiskey, isn't it?'

McSween went into the kitchen where Lara was washing dishes at the sink. Her eyes were hot with

46

tears. McSween put his arms around her. 'Niver ye mind, lassie,' he said. 'He dinna mean it.'

'He hates me.'

'Nae, he doesna.'

'He's never given me one kind word. Never once. Never!'

There was nothing McSween could say.

In the summer, the tourists would arrive at Glace Bay. They came in their expensive cars, wearing beautiful clothes, and shopped along Castle Street and dined at the Cedar House and at Jasper's, and they visited Ingonish Beach and Cape Smoky and the Bird Islands. They were superior beings from another world, and Lara envied them and longed to escape with them when they left at the end of summer. But how?

Lara had heard stories about Grandfather Maxwell.

'The auld bastard tried to keep me frae marryin' his precious daughter,' James Cameron would complain to any of the boarders who would listen. 'He was filthy rich, but do ye think he wad gie me aught? Nae. But I took guid care of his Peggy, anyway . . .'

And Lara would fantasize that one day her grandfather would come to take her away to glamorous cities she had read about: London and Rome and Paris. *And I'll have beautiful clothes to wear. Hundreds of dresses and new shoes.*

But as the months and the years went by, and there was no word, Lara finally came to realize that she would never see her grandfather. She was doomed to spend the rest of her life in Glace Bay.

There were myriad activities for a teenager growing up in Glace Bay: There were football games and hockey games, skating rinks and bowling, and in the summer, swimming and fishing. Carl's Drug Store was the popular after-school hangout. There were two movie theatres, and for dancing, the Venetian Gardens.

Lara had no chance to enjoy any of those things. She rose at five every morning to help Bertha prepare breakfast for the boarders, and make up the beds before she left for school. In the afternoon, she would hurry home to begin preparing supper. She helped Bertha serve, and after supper, Lara cleared the table and washed and dried the dishes.

The boarding house served some favourite Scottish dishes: *Howtowdie* and *hairst bree*, *cabbieclaw* and *skirlie*. Black Bun was a favourite, a spicy mixture encased in a shortpaste jacket made from half a pound of flour.

The conversation of the Scotsmen at supper made the Highlands of Scotland come alive for Lara. Her ancestors had come from the Highlands, and the stories about them gave Lara the only sense of belonging that she had. The boarders talked of the Great Glen containing Lochs Ness, Lochy, and Linnhe, and of the rugged islands off the coast.

There was a battered piano in the sitting room, and sometimes at night, after supper, half a dozen boarders would gather around and sing the songs of home: 'Annie Laurie', and 'Comin' Through the Rye', and 'The Hills of Home', and 'The Bonnie Banks o' Loch Lomon''.

Once a year there was a parade in town, and all the Scotsmen in Glace Bay would proudly put on their kilts or tartans and march through the streets to the loud, raucous accompaniment of bagpipes.

'Why do the men wear skirts?' Lara asked Mungo McSween.

He frowned. 'It's *nae* a skirt, lass. It's a kilt. Our ancestors invented it long ago. I' the Highlands, a plaid covered a mon's body agin the bitter cold, but kept his legs free sae he could race across the heather and peat and escape his enemies. And at night, if he was in the open, the great length of the cloth was both bed and tent for him.'

The names of the Scottish places were poetry to Lara. There was Breadalbane, Glenfinnan and Kilbride, Kilninver and Kilmichael. Lara learned that 'kil' referred to a monk's cell of medieval times. If a name began with 'inver' or 'aber', it meant the village was at the mouth of a stream. If it began with 'strath', it was in a valley. 'Bad' meant the village was in a grove.

There were fierce arguments every night at the

supper table. The Scotsmen argued about everything. Their ancestors had belonged to proud clans and they were still fiercely protective of their history.

'The House of Bruce produced cowards. They lay down for the English like grovelling dogs.'

'You dinna ken wha' you're talking aboot, as usual, Ian. It was the great Bruce himself who stood up to the English. It was the House of Stuart that grovelled.'

'Och, you're a fool, and your clan comes from a long line of fools.'

The argument would grow more heated.

'You ken wha' Scotland needed? Mair leaders like Robert the Second. Now, there was a great mon. He sired twenty-one bairns.'

'Aye, and half of them were bastards!'

And another argument would start.

Lara could not believe that they were fighting over events that had happened more than six hundred years earlier.

Mungo McSween said to Lara, 'Dinna let it bother ye, lassie. A Scotsman wi' start a fight in an empty house.'

It was a poem by Sir Walter Scott that set Lara's imagination on fire.

> *Oh, young Lochinvar is come out of the west,*
> *Through all the wide Border his steed was the best;*
> *And save his good broadsword he weapons had none,*
> *He rode all unarmed, and he rode all alone.*

50

So faithful in love, and so dauntless in war.
There never was knight like the young
Lochinvar.

And the glorious poem went on to tell how Lochinvar risked his life to rescue his beloved, who was being forced to marry another man.

So daring in love, and so dauntless in war,
Have ye e'er heard of gallant like young
Lochinvar?

Some day, Lara thought, *a handsome Lochinvar will come and rescue me.*

One day Lara was working in the kitchen, when she came across an advertisement in a magazine, and her breath caught in her throat. It showed a tall, handsome man, blond, elegantly dressed in tails and white tie. He had blue eyes and a warm smile, and he looked every inch a prince. *That's what my Lochinvar will look like*, Lara thought. *He's out there somewhere, looking for me. He'll come and rescue me from here. I'll be at the sink washing dishes and he'll come up behind me, put his arms around me, and whisper, 'Can I help you?' And I'll turn and look into his eyes. And I'll say, 'Do you dry dishes?'*

Bertha's voice said, 'Do I *what*?'

Lara whirled around. Bertha was standing behind her. Lara had not realized she had spoken aloud.

'Nothing,' Lara blushed.

To Lara, the most fascinating dinner conversations revolved around the stories of the notorious

51

Highland Clearances. She had heard them told over and over but could never get enough of it.

'Tell me again,' she would ask. And Mungo McSween was eager to oblige . . .

'Weel, it began in the year 1792 and it went on for more than sixty years. At first they called it *Bliadhna nan Caorach* – The Year of the Sheep. The landowners in the Highlands had decided that their land would be more profitable with sheep than with tenant farmers, so they brought flocks of sheep into the Highlands, and found that they could survive the cold winters. That was when the clearances began.

'The cry became, "*Mo thruaighe ort a thir, tha'n caoraich mhor a' teachd!*" Woe to thee, oh land, the Great Sheep is coming. First there were a hundred sheep, then a thousand, then ten thousand. It was a bloody invasion.

'The lairds saw riches beyond their dreams, but they maun get rid of the tenants first, who worked their wee patches of land. They had little enough to begin with, God knows. They lived in sma' stone houses with na chimneys and na windows. But the lairds forced them out.'

The young girl was wide-eyed. 'How?'

'The government regiments were ordered to attack the villages and evict the tenants. The soldiers wad come to a little village and gie the tenants six hours to remove their cattle and furniture and get oot. They maun leave their crops behind. Then the soldiers burned their huts to the ground. More than a quarter of a million men, women and children were forced frae their holdings and driven to the shores of the sea.'

'But how could they drive them from their own land?'

'Ah, they niver owned the land, you see. They had the use of an acre or two frae a laird, but it was niver theirs. They paid a fee in goods or labour in order to till the land and grow some tatties and raise a few cattle.'

'What happened if the people wouldn't move?' Lara asked breathlessly.

'The old folk that didn't get out in time were burned in their huts. The government was ruthless. Och, it was a terrible time. The people had naething to eat. Cholera struck, and diseases spread like wildfire.'

'How awful,' Lara said.

'Aye, lassie. Our people lived on tatties and bread and porridge, when they could git it. But there's one thing the government could nae take away frae the Highlanders – their pride. They fought back as best they could. For days after the burning was over, the homeless people remained in the glen, trying to salvage what they could from the ruins. They put canvas over their heids for protection agin the night rain. My great-great-grandfather and my great-great-grandmother were there and suffered through it all. It's part of our history, and it's been burned into our very souls.'

Lara could visualize the thousands of desperate, forlorn people robbed of everything they possessed, stunned by what had happened to them. She could hear the crying of the mourners, and the screams of the terrified children.

'What finally happened to the people?' Lara asked.

'They left for other lands on ships that were death traps. The crowded passengers died of fever or frae dysentery. Sometimes, the ships would hit storms that delayed them for weeks, so they ran out of food. Only the strong were still alive when the ships landed in Canada. But once they landed here, they were able to hae somethin' they niver had before.'

'Their own land,' Lara said.

'That's right, lass.'

Some day, Lara thought fiercely, *I will have my own land, and no one – no one – will ever take it away from me.*

On an evening in early July, James Cameron was in bed with one of the whores at Kirstie's Bawdy House, when he suffered a heart attack. He was quite drunk, and when he suddenly toppled over, his playmate assumed he had simply fallen asleep.

'Oh, no, you don't! I have other customers waitin' for me. Wake up, James! Wake up!'

He was gasping for breath and clutching his chest.

'For Gude's sake,' he moaned, 'git me a doctor.'

An ambulance took him to the little hospital on Quarry Street. Dr Duncan sent for Lara. She walked into the hospital, her heart pounding. Duncan was waiting for her.

'What happened?' Lara asked urgently. 'Is my father dead?'

'No, Lara, but I'm afraid he's had a heart attack.'

She stood there, frozen. 'Is he . . . is he going to live?'

'I don't know. We're doing everything we can for him.'

54

'Can I see him?'

'It would be better if you came back in the morning, lass.'

She walked home, numb with fear. *Please don't let him die, God. He's all I have.*

When Lara reached the boarding house, Bertha was waiting for her. 'What happened?'

Lara told her.

'Oh, God!' Bertha said. 'And today is Friday.'

'What?'

'Friday. The day the rents have to be collected. If I know Sean MacAllister, he'll use this as an excuse to throw us all out into the streets.'

At least a dozen times in the past when James Cameron had been too drunk to handle it himself, he had sent Lara around to collect the rents from the other boarding houses that Sean MacAllister owned. Lara had given the money to her father, and the next day he had taken it to the banker.

'What are we going to do?' Bertha moaned.

And suddenly Lara knew what had to be done.

'Don't worry,' she said. 'I'll take care of it.'

In the middle of supper that evening Lara said, 'Gentlemen, would you listen to me, please?' The conversations stopped. They were all watching her. 'My father has had a . . . a little dizzy spell. He's in the hospital. They want to keep him under observation for a bit. So, until he comes back, I'll be collecting the rents. After supper, I'll wait for you in the parlour.'

'Is he going to be all right?' one of the boarders asked.

'Oh, yes,' Lara said with a forced smile. 'It's nothing serious.'

55

After supper the men came into the parlour and handed Lara their week's rent.

'I hope your father recovers soon, child . . .'

'If there's anything I can do, let me know . . .'

'You're a braw lassie to do this for your father . . .'

'What about the other boarding houses?' Bertha asked Lara. 'He has to collect from four more.'

'I know,' Lara said. 'If you'll take care of the dishes, I'll go collect the rents.'

Bertha looked at her dubiously. 'I wish you luck.'

It was easier than Lara had expected. Most of the boarders were sympathetic, and happy to help out the young girl.

Early the following morning, Lara took the rent envelopes and went to see Sean MacAllister. The banker was seated in his office when Lara walked in.

'My secretary said you wanted to see me.'

'Yes, sir.'

MacAllister studied the scrawny, unkempt girl standing before him. 'You're James Cameron's daughter, aren't you?'

'Yes, sir.'

'Sarah.'

'Lara.'

'Sorry to hear about your father,' MacAllister said. There was no sympathy in his voice. 'I'll have to make other arrangements, of course, now that your father's too ill to carry out his job. I . . .'

'Oh, no, sir!' Lara said quickly. 'He asked me to handle it for him.'

'You?'

'Yes, sir.'

'I'm afraid that won't . . .'

Lara put the envelopes on his desk. 'Here are this week's rents.'

MacAllister looked at her, surprised. 'All of them?'

She nodded.

'And you collected them?'

'Yes, sir. And I'll do it every week until Papa gets better.'

'I see.' He opened the envelopes and carefully counted the money. Lara watched him enter the amount in a large green ledger.

For some time now, MacAllister had intended to replace James Cameron because of his drunkenness and erratic performance, and now he saw his opportunity to get rid of the family.

He was sure that the young girl in front of him would not be able to carry out her father's duties, but at the same time, he realized what the town's reaction would be if he threw James Cameron and his daughter out of the boarding house into the street. He made his decision.

'I'll try you for one month,' he said. 'At the end of that time, we'll see where we stand.'

'Thank you, Mr MacAllister. Thank you very much.'

'Wait.' He handed Lara twenty-five dollars. 'This is yours.'

Lara held the money in her hand, and it was like a taste of freedom. It was the first time she had ever been paid for what she had done.

From the bank, Lara went to the hospital. Dr Duncan was just coming out of her father's room.

Lara felt a sudden sense of panic. 'He isn't . . . ?'

'No . . . no . . . he's going to be all right, Lara.' He hesitated. 'When I say "all right", I mean he is not going to die . . . not yet, at least . . . but he is going to have to stay in bed for a few weeks. He'll need someone to take care of him.'

'I'll take care of him,' Lara said.

He looked at her and said, softly, 'Your father doesn't know it, my dear, but he's a very lucky man.'

'May I go in and see him now?'

'Yes.'

Lara walked into her father's room and stood there staring at him. James Cameron lay in bed, looking pale and helpless, and he suddenly seemed very old. Lara was engulfed by a wave of tenderness. She was finally going to be able to do something for her father, something that would make him appreciate her and love her. She approached the bed.

'Papa . . .'

He looked up and muttered, 'What the bluidy hell are you doin' here? You've work to dae at the boardin' house.'

Lara froze. 'I . . . I know, Papa. I just wanted to tell you that I saw Mr MacAllister. I told him I would collect the rents until you got better and . . .'

'*Ye* collect the rents? Dinna make me laugh.' He was shaken with a sudden spasm. When he spoke again, his voice was weak. 'It's the Fates,' he moaned. 'I'm gang to be thrown oot into the streets.'

He was not even thinking about what would happen to her. Lara stood there looking at him for a long time. Then she turned and walked out.

*

James Cameron was brought home three days later, and put to bed.

'You're not to get out of bed for the next couple of weeks,' Dr Duncan told him. 'I'll come back and check on you in a day or two.'

'I canna stay in bed,' James Cameron protested. 'I'm a busy mon. I have a lot to dae.'

The doctor looked at him and said, quietly, 'You have a choice. You can either stay in bed and live, or get up and die.'

MacAllister's boarders were, at first, delighted to see the innocent young girl come around to collect their rents. But when the novelty wore off, they had a myriad of excuses:

'I was sick this week, and I had medical bills . . .'

'My son sends me money every week, but the mail's been delayed . . .'

'I had to buy some equipment . . .'

'I'll have the money for you next week for sure . . .'

But the young girl was fighting for her life. She listened politely and said, 'I'm so sorry, but Mr MacAllister says that the money is due today, and if you don't have it, you'll have to vacate immediately.'

And somehow, they all managed to come up with the money.

Lara was inflexible.

'It was easier dealing with your father,' one of the boarders grumbled. 'He was always willing to wait a few days.'

But, in the end, they had to admire the young girl's spunk.

If Lara had thought that her father's illness would bring him closer to her, she was sadly mistaken. Lara tried to anticipate his every need, but the more solicitous she was, the more badly he behaved.

She brought him fresh flowers every day, and little treats.

'For Gude's sakes!' he cried. 'Stop hoverin' aboote. Hae ye nae work to dae?'

'I just thought you'd like . . .'

'*Oot!*' He turned his face to the wall.

I hate him, Lara thought. *I hate him*.

At the end of the month, when Lara walked into Sean MacAllister's office with the envelopes filled with rent money, and he had finished counting it, he said, 'I don't mind admitting, young lady, that you've been quite a surprise to me. You've done better than your father.'

The words were thrilling. 'Thank you.'

'As a matter of fact, this is the first month that everybody has paid on time in full.'

'Then my father and I can stay on at the boarding house?' Lara asked eagerly.

MacAllister studied her a moment. 'I suppose so. You must love your father very much.'

'I'll see you next Saturday, Mr MacAllister.'

At seventeen, the spindly, gaunt little girl had grown into a woman. Her face bore the imprint of her Scottish forebears. The gleaming skin, the arched, fine eyebrows, the thundercloud grey eyes, the stormy black hair. And in addition, there was a strain of melancholy that seemed to hover around her, the bleed-through of a people's tragic history. It was hard to look away from Lara Cameron's face.

Most of the boarders were without women, except for the companions they paid for at Madame Kirstie's and some of the other houses of prostitution, and the beautiful young girl was a natural target for them. One of the men would corner her in the kitchen or in his bedroom when she was cleaning it and say, 'Why don't you be nice to me, Lara? I could do a lot for you.'

Or, 'You don't have a boy friend, do you? Let me show you what a man is like.'

Or, 'How would you like to go to Kansas City? I'm leaving next week and I'd be glad to take you with me.'

After one or another of the boarders had tried to persuade Lara to go to bed with him, she would walk into the small room where her father lay helpless, and say, 'You were wrong, Father. All the men want me.' And she would walk out, leaving him staring after her.

James Cameron died on an early morning in spring, and Lara buried him at the Greenwood Cemetery in the Passiondale area. The only other person at the funeral was Bertha. There were no tears.

A new boarder moved in, an American named Bill Rogers. He was in his seventies, bald and fat, an affable man who liked to talk. After supper, he would sit and chat with Lara. 'You're too damned pretty to be stuck in a hick town like this,' he advised her. 'You should go to Chicago or New York. Big time.'

'I will one day,' Lara said.

'You've got your whole life ahead of you. Do you know what you want to do with it?'

'I want to own things.'

'Ah, pretty clothes and . . .'

'No. Land. I want to own land. My father never owned anything. He had to live off other people's favours all his life.'

Bill Rogers' face lit up. 'Real estate was the business I was in.'

'Really?'

'I had buildings all over the Midwest. I even had a chain of hotels once.' His tone was wistful.

'What happened?'

He shrugged. 'I got greedy. Lost it all. But it was sure fun while it lasted.'

After that they talked about real estate almost every night.

'The first rule in real estate,' Rogers told her, 'is OPM. Never forget that.'

'What's OPM?'

'Other people's money. What makes real estate a great business is that the government lets you take deductions on interest and depreciation while your assets keep growing. The three most important things in real estate are location, location and location. A beautiful building up on a hill is a waste of time. An ugly building downtown will make you rich.'

Rogers taught Lara about mortgages and refinancing and the use of bank loans. Lara listened and learned and remembered. She was like a sponge, eagerly soaking up every bit of information.

The most meaningful thing Rogers said to her was, 'You know, Glace Bay has a big housing shortage. It's a great opportunity for someone. If I were twenty years younger . . .'

From that moment on, Lara looked at Glace Bay with different eyes, visualizing office buildings and homes on vacant lots. It was exciting and it was frustrating. Her dreams were there, but she had no money to carry them out.

The day Bill Rogers left town he said, 'Remember – other people's money. Good luck, kid.'

A week later, Charles Cohn moved into the boarding house. He was a small man in his sixties, neat and trim, and well dressed. He sat at the supper table with the other boarders, but said very little. He seemed cocooned in his own private world.

He watched Lara as she worked around the boarding house, smiling, never complaining.

'How long do you plan to stay with us?' Lara asked Cohn.

'I'm not sure. It could be a week or a month or two . . .'

Charles Cohn was a puzzle to Lara. He did not fit in with the other boarders at all. She tried to imagine what he did. He was certainly not a miner or a fisherman, and he did not look like a merchant. He seemed superior to the other boarders, better educated. He told Lara that he had tried to get into the one hotel in town, but that it was full. Lara noticed that at meal times he ate almost nothing.

'If you have a little fruit,' he would say, apologetically, 'or some vegetables . . .'

'Are you on some special kind of diet?' Lara asked.

'In a way. I eat only kosher food, and I'm afraid Glace Bay doesn't have any.'

The next evening, when Charles Cohn sat down to supper, a plate of lamb chops was placed in front of him. He looked up at Lara in surprise. 'I'm sorry. I can't eat this,' he said. 'I thought I explained . . .'

Lara smiled, 'You did. This is kosher.'

'*What*?'

'I found a kosher meat market in Sydney. The *shochet* there sold me this. Enjoy it. Your rent includes two meals a day. Tomorrow you're having a steak.'

From that time on, whenever Lara had a free moment, Cohn made it a point to talk to her, to draw her out. He was impressed by her quick intelligence and her independent spirit.

One day Charles Cohn confided to Lara what he was doing in Glace Bay. 'I'm an executive with Continental Supplies.' It was a famous national chain. 'I'm here to find a location for our new store.'

'That's exciting,' Lara said. *I knew he was in Glace Bay for some important reason.* 'You're going to put up a building?'

'No. We'll find someone else to do that. We just lease our buildings.'

At three o'clock in the morning, Lara awakened out of a sound sleep and sat up in bed, her heart pounding wildly. Had it been a dream? No. Her mind was racing. She was too excited to go back to sleep.

When Charles Cohn came out of his room for breakfast, Lara was waiting for him.

'Mr Cohn . . . I know a great place,' she blurted out.

He stared at her, puzzled. 'What?'

'For the location you're looking for.'

'Oh? Where?'

Lara evaded the question. 'Let me ask you something. If I owned a location that you liked, and if I put up a building on it, would you agree to lease it from me for five years?'

He shook his head. 'That's a rather hypothetical question, isn't it?'

'Would you?' Lara persisted.

'Lara, what do you know about putting up a building?'

'I wouldn't be putting it up,' she said. 'I'd hire an architect and a good construction firm to do that.'

Charles Cohn was watching her closely. 'I see. And where is this wonderful piece of land?'

'I'll show it to you,' Lara said. 'Believe me, you're going to love it. It's perfect.'

After breakfast, Lara took Charles Cohn downtown. At the corner of Main and Commercial Streets in the centre of Glace Bay was a vacant square block. It was a site Cohn had examined two days earlier.

'This is the location I had in mind,' Lara said.

Cohn stood there, pretending to study it. 'You have an *ahf* – a nose. It's a very good location.'

He had already made discreet inquiries and learned that the property was owned by a banker, Sean MacAllister. Cohn's assignment was to locate a site, arrange for someone to construct the building, and then lease it from them. It would not matter to the company who put up the building so long as its specifications were met.

Cohn was studying Lara. *She's too young*, he thought. *It's a foolish idea. And yet . . . 'I found a kosher meat market in Sydney . . . Tomorrow you're having a steak.'* She had such compassion.

Lara was saying, excitedly, 'If I could acquire this land and put up a building to meet your specifications, would you give me a five-year lease?'

He paused, and then said slowly, 'No, Lara. It would have to be a ten-year lease.'

That afternoon, Lara went to see Sean MacAllister. He looked up in surprise as she walked into his office.

'You're a few days early, Lara. Today's only Wednesday.'

'I know. I want to ask a favour, Mr MacAllister.'

66

Sean MacAllister sat there, watching her. *She has really turned into a beautiful-looking girl. Not a girl, a woman.* He could see the swell of her breasts against the cotton blouse she was wearing.

'Sit down, my dear. What can I do for you?'

Lara was too excited to sit. 'I want to take a loan.'

It took him by surprise. 'What?'

'I'd like to borrow some money.'

He smiled indulgently. 'I don't see why not. If you need a new dress or something, I'll be happy to advance . . .'

'I want to borrow two hundred thousand dollars.'

MacAllister's smile died. 'Is this some kind of joke?'

'No, sir.' Lara leaned forward and said earnestly, 'There's a piece of land I want to buy to put up a building. I have an important tenant who's willing to give me a ten-year lease. That will guarantee the cost of the land and the building.'

MacAllister was studying her, frowning. 'Have you discussed this with the owner of the land?'

'I'm discussing it with him now,' Lara said.

It took a moment for it to sink in. 'Wait a minute. Are you telling me that this is land that *I* own?'

'Yes. It's the lot on the corner of Main and Commercial Streets.'

'You came here to borrow money from *me* to buy *my* land?'

'That lot is worth no more than twenty thousand dollars. I checked. I'm offering you thirty. You'll make a profit of ten thousand dollars on the land plus interest on the two hundred thousand dollars you're going to loan me to put up the building.'

MacAllister shook his head. 'You're asking me

to loan you two hundred thousand dollars with no security. It's out of the question.'

Lara leaned forward. 'There *is* security. You'll hold the mortgage on the building and the land, and I've already got the tenant. You can't lose.'

MacAllister sat there studying her, turning her proposal over in his mind. He smiled, 'You know,' he said, 'you have a lot of nerve. But I could never explain a loan like that to my board of directors.'

'You have no board of directors,' Lara told him.

The smile turned to a grin. 'True.'

Lara leaned forward and he could see her breasts touching the edge of his desk.

'If you say yes, Mr MacAllister, you'll never regret it. I promise.'

He could not take his eyes off her breasts. 'You're not a bit like your father, are you?'

'No, sir.' *Nothing, like him*, Lara thought fiercely.

'Supposing, for the sake of argument,' MacAllister said carefully, 'that I was interested. Who is this tenant of yours?'

'His name is Charles Cohn. He's an executive with Continental Supplies.'

'The chain store?'

'Yes.'

MacAllister was suddenly very interested.

Lara went on. 'They want to have a big store built here to supply the miners and lumbermen with equipment.'

To MacAllister, it had the smell of instant success.

'Where did you meet this man?' he asked casually.

'He's staying at the boarding house.'

'I see. Let me think about it, Lara. We'll discuss it again tomorrow.'

68

Lara was almost trembling with excitement. 'Thank you, Mr MacAllister. You won't be sorry.'

He smiled. 'No, I don't think I will be.'

That afternoon, Sean MacAllister went to the boarding house to meet Charles Cohn.

'I just dropped by to welcome you to Glace Bay,' MacAllister said. 'I'm Sean MacAllister. I own the bank here. I heard you were in town. But you shouldn't be staying at my boarding house, you should be staying at my hotel. It's much more comfortable.'

'It was full,' Mr Cohn explained.

'That's because we didn't know who you were.'

Mr Cohn said pleasantly, 'Who am I?'

Sean MacAllister smiled. 'We don't have to play games, Mr Cohn. Word gets around. I understand that you're interested in leasing a building to be put up on a property I own.'

'What property would that be?'

'The lot at Main and Commercial. It's a great location, isn't it? I don't think we'll have any problem making a deal.'

'I already have a deal with someone.'

Sean MacAllister laughed. 'Lara? She's a pretty little thing, isn't she? Why don't you come down to the bank with me and we'll draw up a contract?'

'I don't think you understand, Mr MacAllister. I said I already have a deal.'

'I don't think *you* understand, Mr Cohn. Lara doesn't own that land. I do.'

'She's trying to buy it from you, isn't she?'

'Yes. I don't have to sell it to her.'

'And I don't have to use that lot. I've seen three other lots that will do just as nicely. Thanks for dropping by.'

Sean MacAllister looked at him for a long moment. 'You mean . . . you're serious?'

'Very. I never go into a deal that's not kosher, and I never break my word.'

'But Lara doesn't know anything about building. She . . .'

'She plans to find people who do. Naturally, we'll have final approval.'

The banker was thoughtful. 'Do I understand that Continental Supplies is willing to sign a ten-year lease?'

'That's correct.'

'I see. Well, under the circumstances, I . . . let me think about it.'

When Lara arrived at the boarding house, Charles Cohn told her about his conversation with the banker.

Lara was upset. 'You mean Mr MacAllister went behind my back and . . . ?'

'Don't worry,' Cohn assured her, 'he'll make the deal with you.'

'Do you really think so?'

'He's a banker. He's in business to make a profit.'

'What about you? Why are you doing this for me?' Lara asked.

He had asked himself the same question. *Because you're achingly young*, he thought. *Because you don't belong in this town. Because I wish I had a daughter like you.*

But he said none of those things.

'I have nothing to lose, Lara. I found some other locations that would serve just as well. If you can acquire this land, I'd like to do this for you. It doesn't matter to my company who I deal with. If you get your loan, and I approve your builder, we're in business.'

A feeling of elation swept over Lara. 'I . . . I don't know how to thank you. I'll go to see Mr MacAllister and . . .'

'I wouldn't if I were you,' Cohn advised her. 'Let him come to you.'

She looked worried. 'But what if he doesn't . . . ?'

Cohn smiled, 'He will.'

He handed her a printed lease. 'Here's the ten-year lease we discussed. It's contingent, you understand, on your meeting all our requirements for the building.' He handed her a set of blueprints. 'These are our specifications.'

Lara spent the night studying the pages of drawings and instructions.

The following morning, Sean MacAllister telephoned Lara.

'Can you come down to see me, Lara?'

Her heart was pounding. 'I'll be there in fifteen minutes.'

He was waiting for her.

'I've been thinking about our conversation,' MacAllister said. 'I would need a written agreement for a ten-year lease from Mr Cohn.'

'I already have it,' Lara said. She opened her bag and took out the contract.

Sean MacAllister examined it carefully. 'It seems to be in order.'

'Then we have a deal?' Lara asked. She was holding her breath.

MacAllister shook his head. 'No.'

'But I thought . . .'

His fingers were drumming restlessly on his desk. 'To tell you the truth, I'm really in no hurry to sell that lot, Lara. The longer I hold on to it, the more valuable it will become.'

She looked at him blankly. 'But you . . .'

'Your request is completely unorthodox. You've had no experience. I would need a very special reason to make this loan to you.'

'I don't under . . . what kind of reason?'

'Let's say . . . a little bonus. Tell me, Lara, have you ever had a lover?'

The question caught her completely off-guard.

'I . . . no.' She could feel the deal slipping away from her. 'What does that have . . . ?'

MacAllister leaned forward. 'I'm going to be frank with you, Lara. I find you very attractive. I'd like to go to bed with you. *Quid pro quo*. That means . . .'

'I know what it means.' Her face had turned to stone.

'Look at it this way. This is your chance to make something of yourself, isn't it? To own something, to be somebody. To prove to yourself that you're not like your father.'

Lara's mind was spinning.

'You'll probably never have another chance like this again, Lara. Perhaps you'd like some time to think it over, and . . .'

'No.' Her voice sounded hollow in her own ears. 'I can give you my answer now.' She pressed her arms tightly against her sides to stop her body from trembling. Her whole future, her very life, hung on her next words.

'I'll go to bed with you.'

Grinning, MacAllister rose and moved toward her, his fat arms outstretched.

'Not now,' Lara said. 'After I see the contract.'

The following day, Sean MacAllister handed Lara a contract for the bank loan.

'It's a very simple contract, my dear. It's a ten-year, two-hundred-thousand-dollar loan at eight per cent.' He gave her a pen. 'You can just sign here on the last page.'

'If you don't mind, I'd like to read it first,' Lara said. She looked at her watch, 'But I don't have time now. May I take it with me? I'll bring it back tomorrow.'

Sean MacAliister shrugged. 'Very well.' He lowered his voice. 'About our little date. Next Saturday I have to go into Halifax. I thought we might go there together.'

Lara looked at his leering smile and felt sick to her stomach. 'All right.' It was a whisper.

'Good. You sign the contract and bring it back and we're in business.' He was thoughtful for a moment. 'You're going to need a good builder. Are you familiar with the Nova Scotia Construction Company?'

Lara's face lit up. 'Yes. I know their foreman, Buzz Steele.'

He had put up some of the biggest buildings in Glace Bay.

'Good. It's a fine outfit. I would recommend them.'

'I'll talk to Buzz tomorrow.'

That evening Lara showed the contract to Charles Cohn. She did not dare tell him about the private deal she had made with MacAllister. She was too ashamed. Cohn read the contract carefully, and when he finished, he handed it back to Lara. 'I would advise you not to sign this.'

She was dismayed. 'Why?'

'There's a clause in there that stipulates that the building must be completed by December 31st, or title reverts to the bank. In other words, the building will belong to MacAllister, and my company will become *his* tenant. You forfeit the deal and are still obligated to repay the loan with interest. Ask him to change that.'

MacAllister's words rang in Lara's ears. *I'm really in no hurry to sell that lot. The longer I hold on to it the more valuable it will become.*

Lara shook her head. 'He won't.'

'Then you're taking a big gamble, Lara. You could wind up with nothing, and a debt of two hundred thousand dollars plus interest.'

'But if I bring the building in on time . . .'

'That's a big "if". When you put up a building, you're at the mercy of a lot of other people. You'd be surprised at the number of things that can go wrong.'

'There's a very good construction company in Sydney. They've put up a lot of buildings around here. I know the foreman. I'll talk to him. If he says

74

he can have the building up in time, I want to go ahead.'

It was the desperate eagerness in Lara's voice that made him put aside his doubts. 'All right,' he finally said, 'talk to him.'

Lara found Buzz Steele walking the girders of a five-storey building he was erecting in Sydney. Steele was a grizzled, weather-beaten man in his forties. He greeted Lara warmly. 'This is a nice surprise,' he said. 'How did they let a pretty girl like you get out of Glace Bay?'

'I sneaked out,' Lara told him. 'I have a job for you, Mr Steele.'

He smiled. 'You do? What are we building – a doll's house?'

'No.' She pulled out the blueprints Charles Cohn had given her. 'This is the building.'

Buzz Steele studied it a moment. He looked up, surprised. 'This is a pretty big job. What does it have to do with you?'

'I put the deal together,' Lara said proudly. 'I'm going to own the building.'

Steele whistled softly. 'Well, good for you, honey.'

'There are two catches.'

'Oh?'

'The building has to be finished by December 31st or it reverts to the bank, and it can't cost more than $170,000.'

'December 31st is just ten months away.'

'I know. Can it be done?'

Steele looked at the blueprints again. Lara watched him silently calculating.

Finally he spoke. 'It can be finished by December 31st if you give us the green light now.'

'Then you've got a deal.'

It was all Lara could do not to shout out loud. *I've done it*, she thought. *I've done it!*

They shook hands. 'You're the prettiest boss I've ever had,' Buzz Steele said.

'Thank you. How soon can you get started?'

'Tell you what. I'll go into Glace Bay tomorrow to look over the lot. I'm going to give you a building you'll be proud of.'

When Lara left, she felt that she had wings.

Lara returned to Glace Bay and told Charles Cohn the news.

'Are you sure this company is reliable, Lara?'

'I know it is,' Lara assured him. 'They've put up buildings here and in Sydney, and Halifax and . . .'

Her enthusiasm was contagious.

Cohn smiled. 'Well, then, it looks like we're in business.'

'It does, doesn't it?' Lara beamed. And then she remembered the deal she had made with Sean MacAllister, and her smile faded. *Next Saturday I have to go into Halifax. I thought we might go there together.* Saturday was only two days away.

Lara signed the contracts the following morning. As Sean MacAllister watched her leave the office, he was very pleased with himself. He had no intention of letting her have the new building. And he almost

76

laughed aloud at her naïveté. He would loan her the money, but he would really be loaning it to himself. He thought about making love to that wonderful young body, and he began to get an erection.

Lara had been to Halifax only twice. Compared to Glace Bay, it was a bustling town, full of pedestrians and automobiles, and shops crammed with merchandise. Sean MacAllister drove Lara to a motel on the outskirts of town. He pulled into the parking lot and patted her on the knee. 'You wait here while I register for us, honey.'

Lara sat in the car, waiting, panicky. *I'm selling myself*, she thought. *Like a whore. But it's all I've got to sell, and at least he thinks I'm worth two hundred thousand dollars. My father never saw two hundred thousand dollars in his life. He was always too . . .*

The car door opened and MacAllister was standing there, grinning. 'All set. Let's go.'

Lara suddenly found it hard to breathe. Her heart was pounding so hard she thought it was going to fly out of her chest. *I'm having a heart attack*, she thought.

'Lara . . .' He was looking at her strangely. 'Are you all right?'

No. I'm dying. They'll take me to the hospital and I'll die there. A virgin. 'I'm fine,' she said.

Slowly she got out of the car and followed MacAllister into a drab cabin with a bed, two chairs, a battered dressing table, and a tiny bathroom.

She was caught up in a nightmare.

'So this is your first time, eh?' MacAllister said.

She thought of the boys at school who had fondled

77

her and kissed her breasts and tried to put their hands between her legs. 'Yes,' she said.

'Well, you mustn't be nervous. Sex is the most natural thing in the world.'

Lara watched as MacAllister began to strip off his clothes. His body was pudgy.

'Get undressed,' MacAllister ordered.

Slowly, Lara took off her blouse and skirt and shoes. She was wearing a brassière and panties.

MacAllister looked at her figure and walked over to her. 'You're beautiful, you know that, baby?'

She could feel his male hardness pressing against her body. MacAllister kissed her on the lips and she felt disgust.

'Get the rest of your clothes off,' he said urgently. He walked over to the bed and stripped off his shorts. His penis was hard and red.

That will never fit inside me, Lara thought. *It will kill me.*

'Hurry up.'

Slowly Lara took off her brassière and stepped out of her panties.

'My God,' he said, 'you're fantastic. Come over here.'

Lara walked over to the bed and sat down. MacAllister squeezed her breasts hard and she cried aloud with the pain.

'That felt good, didn't it? It's time you had yourself a man.' MacAllister pushed her down on her back and spread her legs.

Lara was suddenly panicky. 'I'm not wearing anything,' she said. 'I mean . . . I could get pregnant.'

'Don't worry,' MacAllister promised her, 'I won't come inside you.'

An instant later, Lara felt him pushing inside her, hurting her.

'Wait!' she cried, 'I . . .'

MacAllister was past the waiting. He rammed himself into her and the pain was excruciating. He was pounding into her body now, harder and harder, and Lara put her hand to her mouth to keep from screaming. *It will be over in a minute*, she thought, *and I'll own a building. And I can put up a second building. And another* . . .

The pain was becoming unbearable.

'Move your ass,' MacAllister cried. 'Don't just lay there. Move it!'

She tried to move, but it was impossible. She was in too much pain.

Suddenly, MacAllister gave a gasp and Lara felt his body jerk. He let out a satisfied sigh and lay limp against her.

She was horrified. 'You said you wouldn't . . .'

He lifted himself up on his elbows and said earnestly, 'Darling, I couldn't help it, you're just so beautiful. But don't worry. If you get pregnant, I know a doctor who'll take care of you.'

Lara turned her face away so he could not see her revulsion. She limped into the bathroom, sore and bleeding. She stood in the shower, letting the warm water wash over her body, and she thought, *It's over with. I've done it. I own the land. I'm going to be rich.*

Now all she had to do was get dressed and go back to Glace Bay and get her building started.

She walked out of the bathroom and Sean MacAllister said, 'That was so good, we're going to do it again.'

Charles Cohn had inspected five buildings erected by the Nova Scotia Construction Company.

'They're a first rate outfit,' he had told Lara. 'You shouldn't have any problem with them.'

Now, Lara, Charles Cohn, and Buzz Steele were inspecting the new site.

'It's perfect,' Buzz Steele said. 'The measurements come to 43,560 square feet. That will give you the twenty-thousand-square-foot building you want.'

Charles Cohn asked, 'Can you have the building finished by December 31st?' He was determined to protect Lara.

'Sooner,' Steele said. 'I can promise it to you by Christmas Eve.'

Lara was beaming. 'How soon can you get started?'

'I'll have my crew here by the middle of next week. Do I have the go-ahead?'

Cohn looked at Lara and nodded.

'You have the go-ahead,' Lara said happily.

Watching the new building going up was the most exciting thing Lara had ever experienced. She was there every day. 'I want to learn,' she told Charles Cohn. 'This is just the beginning for me. Before I'm through, I'm going to put up a hundred buildings.'

Cohn wondered whether Lara really knew what she was getting into.

The first men to set foot on the project site were members of the survey team. They established the legal geometric borders of the property and drove hubs into the ground at each corner, every hub painted with a fluorescent colour for easy identification. The survey work was finished in two days, and early the following morning, heavy earth-moving equipment – a truck-mounted Caterpillar front-end loader – arrived at the site.

Lara was there, waiting. 'What happens now?' she asked Buzz Steele.

'We clear and grub.'

Lara looked at him. 'What does that mean?'

'The Caterpillar is gonna dig up tree stumps and do some rough grading.'

The next piece of equipment that came in was a backhoe to dig the trenches for foundations, utility conduits, and drainage piping.

By now, the boarders at the house had all heard what was happening, and it became the main topic of conversation at breakfast and supper. They were all cheering for Lara.

'What happens next?' they would ask.

She was becoming an expert. 'This morning, they put the underground piping in place. Tomorrow they start to put in the wood and concrete formwork, so they can wire-tie the steel bars into the skeletal gridiron.' She grinned. 'Do you understand what I'm saying?'

Pouring the concrete was the next step, and when the concrete foundation was cured, large truckloads of lumber rolled in, and crews of carpenters began to assemble the wooden frames. The noise was horrendous, but to Lara it was music. The place was filled with the sounds of rhythmic hammers and whining power saws. After two weeks, the wall panels, punctuated with window and door openings, were stood upright as if the building had suddenly been inflated.

To passers-by, the building was a maze of wood and steel, but to Lara it was something else. It was her dream come to life. Every morning and every evening, she went downtown and stared at what was being built. *I own this*, Lara thought. *This belongs to me*.

After the episode with MacAllister, Lara had been terrified that she might become pregnant. The thought of it made her sick to her stomach. When her period came, she was weak with relief. *Now all I have to worry about is my building*.

She continued to collect the rents for Sean MacAllister because she needed a place to live, but she had to steel herself to go into his office and face him.

'We had a good time in Halifax, didn't we, honey? Why don't we do it again?'

'I'm busy with my building,' Lara said firmly.

The level of activity began to heighten as the sheet metal crews, roofers and carpenters worked simultaneously, the number of men, materials, and trucks tripling.

Charles Cohn had left Glace Bay, but he telephoned Lara once a week.

'How is the building going?' he had asked the last time he called.

'Great!' Lara said enthusiastically.

'Is it on schedule?'

'It's ahead of schedule.'

'That's wonderful. I can tell you now that I wasn't really sure you could do it.'

'But you gave me a chance, anyway. Thank you, Charles.'

'One good turn deserves another. Remember, if it hadn't been for you, I might have starved to death.'

From time to time, Sean MacAllister would join Lara at the building site.

'It's coming along just fine, isn't it?'

'Yes,' Lara said.

MacAllister seemed genuinely pleased. Lara thought: *Mr Cohn was wrong about him. He's not trying to take advantage of me.*

By the end of November, the building was progressing rapidly. The windows and doors were in place, and the exterior walls were set. The structure was ready to accept the network of nerves and arteries.

On Monday, the first week of December, work on the building began to slow down. Lara went to the site one morning and there were only two men there, and they seemed to be doing very little.

'Where's the rest of the crew today?' Lara asked.

'They're on another job,' one of the men explained. 'They'll be here tomorrow.'

The following day no one was there.

Lara took a bus into Halifax to see Buzz Steele. 'What's happening?' Lara asked. 'The work has stopped.'

'Nothing to worry about,' Steele assured her. 'We ran into a little snag on another job and I had to pull my men off temporarily.'

'When will they be coming back to work?'

'Next week. We'll be on schedule.'

'Buzz, you know how much this means to me.'

'Sure, Lara.'

'If the building's not completed on time, I lose it. I lose everything.'

'Don't worry, kid. I won't let that happen.'

When Lara left, she had a feeling of unease.

The following week, the workmen still had not appeared. She went into Halifax again to see Steele.

'I'm sorry,' the secretary said, 'Mr Steele is not in.'

'I must talk to him. When will he be back?'

'He's out of town on a job. I don't know when he'll be back.'

Lara felt the first stirrings of panic. 'This is very important,' Lara insisted. 'He's putting up a building for me. It has to be finished in three weeks.'

'I wouldn't worry, Miss Cameron. If Mr Steele said it will be finished, it will be finished.'

'But nothing's happening,' Lara cried. 'No one's working on it.'

'Would you like to talk to Mr Ericksen, his assistant?'

'Yes, please.'

Ericksen was a giant of a man, broad shouldered and amiable. He radiated reassurance.

'I know why you're here,' he said, 'but Buzz told me to assure you that you have nothing to worry about. We've been held back a little on your project because of some problems on a couple of big construction jobs we're handling, but your building is only three weeks away from completion.'

'There's still so much to do . . .'

'Not to worry. We'll have a crew out there first thing Monday morning.'

'Thank you,' Lara said, relieved. 'I'm sorry to have bothered you, but I'm a little nervous. This means a great deal to me.'

'No problem,' Ericksen smiled. 'You just go home and relax. You're in good hands.'

On Monday morning there was not a single workman at the site. Lara was frantic. She telephoned Charles Cohn.

'The men have stopped working,' she told him, 'and I can't find out why. They keep making promises and breaking them.'

'What's the name of the company – Nova Scotia Construction?'

'That's right.'

'I'll call you back,' Cohn said.

Two hours later, Charles Cohn telephoned. 'Who recommended the Nova Scotia Construction Company to you?'

She thought back. 'Sean MacAllister.'

'I'm not surprised. He owns the company, Lara.'

Lara felt suddenly faint. 'And he's stopping the men from finishing it on time . . . ?'

'I'm afraid it looks that way.'

85

'Oh, my God.'

'He's a *nahash tzefa* – a poisonous snake.'

He was too kind to say that he had warned her. All he managed was, 'Maybe . . . maybe something will turn up.'

He admired the young girl's spirit and ambition, and he despised Sean MacAllister. But he was helpless. There was nothing he could do.

Lara lay awake all night thinking about her folly. The building she had put up would belong now to Sean MacAllister, and she would be left with a staggering debt which she would spend the rest of her life working to repay. The thought of how MacAllister might exact payment made her shudder. Finally, at dawn, exhausted from crying, she fell asleep.

When Lara awakened, she went to see Sean MacAllister.

'Good morning, my dear. You're looking lovely today.'

Lara came right to the point. 'I need an extension. The building won't be ready by the thirty-first.'

MacAllister sat back in his chair and frowned. 'Really? That's bad news, Lara.'

'I need another month.'

MacAllister sighed. 'I'm afraid that's not possible. Oh dear, no. You signed a contract. A deal is a deal.'

'But . . .'

'I'm sorry, Lara. On the thirty-first, the property reverts to the bank.'

*

When the boarders at the house heard what was happening, they were furious.

'That sonofabitch!' one of them cried. 'He can't do this to you.'

'He's done it,' Lara said, despairingly. 'It's over.'

'Are we going to let him get away with this?'

'Hell, no. What have you got left – three weeks?'

Lara shook her head, 'Less. Two and a half weeks.'

The man turned to the others. 'Let's go down and take a look at that building.'

'What good will . . . ?'

'We'll see.'

Soon, half a dozen boarders were standing at the building site, carefully inspecting it.

'The plumbing hasn't been put in,' one of the men said.

'Nor the electricity.'

They stood there, shivering in the freezing December wind, discussing what still remained to be done.

One of the men turned to Lara. 'Your banker's a tricky fellow. He's had the building almost finished so that he wouldn't have much to do when your contract was up.' He turned to the others. 'I would say that this could be finished in two and a half weeks.'

There was a chorus of agreement.

Lara was bewildered. 'You don't understand. The workmen won't come.'

'Look, lassie, in your boarding house you've got plumbers and carpenters and electricians, and we've got lots of friends in town who can handle the rest.'

'I don't have any money to pay you,' Lara said. 'Mr MacAllister won't give me . . .'

'It will be our Christmas gift to you.'

What happened after that was incredible. Word quickly spread around Glace Bay of what was happening. Construction workers on other buildings came to take a look at Lara's property. Half of them were there because they liked Lara, and the other half because they had had dealings with Sean MacAllister and hated him.

'Let's fix the bastard,' they said.

They dropped by to lend a hand after work, working past midnight and on Saturdays and Sundays, and the sound of construction began again, filling the air with a joyful noise. Beating the deadline became a challenge, and the building was soon swarming with carpenters and electricians and plumbers, all eager to pitch in. When Sean MacAllister heard what was happening, he rushed over to the site.

He stood there, stunned. 'What's going on?' he demanded. 'Those aren't my workmen.'

'They're mine,' Lara said defiantly. 'There's nothing in the contract that says I can't use my own men.'

'Well, I . . .' MacAllister sputtered. 'That building had better be up to specifications.'

'It will be,' Lara assured him.

The day before New Year's Eve, the building was completed. It stood proud against the sky, solid and strong, and it was the most beautiful thing Lara had ever seen. She stood there staring at it, dazed.

'It's all yours,' one of the workmen said proudly. 'Are we going to have a party or what?'

That night, it seemed that the whole town of Glace Bay celebrated Lara Cameron's first building.

It was the beginning.

*

There was no stopping Lara after that. Her mind was brimming with ideas.

'Your new employees are going to need places to live in Glace Bay,' she told Charles Cohn. 'I'd like to build houses for them. Are you interested?'

He nodded. 'I'm very interested.'

Lara went to see a banker in Sydney and borrowed enough money on her building to finance the new project.

When the houses were finished, Lara said to Charles Cohn, 'Do you know what else this town needs, Charles? Cabins to accommodate the summer tourists who come here to fish. I know a wonderful place near the Bay where I could build . . .'

Charles Cohn became Lara's unofficial financial advisor, and during the next three years, Lara built an office building, half a dozen sea-shore cottages, and a shopping mall. The banks in Sydney and Halifax were happy to loan her money.

Two years later, when Lara sold out her real estate holdings, she had a certified cheque for three million dollars. She was twenty-one years old.

The following day, she said goodbye to Glace Bay and left for Chicago.

Chicago was a revelation. Halifax had been the largest city Lara had ever seen, but it was like a hamlet compared to the giant of the Midwest. Chicago was a loud and noisy city, bustling and energetic, and everyone seemed to be hurrying to some important destination.

Lara checked into Stevens Hotel. She took one look at the smartly dressed women walking through the lobby and became self-conscious about the clothes she was wearing. *Glace Bay, yes*, Lara thought. *Chicago, no*. The following morning, Lara went into action. She visited Kane's and Ultimo for designer dresses, Joseph's for shoes, Saks Fifth Avenue and Marshall Field's for lingerie, Trabert and Hoeffer for jewellery, and Ware for a mink coat. And every time she bought something, she heard her father's voice saying, *'I'm nae made of money. Get yourself something frae the Salvation Army Citadel.'* Before her shopping spree was over, the closets in her hotel suite were filled with beautiful clothes.

Lara's next move was to look in the yellow pages of the telephone book under real estate brokers. She selected the one that had the largest advertisement,

Parker & Associates. Lara telephoned and asked to speak to Mr Parker.

'May I tell him who's calling?'

'Lara Cameron.'

A moment later, a voice said, 'Bruce Parker speaking. How can I help you?'

'I'm looking for a location where I can put up a beautiful new hotel,' Lara said.

The voice at the other end of the phone grew warmer. 'Well, we're experts at that, Mrs Cameron.'

'*Miss* Cameron.'

'Right. Did you have any particular area in mind?'

'No. To tell you the truth, I'm not really familiar with Chicago.'

'That's no problem. I'm sure we can line up some very interesting properties for you. Just to give me an idea of what we're looking for, how much equity do you have?'

Lara said proudly, 'Three million dollars.'

There was a long silence. 'Three million dollars?'

'Yes.'

'And you want to build a beautiful new hotel?'

'Yes.'

Another silence.

'Were you interested in building or acquiring something in the inner city area, Miss Cameron?'

'Of course not,' Lara said. 'What I have in mind is exactly the opposite. I want to build an exclusive boutique hotel in a nice area that . . .'

'With an equity of three million dollars?' Parker chuckled. 'I'm afraid we're not going to be able to help you.'

'Thank you,' Lara said. She replaced the receiver. She had obviously called the wrong broker.

She went back to the yellow pages again and made half a dozen more calls. By the end of the afternoon, Lara was forced to face reality. None of the brokers was interested in trying to find a prime location where she could build a hotel with a down payment of three million dollars. They had offered Lara a variety of suggestions, and they had all come down to the same thing: A cheap hotel in an inner city area.

Never, Lara thought. *I'll go back to Glace Bay first.*

She had dreamed for months about the hotel she wanted to build and in her mind it was already a reality – beautiful, vivid, three-dimensional. Her plan was to turn a hotel into a real home away from home. It would have mostly suites, and each suite would have a living room and a library with a fireplace in each room, and be furnished with comfortable couches, easy chairs and a grand piano. There would be two large bedrooms and an outside terrace running the length of the apartment. There would be a jacuzzi and a mini-bar. Lara knew exactly what she wanted. The question was how she was going to get it.

Lara walked into a print shop on Lake Street. 'I would like to have a hundred business cards printed up, please.'

'Certainly. And how will the cards read?'

'*Miss Lara Cameron*, and at the bottom, *Real Estate Developer*.'

'Yes, Miss Cameron. I can have them for you in two days.'

'No. I would like them this afternoon, please.'

*

The next step was to get acquainted with the city.

Lara walked along Michigan Avenue and State Street and La Salle, strolled along Lake Shore Drive and wandered through Lincoln Park with its zoo and golf course and lagoon. She visited the Merchandise Mart, and went to Kroch-Brentano's and bought books about Chicago. She read about the famous who had made Chicago their home: Carl Sandburg, Frank Lloyd Wright, Louis Sullivan, Saul Bellow. She read about the pioneer families of Chicago; the John Bairds and Gaylord Donnelleys, the Marshall Fields and Potter Palmers and Walgreens, and she passed by their homes on Lake Shore Drive and their huge estates in suburban Lake Forest. Lara visited the southside and she felt at home there because of all the ethnic groups: Swedes, Poles, Irish, Lithuanians. It reminded her of Glace Bay.

She took to the streets again, looking at buildings with 'For Sale' signs, and she went to see the listed brokers. 'What's the price of that building?'

'Eighty million dollars . . .'

'Sixty million dollars . . .'

'A hundred million dollars . . .'

Her three million dollars was becoming more and more insignificant. Lara sat in her hotel room considering her options. She could either go to one of the slum sections of the city and put up a little hotel there, or she could return home. Neither choice appealed to her.

I've too much at stake to give up now, Lara thought.

*

The following morning, Lara stopped in at a bank on La Salle Street. She walked up to a clerk behind the counter. 'I would like to speak to your vice president, please.'

She handed the clerk her card.

Five minutes later, she was in the office of Tom Peterson, a flaccid, middle-aged man, with a nervous tic. He was studying her card.

'What can I do for you, Miss Cameron?'

'I'm planning to put up a hotel in Chicago. I'll need to borrow some money.'

He gave her a genial smile. 'That's what we're here for. What kind of hotel were you planning to build?'

'A beautiful boutique hotel in a nice area.'

'Sounds interesting.'

'I have to tell you,' Lara said, 'that I only have three million dollars to put down, and . . .'

He smiled. 'No problem.'

She felt a thrill of excitement. 'Really?'

'Three million can go a long way if you know what to do with it.' He looked at his watch. 'I have another appointment now. I wonder if we could get together for dinner tonight and talk about this.'

'Certainly,' Lara said. 'That would be fine.'

'Where are you staying?'

'At the Palmer House.'

'Why don't I pick you up at eight?'

Lara got to her feet. 'Thank you so much. I can't tell you how good you make me feel. Frankly, I was beginning to get discouraged.'

'No need,' he said. 'I'm going to take good care of you.'

At eight o'clock, Tom Peterson picked up Lara and took her to Henrici's for dinner. When they were seated, he said, 'You know, I'm glad that you came to me. We can do a lot for each other.'

'We can?'

'Yes. There's a lot of ass around this town, but none of it as beautiful as yours, honey. You can open a luxury whorehouse and cater to an exclusive . . .'

Lara froze. 'I beg your pardon?'

'If you can get half a dozen girls together we . . .'

Lara was gone.

The following day, Lara visited three more banks. When she explained her plans to the manager of the first, he said, 'I'm going to give you the best advice you'll ever get: Forget it. Real estate development is a man's game. There's no place for women in it.'

'And why is that?' Lara asked tonelessly.

'Because you'd be dealing with a bunch of macho roughnecks. They'd eat you alive.'

'They didn't eat me alive in Glace Bay,' Lara said.

He leaned forward. 'I'm going to let you in on a little secret. Chicago is not Glace Bay.'

At the next bank, the manager said to her, 'We'll be glad to help you out, Miss Cameron. Of course, what you have in mind is out of the question. What I would suggest is to let us handle your money and invest it . . .'

Lara was out of his office before he finished his sentence.

*

At the third bank, Lara was ushered into the office of Bob Vance, a pleasant-looking, grey-haired man who looked exactly as the president of a bank should look. In the office with him was a pale, thin, sandy-haired man in his early thirties, wearing a rumpled suit, and looking completely out of place.

'This is Howard Keller, Miss Cameron, one of our vice presidents.'

'How do you do?'

'What can I do for you this morning?' Bob Vance asked.

'I'm interested in building a hotel in Chicago,' Lara said, 'and I'm looking for finance.'

Bob Vance smiled. 'You've come to the right place. Do you have a location in mind?'

'I know the general area I want. Near the loop, not too far from Michigan Avenue . . .'

'Excellent.'

Lara told him about her boutique hotel idea.

'That sounds interesting,' Vance said. 'And how much equity do you have?'

'Three million dollars. I want to borrow the rest.'

There was a thoughtful pause. 'I'm afraid I can't help you. Your problem is that you have big ideas and a small purse. Now, if you would like us to invest your money for you . . .'

'No, thank you,' Lara said. 'Thanks for your time. Good afternoon, gentlemen.' She turned and left the office, fuming. In Glace Bay three million dollars was a fortune. Here, people seemed to think it was nothing.

As Lara reached the street, a voice said, 'Miss Cameron!'

Lara turned. It was the man she had been introduced to – Howard Keller. 'Yes?'

'I'd like to talk to you,' he said. 'Perhaps we could have a cup of coffee.'

Lara stiffened. *Was everyone in Chicago a sex maniac?*

'There's a good coffee shop just around the corner.'

Lara shrugged. 'All right.'

When they had ordered, Howard Keller said, 'If you don't mind my butting in, I'd like to give you some advice.'

Lara was watching him, wary. 'Go ahead.'

'In the first place, you're going about this all wrong.'

'You don't think my idea will work?' she asked stiffly.

'On the contrary. I think a boutique hotel is a really great idea.'

She was surprised. 'Then why . . . ?'

'Chicago could use a hotel like that, but I don't think you should build it.'

'What do you mean?'

'I would suggest that, instead, you find an old hotel in a good location and remodel it. There are a lot of rundown hotels that can be bought at a low figure. Your three million dollars would be enough equity for a down payment. Then you could borrow enough from a bank to refurbish it and turn it into your boutique hotel.'

Lara sat there thinking. He was right. It was a better approach.

'Another thing, no bank is going to be interested in financing you unless you come in with a solid architect and builder. They'll want to see a complete package.'

Lara thought about Buzz Steele. 'I understand. Do you know a good architect and builder?'

Howard Keller smiled. 'Quite a few.'

'Thanks for your advice,' Lara said. 'If I find the right site, could I come back and talk to you about it?'

'Any time. Good luck.'

Lara was waiting for him to say something like, 'Why don't we talk it over at my apartment?' Instead, all Howard Keller said was, 'Would you care for more coffee, Miss Cameron?'

Lara roamed the downtown streets again, but this time she was looking for something different. A few blocks from Michigan Avenue, on Delaware, Lara passed a pre-war, rundown transient hotel. A sign outside said, 'Cong essi nal Hotel.' Lara started to pass it, then suddenly stopped. She took a closer look. The brick façade was so dirty that it was difficult to tell what its original colour had been. It was eight storeys high. Lara turned and entered the hotel lobby. The interior was even worse than the exterior. A clerk dressed in jeans and a torn sweater was pushing a derelict out of the door. The front desk looked more like a ticket window than a reception area. At one end of the lobby was a staircase leading to what once were meeting rooms, now turned into rented offices. On the mezzanine, Lara could see a travel agency, a theatre ticket service, and an employment agency.

The clerk returned to the front desk. 'You wanna room?'

'No. I wanted to know . . .' She was interrupted by a heavily made-up young woman in a tight-fitting skirt. 'Give me a key, Mike.' There was an elderly man at her side.

The clerk handed her a key.

Lara watched the two of them head for the elevator.

'What can I do for you?' the clerk asked.

'I'm interested in this hotel,' Lara said. 'Is it for sale?'

'I guess everything's for sale. Is your father in the real estate business?'

'No,' Lara said, 'I am.'

He looked at her in surprise. 'Oh. Well, the one you want to talk to is one of the Diamond brothers. They own a chain of these dumps.'

'Where would I find them?' Lara asked.

The clerk gave her an address on State Street.

'Would you mind if I looked around?'

He shrugged. 'Help yourself.' He grinned. 'Who knows, you might wind up being my boss.'

Not if I can help it, Lara thought.

She walked around the lobby, examining it closely. There were old marble columns lining the entrance. On a hunch, Lara pulled up an edge of the dirty, worn carpet. Underneath was a dull marble floor. She walked up to the mezzanine. The mustard-coloured wallpaper was peeling. She pulled away an edge of it and underneath was the same marble. Lara was becoming more and more excited. The handrail of the staircase was painted black. Lara turned to make sure that the room clerk was not watching and took out her key from Stevens Hotel and scratched away some of the paint. She found what she was hoping for, a solid brass railing. She approached the elevators that were painted with the same black paint, scratched a bit away and found more brass.

Lara walked back to the clerk, trying to conceal her excitement. 'I wonder if I might look at one of the rooms.'

He shrugged. 'No skin off my nose.' He handed her a key. 'Four-ten.'

'Thank you.'

Lara got in the elevator. It was slow and antiquated. *I'll have it redone*, Lara thought. *And I'll put a mural inside.*

In her mind, she was already beginning to decorate the hotel.

Room four-ten looked a disaster, but the possibilities were immediately evident. It was a surprisingly large room with antiquated facilities and tasteless furniture. Lara's heart began to beat faster. *It's perfect*, she thought.

She walked downstairs. The stairway was old and had a musty smell. The carpets were worn, but underneath she found the same marble.

Lara returned the key to the desk clerk.

'Did you see what you wanted?'

'Yes,' Lara said. 'Thank you.'

He grinned at her. 'You really going to buy this joint?'

'Yes,' Lara said. 'I'm really going to buy this joint.'

'Cool,' he said.

The elevator door opened and the young hooker and her elderly john emerged. She handed the key and some money to the clerk. 'Thanks, Mike.'

'Have a nice day,' Mike called. He turned to Lara. 'Are you coming back?'

'Oh, yes,' Lara assured him, 'I'm coming back.'

Lara's next stop was at the City Hall of Records. She asked to see the records on the property that she was interested in. For a fee of ten dollars, she was handed a file on the Congressional Hotel. It had been sold to the Diamond brothers five years earlier for six million dollars.

The office of the Diamond brothers was in an old building on a corner in State Street. An oriental receptionist in a tight red skirt greeted Lara as she walked in.

'Can I help you?'

'I'd like to see Mr Diamond.'

'Which one?'

'Either of them.'

'I'll give you John.'

She picked up the phone and spoke into it. 'There's a lady here to see you, John.' She listened a moment then looked up at Lara. 'What's it about?'

'I want to buy one of his hotels.'

She spoke into the mouthpiece again. 'She says she wants to buy one of your hotels. Right.' She replaced the receiver. 'Go right in.'

John Diamond was a huge man, middle-aged and hairy, and he had the pushed-in face of a man who had once played a lot of football. He was wearing a short-sleeved shirt and smoking a large cigar. He looked up as Lara entered his office.

'My secretary said you wanted to buy one of my buildings.' He studied her a moment. 'You don't look old enough to vote.'

'Oh, I'm old enough to vote,' Lara assured him. 'I'm also old enough to buy one of your buildings.'

'Yeah? Which one?'

'The Cong essi nal Hotel.'

'The *what*?'

'That's what the sign says. I assume it means "Congressional".'

'Oh. Yeah.'

'Is it for sale?'

He shook his head. 'Gee, I don't know. That's one of our big money-makers. I'm not sure we could let it go.'

'You *have* let it go,' Lara said.

'Huh?'

'It's in terrible shape. The place is falling apart.'

'Yeah? Then what the hell do *you* want with it?'

'I'd like to buy it and fix it up a little. Of course, it would have to be delivered to me vacant.'

'That's no problem. Our tenants are on a week-to-week basis.'

'How many rooms does the hotel have?'

'A hundred and twenty-five. The gross building area is a hundred thousand square feet.'

Too many rooms, Lara thought. *But if I combine them to create suites, I would end up with sixty to seventy-five keys. It could work.*

It was time to discuss price.

'*If* I decided to buy the building, how much would you want for it?'

Diamond said, '*If* I decided to sell the building,

I'd want ten million dollars, a six million cash down payment . . .'

Lara shook her head, 'I'll offer . . .'

'. . . period. No negotiating.'

Lara sat there, mentally figuring the cost of renovation. It would be approximately eighty dollars per square foot, or eight million dollars, plus furniture, fixtures and equipment.

Lara's mind was furiously calculating. She was sure she could get a bank to finance the loan. The problem was that she needed six million dollars in equity, and she only had three million. Diamond was asking too much for the hotel, but she wanted it. She wanted it more than anything she had ever wanted in her life.

'I'll make you a deal,' Lara said.

He was listening. 'Yeah?'

'I'll give you your asking price . . .'

He smiled. 'So far so good.'

'And I'll give you a down payment of three million in cash.'

He shook his head. 'Can't do it. I've got to have six million in cash up front.'

'You'll have it.'

'Yeah? Where's the other three coming from?'

'From you.'

'What?'

'You're going to give me a second mortgage for three million.'

'You want to borrow money from *me* to buy my building?'

It was the same thing Sean MacAllister had asked her in Glace Bay.

'Look at it this way,' Lara said. 'You're really

borrowing the money from yourself. You'll own the building until I pay it off. There's no way you can lose.'

He thought about it and grinned. 'Lady, you just bought yourself a hotel.'

Howard Keller's office in the bank was a cubicle with his name on the door. When Lara walked in, he looked more rumpled than ever.

'Back so soon?'

'You told me to come and see you when I found a hotel. I found one.'

Keller leaned back in his chair. 'Tell me about it.'

'I found an old hotel called the Congressional. It's on Delaware. It's a few blocks from Michigan Avenue. It's rundown and seedy, and I want to buy it and turn it into the best hotel in Chicago.'

'Tell me the deal.'

Lara told him.

Keller sat there, thinking. 'Let's run it past Bob Vance.'

Bob Vance listened and made some notes. 'It might be possible,' he said, 'but . . .' He looked at Lara. 'Have you ever run a hotel before, Miss Cameron?'

Lara thought about all the years of running the boarding house in Glace Bay, making the beds, scrubbing the floors and doing the laundry and the dishes, trying to please the different personalities, and keep the peace.

'I ran a boarding house full of miners and lumbermen. A hotel will be a cinch.'

104

Howard Keller said, 'I'd like to take a look at the property, Bob.'

Lara's enthusiasm was irresistible. Howard Keller watched Lara's face as they walked through the seedy hotel rooms, and he saw them through her eyes.

'This will be a beautiful suite with a sauna,' Lara said excitedly. 'The fireplace will be here, and the grand piano in that corner.' She began to pace back and forth. 'When affluent travellers come to Chicago, they stay at the best hotels, but they're all the same – cold rooms without any character. If we can offer them something like this, even though it may cost a little more, there's no doubt about which they'll choose. This will *really* be a home away from home.'

'I'm impressed,' Howard Keller said.

Lara turned to him eagerly. 'Do you think the bank will loan me the money?'

'Let's find out.'

Thirty minutes later, Howard Keller was in conference with Vance.

'What do you think about it?' Vance asked.

'I think the lady's on to something. I like her idea about a boutique hotel.'

'So do I. The only problem is that she's so young and inexperienced. It's a gamble.' They spent the next half hour discussing costs and projected earnings.

'I think we should go ahead with it,' Keller finally

said. 'We can't lose.' He grinned. 'If worse comes to worst, you and I can move into the hotel.'

Howard Keller telephoned Lara at the Stevens Hotel. 'The bank has just approved your loan.'

Lara let out a shriek. 'Do you mean it? That's wonderful! Oh, thank you, thank you!'

'We have a few things to talk about,' Howard Keller said. 'Are you free for dinner this evening?'

'Yes.'

'Fine. I'll pick you up at seven thirty.'

They had dinner at the Imperial House. Lara was so excited that she barely touched her food.

'I can't tell you how thrilled I am,' she said. 'It's going to be the most beautiful hotel in Chicago.'

'Easy,' Keller warned, 'there's a long way to go.' He hesitated. 'May I be frank with you, Miss Cameron?'

'Lara.'

'Lara. You're a dark horse. You have no track record.'

'In Glace Bay . . .'

'This isn't Glace Bay. To mix metaphors, it's a different ballpark.'

'Then why is the bank doing this?' Lara asked.

'Don't get me wrong. We're not a charitable organization. The worst thing that can happen is that the bank will break even. But I have a feeling about you. I believe you're going to make it. I think there could be a big upside. You don't intend to stop with this one hotel, do you?'

'Of course not,' Lara said.

'I didn't think so. What I want to say is that when we make a loan, we don't usually get personally involved in the project. But in this case, I'd like to give you whatever help you might need.'

And Howard Keller intended to get personally involved with her. He had been attracted to Lara from the moment he had seen her. He was captivated by her enthusiasm and determination. She was a beautiful woman-child. He wanted desperately to impress her. *Maybe*, Keller thought, *one day I'll tell her how close I came to being famous* . . .

It was the final game of the World Series and Wrigley Field was packed with 38,710 screaming fans. 'It's the top of the ninth, with the score Cubs – 1, Yankees – 0. The Yankees are up at bat, with two outs. The bases are loaded with Tony Kubek on first, Whitey Ford on second, and Yogi Berra on third.'

As Mickey Mantle stepped up to the plate, the crowd roared. 'The Mick' had hit .304 for the season and had 42 homeruns under his belt for the year.

Jack Brickhouse, the Wrigley Field announcer said, excitedly, 'Oh, oh . . . it looks like they're going to change pitchers. They're taking out Moe Drabowsky . . . Cub Manager, Bob Scheffing is talking to the umpire . . . let's see who's coming in . . . it's Howard Keller! Keller is walking up to the pitcher's mound, and the crowd is screaming! The whole burden of the World Series rests on this youngster's shoulders. Can he strike out the great Mickey Mantle? We'll know in a moment! Keller is on the mound now . . . he looks around the loaded bases . . . takes a deep breath, and winds up. Here's the pitch . . . Mantle hauls back the bat . . . takes a swing, and misses! Strike one!'

The crowd had become hushed. Mantle moved forward a little, his face grim, his bat cocked, ready to swing. Howard Keller checked the runners. The pressure was enormous, but he seemed to be cool and *composed. He turned to the catcher, looked in for the sign, and wound up for another pitch.*

'There's the wind up and the pitch!' the announcer yelled. 'It's Keller's famous curve ball . . . Mantle swings on and misses! Strike Two! If young Keller can strike out "The Mick", the Chicago Cubs will win the World Series! We're watching David and Goliath, ladies and gentlemen! Young Keller has only played in the big leagues for one year, but during that time, he has made an enviable reputation for himself. Mickey Mantle is Goliath . . . can the rookie Keller beat him? Everything is riding on this next pitch.

'Keller checks the runners again . . . here's the wind up . . . and here we go! It's the curve . . . Mantle bails out as it curves right over the heart of the plate . . . Strike Three called!' The announcer was screaming now. 'Mantle is caught looking! The mighty Mick has struck out, ladies and gentlemen! Young Howard Keller struck out the great Mickey Mantle! The game is over – the World Series belongs to the Chicago Cubs! The fans are on their feet going crazy!'

On the field, Howard Keller's teammates raced up to him and picked him up on their shoulders and started to cross the . . .

'Howard, what in the world are you doing?'

'My homework, Mom.' Guiltily the fifteen-year-old Howard Keller turned off the television set. The ball game was almost over anyway.

Baseball was Howard's passion and his life. He knew that one day he would play in the Major leagues. At the age of six he was competing against kids twice his age in Stickball, and when he was twelve, he began pitching for an American Legion team. At fifteen, a scout for the Chicago Cubs was told about the young boy. 'I've never seen anything like him,' his informant said. 'The kid has an outstanding curve, and a mean slider, and a change-up you wouldn't believe!'

The scout was sceptical. Grudgingly, he said, 'All right. I'll take a look at the kid.' He went to the next American Legion game that Howard Keller played in and he became an instant convert. He sought out the young boy after the game. 'What do you want to do with your life, son?'

'Play baseball,' said Keller promptly.

'I'm glad to hear that. We're going to sign you to a contract with our minor league team.'

Howard couldn't wait to tell his parents the exciting news.

The Kellers were a close-knit, Catholic family. They went to Mass every Sunday and they saw to it that their son attended church. Howard Keller, Sr was a typewriter salesman, and he was on the road a great deal. When he was at home, he spent as much time as possible with his son. Howard was close to both his parents. His mother made it a point to attend all the ball games when her son was playing, and cheer him on. Howard got his first glove and uniform when he was six years old. He was a fanatic about baseball. He had an encyclopaedic memory for the statistics of games that were played before he was even born. He knew all the stats of the winning pitchers – the strikes, the outs, the number of saves and shut-outs. He won money betting with his schoolmates that he could name the starting pitchers in any team line-up.

'Nineteen forty-nine.'

'That's easy,' Howard said. 'Newcombe, Roe,

110

Hatten and Branca for the Dodgers. Reynolds, Raschi, Byrne and Lopat for the Yankees.'

'All right,' one of his teammates challenged. 'Who played the most consecutive games in major league history?' The challenger was holding the *Guinness Book of Records* in front of him.

Howard Keller didn't even pause. 'Lou Gehrig – 2,130.'

'Who had the record for the most shut-outs?'

'Walter Johnson – one hundred and thirteen.'

'Who hit the most homeruns in his career?'

'Babe Ruth – seven hundred and fourteen.'

Word of the young player's ability began to circulate, and professional scouts came to take a look at the young phenomenon who was playing on the Chicago Cubs minor league team. They were stunned. By the time Keller was seventeen, he had been approached by scouts from the St Louis Cardinals and the Baltimore Orioles and the New York Yankees.

Howard's father was proud of him. 'He takes after me,' he would boast. 'I used to play baseball when I was a youngster.'

During the summer of his senior year in high school, Howard Keller worked as a junior clerk in a bank owned by one of the sponsors of his American Legion team.

Howard was going steady with a pretty schoolmate named Betty Quinlan. It was understood that when they finished college they would get married. Howard would talk baseball by the hour with her, and because she cared for him, she listened patiently. Howard loved the anecdotes about his favourite ballplayers and every time he heard a new one, he would rush to tell it to Betty.

'Casey Stengel said, "The secret of managing is to keep the five guys who hate you away from the five who are undecided."

'Someone asked Yogi Berra what time it was, and he said, "You mean right now?"'

And when a player was hit in the shoulder by a pitched ball, his teammate said, 'There's nothing wrong with his shoulder except some pain – and pain doesn't hurt you.'

Young Keller knew that he was soon going to join the pantheon of the great players. But the gods had other plans for him.

Howard came home from school one day with his best friend, Jesse, who played shortstop on the team. There were two letters waiting for Keller. One offered him a baseball scholarship at Princeton, and the other a baseball scholarship at Harvard.

'Gee, that's great!' Jesse said. 'Congratulations!' And he meant it. Howard Keller was his idol.

'Which one do you think you're going to take?' Howard's father asked.

'Why do I have to go to college at all?' Howard wondered. 'I could get on one of the big league teams now.'

His mother said firmly, 'There's plenty of time for that, son. You're going to get a good education first, then when you're through playing baseball, you'll be fit to do anything you like.'

'All right,' Howard said. 'Harvard. Betty is going to Wellesley and I can be near her.'

Betty Quinlan was delighted when Howard told her what he had decided.

'We'll get to see each other over the weekends!' she said.

His buddy, Jesse, said, 'I'm sure going to miss you.'

The day before Howard Keller was to leave for the university, his father ran off with the secretary of one of his customers.

The young boy was stunned. 'How could he do that?'

His mother was in shock. 'He . . . he must be going through a change of life,' she stammered. 'Your . . . your father loves me very much. He'll . . . he'll come back. You'll see . . .'

The following day, Howard's mother received a letter from an attorney, formally stating that his client, Howard Keller, Sr, wanted a divorce, and since he had no money to pay for alimony, was willing to let his wife have their small house.

Howard held his mother in his arms. 'Don't worry, Mom, I'm going to stay here and take care of you.'

'No. I don't want you to give up college for me. From the day you were born, your father and I planned for you to go to college.' Then quietly, after a moment, 'Let's talk about it in the morning. I'm very tired.'

Howard stayed up all night, thinking about his choices. He could go to Harvard on a baseball scholarship or take one of the offers in the major leagues. Either way he would be leaving his mother alone. It was a difficult decision.

When his mother didn't appear at breakfast the next morning, Howard went into her bedroom. She was sitting up in bed, unable to move, her face pulled up on one side. She had suffered a stroke.

With no money to pay for the hospital or doctors, Howard went back to work at the bank, full-time. He was finished at four o'clock, and each afternoon he hurried home to take care of his mother.

It was a mild stroke, and the doctor assured Howard that in time his mother would be fine. 'She's had a terrible shock, but she's going to recover.'

Howard still got calls from scouts from the major leagues, but he knew that he could not leave his mother. *I'll go when she's better*, he told himself.

The medical bills kept piling up.

In the beginning, he talked to Betty Quinlan once a week, but after a few months the calls became less and less frequent.

Howard's mother did not seem to be improving. Howard talked to the doctor. 'When is she going to be all right?'

'In a case like this, it's hard to tell, son. She could go on for months like this, or even years. Sorry I can't be more specific.'

The year ended and another began, and Howard was still living with his mother and working at the bank. One day he received a letter from Betty Quinlan, telling him that she had fallen in love with someone else, and that she hoped his mother was feeling better. The calls from scouts became less frequent and finally stopped altogether. Howard's life centred on taking care of his mother. He did the shopping and the cooking, and carried on with his job. He no longer thought about baseball. It was difficult enough just getting through each day.

When his mother died four years later, Howard Keller was no longer interested in baseball. He was now a banker.

His chance of fame had vanished.

Howard Keller and Lara were having dinner.

'How do we get started?' Lara asked.

'First of all, we're going to get you the best team money can buy. We'll start out with a real estate lawyer to work out the contract with the Diamond brothers. Then we want to get you a top architect. I have someone in mind. After that, we want to hire a top construction company. I've done a little arithmetic of my own. The soft costs for the project will come to about three hundred thousand dollars a room. The cost of the hotel will be about seven million dollars. If we plan it right, it can work.'

The architect's name was Ted Tuttle, and when he heard Lara's plans, he grinned and said, 'Bless you. I've been waiting for someone to come along with an idea like this.'

Ten working days later, he had rendered his drawings. They were everything Lara had dreamed.

'Originally, the hotel had a hundred and twenty-five rooms,' the architect said. 'As you can see, I've cut it down to seventy-five keys, as you've asked.'

In the drawing there were fifty suites and twenty-five deluxe rooms.

'It's perfect,' Lara said.

Lara showed the plans to Howard Keller. He was equally enthusiastic.

'Let's go to work. I've set up a meeting with a contractor. His name is Steve Rice.'

Steve Rice was one of the top contractors in Chicago. Lara liked him immediately. He was a rugged, no-nonsense, down-to-earth type.

Lara said, 'Howard Keller tells me that you're the best.'

'He's right,' Rice said. 'Our motto is "We build for posterity."'

'That's a good motto.'

Rice grinned. 'I just made it up.'

The first step was to break down each element into a series of drawings. The drawings were sent to potential subcontractors; steel manufacturers, brick-layers, window companies, electrical contractors. All in all, more than sixty subcontractors were involved.

The day escrow closed, Howard Keller took the afternoon off to celebrate with Lara.

'Does the bank mind your taking this time off?' Lara asked.

'No,' Keller lied. 'It's part of my job.' The truth was that he was enjoying this more than he had enjoyed anything in years. He loved being with Lara, he loved talking to her, looking at her. He wondered how she felt about marriage.

Lara said, 'I read this morning that they've almost completed the Sears Tower. It's a hundred and ten storeys – the tallest building in the world.'

117

'That's right,' Keller said.

Lara said gravely, 'Some day I'm going to build a higher one, Howard.'

He believed her.

They were having lunch with Steve Rice at the Whitehall. 'Tell me what happens next,' Lara asked.

'Well,' Rice said, 'first we're going to clean up the interior of the building. We'll keep the marble. We'll remove all the windows and gut the bathrooms. We'll take out the electrical risers for the installation of the new electrical wiring, and update the plumbing. When the demolition company is through, we'll be ready to begin building your hotel.'

'How many people will be working on it?'

Rice laughed. 'A mob, Miss Cameron. There'll be a window team, a bathroom team, a corridor team. These teams work floor by floor, usually from the top floor down. The hotel is scheduled to have two restaurants, and you'll have room service.'

'How long is all this going to take?'

'I would say – equipped and furnished – eighteen months.'

'I'll give you a bonus if you finish it in a year,' Lara told him.

'Great. The Congressional should . . .'

'I'm changing the name. It's going to be called the Cameron Palace.' Lara felt a thrill just saying the words. It was almost a sexual feeling. Her name was going to be on a building for all the world to see.

At six o'clock on a rainy September morning, the reconstruction of the hotel began. Lara was at the site eagerly watching as the workmen trooped into the lobby and began to tear it apart.

To Lara's surprise, Howard Keller appeared.

'You're up early,' Lara said.

'I couldn't sleep,' Keller grinned. 'I have a feeling this is the beginning of something big.'

Twelve months later, the Cameron Palace opened to rave reviews and land office business.

The architectural critic for the *Chicago Tribune* wrote, 'Chicago finally has a hotel that lives up to the motto: "Your home away from home!" Lara Cameron is someone to keep an eye on . . .'

By the end of the first month, the hotel was full and had a long waiting list.

Howard Keller was enthusiastic. 'At this rate,' he said, 'the hotel will be paid off in twelve years. That's wonderful. We . . .'

'Not good enough,' Lara said. 'I'm raising the rates.' She saw the expression on Keller's face. 'Don't worry. They'll pay it. Where else can they get two fireplaces, a sauna, and a grand piano?'

Two weeks after the Cameron Palace opened, Lara had a meeting with Bob Vance and Howard Keller.

'I found another great site for a hotel,' Lara said. 'It's going to be like the Cameron Palace, only bigger and better.'

Howard Keller grinned. 'I'll take a look at it.'

*

The site was perfect, but there was a problem.

'You're too late,' the broker told Lara. 'A developer named Steve Murchison was here this morning, and he made me an offer. He's going to buy it.'

'How much did he offer?'

'Three million.'

'I'll give you four. Draw up the papers.'

The broker only blinked once. 'Right.'

Lara received a telephone call the following afternoon.

'Lara Cameron?'

'Yes.'

'This is Steve Murchison. I'm going to let it go this time, bitch, because I don't think you know what the hell you're doing. But in the future, stay out of my way – you could get hurt.'

And the line went dead.

It was 1974 and momentous events were occurring around the world. President Nixon resigned to avoid impeachment, and Gerald Ford stepped into the White House. OPEC ended its oil embargo, and Isabel Perón became the President of Argentina. And in Chicago, Lara started construction on her second hotel, the Chicago Cameron Plaza. It was completed eighteen months later, and it was an even bigger success than the Cameron Palace. There was no stopping Lara after that. As *Forbes* magazine was to write later, 'Lara Cameron is a phenomenon. Her innovations are changing the concept of hotels. Miss Cameron has invaded the traditionally male turf of real estate developers and has proved that a woman can outshine all of them.'

Lara received a telephone call from Charles Cohn.

'Congratulations,' he said. 'I'm proud of you. I've never had a protégée before.'

'I've never had a mentor before. Without you, none of this would have happened.'

'You would have found a way,' Cohn said.

In 1975, the movie *Jaws* swept the country, and people stopped going into the ocean. The world population passed four billion, reduced by one when Teamster President James Hoffa disappeared. When Lara heard the four billion population figure, she said to Keller, 'Do you have any idea how much housing that would require?'

He was not sure whether she was joking.

Over the next three years, two apartment buildings and a condominium were completed. 'I want to put up an office building next,' Lara told Keller, 'right in the heart of the loop.'

'There's an interesting piece of property coming on the market,' Keller told her. 'If you like it, we'll finance you.'

That afternoon, they went to look at it. It was on the waterfront, in a choice location.

'What's it going to cost?' Lara asked.

'I've done the numbers. It will come to a hundred and twenty million dollars.'

Lara swallowed. 'That scares me.'

'Lara, in real estate the name of the game is to borrow.'

Other people's money, Lara thought. That's what

Bill Rogers had told her at the boarding house. All that seemed so long ago, and so much had happened since then. *And it's only the beginning*, Lara thought. *It's only the beginning*.

'Some developers put up buildings with almost no cash of their own.'

'I'm listening.'

'The idea is to rent or resell the building for enough money to pay off the debt on it, and still have money left over to buy some more property with that cash, and then borrow more money for another property. It's an inverted pyramid – a real estate pyramid – that you can build on a very small initial cash investment.'

'I understand,' Lara said.

'Of course, you have to be careful. The pyramid is built on paper – the mortgages. If anything goes wrong, if the profit from one investment fails to cover the debt on the next one, the pyramid can topple and bury you.'

'Right. How can I acquire the waterfront property?'

'We'll set up a joint venture for you. I'll talk to Vance about it. If it's too big for our bank to handle, we'll go to an insurance company or a savings and loan. You'll take out a fifty-million-dollar mortgage loan. You'll get their mortgage coupon rate – that would be five million and a ten per cent rate, plus amortization on the mortgage – and they'll be your partners. They'll take the first ten per cent of the earnings, but you'll get your property, fully financed. You can get your cash repaid and keep one hundred per cent of the depreciation, because financial institutions have no use for losses.'

Lara was listening, absorbing every word.

'Are you with me so far?'

'I'm with you.'

'In five or six years, after the building is leased, you sell it. If the property sells for seventy-five million, after you pay off the mortgage, you'll net twelve and a half million dollars. Besides that, you'll have a tax sheltered earning stream of eight million in depreciation that you can use to reduce taxes on other income. All of this for a cash investment of ten million.'

'That's fantastic!' Lara said.

Keller grinned. 'The government wants you to make money.'

'How would *you* like to make some money, Howard? Some real money?'

'I beg your pardon?'

'I want you to come to work for me.'

Keller was suddenly quiet. He knew he was facing one of the most important decisions of his life, and it had nothing to do with money. It was Lara. He had fallen in love with her. There had been one painful episode when he had tried to tell her. He had practised his marriage proposal all night, and the following morning, he had gone to her and stammered, 'Lara, I love you,' and before he could say more, she had kissed him on the cheek and said, 'I love you, too, Howard. Take a look at this new production schedule.' And he had not had the nerve to try again.

Now she was asking him to be her partner. He would be working near her every day, unable to touch her, unable to . . .

'Do you believe in me, Howard?'

'I'd be crazy not to, wouldn't I?'

'I'll pay you twice whatever you're making now, and give you five per cent of the company.'

'Can I . . . can I think about it?'

'There's really nothing to think about, is there?'

He made his decision. 'I guess not . . . partner.'

Lara gave him a hug. 'That's wonderful! You and I are going to build beautiful things. There are so many ugly buildings around. There's no excuse for them. Every building should be a tribute to this city.'

He put his hand on her arm. 'Don't ever change, Lara.'

She looked at him hard.

'I won't.'

The late 1970s were years of growth and change and excitement. In 1976 there was a successful Israeli raid on Entebbe, and Mao Tse-tung died, and James Earl Carter, Jr was elected President of the United States.

Lara erected another office building.

In 1977, Charlie Chaplin died, and Elvis Presley temporarily died.

Lara built the largest shopping mall in Chicago.

In 1978 Reverend Jim Jones and nine hundred and eleven followers committed mass suicide in Guyana. The United States recognized Communist China, and the Panama Canal Treaties were ratified.

Lara built a series of high-rise condominiums in Rogers Park.

In 1979, Israel and Egypt signed a peace treaty at Camp David; there was a nuclear accident at Three Mile Island, and Muslim fundamentalists seized the United States Embassy in Iran.

Lara built a skyscraper and a glamorous resort and country club in Deerfield, north of Chicago.

Lara seldom went out socially, and when she did, she usually went to a club where jazz was played. She liked Andy's, a club where the top jazz artists performed. She listened to Von Freeman, the great saxophonist, and Eric Schneider, and reed man Anthony Braxton, and Art Hodes at the piano.

Lara had no time to feel lonely. She spent every day with her family: The architects and the construction crew, the carpenters, the electricians and surveyors and plumbers. She was obsessed with the buildings she was putting up. Her stage was Chicago and she was the star.

Her professional life was proceeding beyond her wildest dreams, but she had no personal life. Her experience with Sean MacAllister had soured her on sexual relationships, and she never met anyone she was interested in seeing for more than an evening or two. In the back of Lara's mind was an elusive image, someone she had once met and wanted to meet again. But she could never seem to capture it. For a fleeting moment she would recall it, and then it was gone.

There were plenty of suitors. They ranged from business executives to oil men to poets, and even included some of her employees. Lara was pleasant to all of the men, but she never permitted any relationship to go further than a goodnight handshake at the door.

But then Lara found herself attracted to Pete Ryan, the head foreman on one of Lara's building jobs, a handsome strapping young man with an Irish brogue and a quick smile, and Lara started visiting the project Ryan was working on, more and more often. They would talk about construction problems, but underneath they were both aware that they were speaking about other things.

'Are you going to have dinner with me?' Ryan asked. The word 'dinner' was stretched out slowly.

Lara felt her heart give a little jump. 'Yes.'

Ryan picked Lara up at her apartment, but they never got to dinner. 'My God, you're a lovely thing,' he said. And his strong arms went around her.

She was ready for him. Their foreplay had been going on for months. Ryan picked her up and carried her into the bedroom. They undressed together, quickly, urgently. He had a lean, hard build, and Lara had a quick mental picture of Sean MacAllister's heavy, pudgy body. The next moment she was in bed and Ryan was on top of her, his hands and tongue all over her, and she cried aloud with the joy of what was happening to her.

When they were both spent, they lay in each other's arms. 'My God,' Ryan said softly, 'you're a bloody miracle.'

'So are you,' Lara whispered.

She could not remember when she had been so happy. Ryan was everything she wanted. He was intelligent and warm, and they understood each other, they spoke the same language.

Ryan squeezed her hand. 'I'm starved.'

'So am I. I'll make us some sandwiches.'

'Tomorrow night,' Ryan promised, 'I'll take you out for a proper dinner.'

Lara held him close. 'It's a date.'

The following morning, Lara went to visit Ryan at the building site. She could see him high up on one of the steel girders, giving orders to his men. As Lara walked toward the work elevator, one of the workmen grinned at her. 'Mornin', Miss Cameron.' There was an odd note in his voice.

Another workman passed her and grinned. 'Mornin', Miss Cameron.'

Two other workmen were leering at her. 'Morning, boss.'

Lara looked around. Other workmen were watching her, all smirking. Lara's face turned red. She stepped into the work elevator and rode up to the level where Ryan was. As she stepped out, Ryan saw her and smiled.

'Morning, sweetheart,' Ryan said. 'What time is dinner tonight?'

'You'll starve first,' Lara said fiercely. 'You're fired.'

Every building Lara put up was a challenge. She erected small office buildings with floor spaces of five thousand square feet, and large office buildings and hotels. But no matter what type of building it was, the most important thing to her was the location.

Bill Rogers had been right. *Location, location, location.*

Lara's empire kept expanding. She was beginning to get recognition from the City Fathers and from the press and the public. She was a glamorous figure, and when she went to charity events or to the opera or a museum, photographers were always eager to take her picture. She began to appear in the media more and more often. All her buildings were successes, and still she was not satisfied. It was as though she were waiting for something wonderful to happen to her, waiting for a door to open, waiting to be touched by some unknown magic.

Keller was puzzled. 'What do you want, Lara?'

'More.'

And it was all he could get out of her.

One day Lara said to Keller, 'Howard, do you know how much we're paying every month for janitors and linen service and window washers?'

'It goes with the territory,' Keller said.

'Then let's buy the territory.'

'What are you talking about?'

'We're going to start a subsidiary. We'll supply those services to ourselves and to other builders.'

The idea was a success from the beginning. The profits kept pouring in.

It seemed to Keller that Lara had built an emotional wall around herself. He was closer to her than anyone else, and yet Lara never spoke to him about her family or her background. It was as though she had emerged full blown out of the mists of nowhere. In the beginning, Keller had been Lara's mentor, teaching her and guiding her, but now Lara made all the decisions alone. The pupil had out-grown the teacher.

Lara let nothing stand in her way. She was becoming an irresistible force, and there was no stopping her. She was a perfectionist. She knew what she wanted and insisted on getting it.

At first, some of the workmen tried to take advantage of her. They had never worked for a woman before, and the idea amused them. They were in for a shock. When Lara caught one of the foremen pencil-whipping – signing off for work that had not been done – she called him in front of the crew and fired him. She was at the building site every morning. The crew would arrive at six o'clock and find Lara already there, waiting for them. There was rampant sexism. The men would wait until Lara was in earshot and exchange lewd jokes.

'Did you hear about the talking pussy at the farm? It fell in love with a cock and . . .'

'So the little girl said, "Can you get pregnant swallowing a man's seed?" And her mama said, "No. From that, darling, you get jewellery . . ."'

There were some overt gestures. Occasionally, one of the workmen passing Lara would 'accidentally' brush his arm across her breasts or press against her bottom.

'Oops, sorry.'

'No problem,' Lara said. 'Pick up your cheque and get out of here.'

Their amusement eventually began to change to respect.

One day, when Lara was driving along Kedzie Avenue with Howard Keller, she came to a block filled with small shops. She stopped the car.

'This block is being wasted,' Lara said. 'There should be a high-rise here. These little shops can't bring much of an income.'

'Yeah, but the problem is, you'd have to persuade every one of these tenants to sell out,' Keller said. 'Some of them may not want to.'

'We can buy them out,' Lara declared.

'Lara, if even one tenant refuses to sell, you could be stuck for a bundle. You'll have bought a lot of little shops you don't want and you won't be able to put up your building. And if the tenants get wind that a big high-rise is going up here, they'll hold you up.'

'We won't let them know what we're doing,' Lara said. She was beginning to get excited. 'We'll have different people approach the owners of the shops.'

'I've been through this before,' Keller warned. 'If word leaks out, they're going to gouge you for every penny they can get.'

'Then we'll have to be careful. Let's get an option on the property.'

The block on Kedzie Avenue consisted of more than a dozen small stores and shops. There was a bakery, a hardware store, a barber shop, a clothing store, a butcher, a tailor, a drug store, a stationery store, a coffee shop, and a variety of other businesses.

'Don't forget the risk,' Keller warned Lara. 'If there's one hold-out, you've lost all the money you've put in to buy those businesses.'

'Don't worry,' Lara said. 'I'll handle it.'

A week later, a stranger walked into the two-chair barber shop. The barber was reading a magazine. As the door opened, he looked up and nodded. 'Can I help you, sir? Hair cut?'

The stranger smiled. 'No,' he said. 'I just arrived in town. I had a barber shop in New Jersey, but my wife wanted to move here to be near her mother. I'm looking for a shop I can buy.'

'This is the only barber shop in the neighbourhood,' the barber said. 'It's not for sale.'

The stranger smiled. 'When you come right down

to it, everything's for sale, isn't it? At the right price, of course. What's this shop worth – about fifty, sixty thousand dollars?'

'Something like that,' the barber admitted.

'I really am anxious to have my own shop again. I'll tell you what. I'll give you seventy-five thousand dollars for this place.'

'No, I couldn't think of selling it.'

'A hundred.'

'Really, mister, I don't . . .'

'And you can take all the equipment with you.'

The barber was staring at him. 'You'll give me a hundred thousand and let me take the barber chairs and the rest of the equipment?'

'That's right. I have my own equipment.'

'Can I think about it? I'll have to talk to my wife.'

'Sure. I'll drop back tomorrow.'

Two days later, the barber shop was acquired.

'That's one down,' Lara said.

The bakery was next. It was a small family bakery owned by a husband and wife. The ovens in the back room permeated the store with the smell of fresh bread. A woman was talking to one of the owners.

'My husband died and left me his insurance money. We had a bakery in Florida. I've been looking for a place just like this. I'd like to buy it.'

'It's a comfortable living,' the owner said. 'My wife and I have never thought about selling.'

'If you *were* interested in selling, how much would you want?'

The owner shrugged. 'I don't know.'

'Would you say the bakery's worth sixty thousand dollars?'

'Oh, at least seventy-five,' the owner said.

'I'll tell you what,' the woman said. 'I'll give you a hundred thousand dollars for it.'

The owner stared at her. 'Are you serious?'

'I've never been more serious in my life.'

The next morning, Lara said, 'That's two down.'

The rest of the deals went just as smoothly. They had a dozen men and women going around impersonating tailors, bakers, pharmacists and butchers. Over the period of the next six months, Lara bought out the stores, then hired people to come in and run the different operations. The architects had already started to draw up plans for the high-rise.

Lara was studying the latest reports. 'It looks like we've done it,' she told Keller.

'I'm afraid we have a problem.'

'Why? The only one left is the coffee shop.'

'That's our problem. He's there on a five-year lease, but he won't give up the lease.'

'Offer him more money . . .'

'He says he won't give it up at any price.'

Lara was staring at him. 'Does he know about the high-rise going up?'

'No.'

'All right. I'll go talk to him. Don't worry, he'll get out. Find out who owns the building he's in.'

The following morning, Lara paid a visit to the site. Haley's Coffee Shop was at the far end of the southwest corner of the block. The shop was small, with half a dozen stools along the counter and four booths. A man Lara presumed to be the proprietor was behind the counter. He appeared to be in his late sixties.

Lara sat down at a booth.

'Morning,' the man said pleasantly. 'What can I bring you?'

'Orange juice and coffee, please.'

'Coming up.'

She watched him squeeze some fresh orange juice.

'My waitress didn't show up today. Good help's hard to get these days.' He poured the coffee and came from behind the counter. He was in a wheelchair. He had no legs. Lara watched silently as he brought the coffee and orange juice to the table.

'Thank you,' Lara said. She looked around. 'Nice place you have here.'

'Yep. I like it.'

'How long have you been here?'

'Ten years.'

'Did you ever think of retiring?'

He shook his head. 'You're the second person who asked me that this week. No, I'll never retire.'

'Maybe they didn't offer you enough money,' Lara suggested.

'It has nothing to do with money, Miss. Before I came here, I spent two years in a veterans' hospital. No friends. Not much point to life. And then someone talked me into leasing this place.' He smiled. 'It changed my whole life. All the people in the neighbourhood drop in here. They've become my friends, almost like my family. It's given me a reason for living.' He shook his head. 'No. Money has nothing to do with it. Can I bring you more coffee?'

Lara was in a meeting with Howard Keller and the architect. 'We don't even have to buy out his lease,'

134

Keller was saying. 'I just talked to the landlord. There's a forfeiture clause if the coffee shop doesn't gross a certain amount each month. For the last few months he's been under that gross, so we can close him out.'

Lara turned to the architect. 'I have a question for you.' She looked down at the plans spread out on the table. and pointed to the south-west corner of the drawing. 'What if we built a set-back here, eliminated this little area and let the coffee shop stay? Could the building still be put up?'

The architect studied the plan. 'I suppose so. I could slope that side of the building and counterbalance it on the other side. Of course it would look better if we didn't have to do that . . .'

'But it *could* work,' Lara pressed.

'Yes.'

Keller said, 'Lara, I told you we can force him out of there.'

Lara shook her head. 'We've bought up the rest of the block, haven't we?'

Keller nodded. 'You bet. You're the proud owner of a clothing store, a tailor shop, a stationery store, a drug store, a bakery, a . . .'

'All right,' Lara said. 'The tenants of the new highrise are going to have a coffee shop to drop in on. And so do we. Haley stays.'

On her father's birthday, Lara said to Keller, 'Howard, I want you to do me a favour.'

'Sure.'

'I want you to go to Scotland for me.'

'Are we going to build something in Scotland?'

135

'We're going to buy a castle.'

He stood there, listening.

'There's a place in the Highlands called Loch Morlich. It's on the road to Glenmore near Aviemore. There are castles all around there. Buy one.'

'Kind of a summer home?'

'I don't plan to live in it. I want to bury my father in the grounds.'

Keller said, slowly, 'You want me to buy a castle in Scotland to bury your father in?'

'That's right. I haven't time to go over myself. You're the only one I can trust to do it. My father is in the Greenwood Cemetery at Glace Bay.'

It was the first real insight Keller ever had into Lara's feelings about her family.

'You must have loved your father very much.'

'Will you do it for me?'

'Certainly.'

'After he's buried, arrange for a caretaker to tend the grave.'

Three weeks later, Keller returned from Scotland and said, 'It's all taken care of. You own a castle. Your father's resting in the grounds. It's a beautiful place in the hills and with a small lochan close by. You'll love it. When are you going over?'

Lara looked up in surprise. 'Me? I'm not,' she said.

Book Two

In 1984, Lara Cameron decided that the time had come to conquer New York. When she told Keller her plan, he was appalled.

'I don't like the idea,' he said flatly. 'You don't know New York. Neither do I. It's a different city, Lara. We . . .'

'That's what they told me when I came from Glace Bay to Chicago,' Lara pointed out. 'Buildings are the same whether you put them up in Glace Bay, Chicago, New York or Tokyo. We all play by the same rules.'

'But you're doing so great here,' Keller protested. 'What is it you want?'

'I told you. *More*. I want my name up on the New York skyline. I'm going to build a Cameron Plaza there, and a Cameron Center. And one day, Howard, I'm going to build the tallest skyscraper in the world. *That's* what I want. Cameron Enterprises is moving to New York.'

New York was in the middle of a building boom, and it was peopled by real estate giants – the Zeckendorfs, Harry Helmsley, Donald Trump, the Urises and the Rudins.

'We're going to join the club,' Lara told Keller.

They checked into the Regency and began to explore the city. Lara could not get over the size and dynamics of the bustling metropolis. It was a canyon of skyscrapers, with rivers of cars running through it.

'It makes Chicago look like Glace Bay!' Lara said. She could not wait to get started.

'The first thing we're going to do is assemble a team. We'll find the best real estate lawyer in New York. Then a great management team. Find out who Rudin uses. See if you can lure them away.'

'Right.'

Lara said, 'Here's a list of buildings I like the look of. Find out who the architects are. I want to meet with them.'

Keller was beginning to feel Lara's excitement. 'I'll open up a line of credit with the banks. With the assets we have in Chicago, that won't be any problem. I'll make contacts with some savings and loan companies, and some real estate brokers.'

'Fine.'

'Lara, before we start to get involved in all this, don't you think you should decide what your next project is going to be?'

Lara looked up and asked innocently, 'Didn't I tell you? We're going to buy Manhattan Central Hospital.'

Several days earlier, Lara had gone to a hairdresser on Madison Avenue. While she was having her hair done, she had overheard a conversation in the next booth.

140

'. . . We're going to miss you, Mrs Walker.'

'Same here, Darlene. How long have I been coming here?'

'Almost fifteen years.'

'Time certainly flies, doesn't it? I'm going to miss New York.'

'When will you be leaving?'

'Right away. We just got the closing notice this morning. Imagine – a hospital like Manhattan Central closing down because they've run out of cash. I've been supervisor there for almost twenty years, and they send me a memo telling me I'm through! You'd think they'd have the decency to do it in person, wouldn't you? What's the world coming to?'

Lara was now listening intently.

'I haven't seen anything about the closing in the papers.'

'No. They're keeping it quiet. They want to break the news to the employees first.'

Her beautician was in the middle of blow drying Lara's hair. Lara started to get up.

'I'm not through yet, Miss Cameron.'

'Never mind,' Lara said, 'I'm in a hurry.'

Manhattan Central Hospital was a dilapidated, ugly-looking building located on the East Side between 68th and 69th Streets, and it took up an entire block. Lara stared at it for a long time, and what she was seeing in her mind was a majestic new skyscraper with chic retail stores on the ground floor and luxury condominiums on the upper floors.

Lara walked into the hospital and asked the name

of the corporation that owned it. She was sent to the offices of a Roger Burnham on Wall Street.

'What can I do for you, Miss Cameron?'

'I hear that Manhattan Central Hospital is for sale.'

He looked at her in surprise. 'Where did you hear that?'

'Is it true?'

He hedged. 'It might be.'

'I might be interested in buying it,' Lara said. 'What's your price?'

'Look, lady . . . I don't know you from Adam. You can't walk in off the street and expect me to discuss a ninety-million-dollar deal with you. I . . .'

'Ninety million?' Lara had a feeling it was high, but she wanted that site. It would be an exciting beginning. 'Is that what we're talking about?'

'We're not talking about anything.'

Lara handed Roger Burnham a hundred-dollar bill.

'What's this for?'

'That's for a forty-eight hour option. All I'm asking is forty-eight hours. You weren't ready to announce that it was for sale, anyway. What can you lose? If I meet your asking price, you've got what you wanted.'

'I don't know anything about you.'

'Call the Mercantile Bank in Chicago. Ask for Bob Vance. He's the president.'

He stared at her for a long moment, shook his head and muttered something with the word 'crazies' in it.

He looked up the telephone number himself. Lara sat there while his secretary got Bob Vance for him.

'Mr Vance? This is Roger Burnham in New York. I have a Miss . . .' He looked up at her.

'Lara Cameron.'

'Lara Cameron here. She's interested in buying a property of ours here, and she says that you know her.'

He sat there listening.

'She is . . . ? I see . . . Really . . . ? No, I wasn't aware of that . . . Right . . . Right.' After a long time, he said, 'Thank you very much.'

He replaced the receiver and stared at Lara. 'You seem to have made quite an impression in Chicago.'

'I intend to make quite an impression in New York.'

Burnham looked at the hundred dollar bill. 'What am I supposed to do with this?'

'Buy yourself some Cuban cigars. Do I have the option if I meet your price?'

He sat there, studying her. 'It's a little unorthodox . . . but, yes. I'll give you forty-eight hours.'

'We have to move fast on this,' Lara had told Keller. 'We have forty-eight hours to line up our financing.'

'Do you have any figures on it?'

'Ballpark. Ninety million for the property, and I estimate another two hundred million to demolish the hospital and put up the building.'

Keller was staring at her. 'That's two hundred and ninety million dollars.'

'You were always quick with figures,' Lara said.

He ignored it. 'Lara, where's that kind of money coming from?'

'We'll borrow it,' Lara said. 'Between my collateral in Chicago and the new property, it shouldn't be any problem.'

'It's a big risk. A hundred things could go wrong. You'll be gambling everything you have on . . .'

'That's what makes it exciting,' Lara said, 'the gamble. And winning.'

Getting finance for a building in New York was even simpler than in Chicago. Mayor Koch had instituted a tax programme called the 421-A, and under it, a developer replacing a functionally obsolete building could claim tax exemptions, with the first two years tax free.

When the banks and savings and loan companies checked on Lara Cameron's credit, they were more than eager to do business with her.

Before forty-eight hours had passed, Lara walked into Burnham's office and handed him a cheque for three million dollars.

'This is a down payment on the deal,' Lara said. 'I'm meeting your asking price. By the way, you can keep the hundred dollars.'

During the next six months, Keller worked with banks on financing, and Lara worked with architects on planning.

Everything was proceeding smoothly. The architects and builders and marketing people were on schedule. Work was to begin on the demolition of the hospital and the construction of the new building in April.

Lara was restless. At six o'clock every morning, she was at the construction site watching the new building going up. She felt frustrated because at this stage the building belonged to the workmen. There was nothing for her to do. She was used to more action. She liked to have a half a dozen projects going at once.

'Why don't we look around for another deal?' Lara asked Keller.

'Because you're up to your ears in this one. If you even breathe hard this whole thing is going to collapse. Do you know you've leveraged every penny you have to put this building up? If anything goes wrong . . .'

'Nothing is going to go wrong.' She was watching his expression. 'What's bothering you?'

'The deal you made with the savings and loan company . . .'

'What about it? We got our financing, didn't we?'

'I don't like the completion date clause. If the building's not finished by March 15th, they'll take it over, and you stand to lose everything you have.'

Lara thought of the building she had put up in Glace Bay, and how her friends had pitched in and finished it for her. But this was different.

'Don't worry,' she told Keller. 'The building will be finished. Are you sure we can't look around for another project?'

Lara was talking to the marketing people.

'The downstairs retail stores are already signed

up,' the marketing manager told Lara. 'And more than half the condominiums have been taken. We estimate we'll have sold three-fourths of them before the building is finished, and the rest of them shortly after.'

'I want them *all* sold before the building is completed,' Lara said. 'Step up the advertising.'

'Very well.'

Keller came into the office. 'I have to hand it to you, Lara. You were right. The building's on schedule.'

'This is going to be a money machine.'

On January 15th, sixty days before the date of completion, the huge girders and walls were finished, and the workers were already installing the electrical wiring and plumbing lines.

Lara stood there watching the men working on the girders high above. One of the workmen stopped to pull out a pack of cigarettes, and as he did so, a wrench slipped from his hand and fell to the ground far below. Lara watched in disbelief as the wrench came hurtling down toward her. She leaped out of the way, her heart pounding. The workman was looking down. He waved a 'sorry'.

Grim-faced, Lara got into the construction elevator and took it to the level where the workman was. Ignoring the dizzying empty space below, she walked across the scaffolding to the man.

'Did you drop that wrench?'

'Yeah, sorry.'

She slapped him hard across the face. 'You're fired. Now get off my building.'

'Hey,' he said, 'it was an accident. I . . .'

'Get out of here.'

The man glared at her for a moment then walked away and took the elevator down.

Lara took a deep breath to control herself. The other workers were watching her.

'Get back to work,' she ordered.

Lara was having lunch with Sam Gosden, the New York attorney who handled her contracts for her.

'I hear everything's going very well,' Gosden said.

Lara smiled. 'Better than very well. We're only a few weeks away from completion.'

'Can I make an admission?'

'Yes, but be careful not to incriminate yourself.'

He laughed. 'I was betting that you couldn't do it.'

'Really? Why?'

'Real estate development on the level where you're operating is a man's game. The only women who should be in real estate are the little old blue-haired ladies who sell co-ops.'

'So you were betting against me,' Lara said.

Sam Gosden smiled. 'Yeah.'

Lara leaned forward. 'Sam . . .'

'Yes?'

'No one on my team bets against me. You're fired.'

He sat there open-mouthed as Lara got up and walked out of the restaurant.

On the following Monday morning, as Lara drove toward the building site, she sensed that something was wrong. And suddenly she realized what it was. It was the silence. There were no sounds of hammers or drills. When Lara arrived at the construction site, she stared in disbelief. The workmen were collecting their equipment and leaving. The foreman was packing up his things. Lara hurried up to him.

'What's going on?' Lara demanded. 'It's only seven o'clock.'

'I'm pulling the men.'

'What are you talking about?'

'There's been a complaint, Miss Cameron.'

'What kind of complaint?'

'Did you slap one of the workmen?'

'What?' She had forgotten. 'Yes. He deserved it. I fired him.'

'Did the City give you a licence to go around slapping the people who work for you?'

'Wait a minute,' Lara said. 'It wasn't like that. He dropped a wrench. It almost killed me. I suppose I lost my temper. I'm sorry, but I don't want him back here.'

'He won't be coming back here,' the foreman said. 'None of us will.'

Lara stared at him. 'Is this some kind of joke?'

'My union doesn't think it's a joke,' the foreman told her. 'They gave us orders to walk. We're walking.'

'You have a contract.'

'You broke it,' the foreman told her. 'If you have any complaints, take it up with the union.'

He started to walk away.

'Wait a minute. I said I'm sorry. I'll tell you what. I . . . I'm willing to apologize to the man, and he can have his job back.'

'Miss Cameron, I don't think you get the picture. He doesn't want his job back. We've all got other jobs waiting for us. This is a busy city. And I'll tell you something else, lady. We're too goddamn busy to let our bosses slap us around.'

Lara stood there watching him walk away. It was her worst nightmare.

Lara hurried back to the office to tell the news to Keller.

Before she could speak, he said, 'I heard. I've been on the phone talking to the union.'

'What did they say?' Lara asked eagerly.

'They're going to hold a hearing next month.'

Lara's face filled with dismay. 'Next month! We've less than two months left to finish the building.'

'I told them that.'

'And what did they say?'

'That it's not their problem.'

Lara sank onto the couch. 'Oh, my God. What are we going to do?'

'I don't know.'

'Maybe we could persuade the bank to . . .' She saw the look on his face. 'I guess not.' Lara suddenly brightened. 'I know. We'll hire another construction crew and . . .'

'Lara, there isn't a union worker who will touch that building.'

'I should have killed that bastard.'

'Right. That would have helped a lot,' Keller said dryly.

Lara got up and began pacing. 'I could ask Sam Gosden to . . .' she suddenly remembered. 'No, I fired him.'

'Why?'

'Never mind.'

Keller was thinking aloud. 'Maybe if we got hold of a good labour lawyer . . . someone with clout.'

'That's a good idea. Someone who can move fast. Do you know anybody?'

'No. But Sam Gosden mentioned someone in one of our meetings. A man named Martin. Paul Martin.'

'Who is he?'

'I'm not sure, but we were talking about union problems and his name came up.'

'Do you know what firm he's with?'

'No.'

Lara buzzed her secretary. 'Kathy, there's a lawyer in Manhattan named Paul Martin. Get me his address.'

Keller said, 'Don't you want his phone number so you can make an appointment?'

'There's no time. I can't afford to sit around waiting for an appointment. I'm going to see him today. If he can help us, fine. If he can't, we'll have to come up with something else.'

But Lara was thinking to herself, *There is nothing else*.

Paul Martin's office was on the twenty-fifth floor in an office building on Wall Street. The frosted sign on the door read, 'Paul Martin, Attorney at Law.'

Lara took a deep breath and stepped inside. The reception office was smaller than she had expected. It contained one scarred desk with a bottle-blonde secretary behind it.

'Good morning. Can I help you?'

'I'm here to see Mr Martin,' Lara said.

'Is he expecting you?'

'Yes, he is.' There was no time for explanations.

'And your name?'

'Cameron. Lara Cameron.'

The secretary looked at her quizzically. 'Just a moment. I'll see whether Mr Martin can see you.'

The secretary got up from behind the desk and disappeared into the inner office.

He's got to see me, Lara thought.

A moment later, the secretary emerged. 'Yes, Mr Martin will see you.'

Lara concealed a sigh of relief. 'Thank you.'

She walked into the inner office. It was small and simply furnished. A desk, two couches, a coffee table and a few chairs. *Not exactly a citadel of power*, Lara thought. The man behind the desk appeared to be in his early sixties. He had a deeply-lined face, a hawk nose, and a mane of white hair. There was a feral, animal-like vitality about him. He was wearing an old-fashioned pin-stripe double-breasted grey suit and a white shirt with a narrow collar. When he spoke, his voice was raspy, low, somehow compelling.

'My secretary said that I was expecting you.'

'I'm sorry,' Lara said. 'I had to see you. It's an emergency.'

'Sit down, Miss . . .'

'Cameron. Lara Cameron.' She took a chair.

'What can I do for you?'

Lara took a deep breath. 'I have a little problem.' *A skeleton twenty-four storeys of uncompleted steel and concrete standing idle.* 'It's about a building.'

'What about it?'

'I'm a real estate developer, Mr Martin. I'm in the middle of putting up an office building on the East Side, and I'm having a problem with the union.'

He was listening, saying nothing.

Lara hurried on. 'I lost my temper and slapped one of the workmen, and the union called a strike.'

He was studying her, puzzled. 'Miss Cameron . . . what does all this have to do with me?'

'I heard you might be able to help me.'

'I'm afraid you heard wrong. I'm a corporate attorney. I'm not involved with buildings and I don't deal with unions.'

Lara's heart sank. 'Oh, I thought . . . isn't there anything you can do?'

He placed the palms of his hands on the desk, as though he were about to rise. 'I can give you a couple of pieces of advice. Get hold of a labour lawyer. Have him take the union to court and . . .'

'There's no time. I'm up against a deadline. I . . . what's the second piece of advice?'

'Get out of the building business.' His eyes were fixed on her breasts. 'You don't have the right equipment for it.'

'*What?*'

'It's no place for a woman.'

'And what *is* the place for a woman?' Lara asked angrily. 'Barefoot, pregnant and in the kitchen?'

'Something like that. Yeah.'

Lara rose to her feet. It was all she could do to control herself. 'You must come from a long line of dinosaurs. Maybe you haven't heard the news. Women are free now.'

Paul Martin shook his head. 'No. Just noisier.'

'Goodbye, Mr Martin. I'm sorry I took up your valuable time.'

Lara turned and strode out of the office, slamming the door behind her. She stopped in the corridor, and took a deep breath. *This was a mistake*, she thought. She had finally reached a dead end. She had risked everything it had taken her years to build up, and she had lost it in one swift instant. There was no one to turn to. Nowhere to go.

It was over.

Lara walked the cold, rainy streets. She was completely unaware of the icy wind and her surroundings. Her mind was filled with the terrible disaster that had befallen her. Howard Keller's warning was ringing in her ears. *You put up buildings and borrow on them. It's like a pyramid, only if you're not care-ful, that pyramid can fall down.* And it had. The banks in Chicago would foreclose on her properties there, and she would lose all the money she had invested in the new building. She would have to start all over, from the beginning. *Poor Howard,* she thought. *He believed in my dreams and I've let him down.*

The rain had stopped and the sky was beginning to clear. A pale sun was fighting its way through the clouds. She suddenly realized it was dawn. She had walked all night. Lara looked around and saw where she was for the first time. She was only two blocks from the doomed property. *I'll take a last look at it,* Lara thought, resignedly.

She was a full block away when she first heard it. It was the sound of pneumatic drills and hammers, and the roar of cement mixers filling the air. Lara stood there, listening for an instant, then started run-ning toward the building site. When she reached it, she stood there, staring, unbelievingly.

The full crew was there, hard at work.

The foreman came up to her, smiling. 'Morning, Miss Cameron.'

Lara finally found her voice. 'What . . . What's happening? I . . . I thought you were pulling your men off the job.'

He said sheepishly. 'That was a little misunder-standing, Miss Cameron. Bruno could have killed you when he dropped that wrench.'

Lara swallowed. 'But he . . .'

'Don't worry. He's gone. Nothing like that will

154

happen again. You don't have a thing to worry about. We're right back on schedule.'

Lara felt as though she were in a dream. She stood there watching the men swarming over the skeleton of the building and she thought, *I got it all back again. Everything. Paul Martin.*

Lara telephoned him as soon as she returned to her office. His secretary said, 'I'm sorry, Mr Martin is not available.'

'Would you ask him to call me, please?' Lara left her number.

At three o'clock in the afternoon, she still had not heard from him. She called him again.

'I'm sorry. Mr Martin is not available.'

He did not return her call.

At five o'clock, Lara went to Paul Martin's office.

She said to the blonde secretary, 'Would you please tell Mr Martin that Lara Cameron is here to see him.'

The secretary looked uncertain. 'Well, I'll . . . Just a moment.' She disappeared into the inner office and returned a minute later. 'Go right in, please.'

Paul Martin looked up as Lara walked in.

'Yes, Miss Cameron?' His voice was cool, neither friendly nor unfriendly. 'What can I do for you?'

'I came to thank you.'

'Thank me for what?'

'For . . . for straightening things out with the union.'

He frowned. 'I don't know what you're talking about.'

'All the workmen came back this morning, and

everything's wonderful. The building is back on schedule.'

'Well, congratulations.'

'If you'll send me a bill for your fee . . .'

'Miss Cameron, I think you're a little confused. If your problem is solved, I'm glad. But I had nothing to do with it.'

Lara looked at him for a long time. 'All right. I'm . . . I'm sorry I bothered you.'

'No problem.' He watched her leave the office.

A moment later his secretary came in. 'Miss Cameron left a package for you, Mr Martin.'

It was a small package, tied with bright ribbon. Curious, he opened it. Inside was a silver knight in full armour, ready to do battle. An apology. *What did she call me? A dinosaur.* He could still hear his grandfather's voice. *Those were dangerous times, Paul. The young men decided to take control of the mafia, to get rid of the old-timers, the moustache Petes, the dinosaurs. It was bloody, but they did it.*

But all that was a long, long time ago, in the old country. Sicily.

13

Gibellina, Sicily, 1879

The Martinis were *stranieri* – outsiders, in the little Sicilian village of Gibellina. The countryside was desolate, a barren land of death, bathed in blazing, pitiless sunlight, a landscape painted by a sadistic artist. In a land where the large estates belonged to the *gabelloti*, the wealthy landowners, the Martinis had bought a small farm and tried to run it themselves.

The *soprintendente* had come calling on Giuseppe Martini one day.

'This little farm of yours,' he said, 'the land is too rocky. You will not be able to make a decent living on it, growing olives and grapes.'

'Don't worry about me,' Martini said. 'I've been farming all my life.'

'We're all worried about you,' the *soprintendente* insisted. 'Don Vito has some good farmland that he is willing to lease to you.'

'I know about Don Vito and his land,' Giuseppe Martini snorted. 'If I sign a *mezzadria* with him to farm his land, he will take three-fourths of my crops and charge me a hundred per cent interest on the seed. I will end up with nothing, like the other fools who deal with him. Tell him I said "no, thank you."'

'You are making a big mistake, *signore*. This is dangerous country. Serious accidents can happen here.'

'Are you threatening me?'

'Certainly not, *signore*. I was merely pointing out . . .'

'Get off my land,' Giuseppe Martini said.

The overseer looked at him for a long time then shook his head sadly. 'You are a stubborn man.'

Giuseppe Martini's young son Ivo said, 'Who was that, Papa?'

'He's the overseer for one of the large landowners.'

'I don't like him,' the young boy said.

'I don't like him either, Ivo.'

The following night, Giuseppe Martini's crops were set on fire and the few cattle he had disappeared.

That was when Giuseppe Martini made his second mistake. He went to the Guardia in the village.

'I demand protection,' he said.

The chief of police studied him noncommittally. 'That's what we are here for,' he said. 'What is your problem, *signore*?'

'Last night Don Vito's men burned my crops and stole my cattle.'

'That is a serious charge. Can you prove it?'

'His *soprintendente* came to me and threatened me.'

'Did he tell you they were going to burn your crops and steal your cattle?'

'Of course not,' Giuseppe Martini said.

158

'What *did* he say to you?'

'He said that I should give up my farm and lease land from Don Vito.'

'And you refused?'

'Naturally.'

'*Signore*, Don Vito is a very important man. Do you wish me to arrest him simply because he offered to share his rich farmland with you?'

'I want you to protect me,' Giuseppe Martini demanded. 'I'm not going to let them drive me off my land.'

'*Signore*, I am most sympathetic. I will certainly see what I can do.'

'I would appreciate that.'

'Consider it done.'

The following afternoon, as young Ivo was returning from town, he saw half a dozen men ride up to his father's farm. They dismounted and went into the house.

A few minutes later, Ivo saw his father dragged out to the field.

One of the men took out a gun. 'We are going to give you a chance to escape. Run for it.'

'No! This is my land! I . . .'

Ivo watched, terrified, as the man shot at the ground near his father's feet.

'Run!'

Giuseppe Martini started to run.

The *campagni* got on their horses and began circling Martini, yelling all the while.

Ivo hid, watching in horror at the terrible scene that was unfolding before his eyes.

*

159

The mounted men watched the farmer run across the field, trying to escape. Each time he reached the edge of the dirt road, one of them raced to cut him off and knock him to the ground. The man was bleeding and exhausted. He was slowing down.

The *campagni* decided they had had enough sport. One of them put a rope around the man's neck and dragged him toward the well.

'Why?' he gasped. 'What have I done?'

'You went to the Guardia. You should not have done that.'

They pulled down the victim's trousers and one of the men took out a knife, while the others held him down.

'Let this be a lesson to you.'

The man screamed, 'No, please! I'm sorry.'

The *campagni* smiled. 'Tell that to your wife.'

He reached down, grabbed the man's member, and slashed through it with the knife.

His screams filled the air.

'You won't need this any more,' the captain assured him.

He took the member and stuffed it in the man's mouth. He gagged and spat it out.

The captain looked at the other *campagni*. 'He doesn't like the taste of it.'

'*Uccidi quel figlio di puttana!*'

One of the *campagni* dismounted from his horse and picked up some heavy stones from the field. He pulled up the victim's bloodied trousers and filled his pockets with the stones.

'Up you go.' They lifted the man and carried him to the top of the well. 'Have a nice trip.'

They dumped him in the well.

160

'That water's going to taste like piss,' one of them said.

Another one laughed, 'The villagers won't know the difference.'

They stayed for a moment, listening to the diminishing sounds and finally the silence, then mounted their horses and rode toward the house.

Ivo Martini stayed in the distance, watching in horror, hidden by the brush. The ten-year-old boy hurried to the well.

He looked down and whispered, 'Papa . . .'

But the well was deep, and he heard nothing.

When the *campagni* had finished with Giuseppe Martini, they went to find his wife Maria. She was in the kitchen when they entered.

'Where's my husband?' she demanded.

A grin. 'Getting a drink of water.'

Two of the men were closing in on her. One of them said, 'You're too pretty to be married to an ugly man like that.'

'Get out of my house,' Maria ordered.

'Is that a way to treat guests?' One of the men reached out and tore her dress. 'You're going to be wearing widow's clothes, so you won't need that any more.'

'Animal!'

There was a boiling pot of water on the stove. Maria reached for it and threw it in the man's face.

He screamed in pain. '*Fica!*' He pulled out his gun and fired at her.

She was dead before she hit the floor.

The captain shouted, '*Idiot! First* you fuck them, *then* you shoot them. Come on, let's report back to Don Vito.'

Half an hour later, they were back at Don Vito's *azienda*.

'We took good care of the husband and wife,' the captain reported.

'What about the son?'

The captain looked at Don Vito in surprise. 'You didn't say anything about a son.'

'*Cretino!* I said to take care of the family.'

'But he's only a boy, Don Vito.'

'Boys grow up to be men. Men want their vengeance. Kill him.'

'As you say.'

Two of the men rode back to the Martini farm.

Ivo was in a state of shock. He had watched both his parents murdered. He was alone in the world with no place to go and no one to turn to. *Wait!* There *was* one person to turn to: His father's brother, Nuncio Martini, in Palermo. Ivo knew that he had to move quickly. Don Vito's men would be coming back to kill him. He wondered why they had not done so already. The young boy threw some food into a knapsack, slung it over his shoulder and hurriedly left the farm.

Ivo made his way to the little dirt road that led away from the village, and started walking. Whenever he heard a cart coming, he moved off the road and hid in the trees.

An hour after he had started his journey, he saw

a group of *campagni* riding along the road searching for him. Ivo stayed hidden, motionless until long after they were gone. Then he began walking again. At night, he slept in the orchards and he lived off the fruit from the trees and the vegetables in the fields. He walked for three days.

When he felt he was safe from Don Vito, he approached a small village, where there was a market. An hour later, he was in the back of a farm cart headed for Palermo.

Ivo reached the house of his uncle in the middle of the night. Nuncio Martini lived in a large, prosperous-looking house on the outskirts of the city. It had a spacious balcony, terraces, and a courtyard. Ivo pounded on the front door. There was a long silence, and then a deep voice called out, 'Who the hell is it?'

'It's Ivo, Uncle Nuncio.'

Moments later, Nuncio Martini opened the door. Ivo's uncle was a large, middle-aged man with a generous Roman nose and flowing white hair. He was wearing a nightshirt. He looked at the boy in surprise. 'Ivo! What are you doing here in the middle of the night? Where are your mother and father?'

'They're dead,' Ivo sobbed.

'Dead? Come in, come in.'

Ivo stumbled into the house.

'That's terrible news. Was there some kind of an accident?'

Ivo shook his head. 'Don Vito had them murdered.'

'Murdered? But why?'

163

'My father refused to lease land from him.'

'Ah.'

'Why would he have them killed? They never did anything to him.'

'It was nothing personal,' Nuncio Martini said.

Ivo stared at him. '*Nothing personal?* I don't understand.'

'Everyone knows of Don Vito. He has a reputation. He is an *uomo rispettato* – a man of respect and power. If he let your father defy him, then others would try to defy him and he would lose his power. There is nothing that can be done.'

The boy was watching him, aghast. 'Nothing?'

'Not now, Ivo. Not now. Meanwhile, you look as though you could use a good night's sleep.'

In the morning, at breakfast, they talked.

'How would you like to live in this fine house and work for me?' Nuncio Martini was a widower.

'I think I would like that,' Ivo said.

'I can use a smart boy like you. And you look strong.'

'I am strong,' Ivo told him.

'Good.'

'What business are you in, Uncle?' Ivo asked.

Nuncio Martini smiled. 'I protect people.'

The Mafia, originally known as 'The Black Hand', had sprung up throughout Sicily and other poverty-stricken parts of Italy to protect the people from a ruthless, autocratic government. The Mafia corrected injustices and avenged wrongs, and finally became so powerful that the government itself feared it, and merchants and farmers paid tribute to it.

Legend had it that the word Mafia was coined after an incident where a young girl was raped and murdered, and her anguished mother ran into the night screaming for her daughter, '*Ma fia! Ma fia!*'

Nuncio Martini was the Mafia *capo* in Palermo. He saw to it that proper tribute was collected and that those who did not pay were punished. Punishment could range from a broken arm or leg to a slow and painful death.

Ivo went to work for his uncle.

For the next fifteen years, Palermo was Ivo's school, and his Uncle Nuncio was his teacher. Ivo started out as an errand boy, then moved up to collector, and finally became his uncle's trusted lieutenant.

When Ivo was twenty-five years old, he married Carmela, a buxom Sicilian girl, and a year later, they had a son, Gian Carlo. Ivo moved his family into their own house. When his uncle died, Ivo took his position and became even more successful and prosperous. But he had some unfinished business to attend to.

One day, he said to Carmela, 'Start packing, We're moving to America.'

She looked at him in surprise. 'Why are we going to America?'

Ivo was not accustomed to being questioned. 'Just do as I say. I'm leaving now. I'll be back in two or three days.'

'Ivo . . .'

'Pack.'

*

Three black carriages pulled up in front of the Guardia headquarters in Gibellina. The captain, now heavier by thirty pounds, was seated at his desk when the door opened and half a dozen men walked in. They were well dressed and prosperous looking.

'Good morning, gentlemen. Can I help you?'

'We have come to help *you*,' Ivo said. 'Do you remember me? I'm the son of Giuseppe Martini.'

The police captain's eyes widened. '*You*,' he said. 'What are you doing here? It is dangerous for you.'

'I came because of your teeth.'

'My teeth?'

'Yes.' Two of Ivo's men closed in on the captain and pinned his arms to his side. 'You need dental work. Let me fix them.'

Ivo shoved the gun into the chief's mouth and pulled the trigger.

Ivo turned to his companions. 'Let's go.'

Fifteen minutes later, the three carriages drove up to Don Vito's house. There were two guards outside. They watched the procession curiously. When the cars came to a stop, Ivo got out.

'Good morning. Don Vito's expecting us,' he said.

One of the guards frowned. 'He didn't say anything about . . .'

In the next instant, the guards were gunned down. The guns were loaded with *lupare*, cartridges with large leaden balls, a hunter's trick to spread the pellets. The guards were cut to pieces.

Inside the house, Don Vito heard the shooting. When he looked out of the window and saw what was happening, he quickly crossed to a drawer and pulled out a gun. 'Franco!' he called, 'Antonio! Quickly!'

There were more sounds of shots from outside.

A voice said, 'Don Vito . . .'

He spun around.

Ivo stood there, a gun in his hand. 'Drop your gun.'

'I . . .'

'Drop it.'

Don Vito let his gun fall to the floor. 'Take whatever you want and get out.'

'I don't want anything,' Ivo said. 'As a matter of fact, I came here because I owe you something.'

Don Vito said, 'Whatever it is, I'm prepared to forget it.'

'I'm not. Do you know who I am?'

'No.'

'Ivo Martini.'

The old man frowned, trying to remember. He shrugged. 'It means nothing to me.'

'More than fifteen years ago. Your men killed my mother and father.'

'That's terrible,' Don Vito exclaimed. 'I will have them punished, I'll . . .'

Ivo reached out and smashed him across his nose with his gun. Blood started pouring out. 'This isn't necessary,' Don Vito gasped. 'I . . .'

Ivo pulled out a knife. 'Take down your trousers.'

'Why? You can't . . .'

Ivo raised the gun. 'Take down your trousers.'

'No!' It was a scream. 'Think about what you're doing. I have sons and brothers. If you harm me, they will track you down and kill you like a dog.'

'If they can find me,' Ivo said. 'Your trousers.'

'No.'

Ivo shot one of his kneecaps. The old man screamed out in pain.

'Let me help you,' Ivo said. He reached out and pulled the old man's trousers down, and then his underwear. 'There's not much there, is there? Well, we'll have to do the best we can.' He grabbed Don Vito's member and slashed it off with a knife.

Don Vito fainted.

Ivo took the penis and shoved it into the man's mouth. 'Sorry I don't have a well to drop you into,' Ivo said. As a parting gesture, he shot the old man in the head then turned and walked out of the house to the car.

His friends were waiting for him.

'Let's go.'

'He has a large family, Ivo. They'll come after you.'

'Let them.'

Two days later, Ivo, his wife and son Gian Carlo were on a boat to New York.

At the end of the last century, the new world was a land of opportunity. New York had a large population of Italians. Many of Ivo's friends had already emigrated to the big city and decided to use their expertise in what they knew best: The protection racket. The Mafia began spreading its tentacles. Ivo anglicized his family name from Martini to Martin, and enjoyed uninterrupted prosperity.

Gian Carlo was a big disappointment to his father. He had no interest in working. When he was twenty-seven, he got an Italian girl pregnant, married her in a quiet and hurried ceremony, and three months later they had a son, Paul.

Ivo had big plans for his grandson. Lawyers were very important in America, and Ivo decided that his grandson should be an attorney. The young boy was ambitious and intelligent, and when he was twenty-two, he was admitted to Harvard Law School. When Paul was graduated, Ivo arranged for him to join a prestigious law firm and he soon became a partner. Five years later, Paul opened his own law firm. By this time, Ivo had invested heavily in legitimate businesses, but he still kept his contacts with the Mafia, and his grandson handled his business affairs for him. In 1967, the year Ivo died, Paul married an Italian girl, Nina, and a year later his wife gave birth to twins.

In the '70s Paul was kept busy. His main clients were the unions, and because of that, he was in a position of power. Heads of businesses and industries deferred to him.

One day, Paul was having lunch with a client, Bill Rohan, a respected banker who knew nothing of Paul's family background.

'You should join Sunnyvale, my golf club,' Bill Rohan said. 'You play golf, don't you?'

'Occasionally,' Paul said. 'When I have time.'

'Fine. I'm on the admissions board. Would you like me to put you up for membership?'

'That would be nice.'

The following week the board met to discuss new members. Paul Martin's name was brought up.

'I can recommend him,' Bill Rohan said. 'He's a good man.'

John Hammond, another member of the board, said, 'He's Italian, isn't he? We don't need any dagos in this club, Bill.'

The banker looked at him. 'Are you going to blackball him?'

'You're damn right I am.'

'Okay, then we'll pass on him. Next . . .'

The meeting continued.

Two weeks later, Paul Martin was having lunch with the banker again. 'I've been practising my golf,' Paul joked.

Bill Rohan was embarrassed. 'There's been a slight hitch, Paul.'

'A hitch?'

'I did propose you for membership. But I'm afraid one of the members of the board blackballed you.'

'Oh? Why?'

'Don't take this personally. He's a bigot. He doesn't like Italians.'

Paul smiled. 'That doesn't bother me, Bill. A lot of people don't like Italians. This Mr . . .'

'Hammond. John Hammond.'

'The meat packer?'

'Yes. He'll change his mind. I'll talk to him again.'

Paul shook his head. 'Don't bother. To tell you the truth, I'm really not that crazy about golf anyway.'

Six months later, in the middle of July, four Hammond Meat Packing Company refrigerated trucks loaded with pork and steaks and headed from the packing house in Minnesota to supermarkets in

Buffalo and New Jersey pulled off the road. The drivers opened the back doors of the trucks and walked away.

When John Hammond heard the news, he was furious. He called in his manager.

'What the hell is going on?' he demanded. 'A million and a half dollars' worth of meat spoiled in the sun. How could that happen?'

'The union called a strike,' the supervisor said.

'Without telling us? What are they striking about? More money?'

The supervisor shrugged. 'I don't know. They didn't say anything to me. They just walked.'

'Tell the local union guy to come in and see me. I'll settle it,' Hammond said.

That afternoon, the union representative was ushered into Hammond's office.

'Why wasn't I told there was going to be a strike?' Hammond demanded.

The representative said, apologetically, 'I didn't know it myself, Mr Hammond. The men just got mad and walked out. It happened very suddenly.'

'You know I've always been a reasonable man to deal with. What is it they want? A raise?'

'No, sir. It's soap.'

Hammond stared at him. 'Did you say *soap*?'

'That's right. They don't like the soap you're using in their bathrooms. It's too strong.'

Hammond could not believe what he was hearing. '*The soap was too strong?* And that's why I lost a million and a half dollars?'

'Don't blame me,' the foreman said. 'It's the men.'

'Jesus,' Hammond said. 'I can't believe this. What

171

kind of soap would they like – fairy soap?' He slammed his fist on the desk. 'The next time the men have any problem, you come to me first. You hear me?'

'Yes, Mr Hammond.'

'You tell them to get back to work. There will be the best soap money can buy in those washrooms by six o'clock tonight. Is that clear?'

'I'll tell them, Mr Hammond.'

John Hammond sat there for a long time fuming. *No wonder this country is going to hell*, he thought. *Soap*!

Two weeks later, at noon on a hot day in August, five Hammond Meat Packing trucks on their way to deliver meat to Syracuse and Boston pulled off the road. The drivers opened the back doors of the refrigerated trucks and left.

John Hammond got the news at six o'clock that evening.

'What the hell are you talking about?' he screamed. 'Didn't you put in the new soap?'

'I did,' his manager said, 'the same day you told me to.'

'Then what the hell is it this time?'

The manager said helplessly, 'I don't know. There haven't been any complaints. No one said a word to me.'

'Get the goddamned union representative in here.'

At seven o'clock that evening, Hammond was talking to the union representative.

'Two million dollars' worth of meat was ruined

this afternoon because of your men,' Hammond screamed. 'Have they gone crazy?'

'Do you want me to tell the president of the union you asked that, Mr Hammond?'

'No, no,' Hammond said quickly. 'Look, I've never had any problem with you fellows before. If the men want more money, just come to me and we'll discuss it like reasonable people. How much are they asking for?'

'Nothing.'

'What do you mean?'

'It isn't the money, Mr Hammond.'

'Oh? What is it?'

'Lights.'

'Lights?' Hammond thought he had misunderstood him.

'Yes. The men are complaining that the lights in the washrooms are too dim.'

John Hammond sat back in his chair, suddenly quiet. 'What's going on here?' he asked softly.

'I told you, the men think that . . .'

'Never mind that crap. What's going on?'

The union representative said, 'If I knew, I would tell you.'

'Is someone trying to put me out of business? Is that it?'

The union representative was silent.

'All right,' John Hammond said. 'Give me a name. Who can I talk to?'

'There's a lawyer who might be able to help you. The union uses him a lot. His name is Paul Martin.'

'Paul . . . ?' And John Hammond suddenly remembered. 'Why that blackmailing guinea bastard. Get out of here,' he yelled. '*Out!*'

173

Hammond sat there seething. *No one blackmails me. No one.*

One week later, six more of his refrigerated trucks were abandoned on side roads.

John Hammond arranged a luncheon with Bill Rohan. 'I've been thinking about your friend, Paul Martin,' Hammond said. 'I may have been a bit hasty in blackballing him.'

'Why, it's very generous of you to say that, John.'

'I'll tell you what. You propose him for membership next week and I'll give him my vote.'

The following week, when Paul Martin's name came up, he was accepted unanimously by the membership committee.

John Hammond personally put in a call to Paul Martin. 'Congratulations, Mr Martin,' he said. 'You've just been accepted as a member of Sunnyvale. We're delighted to have you aboard.'

'Thank you,' Paul said. 'I appreciate the call.'

John Hammond's next call was to the district attorney's office. He made an appointment to meet him the following week.

On Sunday, John Hammond and Bill Rohan were part of a foursome at the club.

'You haven't met Paul Martin yet, have you?' Bill Rohan asked.

John Hammond shook his head. 'No. I don't think he's going to be playing a lot of golf. The Grand Jury is going to be keeping your friend too busy.'

'What are you talking about?'

'I'm going to give information about him to the district attorney that will certainly interest a Grand Jury.'

Bill Rohan was shocked. 'Do you know what you're doing?'

'You bet I do. He's a cockroach, John. I'm going to step on him.'

The following Monday, on his way to the district attorney's office, John Hammond was killed in a hit and run accident. There were no witnesses. The police never found the driver.

Every Sunday after that, Paul Martin took his wife and the twins to the Sunnyvale club for lunch. The buffet there was delicious.

Paul Martin took his marriage vows seriously. For instance, he would never have dreamed of dishonouring his wife by taking her and his mistress to the same restaurant. His marriage was one part of his life, his affairs were another. All of Paul Martin's friends had mistresses. It was part of their accepted lifestyle. What bothered Martin was to see old men taking out young girls. It was undignified, and Paul Martin placed great value on dignity. He resolved that when he reached the age of sixty he would stop having mistresses. And on his sixtieth birthday, two years earlier, he had stopped. His wife, Nina, was a good companion to him. That was enough. *Dignity.*

It was this man to whom Lara Cameron had come to ask for help. Martin had been aware of Lara Cameron by name, but he was stunned by how young and beautiful she was. She was ambitious and angrily independent, and yet she was very feminine. He found himself strongly attracted to her. *No*, he thought, *she's a young girl. I'm an old man. Too old.*

When Lara had stormed out of his office on her first visit, Paul Martin sat there for a long time, thinking about her. And then he had picked up the telephone and made a call.

The new building was progressing on schedule. Lara visited the site every morning and every afternoon, and there was a new respect in the attitude of the men toward her. She sensed it in the way they looked at her, talked to her and worked for her. She knew it was because of Paul Martin, and, disturbingly, she found herself thinking more and more about the ugly-attractive man with the strangely compelling voice.

Lara telephoned him again.

'I wondered if we might have lunch, Mr Martin?'

'Are you having another problem of some kind?'

'No. I just thought it would be nice if we got to know each other better.'

'I'm sorry, Miss Cameron. I never have lunch.'

'What about dinner one evening?'

'I'm a married man, Miss Cameron. I have dinner with my wife and children.'

'I see. If . . .' The line went dead. *What's the matter with him?* Lara wondered. *I'm not trying to go to bed with the man, I just want to find some way to thank him.* She tried to put him out of her mind.

Paul Martin was disturbed by how pleased he was to hear Lara Cameron's voice. He told his secretary,

'If Miss Cameron calls again, tell her I'm not in.' He did not need temptation, and Lara Cameron was temptation.

Howard Keller was delighted with the way things were progressing.

'I must admit, you had me a little worried there for a while,' he said. 'It looked as though we were going right down the tube. You pulled off a miracle.'

It wasn't my miracle, Lara thought. *It was Paul Martin's*. Perhaps he was angry with her because she had not paid him for his services.

On an impulse, Lara sent Paul a cheque for fifty thousand dollars.

The following day, the cheque was returned with no note.

Lara telephoned him again. His secretary said, 'I'm sorry, Mr Martin is not available.'

Another snub. It was as though he could not be bothered with her. *And if he can't be bothered with me*, Lara wondered, *why did he go out of his way to help me?*

She dreamed about him that night.

Howard Keller walked into Lara's office.

'I've got two tickets for the new Andrew Lloyd Webber musical, *Song and Dance*. I have to go to Chicago. Can you use the tickets?'

'No, I . . . wait.' She was quiet for a moment. 'Yes, I think I can use them. Thank you, Howard.'

That afternoon Lara put one of the tickets in an

178

envelope and addressed it to Paul Martin at his office.

When he received the ticket the next day, he looked at it, puzzled. Who would send him a single ticket to the theatre? *The Cameron girl. I'll have to put a stop to this*, he thought.

'Am I free Friday evening?' he asked his secretary.

'You're having dinner with your brother-in-law, Mr Martin.'

'Cancel it.'

Lara sat through the first act, and the seat next to her remained empty. *So he's not coming*, Lara thought. *Well, to hell with him. I've done everything I can.*

As the first act curtain came down, Lara debated whether she should stay for the second act or leave. A figure appeared at the seat next to hers.

'Let's get out of here,' Paul Martin commanded.

They had dinner at a bistro on the east side. He sat across the table from her, studying her, quiet and wary. The waiter came to take their drink order.

'I'll have a Scotch and soda,' Lara said.

'Nothing for me.'

Lara looked at him in surprise.

'I don't drink.'

After they had ordered dinner, Paul Martin said, 'Miss Cameron, what do you want from me?'

'I don't like owing anyone anything,' Lara said. 'I

owe you something, and you won't let me pay you. That bothers me.'

'I told you before . . . you don't owe me anything.'

'But I . . .'

'I hear your building is coming along well.'

'Yes.' She started to say 'thanks to you,' then thought better of it.

'You're good at what you do, aren't you?'

Lara nodded. 'I want to be. It's the most exciting thing in the world to have an idea and watch it grow into concrete and steel, and become a building that people work in and live in. In a way, it becomes a monument, doesn't it?' Her face was vibrant and alive.

'I suppose it does. And is one monument going to lead to another?'

'You bet it is,' Lara said enthusiastically. 'I intend to become the most important real estate developer in this city.'

There was a sexuality about her that was mesmerizing.

Paul Martin smiled. 'I wouldn't be surprised.'

'Why did you decide to come to the theatre tonight?' Lara asked.

He had come to tell her to leave him alone, but being with her now, being this close to her, he could not bring himself to say it. 'I heard good things about the show.'

Lara smiled. 'Maybe we'll go again and see it together, Paul.'

He shook his head. 'Miss Cameron, I'm not only married, I'm very much married. I happen to love my wife.'

'I admire that,' Lara said. 'The building will be

finished on the fifteenth of March. We're having a party to celebrate. Will you come?'

He hesitated a long time trying to word his refusal as gently as possible. When he finally spoke, he said, 'Yes. I'll come.'

The celebration for the opening of the new building was a moderate success. Lara Cameron's name was not big enough to attract many members of the press nor any of the city's important dignitaries. But the mayor's assistant was there and a reporter from the *Post*.

'The building is almost fully leased out,' Keller told Lara. 'And we have a flood of inquiries.'

'Good,' Lara said absently. Her mind was on something else. She was thinking about Paul Martin and wondering whether he would appear. For some reason it was important to her. He was an intriguing mystery. He denied that he had helped her, and yet . . . She was pursuing a man old enough to be her father. Lara put the connection out of her mind.

Lara attended to her guests. Hors d'oeuvres and drinks were being served, and everyone seemed to be having a good time. In the midst of the festivities, Paul Martin arrived, and the tone of the party immediately changed. The workmen greeted him as though he were royalty. They were obviously in awe of him.

I'm a corporate attorney. I don't deal with unions.

Martin shook hands with the mayor's assistant and some of the union officials there, then went up to Lara.

'I'm glad you could come,' Lara said.

Paul Martin looked around at the huge building and said, 'Congratulations. You've done a good job.'

181

'Thank you.' She lowered her voice. 'And I do mean thank you.'

He was staring at her, bemused by how ravishing Lara looked, and the way he felt, looking at her.

'The party's almost over,' Lara said. 'I was hoping you would take me to dinner.'

'I told you, I have dinner with my wife and children.' He was looking into her eyes. 'I'll buy you a drink.'

Lara smiled. 'That will do nicely.'

They stopped at a small bar on Third Avenue. They talked, but afterward neither of them would remember what they talked about. The words were camouflage for the sexual tension between them.

'Tell me about yourself,' Paul Martin said. 'Who are you? Where are you from? How did you get started in this business?'

Lara thought of Sean McAllister and his repulsive body on top of hers. *'Come back to bed, honey. That was so good we're going to do it again.'*

'I come from a little town in Nova Scotia,' Lara said. 'Glace Bay. My father collected rents from some boarding houses there. When he died, I took over. One of the boarders helped me buy a lot, and I put up a building on it. That was the beginning.'

He was listening closely.

'After that, I went to Chicago and developed some buildings there. I did well and came to New York.' She smiled. 'That's really the whole story.' *Except for the agony of growing up with a father who hated her, the shame of poverty, of never owning anything, of giving her body to Sean McAllister . . .*

As though reading her mind, Paul Martin said, 'I'll bet it wasn't really all that easy, was it?'

'I'm not complaining.'

'What's your next project?'

Lara shrugged. 'I'm not sure. I've looked at a lot of possibilities, but there's nothing I'm really wild about.'

He could not take his eyes off her.

'What are you thinking?' Lara asked.

He took a deep breath. 'The truth? I was thinking that if I weren't married, I would tell you that you're one of the most exciting women I've ever met. But I am married, so you and I are going to be just friends. Do I make myself clear?'

'Very clear.'

He looked at his watch. 'Time to go.' He turned to the waiter. 'Check, please.' He rose to his feet.

'Can we have lunch next week?' Lara asked.

'No. Maybe I'll see you again when your next building is finished.'

And he was gone.

That night, Lara dreamed they were making love. Paul Martin was on top of her, stroking her body with his hands and whispering in her ear.

'Ye ken, I maun hae ye, and onie ye . . . Gude forgie me, my bonnie darlin', for I've niver tauld you how meikle I love ye, love ye, love ye . . .'

And then he was inside her and her body was suddenly molten. She moaned and her moans awakened her. She sat up in bed, trembling.

*

183

Two days later, Paul Martin telephoned. 'I think I have a location you might be interested in,' he said crisply. 'It's over on the West Side, on 69th Street. It's not on the market yet. It belongs to a client of mine who wants to sell.'

Lara and Howard Keller went to look at it that morning. It was a prime piece of property.

'How did you hear about this?' Keller asked.

'Paul Martin.'

'Oh. I see.' There was disapproval in his voice.

'What is that supposed to mean?'

'Lara . . . I checked on Martin. He's Mafia. Stay away from him.'

She said indignantly, 'He has nothing to do with the Mafia. He's a good friend. Anyway, what does that have to do with this site? Do you like it?'

'I think it's great.'

'Then let's buy it.'

Ten days later, they closed the deal.

Lara sent Paul Martin a large bouquet of flowers. There was a note attached: 'Paul – please don't send these back. They're very sensitive.'

She received a call from him that afternoon.

'Thanks for the flowers. I'm not used to getting flowers from beautiful women.' His voice sounded gruffer than usual.

'Do you know your problem?' Lara said. 'No one has ever spoiled you enough.'

'Is that what you want to do, spoil me?'

'Rotten.'

Paul laughed.

'I mean it.'

'I know you do.'

'Why don't we talk about it at lunch?' Lara asked.

Paul Martin had not been able to get Lara out of his mind. He knew that he could easily fall in love with her. There was a vulnerability about her, an innocence, and at the same time, something wildly sensual. He knew that he would be smart never to see her again, but he was unable to control himself. He was drawn to her by something more powerful than his will.

They had lunch at the Twenty-One Club.

'When you're trying to hide something,' Paul Martin advised, 'always do it out in the open. Then no one will believe you're doing anything wrong.'

'Are we trying to hide something?' Lara asked softly.

He looked at her and made his decision. *She's beautiful and smart, but so are a thousand other women. It will be easy to get her out of my system. I'll go to bed with her once and that will be the end of it.*

As it turned out, he was wrong.

When they arrived at Lara's apartment, Paul was unaccountably nervous.

'I feel like a fuckin' schoolboy,' Paul said. 'I'm out of practice.'

'It's like riding a bicycle,' Lara murmured. 'It will come back to you. Let me undress you.'

She took off his jacket and tie and started unbuttoning his shirt.

185

'You know that this could never become serious, Lara.'

'I know that.'

'I'm sixty-two years old. I could be your father.'

She went still for an instant, remembering her dream. 'I know.' She finished undressing him. 'You have a beautiful body.'

'Thanks.' His wife never told him that.

Lara slid her arms along his thighs. 'You're very strong, aren't you?'

He found himself standing straighter. 'I played basketball when I was in . . .'

Her lips were on his and they were in bed, and he experienced something that had never happened to him before in his life. He felt as though his body were on fire. They were making love and it was without a beginning or an ending, a river that swept him along faster and faster, and the tide began to pull at him, sucking him down and down, deeper and deeper, into a velvet darkness that exploded into a thousand stars. And the miracle was that it happened again, and once again, until he lay there panting and exhausted.

'I can't believe this,' he said.

His love-making with his wife had always been conventional, routine. But with Lara it was an incredibly sensual experience. Paul Martin had had many women before, but Lara was like no one he had ever known. She had given him a gift no woman had ever given him: She made him feel young.

When Paul was getting dressed, Lara asked, 'Will I see you again?'

'Yes.' *God help me*. 'Yes.'

*

186

The 1980s were a time of changes. Ronald Reagan was elected President of the United States and Wall Street had the busiest day in its history. The Shah of Iran died in exile, and Anwar Sadat was assassinated. The public debt hit one trillion dollars, and the American hostages in Iran were freed. Sandra Day O'Connor became the first woman to serve on the Supreme Court.

Lara was in the right place at the right time. Real estate development was booming. Money was abundant and banks were willing to finance projects that were both speculative and highly leveraged.

Savings and loan companies were a big source of equity. High yield and high risk bonds – nicknamed junk bonds – had been popularized by a young financial genius named Mike Milken, and they were manna to the real estate industry. The financing was there for the asking.

'I'm going to put up a hotel on the 69th Street property, instead of an office building.'

'Why?' Howard Keller asked. 'It's a perfect location for an office building. With a hotel, you have to run it twenty-four hours a day. Tenants come and go like ants. With an office building, you only have to worry about a lease every five or ten years.'

'I know, but in a hotel you have drop-dead power, Howard. You can give important people suites and entertain them in your own restaurant. I like that idea. It's going to be a hotel. I want you to set up meetings with the top architects in New York: Skidmore, Owings and Merrill, Peter Eisenman and Philip Johnson.'

The meetings took place over the next two weeks. Some of the architects were patronizing. They had never worked for a female developer before.

One of them said, 'If you'd like us to copy . . .'

'No. We're going to build a hotel that *other* builders will copy. If you want a buzzword, try "elegance". I see an entry way flanked by twin fountains, a lobby with Italian marble. Off the lobby we'll have a comfortable conference room where . . .'

By the end of the meeting, they were impressed.

Lara put together a team. She hired a lawyer named Terry Hill, an assistant named Jim Belon, a project manager named Tom Chriton, and an advertising agency headed by Tom Scott. She hired the architectural firm of Higgins, Almont & Clark, and the project was under way.

'We'll meet once a week,' Lara told the group, 'but I'll want daily reports from each of you. I want this hotel to go up on schedule and on budget. I selected all of you because you're the best at what you do. Don't let me down. Are there any questions?'

The next two hours were spent in answering them.

Later Lara said to Keller, 'How do you think the meeting went?'

'Fine, boss.'

It was the first time he had called her that. She liked it.

Charles Cohn telephoned.

'I'm in New York. Can we have lunch?'

'You bet we can!' Lara said.

They had lunch at Sardi's.

'You look wonderful,' Cohn said. 'Success agrees with you, Lara.'

'It's only the beginning,' Lara said. 'Charles . . . how would you like to join Cameron Enterprises? I'll give you a piece of the company and . . .'

He shook his head. 'Thanks, but no. You've just started the journey. I'm near the end of the road. I'll be retiring next summer.'

'Let's stay in touch,' Lara said. 'I don't want to lose you.'

The next time Paul Martin came to Lara's apartment, she said, 'I have a surprise for you, darling.'

She handed him half a dozen packages.

'Hey! It's not my birthday.'

'Open them.'

Inside were a dozen Bergdorf Goodman shirts and a dozen Pucci ties.

'I have shirts and ties,' he laughed.

'Not like these,' Lara told him. 'They'll make you feel younger. I got the name of a good tailor for you, too.'

The following week Lara had a new barber style Paul's hair.

Paul Martin looked at himself in the mirror and thought, *I do look younger*. Life had become exciting. *And all because of Lara*, he thought.

Paul's wife tried not to notice the change in her husband.

They were all there for the meeting: Keller, Tom Chriton, Jim Belon and Terry Hill.

'We're going to fast track the hotel,' Lara announced.

The men looked at one another. 'That's dangerous,' Keller said.

'Not if you do it right.'

Tom Chriton spoke up. 'Miss Cameron, the safe way to do this is to complete one phase at a time. You do your grading, and when that's done, you begin digging the trenches for foundations. When that's done, you put in the utility conduits and drainage piping. Then . . .'

Lara interrupted. '. . . You put in the wooden concrete formwork and the skeletal gridiron. I know all that.'

'Then why . . . ?'

'Because that will take two years. I don't want to wait two years.'

Jim Belon said, 'If we fast track it, that means starting all the different steps at once. If anything goes wrong, nothing will fit together. You could have a lopsided building with electric circuits in the wrong place and . . .'

'Then we have to see to it that nothing goes wrong, don't we?' Lara said. 'If we do it this way, we'll get the building up in a year instead of two, and we'll save close to twenty million dollars.'

'True, but it's taking a big chance.'

'I like taking chances.'

Lara told Paul Martin about her decision to fast track the hotel, and the discussion she had had with the committee.

'They may have been right,' Paul said. 'What you're doing could be dangerous.'

'Trump does it. Uris does it.'

Paul said gently, 'Baby, you're not Trump or Uris.'

'I'm going to be bigger than they are, Paul. I'm going to put up more buildings in New York than anyone ever has before. It's going to be my city.'

He looked at her for a long moment. 'I believe you.'

Lara had an unlisted telephone installed in her office. Only Paul Martin had the number. He installed a telephone in his office for Lara's calls. They spoke to each other several times a day.

Whenever they could get away in the afternoon, they went to Lara's apartment. Paul Martin looked forward to those trysts more than he had ever believed possible. Lara had become an obsession with him.

When Keller became aware of what was happening, he was concerned.

'Lara,' he said, 'I think you're making a mistake. He's dangerous.'

'You don't know him. He's wonderful.'

'Are you in love with him?'

Lara thought about it. Paul Martin fulfilled a need in her life. But was she in love with him?

'No.'

'Is he in love with you?'

'I think so.'

'Be careful. Be very careful.'

Lara smiled. Impulsively, she kissed Keller's cheek. 'I love the way you take care of me, Howard.'

Lara was at the construction site, studying a report.

'I notice we're paying for an awful lot of lumber,' Lara said. She was talking to Pete Reese, the new project manager.

'I didn't want to mention it before, Miss Cameron, because I wasn't sure – but you're right. A lot of our lumber's missing. We've had to double order it.'

She looked up at him. 'You mean someone is stealing it?'

'It looks that way.'

'Do you have any idea who?'

'No.'

'We have night watchmen here, don't we?'

'One watchman.'

'And he hasn't seen anything?'

'No. But with all this activity going on, it could be happening during the day. It could be anybody.'

Lara was thoughtful. 'I see. Thanks for letting me know, Pete. I'll take care of it.'

That afternoon, Lara hired a private detective, Steve Kane.

'How does anyone walk away in broad daylight with a load of lumber?' Kane asked.

'You tell me.'

'You say there's a night watchman at the site?'

'Yes.'

'Maybe he's in on it.'

'I'm not interested in maybes,' Lara said. 'Find out who's behind it and get back to me.'

'Can you get me hired as a member of the construction crew?'

'I'll take care of it.'

Steve Kane went to work at the site the next day.

When Lara told Keller what was happening, he said, 'You didn't have to get involved in this. I could have handled it for you.'

'I like handling things myself,' Lara said.

That was the end of the conversation.

Five days later, Kane appeared at Lara's office.

'Have you found out anything?'

'Everything,' he said.

'Was it the watchman?'

'No. The lumber wasn't stolen from the building site.'

'What do you mean?'

'I mean it never reached there. It was sent to another construction site in Jersey and double billed. The invoices were doctored.'

'Who's behind it?' Lara asked.

Kane told her.

The following afternoon, there was a meeting of the committee. Terry Hill, Lara's lawyer, was there,

Howard Keller, Jim Belon, the project manager, and Pete Reese. There was also a stranger at the conference table. Lara introduced him as Mr Conroy.

'Let's have a report,' Lara said.

Pete Reese said, 'We're right on schedule. We estimate four more months. You were right about going fast track. It's all going smooth as silk. We've already started on the electrical and plumbing.'

'Good,' Lara said.

'What about the stolen lumber?' Keller asked.

'Nothing new on it yet,' Pete Reese said. 'We're keeping an eye open.'

'I don't think we have to worry about that any more,' Lara announced. 'We found out who's stealing it.' She nodded toward the stranger. 'Mr Conroy is with the Special Fraud Squad. It's actually *Detective* Conroy.'

'What's he doing here?' Pete Reese asked.

'He's come to take you away.'

Reese looked up, startled. 'What?'

Lara turned to the group. 'Mr Reese has been selling our lumber to another construction job. When he found out that I was checking the reports, he decided to tell me there was a problem.'

'Wait a minute,' Pete Reese said. 'I . . . I . . . You have it wrong.'

She turned to Conroy. 'Would you please get him out of here?'

She turned to the others. 'Now, let's discuss the opening of the hotel.'

As the hotel grew nearer completion, the pressure became more intense. Lara was becoming impossible. She badgered everyone constantly. She made phone calls in the middle of the night.

'Howard, did you know the shipment of wallpaper hasn't arrived yet?'

'For God's sakes, Lara, it's four o'clock in the morning.'

'It's ninety days to the opening of the hotel. We can't open a hotel without wallpaper.'

'I'll check it out in the morning.'

'This *is* morning. Check it out now.'

Lara's nervousness increased as the deadline grew closer. She met with Tom Scott, head of the advertising agency.

'Do you have small children, Mr Scott?'

He looked at her in surprise. 'No. Why?'

'Because I just went over the new advertising campaign and it seems to have been devised by a small retarded child. I can't believe that grown men sat down and thought up this junk.'

Scott frowned. 'If there's something about it that displeases you . . .'

'Everything about it displeases me,' Lara said. 'It lacks excitement. It's bland. It could be about any hotel anywhere. This isn't *any* hotel, Mr Scott. This is the most beautiful, most modern hotel in New York. You make it sound like a cold, faceless building. It's a warm, exciting home. Let's spread the word. Do you think you can handle that?'

'I assure you we can handle it. We'll revise the campaign and in two weeks . . .'

'Monday,' Lara said flatly. 'I want to see the new campaign Monday.'

*

The new ads went out in newspapers and magazines and billboards all over the country.

'I think the campaign turned out great,' Tom Scott said. 'You were right.'

Lara looked at him and said quietly, 'I don't want to be right. I want *you* to be right. That's what I pay you for.'

She turned to Jerry Townsend, in charge of publicity.

'Have the invitations all been sent out?'

'Yes. We've got most of our replies already. Everybody's coming to the opening. It's going to be quite a party.'

'It should be,' Keller grumbled, 'it's costing enough.'

Lara grinned. 'Stop being a banker. We'll get a million dollars' worth of publicity. We're going to have dozens of celebrities there and . . .'

He held up his hand. 'All right, all right.'

Two weeks before the opening, everything seemed to be happening at once. The wallpaper had arrived and carpets were being installed, halls were being painted and pictures were being hung. Lara inspected every suite, accompanied by a staff of five.

She walked into one suite and said, 'The drapes are wrong. Switch them with the suite next door.'

In another suite, she tried the piano. 'It's out of tune. Take care of it.'

In a third suite the electric fireplace didn't work. 'Fix it.'

It seemed to the harried staff that Lara was trying to do everything herself. She was in the kitchen and in the laundry room and in the utility closets. She was everywhere, demanding, complaining, fixing.

The man whom she had hired to manage the hotel said, 'Don't get so excited, Miss Cameron. At the opening of any hotel, little things always go wrong.'

'Not in my hotels,' Lara said. 'Not in my hotels.'

The day of the opening, Lara was up at four a.m., too nervous to sleep. She wanted desperately to talk to Paul Martin, but there was no way she could call him at that hour. She dressed and went for a walk.

Everything is going to be fine, she told herself. *The reservation computer is going to be fixed. They'll get the third oven working. The lock on suite seven will be repaired. We'll find a replacement for the maids who quit yesterday. The air conditioning unit in the penthouse will work . . .*

At six o'clock that evening, the invited guests began to arrive. A uniformed guard at each entrance to the hotel examined their invitations before admitting them. There was a mix of celebrities, famous athletes and corporation executives. Lara had gone over the list carefully, eliminating the names of the freeloaders and the hangers-on.

She stood in the spacious lobby greeting the newcomers as they arrived. 'I'm Lara Cameron. So nice of you to come . . . Please feel free to look around.'

Lara took Keller aside. 'Why isn't the mayor coming?'

'He's pretty busy, you know, and . . .'

'You mean he thinks I'm not important enough.'

'One day he'll change his mind.'

One of the mayor's assistants arrived.

'Thank you for coming,' Lara said. 'This is an honour for the hotel.'

Lara kept looking nervously for Todd Grayson, the architectural critic for the *New York Times*, who had been invited. *If he likes it*, Lara thought, *we have a winner*.

Paul Martin arrived with his wife. It was the first time Lara had seen Mrs Martin. She was an attractive, elegant looking woman. Lara felt an unexpected pang of guilt.

Paul walked up to Lara. 'Miss Cameron, I'm Paul Martin. This is my wife, Nina. Thank you for inviting us.'

Lara gripped his hand a second longer than necessary. 'I'm delighted that you're here. Please make yourself at home.'

Paul looked around the lobby. He had seen it half a dozen times before. 'It's beautiful,' he exclaimed. 'I think you're going to be very successful.'

Nina Martin was staring at Lara. 'I'm sure she will be.'

And Lara wondered if she knew.

The guests began to stream in.

An hour later, Lara was standing in the lobby when Keller rushed up to her. 'For God's sakes,' he said, 'everyone's looking for you. They're all in the ballroom, eating. Why aren't you in there?'

'Todd Grayson hasn't arrived. I'm waiting for him.'

'*The Times*' architectural critic? I saw him an hour ago.'

'*What?*'

'Yes. He went on a tour of the hotel with the others.'

'Why didn't you tell me?'

'I thought you knew.'

'What did he say?' Lara asked eagerly. 'How did he look? Did he seem impressed?'

'He didn't say anything. He looked fine. And I don't know whether he was impressed or not.'

'Didn't he say *anything*?'

'No.'

Lara frowned. 'He would have said something if he had liked it. It's a bad sign, Howard.'

The party was a huge success. The guests ate and drank and toasted the hotel. When the evening was over, Lara was showered with compliments.

'It's such a lovely hotel, Miss Cameron . . .'

'I'll certainly stay here when I come back to New York . . .'

'What a great idea, having a piano in every living room . . .'

'I love the fireplaces . . .'

'I'll certainly recommend this to all my friends . . .'

Well, Lara thought, *even if the New York Times hates it, it's going to be a success*.

Lara saw Paul Martin and his wife as they were leaving.

'I think you really have a winner here, Miss Cameron. It's going to be the talk of New York.'

'You're very kind, Mr Martin,' Lara said. 'Thank you for coming.'

199

Nina Martin said quietly, 'Goodnight, Miss Cameron.'

'Goodnight.'

As they were walking out of the lobby door, Lara heard her say, 'She's very beautiful, isn't she, Paul?'

The following Thursday, when the first edition of the *New York Times* came out, Lara was at the newsstand at 42nd Street and Broadway at four o'clock in the morning to pick up a copy. She hurriedly turned to the Home Section. Todd Grayson's article began:

> Manhattan has long needed a hotel that does not remind travellers that they're staying in a hotel. The suites at the Cameron Plaza are large and gracious, and done in beautiful taste. Lara Cameron has finally given New York . . .

She yelled aloud with joy. She telephoned Keller and woke him up.

'We're in!' she said. '*The Times* loves us.'

He sat up in bed, groggy. 'That's great. What did they say?'

Lara read the article to him. 'All right,' Keller said, 'now you can get some sleep.'

'Sleep? Are you joking? I have a new site picked out. As soon as the banks open, I want you to start negotiating a loan . . .'

The New York Cameron Plaza was a triumph. It was completely booked, and there was a waiting list.

'It's only the beginning,' Lara told Keller. 'There are ten thousand builders in the metropolitan area but only a handful of the big boys – the Tisches, the Rudins, the Rockefellers, the Sterns. Well, whether they like it or not, we're going to play in their sandbox. We're going to change the skyline. We're going to invent the future.'

Lara began to get calls from banks offering her loans. She cultivated the important real estate brokers, taking them to dinner and the theatre. She had power breakfasts at the Regency, and was told about properties that were about to come on the market. She acquired two more downtown sites and began construction.

Paul Martin telephoned Lara at the office. 'Have you seen *Business Week*? You're a hot ticket,' he said. 'The word's out that you're a shaker. You get things done.'

'I try.'

'Are you free for dinner?'

'I'll make myself free.'

Lara was in a meeting with the partner of a top architectural firm. She was examining the blueprints and drawings they had brought.

'You're going to like this,' the chief architect said. 'It has grace and symmetry, and the scope that you asked for. Let me explain some of the details . . .'

'That won't be necessary,' Lara said. 'I understand them.' She looked up. 'I want you to turn these plans over to an artist.'

'What?'

'I want large colour drawings of the building. I

want drawings of the lobby, the corridors and the offices. Bankers have no imagination. I'm going to *show* them what the building is going to look like.'

'That's a great idea.'

Lara's secretary appeared. 'I'm sorry I'm late.'

'This meeting was called for nine o'clock, Kathy. It's nine fifteen.'

'I'm sorry, Miss Cameron, my alarm didn't go off and . . .'

'We'll discuss it later.'

She turned to the architects. 'I want a few changes made . . .'

Two hours later, Lara had finished discussing the changes she wanted. When the meeting was over, she said to Kathy, 'Don't leave. Sit down.'

Kathy sat.

'Do you like your job?'

'Yes, Miss Cameron.'

'This is the third time you've been late this week. I won't put up with that again.'

'I'm terribly sorry, I . . . I haven't been feeling well.'

'What's your problem?'

'It's nothing, really.'

'It's obviously enough to keep you from coming in on time. What is it?'

'I haven't been sleeping very well lately. To tell you the truth, I . . . I'm scared.'

'Scared of what?' Lara asked impatiently.

'I . . . I have a lump.'

'Oh.' Lara was silent for a moment. 'Well, what did the doctor say?'

Kathy swallowed. 'I haven't seen a doctor.'

'Not seen one!' Lara exploded. 'For God's sakes, do you come from a family of ostriches? Of course you've got to see a doctor.'

Lara picked up the phone. 'Get me Dr Peters.'

She replaced the receiver. 'It's probably nothing, but you can't let it go.'

'I have a mother and brother who died of cancer,' Kathy said miserably. 'I don't want a doctor to tell me I have it.'

The telephone rang. Lara picked it up. 'Hello? He what? I don't care if he is. You tell him I want to talk to him *now*.'

She replaced the receiver.

A few moments later the phone rang again. Lara picked it up. 'Hello, Alan . . . no, I'm fine. I'm sending my secretary over to see you. Her name is Kathy Turner. She'll be there in half an hour. I want her examined this morning, and I want you to stay on top of it . . . I know you are . . . I appreciate it . . . thanks.'

She replaced the receiver. 'Get over to Sloan-Kettering Hospital. Dr Peters will be waiting for you.'

'I don't know what to say, Miss Cameron.'

'Say that you'll be on time tomorrow.'

Howard Keller came into the office. 'We have a problem, boss.'

'Go.'

'It's the property on Fourteenth Street. We've cleared the tenants out of the whole block except for one apartment house. The Dorchester Apartments.

Six of the tenants refuse to leave, and the City won't let us force them out.'

'Offer them more money.'

'It's not a question of money. Those people have lived there a long time. They don't want to leave. They're comfortable there.'

'Then let's make them *un*comfortable.'

'What do you mean?'

Lara got up. 'Let's go take a look at the building.'

On the drive down they passed bag ladies and homeless people roaming the streets, asking for handouts.

'In a country as wealthy as this,' Lara said, 'that's a disgrace.'

The Dorchester Apartments was a six-storey brick building in the middle of a block filled with old structures waiting for the bulldozers.

Lara stood in front of it, examining it. 'How many tenants are in there?'

'We got sixteen out of the apartments. Six are still hanging on.'

'That means we have sixteen apartments available.'

He looked at her, puzzled. 'That's right. Why?'

'Let's fill those apartments.'

'You mean lease them? What's the point . . . ?'

'We're not going to lease them. We're going to donate them to the homeless. There are thousands of homeless people in New York. We're going to take care of some of them. Crowd in as many as you can. See that they're given some food.'

Keller frowned. 'What makes me think this isn't one of your better ideas?'

'Howard, we're going to become benefactors. We're going to do something the City can't do – shelter the homeless.'

Lara was studying the building more closely, looking at the windows. 'And I want those windows boarded up.'

'What?'

'We're going to make the building look like an old derelict. Is the top floor apartment still occupied, the one with the roof garden?'

'Yes.'

'Put up a big billboard on the roof to block the view.'

'But . . .'

'Get to work on it.'

When Lara returned to the office, there was a message for her. 'Dr Peters would like you to call him,' Tricia said.

'Get him for me.'

He came on the phone almost immediately.

'Lara, I examined your secretary.'

'Yes?'

'She has a tumour. I'm afraid it's malignant. I recommend an immediate mastectomy.'

'I want a second opinion,' Lara said.

'Of course, if you wish, but I *am* head of the department and . . .'

'I still want a second opinion. Have someone else examine her. Get back to me as soon as possible. Where is Kathy now?'

'She's on her way back to your office.'

'Thanks, Alan.'

Lara replaced the receiver. She pressed down the intercom button. 'When Kathy returns, send her in to me.'

Lara studied the calendar on her desk. She had only thirty days left to clear out the Dorchester Apartments before construction was scheduled to start.

Six stubborn tenants. All right, Lara thought, *let's see how long they can hold out.*

Kathy walked into Lara's office. Her face was puffy and her eyes were red.

'I heard the news,' Lara told her. 'I'm so sorry, Kathy.'

'I'm going to die,' Kathy said.

Lara rose and put her arms around her, holding her close. 'You're not going to do anything of the kind. They've made a lot of progress with cancer. You're going to have the operation and you're going to be all right.'

'Miss Cameron, I can't afford . . .'

'Everything will be taken care of. Dr Peters is going to see that you have one more examination. If it verifies his diagnosis, you should have the operation right away. Now go home and get some rest.'

Kathy's eyes filled with tears again. 'I . . . thank you.'

As Kathy walked out of the office she thought, *No one really knows that lady.*

The following Monday, Lara had a visitor.

'There's a Mr O'Brian here to see you from the city Housing Commissioner's office, Miss Cameron.'

'What about?'

'He didn't say.'

Lara buzzed Keller on the intercom. 'Will you come in here, Howard?' She said to the secretary, 'Send Mr O'Brian in.'

Andy O'Brian was a burly red-faced Irishman with a slight brogue. 'Miss Cameron?'

Lara remained seated behind her desk. 'Yes. What can I do for you, Mr O'Brian?'

'I'm afraid you're in violation of the law, Miss Cameron.'

'Really? What is this all about?'

'You own the Dorchester Apartments on East Fourteenth Street?'

'Yes.'

'We have a report that about a hundred homeless people have crowded into those apartments.'

'Oh, that.' Lara smiled. 'Yes, I thought that since the City wasn't doing anything about the homeless, I would help out. I'm giving them shelter.'

Howard Keller walked into the room.

'This is Mr Keller. Mr O'Brian.'

The two men shook hands.

Lara turned to Keller. 'I was just explaining how

we're helping the City out by providing housing.'

'You invited them in, Miss Cameron?'

'That's right.'

'Do you have a licence from the City?'

'A licence for what?'

'If you're setting up a shelter, it has to be approved by the City. There are certain strict conditions that are enforced.'

'I'm sorry. I wasn't aware of that. I'll arrange for the licence immediately.'

'I don't think so.'

'What does that mean?'

'We've had complaints from the tenants in that building. They say you're trying to force them out.'

'Nonsense.'

'Miss Cameron, the City is giving you forty-eight hours to move those homeless people out of there. And when they leave, we have an order for you to take down the boards that you put up to cover the windows.'

Lara was furious. 'Is that all?'

'No, ma'am. The tenant who has the roof garden says you put up a sign blocking his view. You'll have to take that down, too.'

'What if I won't?'

'I think you will. All this comes under harassment. You'll save yourself a lot of trouble and unpleasant publicity by not forcing us to take you to court.' He nodded and said, 'Have a nice day.'

They watched him walk out of the office.

Keller turned to Lara. 'We'll have to get all those people out of there.'

'No.' She sat there, thinking.

'What do you mean "no"? The man said . . .'

'I know what he said. I want you to bring in *more* homeless. I want that building packed with street people. We're going to stall. Call Terry Hill. Tell him the problem. Have him get a stay or something. We've got to get those six tenants out by the end of the month or it's going to cost us three million dollars.'

The intercom buzzed. 'Dr Peters is on the phone.'

Lara picked up the telephone. 'Hello, Alan.'

'I just wanted to tell you that we finished the operation. It looks like we got it all. Kathy's going to be fine.'

'That's wonderful news. When can I visit her?'

'You can come by this afternoon.'

'I'll do that. Thanks, Alan. See that I get all the bills, will you?'

'Will do.'

'And you can tell the hospital to expect a donation. Fifty thousand dollars.'

Lara said to Tricia, 'Fill her room with flowers.' She looked at her schedule. 'I'll go down to see her at four o'clock.'

Terry Hill arrived at the office. 'There's a warrant for your arrest coming in.'

'What?'

'Weren't you warned to get those homeless people out of the building?'

'Yes, but . . .'

'You can't get away with this, Lara. There's an old adage: "Don't fight City Hall, you can't win."'

'Are they really going to arrest me?'

'You're damn right they are. You were given

notice by the City to get those people out of there.'

'All right,' Lara said. 'Let's get them out.' She turned to Keller. 'Remove them. But don't put them out on the street. That's not right. We have those empty rooming houses that we're waiting to convert in the West 20s. Let's put them there. Take all the help you need. I want them gone in an hour.'

She turned to Terry Hill. 'I'll be out of here, so they can't serve me. By the time they do, the problem will be solved.'

The intercom buzzed. 'There are two gentlemen here from the district attorney's office.'

Lara motioned to Howard Keller. He walked over to the intercom and said, 'Miss Cameron isn't here.'

There was a silence. 'When do you expect her?'

Keller looked at Lara. Lara shook her head. Keller said into the intercom, 'We don't know.' He flicked the key up.

'I'll go out the back way,' Lara said.

Lara hated hospitals. A hospital was her father lying in bed, pale and suddenly old. *'What the bluidy hell are you doin' here? You've work to dae at the boardin' house.'*

Lara walked into Kathy's room. It was filled with flowers. Kathy was sitting up in bed.

'How do you feel?' Lara asked.

Kathy smiled. 'The doctor said I'm going to be fine.'

'You'd better be. Your work is piling up. I need you.'

'I . . . I don't know how to thank you for all this.'

'Don't.'

210

Lara picked up the bedside phone and put a call through to her office. She spoke to Terry Hill.

'Are they still there?'

'They're still here. They intend to stay until you return.'

'Check with Howard. As soon as he clears the street people out of the building, I'll come back.'

Lara replaced the receiver.

'If you need anything, let me know,' Lara said. 'I'll be back to see you tomorrow.'

Lara's next stop was at the architectural offices of Higgins, Almont & Clark. She was ushered in to see Mr Clark. He rose as she walked into his office.

'What a nice surprise. What can I do for you, Miss Cameron?'

'Do you have the plans here for the project on Fourteenth Street?'

'Yes, indeed.'

He went over to his drawing board. 'Here we are.'

There was a sketch of a beautiful high-rise complex with apartment buildings and shops around it.

'I want you to redraw it,' Lara said.

'What?'

Lara pointed to a space in the middle of the block. 'There's a building still standing in this area. I want you to draw the same concept, but construct it *around* that building.'

'You mean you want to put up the project with one of the old buildings still standing? It would never work. First of all, it would look terrible and . . .'

'Just do it, please. Send it over to my office this afternoon.'

And Lara was gone.

From the car, she telephoned Terry Hill. 'Have you heard from Howard yet?'

'Yes. The squatters have all been cleared out.'

'Good. Get the district attorney on the phone. Tell him that I had ordered those squatters out two days ago, and that there was a lack of communication. The minute I heard about it, today, I had them evicted. I'm on my way back to the office now. See if he still wants to arrest me.'

She said to the driver, 'Drive through the park. Take your time.'

Thirty minutes later, when Lara reached her office, the men with the warrant were gone.

Lara was in a meeting with Howard Keller and Terry Hill.

'The tenants still won't budge,' Keller said. 'I even went back and offered them more money. They're not leaving. We've only got five days left before we have to begin bulldozing.'

Lara said, 'I asked Mr Clark to draw up a new blueprint for the project.'

'I saw it,' Keller said. 'It doesn't make any sense. We can't leave that old building standing in the middle of a new giant construction. We're going to have to go to the bank and ask them if they'll move back the start date.'

'No,' Lara said. 'I want to move it *up*.'

'*What*?'

'Get hold of the contractor. Tell him we want to start bulldozing tomorrow.'

'*Tomorrow*? Lara . . .'

'First thing in the morning. And take that blue-print and give it to the foreman of the construction crew.'

'What good will that do?' Keller asked.

'We'll see.'

The following morning, the remaining tenants of the Dorchester Apartments were awakened by the roar of a bulldozer. They looked out of their windows. Halfway down the block, as they watched, a mechanical behemoth was moving toward them, levelling everything in its path. The tenants were stunned.

Mr Hershey, who lived on the top floor, rushed outside and hurried over to the foreman. 'What do you think you're doing?' he screamed. 'You can't go ahead with this.'

'Who says so?'

'The City does.' Hershey pointed to the building he lived in. 'You're not permitted to touch that building.'

The foreman looked at the blueprint in front of him. 'That's right,' he said. 'We have orders to leave that building standing.'

Hershey frowned. 'What? Let me see that.' He looked at the plan and gasped. 'They're going to put up the plaza and leave this building *standing*?'

'That's right, mister.'

'But they can't do that! The noise and dirt!'

'That's not my problem. Now, if you'll get out of my way, I'd like to get back to work.'

*

Thirty minutes later, Lara's secretary said, 'There's a Mr Hershey on line two, Miss Cameron.'

'Tell him I'm not available.'

When Hershey called for the third time that afternoon, Lara finally picked up the phone and spoke with him.

'Yes, Mr Hershey. What can I do for you?'

'I'd like to come in and see you, Miss Cameron.'

'I'm afraid I'm rather busy. Whatever it is you have to say you can say on the phone.'

'Well, you'll be glad to know that I've talked to the other tenants in our building and we've agreed that it might be best after all to take your offer and vacate our apartments.'

'That offer is no longer good, Mr Hershey. You can all stay where you are.'

'If you build around us, we're never going to get any sleep!'

'Who told you we were going to build around you?' Lara demanded. 'Where did you get that information?'

'The foreman on the job showed me a blueprint and . . .'

'Well, he's going to be fired.' There was fury in Lara's voice. 'That was confidential information.'

'Wait a minute. Let's talk like two reasonable people, okay? Your project would be better off if we got out of here, and I think we'd be better off leaving. I don't want to live in the middle of a damned high-rise.'

Lara said, 'It doesn't matter to me whether you go or stay, Mr Hershey.' Her voice softened. 'I'll tell you what I'll do. If that building is vacated by next month, I'm willing to go with our first offer.'

She could hear him thinking it over.

Finally he said reluctantly, 'Okay. I'll talk to the others, but I'm sure it will be all right. I really appreciate this, Miss Cameron.'

Lara said, 'It's been my pleasure, Mr Hershey.'

The following month, work on the new project began in earnest.

Lara's reputation was growing. Cameron Enterprises was putting up a high-rise in Brooklyn, a shopping centre in Westchester, a mall in Washington, DC. There was a low-cost housing project being constructed in Dallas and a block of condominiums in Los Angeles. Capital flowed in from banks, savings and loan companies and eager private investors. Lara had become a Name.

Kathy had returned to work.

'I'm back.'

Lara studied her a moment. 'How do you feel?'

Kathy smiled. 'Great. Thanks to . . .'

'Do you have a lot of energy?'

She was surprised at the question. 'Yes, I . . .'

'Good. You're going to need it. I'm making you my executive assistant. There will be a nice raise for you.'

'I don't know what to say. I . . .'

'You've earned it.'

Lara saw the memo in Kathy's hand. 'What's that?'

'*Gourmet* magazine would like to publish your favourite recipe. Are you interested?'

'No. Tell them I'm too . . . wait a minute.' She sat there a moment, lost in thought. Then she said softly, 'Yes. I'll give them a recipe.'

The recipe appeared in the magazine three months later. It began:

> Black Bun – A classic Scottish dish. A mixture encased in a shortpaste jacket made from half a pound of flour, a quarter pound of butter, a touch of cold water, and a half a teaspoon of baking powder. Inside are two pounds of raisins, half a pound of chopped almonds, three-quarters of a pound of flour, half a pound of sugar, two teaspoons of allspice, a teaspoon each of ground ginger and ground cinnamon, a half teaspoon of baking powder, and a dash of brandy . . .

Lara looked at the article for a long time, and it brought back the taste of it, the smell of the boarding house kitchen, the noise of the boarders at supper. Her father helpless in his bed. She put the magazine away.

People recognized Lara on the street, and when she walked into a restaurant, there were always excited whispers. She was escorted around town by half a dozen eligible suitors and had flattering proposals, but she was not interested. In a strange, almost eerie way, she was still looking for someone. Someone familiar. Someone she had never met.

Lara would wake up at five o'clock every morning and have her driver, Max, take her to one of the buildings under construction. She would stand there, staring at what she was creating, and she thought, *You were wrong, Father. I can collect the rents.*

For Lara, the sounds of the day began with the

rat-a-tat-tat of the jackhammers, the roar of the bull-dozers, the clanging of heavy metal. She would ride the rickety construction elevator to the top, and stand on the steel girders with the wind blowing in her face, and she thought, *I own this city*.

Paul Martin and Lara were in bed.

'I hear you chewed out a couple of your construction workers pretty good today.'

'They deserved it,' Lara said. 'They were doing sloppy work.'

Paul grinned. 'At least you've learned not to slap them.'

'Look what happened when I *did* slap one.' She snuggled up to him. 'I met you.'

'I have to take a trip to LA,' Paul said. 'I'd like you to come with me. Can you get away for a few days?'

'I'd love to, Paul, but it's impossible. I schedule my days with a stopwatch.'

He sat up and looked down at her. 'Maybe you're doing too much, baby. Don't ever get too busy for me.'

Lara smiled and began to stroke him. 'Don't worry about that. It will never happen.'

It had been there in front of her all the time, and she had not seen it. It was a huge waterfront property in the Wall Street area, near the World Trade Center. And it was for sale. Lara had passed it a dozen times, but she looked at it now and saw what should have been there all along: In her mind, she could see the world's tallest building. She knew what Howard was going to say: *You're getting in over your head, Lara. You can't get involved with this*. But she knew that nothing was going to stop her.

When she got to the office, she called a meeting of her staff.

'The Wall Street property on the waterfront,' Lara said. 'We're going to buy it. We're going to put up the tallest skyscraper in the world.'

'Lara . . .'

'Before you say anything, Howard, let me point out a few things. The location is perfect. It's in the heart of the business district. Tenants will be fighting to get office space there. And remember, it's going to be the tallest skyscraper in the world. That's a big sizzle. It's going to be our flagship. We'll call it Cameron Towers.'

'Where's the money coming from?'

Lara handed him a piece of paper.

Keller was examining the figures. 'You're being optimistic.'

'I'm being realistic. We're not talking about just any building. We're talking about a jewel, Howard.'

He was thinking hard. 'You'll be stretching yourself thin.'

Lara smiled. 'We've done that before, haven't we?'

Keller said, thoughtfully, 'The tallest skyscraper in the world . . .'

'That's right. And the banks call us every day, throwing money at us. They'll jump at this.'

'They probably will,' Keller said. He looked at Lara. 'You really want this, don't you?'

'Yes.'

Keller sighed. He looked around at the group. 'All right. The first step is to take an option on the property.'

Lara smiled. 'I've already done that. And I have some other news for you. Steve Murchison was negotiating for that property.'

'I remember him. We took that hotel site away from him in Chicago.'

I'm going to let it go this time, bitch, because I don't think you know what the hell you're doing. But in the future, stay out of my way – you could get hurt.

'Right.' Murchison had become one of the most ruthless and successful real estate developers in New York.

Keller said, 'Lara, he's bad news. He enjoys destroying people.'

'You worry too much.'

The financing for Cameron Towers went smoothly. Lara had been right. The bankers felt that there was a sizzle to the tallest skyscraper in the world. And the name of Cameron was an added cachet. They were eager to be associated with her.

Lara was more than a glamorous figure. She was a symbol to the women of the world, an icon. *If she can accomplish this, why not me?* A perfume was named after her. She was invited to all the important social events, and hostesses were eager to have her at their dinner parties. Her name on a building seemed to ensure success.

*

'We're going to start our own construction company,' Lara decided one day. 'We have the crews. We'll rent them out to other builders.'

'That's not a bad idea,' Keller said.

'Let's go for it. How soon are we going to break ground for Cameron Towers?'

'The deal's in place. I would say three months from now.'

Lara sat back in her chair. 'Can you imagine it, Howard? The tallest skyscraper in the world.'

He wondered what Freud would have made of that.

The ground-breaking ceremony for Cameron Towers had the atmosphere of a three-ring circus. America's Princess, Lara Cameron, was the main attraction. The event had been heavily publicized in the newspapers and on television, and a crowd of more than two hundred people had gathered, waiting for Lara to arrive. When her white limousine pulled up to the building site, there was a roar from the crowd.

'There she is!'

As Lara stepped out of the car and moved toward the building site to greet the mayor, police and security guards held the crowd back. The people pushed forward, screaming and calling her name, and the photographers' flashbulbs began popping.

In a special roped-off section were the bankers, heads of advertising agencies, company directors, contractors, project managers, community representatives, and architects. One hundred feet away, large bulldozers and backhoes were standing by, ready to go to work. Fifty trucks were lined up to cart the rubble away.

Lara was standing next to the mayor and the Manhattan borough president. It had started to drizzle. Jerry Townsend, head of public relations for Cameron Enterprises, hurried toward Lara with an umbrella. She smiled and waved him away.

The mayor spoke into the cameras. 'Today is a great day for Manhattan. This ground-breaking ceremony at Cameron Towers marks the beginning of one of the largest real estate projects in Manhattan's history. Six blocks of Manhattan real estate will be converted into a modern community that will include apartment buildings, two shopping centres, a convention centre, and the tallest skyscraper in the world.'

There was applause from the crowd.

'Wherever you look,' the mayor continued, 'you can see Lara Cameron's contribution written in concrete.' He pointed. 'Uptown is the Cameron Center. And near it, Cameron Plaza and half a dozen housing projects. And across the country is the great Cameron Hotel chain.'

The mayor turned to Lara and smiled. 'And she's not only brainy, she's beautiful.'

There was laughter and more applause.

'Lara Cameron, ladies and gentlemen.'

Lara looked into the television cameras and smiled. 'Thank you, Mr Mayor. I'm very pleased to have made some small contribution to this fabulous city of ours. My father always told me that the reason we were put on this earth was . . .' she hesitated. Out of the corner of her eye, she had seen a familiar face in the crowd. Steve Murchison. She had seen

221

his photograph in the newspapers. What was he doing here? Lara went on, '. . . was to leave it a better place than when we came into it. Well, I hope that in my own small way, I've been able to do that.'

There was more applause. Lara was handed a ceremonial hard hat and a chrome-plated shovel.

'Time to go to work, Miss Cameron.'

The flashbulbs began to pop again.

Lara pushed the shovel into the dirt and dug up the first bit of earth.

At the conclusion of the ceremony, refreshments were served, while the television cameras kept recording the event. When Lara looked around again, Murchison was nowhere in sight.

Thirty minutes later, Lara Cameron was back in the limousine headed for the office. Jerry Townsend was seated next to her.

'I thought it went great,' he said. 'Just great.'

'Not bad,' Lara grinned. 'Thanks, Jerry.'

The executive suites of Cameron Enterprises occupied the entire fiftieth floor of Cameron Center.

Lara got off at the fiftieth floor, and by then word had got around that she was arriving. The secretaries and staff were busily at work.

Lara turned to Jerry Townsend. 'Come into my office.'

The office was an enormous corner suite overlooking the city.

Lara glanced at some papers on her desk and looked up at Jerry.

'How's your father? Is he any better?'

What did she know about his father?

'He's . . . he's not well.'

'I know. He has Huntington's Chorea, hasn't he, Jerry?'

'Yes.'

It was a terrible disease. It was progressive and degenerative, characterized by spasmodic involuntary movements of the face and extremities, accompanied by the loss of mental faculties.

'How do you know about my father?'

'I'm on the board at the hospital where he's being treated. I heard some doctors discussing his case.'

Jerry said tightly, 'It's incurable.'

'Everything is incurable until they find the cure,' Lara said. 'I did some checking. There's a doctor in Switzerland who's doing some advanced research on the disease. He's willing to take on your father's case. I'll handle the expenses.'

Jerry stood there, stunned.

'Okay?'

He found it difficult to speak. 'Okay.' *I don't know her*, Jerry Townsend thought. *Nobody knows her.*

History was being made, but Lara was too busy to notice. Ronald Reagan had been re-elected, and a man named Mikhail Gorbachev had succeeded Chernenko as leader of the USSR.

Lara built a low-income housing development in Detroit.

In 1986, Ivan Boesky had been fined a hundred million dollars in an insider trading scandal and sentenced to three years in prison.

Lara started development on condominiums in Queens. Investors were eager to be a part of the

223

magic of her name. A group of German investment bankers flew to New York to meet with Lara. She arranged for the meeting immediately after their plane landed. They had protested, but Lara said, 'I'm so sorry, gentlemen. It's the only time I have. I'm leaving for Hong Kong.'

The Germans were served coffee. Lara had tea. One of the Germans complained about the taste of the coffee. 'It's a special brand made for me,' Lara explained. 'The flavour will grow on you. Have another cup.'

By the end of the negotiations, Lara had won all her points.

Life was a series of serendipities, except for one disturbing incident. Lara had had several run-ins with Steve Murchison over various properties and she had always managed to outwit him.

'I think we should back off,' Keller warned.

'Let him back off.'

And one morning a beautiful package wrapped in rose paper arrived from Bendels. Kathy laid it on Lara's desk.

'It's awfully heavy,' Kathy said. 'If it's a hat, you're in trouble.'

Curious, Lara unwrapped it and opened the lid. The box was packed with dirt. A printed card inside read: *The Frank E. Campbell Funeral Chapel.*

The building projects were all going well. When Lara read about a proposed inner-city playground that was stymied because of bureaucratic redtape, she stepped in, had her company build it and donated it to the City. The publicity she received on it was enormous. One headline read: *Lara Cameron stands for 'CAN DO.'*

She was seeing Paul once or twice a week, and she talked to him every day.

Lara bought a house in Southampton and lived in a fantasy world of expensive jewels and furs and limousines. Her closets were filled with beautiful designer clothes. *'I need some clothes for school.' 'Weel, I'm nae made of money. Get yourself somethin' frae the Salvation Army Citadel.'*

And Lara would order another outfit.

Her employees were her family. She worried about them, and was generous with them. They were all she had. She remembered their birthdays and anniversaries. She helped get their children into good schools, and set up scholarship funds for them. When they tried to thank her, Lara was embarrassed. It was difficult for her to express her emotions. Her father had ridiculed her when she had tried. Lara had built a protective wall around herself. *No one is ever going to hurt me again*, she vowed. *No one*.

Book Three

'I'm leaving for London in the morning, Howard.'

'What's up?' Keller asked.

'Lord MacIntosh has invited me to come over and take a look at a property he's interested in. He wants to go into partnership.'

Brian MacIntosh was one of the wealthiest real estate developers in England.

'What time do we leave?' Keller asked.

'I've decided to go alone.'

'Oh?'

'I want you to keep an eye on things here.'

He nodded. 'Right. I'll do that.'

'I know you will. I can always count on you.'

The trip to London was uneventful. The private 727 she had purchased took off in the morning and landed at the Magec Terminal at Luton Airport outside London. She had no idea her life was about to change.

When Lara arrived at the lobby of Claridge's, Ronald Jones, the manager, was there to greet her. 'It's a pleasure to have you back, Miss Cameron. I'll show you to your suite. By the way, we have some messages for you.' There were more than two dozen.

The suite was lovely. There were flowers from Brian MacIntosh and from Paul Martin, and champagne and hors d'oeuvres from the management. The phone began to ring the minute Lara walked in. The calls were from all over the United States.

'The architect wants to make some changes in the plans. It will cost a fortune . . .'

'There's a hold-up on the cement delivery . . .'

'The First National Savings and Loan wants in on our next deal . . .'

'The mayor wants to know if you can be in LA for the opening. He'd like to plan a big ceremony . . .'

'The toilets haven't arrived . . .'

'Bad weather is holding us up. We're falling behind schedule . . .'

Each problem required a decision, and when Lara finally finished with her calls, she was exhausted. She had dinner in her room alone and sat looking out of the window, at the Rolls-Royces and Bentleys pulling up to the Brook Street entrance, and a feeling of elation swept over her. *The little girl from Glace Bay has come a long way, Daddy.*

The following morning Lara went with Brian MacIntosh to look at the proposed site. It was enormous – two miles of riverside frontage filled with old rundown buildings and storage sheds.

'The British Government will give us a lot of tax relief on this,' Brian MacIntosh explained, 'because we're going to rehabilitate this whole section of the city.'

'I'd like to think about it,' Lara said. She had already made up her mind.

'By the way, I have tickets to a concert tonight,' Brian MacIntosh told her. 'My wife has a club meeting. Do you like classical music?'

Lara had no interest in classical music. 'Yes.'

'Philip Adler is playing Rachmaninoff.' He looked at Lara as though expecting her to say something. She had never heard of Philip Adler.

'It sounds wonderful,' Lara said.

'Good. We'll have supper afterward at Scott's. I'll pick you up at seven.'

Why did I say I liked classical music? Lara wondered. It was going to be a boring evening. She would have preferred to take a hot bath and go to sleep. *Oh, well, one more evening won't hurt me. I'll fly back to New York in the morning.*

The Festival Hall was crowded with music aficionados. The men wore dinner jackets and the women were dressed in beautiful evening gowns. It was a gala evening and there was a feeling of excited expectation in the large hall.

Brian MacIntosh purchased two programmes from the usher, and they were seated. He handed Lara a programme. She barely glanced at it. The London Philharmonic Orchestra . . . Philip Adler playing Rachmaninoff's piano concerto no. 3 in D minor, Opus 30.

I've got to call Howard and remind him about the revised estimates on the Fifth Avenue site.

The conductor appeared on stage and the audience applauded. Lara paid no attention. *The contractor in Boston is moving too slowly. He needs a carrot. I'll tell Howard to offer him a bonus.*

There was another loud round of applause from the audience. A man was taking his place at the piano at centre stage. The conductor gave a down-beat and the music began.

Philip Adler's fingers flashed across the keys.

A woman seated behind Lara said with a loud Texas accent, 'Isn't he fantastic? I *told* you, Agnes!'

Lara tried to concentrate again. *The London deal is out. It's the wrong neighbourhood*, Lara thought. *People aren't going to want to live there. Location. Location. Location.* She thought about a project that had been brought to her, near Columbus Circle. *Now that one could work.*

The woman behind Lara said, loudly, 'His *expression* . . . he's fabulous! He's one of the most . . .'

Lara tried to tune her out.

The cost of an office building there would be approximately four hundred dollars per rentable square foot. If I can bring in the construction cost at one hundred and fifty million, the land costs at one hundred twenty-five million, the soft costs . . .

'My God!' the woman behind Lara exclaimed.

Lara was startled out of her reverie.

'He's so brilliant!'

There was a drum roll from the orchestra and Philip Adler played four bars alone, and the orchestra began to play faster and faster. The drums began to beat . . .

The woman could not contain herself. 'Listen to that! The music is going from *più vivo* to *più mosso*. Have you ever heard anything so exciting?'

Lara gritted her teeth.

The minimum break-even should work out all

right, she thought. *The cost of the rentable square feet would be three hundred and fifty million, the interest at ten per cent would be thirty-five million, plus ten million in operating expenses . . .*

The tempo of the music was increasing, reverberating through the hall. The music came to a sudden climax and stopped, and the audience was on its feet, cheering. There were calls of *bravo!* The pianist had risen and was taking bows.

Lara did not even bother to look up. *Taxes would be about six, free rent concessions would come to two. We're talking about fifty-eight million.*

'He's incredible, isn't he?' Brian MacIntosh said.

'Yes.' Lara was annoyed at having her thoughts interrupted again.

'Let's go backstage. Philip is a friend of mine.'

'I really don't . . .'

He took Lara's hand and they were moving toward an exit.

'I'm glad I'll have a chance to introduce you to him,' Brian MacIntosh said.

It's six o'clock in New York, Lara thought. *I'll be able to call Howard and tell him to start negotiations.*

'He's a once in a lifetime experience, isn't he?'

Once is enough for me, Lara thought. 'Yes.'

They had reached the outside artists' entrance. There was a large crowd waiting. Brian MacIntosh knocked on the door. A doorman opened it.

'Yes, sir?'

'Lord MacIntosh to see Mr Adler.'

'Right, My Lord. Come in, please.' He opened the door wide enough to let Brian MacIntosh and Lara enter, then closed it against the crowd.

'What do all these people want?' Lara asked.

He looked at her in surprise. 'They're here to see Philip.'

She wondered why.

The doorman said, 'Go right into the green room, My Lord.'

'Thank you.'

Five minutes, Lara thought, *and I'll say I have to leave*.

The green room was noisy and already full. People were crowded around a figure Lara could not see. The crowd shifted and for an instant he was clearly visible. Lara froze, and for a moment she felt her heart stop. The vague, evanescent image that had been at the back of her mind all those years had suddenly materialized out of nowhere. Lochinvar, the vision in her fantasies, had come to life! The man at the centre of the crowd was tall and blond, with delicate, sensitive features. He was wearing white tie and tails, and a feeling of *déjà vu* swept over Lara: *She was standing at the kitchen sink in the boarding house, and the handsome young man in white tie and tails came up behind her and whispered, 'Can I help you?'*

Brian MacIntosh was watching Lara, concerned. 'Are you all right?'

'I . . . I'm fine.' She was finding it difficult to breathe.

Philip Adler was moving toward them, smiling, and it was the same warm smile Lara had imagined. He held out his hand. 'Brian, how good of you to come.'

'I wouldn't have missed it,' MacIntosh said. 'You were simply marvellous.'

'Thank you.'

'Oh, Philip, I would like you to meet Lara Cameron.'

Lara was looking into his eyes and the words came out unbidden. 'Do you dry?'

'I beg your pardon?'

Lara turned red. 'Nothing. I . . .' She was suddenly tongue-tied.

People were crowding around Philip Adler, heaping praise on him.

'You've never played better . . .'

'I think Rachmaninoff was with you tonight . . .'

The praise went on and on. The women in the room were crowding around him, touching and pulling at him. Lara stood there watching, mesmerized. Her childhood dream had come true. Her fantasy had become flesh and blood.

'Are you ready to go?' Brian MacIntosh asked Lara.

No. She wanted nothing more than to stay. She wanted to talk to the vision again, to touch him, to make sure he was real. 'I'm ready,' Lara said reluctantly.

The following morning, Lara was on her way back to New York. She wondered whether she would ever see Philip Adler again.

She was unable to get him out of her mind. She tried to tell herself that it was ridiculous, that she was trying to relive a childhood dream, but it was no use. She kept seeing his face, hearing his voice. *I must see him again*, Lara thought.

Early the next morning, Paul Martin telephoned. 'Hi, baby. I missed you. How was London?'

'Fine,' Lara said carefully. 'Just fine.'

When they had finished talking, Lara sat at her desk thinking about Philip Adler.

'They're waiting for you in the conference room, Miss Cameron.'

'I'm coming.'

'We lost the Queens deal,' Keller said.

'Why? I thought it was all set.'

'So did I, but the Community Board refuses to change the zoning.'

Lara looked around at the Executive Committee assembled in the room. There were architects, lawyers, publicity men, and construction engineers.

Lara said, 'I don't understand. Those tenants have an average income of nine thousand dollars a year, and they're paying less than two hundred dollars a month in rent. We're going to rehabilitate the apartments for them, at no increase in rent, and we're going to provide new apartments for some of the other residents in the neighbourhood. We're giving them Christmas in July and they turned you down? What's the problem?'

'It's not the board so much. It's their chairman. A lady named Edith Benson.'

'Set up another meeting with her. I'll go there myself.'

Lara took her chief construction supervisor, Bill Whitman, to the meeting.

236

Lara said, 'Frankly, I was stunned when I heard that your Board turned us down. We're going to put up over a hundred million dollars to improve this neighbourhood and yet you refuse to . . .'

Edith Benson cut her short. 'Let's be honest, Miss Cameron. You're not putting up the money to improve the neighbourhood. You're putting up the money so Cameron Enterprises can make more money.'

'Of course we expect to make money,' Lara said. 'But the only way we can do that is to help you people. We're going to make the living conditions in your area better, and . . .'

'Sorry. I don't agree. Right now, we're a quiet little neighbourhood. If we let you in, we're going to become a higher density area – more traffic, more automobiles, more pollution. We don't want any of that.'

'Neither do I,' Lara said. 'We don't intend to put up Dingbats that . . .'

'Dingbats?'

'Yes, those ugly, stripped-down, three-storey stucco boxes. We're interested in designs that won't increase the noise level or reduce the light or change the feel of the neighbourhood. We're not interested in hot-dog, show-off architecture. I've already hired Stanton Fielding, the top architect in the country, to design this project, and Andrew Burton from Washington to do the landscaping.'

Edith Benson shrugged. 'I'm sorry. It's no use. I don't think there's anything more to discuss.' She started to rise.

I can't lose this, Lara thought desperately. *Can't they see it's for the good of their neighbourhood? I'm trying to do something for them and they won't let me.* And suddenly she had a wild idea.

'Wait a minute,' Lara said. 'I understand that the other members of the Board are willing to make the deal but you are the one blocking it.'

'That's correct.'

Lara took a deep breath. 'There *is* something to discuss.' She hesitated. 'It's very personal.' She was fidgeting now. 'You say I'm not worried about pollution and what happens to the environment in this neighbourhood if we move in? I'm going to tell you something that I hope you will keep in confidence. I have a ten-year-old daughter that I'm crazy about, and she's going to live in the new building with her father. He has custody of her.'

Edith Benson was looking at her in surprise. 'I . . . I didn't know you had a daughter.'

'No one does,' Lara said quietly. 'I've never been married. That's why I'm asking you to keep this confidential. If it gets out, it could be very damaging to me. I'm sure you understand that.'

'I do understand.'

'I love my daughter very much, and I assure you that I would never do anything in the world that would hurt her. I intend to do everything I can to make this project wonderful for all the people who live here. And she'll be one of them.'

There was a sympathetic silence. 'I must say, this . . . this puts quite a different complexion on things, Miss Cameron. I'd like to have some time to think about it.'

'Thank you. I appreciate that.' *If I did have a*

daughter, Lara thought, *it would be safe for her to live here.*

Three weeks later, Lara got the approval from the Community Board to go ahead with the project.

'Great,' Lara said. 'Now we'd better get hold of Stanton Fielding and Andrew Burton and see if they're interested in working on the project.'

Howard Keller could not believe the news. 'I heard what happened,' he said. 'You conned her! That's incredible. You don't *have* a daughter!'

'They need this project,' Lara said. 'This was the only way I could think of to change their minds.'

Bill Whitman was listening. 'There'll be hell to pay if they ever find out.'

In January, construction was completed on a new building on East 63rd Street. It was a forty-five storey apartment building, and Lara reserved the duplex penthouse for herself. The rooms were large, and the apartment had terraces that covered a full block. She brought in a top decorator to do the apartment. There was a housewarming for a hundred people.

'All it lacks is a man,' one of the lady guests said cattily.

And Lara thought of Philip Adler and wondered where he was and what he was doing.

Lara and Howard Keller were in the middle of a discussion when Bill Whitman came into the office.

'Hi, boss. Got a minute?'

Lara looked up from her desk. 'Just about, Bill. What's the problem?'

'My wife.'

'If you're having marital difficulties . . .'

'It's not that. She thinks we ought to go away for a while on vacation. Maybe go to Paris for a few weeks.'

Lara frowned. 'Paris? We're in the middle of half a dozen jobs.'

'I know, but I've been working long hours lately, and I don't get to see much of my wife. You know what she said to me this morning? She said, "Bill, if you got a promotion and a nice raise, you wouldn't have to work so hard."' He smiled.

Lara sat back in her chair, studying him. 'You aren't due for a raise until next year.'

Whitman shrugged. 'Who knows what can happen in a year? We might run into problems with that Queens deal, for instance. You know, old Edith Benson might hear something that would make her change her mind. Right?'

Lara sat very still. 'I see.'

Bill Whitman got to his feet. 'Think about it, and let me know.'

Lara forced a smile. 'Yes.'

She watched him walk out of her office, her face grim.

'Jesus,' Keller said. 'What was that all about?'

'It's called blackmail.'

The following day, Lara had lunch with Paul Martin.

Lara said, 'Paul, I have a problem. I'm not sure

how to handle it.' She told him about her conversation with Bill Whitman.

'Do you think he'll really go back to the old lady?' Paul Martin asked.

'I don't know. But if he does, I could get in a lot of trouble with the Building Commission.'

Paul shrugged. 'I wouldn't worry about him. He's probably bluffing.'

Lara sighed. 'I hope so.'

'How would you like to go to Reno?' Paul asked.

'I'd love to, but I can't get away.'

'I'm not asking you to get away. I'm asking if you'd like to buy a hotel and casino there.'

Lara studied him. 'Are you serious?'

'I got word that one of the hotels is going to lose its licence. The place is a gold mine. When the news gets out, everyone is going to be after it. The hotel's going on auction, but I think I can fix it for you to get it.'

Lara hesitated. 'I don't know. I'm pretty heavily committed. Howard Keller says the banks won't lend me any more until I can pay off some loans.'

'You don't have to go to a bank.'

'Then where . . . ?'

'Junk bonds. A lot of Wall Street firms offer them. There are savings and loan companies. You put up five per cent equity, and a savings and loan company will put up sixty-five per cent in high-yield notes. That leaves thirty per cent uncovered. You can get that from a foreign bank that invests in casinos. You've got choices – Switzerland, Germany, Japan. There are half a dozen banks that will put up the thirty per cent in commercial notes.'

Lara was beginning to get excited. 'It sounds great.

241

Do you really think you can get the hotel for me?'

Paul grinned. 'It will be your Christmas present.'

'You're wonderful. Why are you so good to me?'

'I haven't the vaguest idea,' he teased. But he knew the answer. He was obsessed with her. Lara made him feel young again, and she made everything exciting for him. *I never want to lose you*, he thought.

Keller was waiting for Lara when she walked into the office.

'Where have you been?' he asked. 'There was a two o'clock meeting that . . .'

'Tell me about junk bonds, Howard. We've never dealt with them. How are bonds rated?'

'Well, at the top you have Triple A. That would be a company like AT&T. Down the ladder you have Double A, Single A, BAA, and at the bottom of the ladder, Double B – those are the junk bonds. An investment bond will pay nine per cent. A junk bond will pay fourteen per cent. Why do you ask?'

Lara told him.

'A *casino*, Lara? Jesus! Paul Martin is behind this, isn't he?'

'No, Howard. If I go ahead with this, *I'm* behind it. Did we get an answer on our offer on the Battery Park property?'

'Yes. She won't sell to us.'

'The property is up for sale, isn't it?'

'In a way.'

'Stop talking in circles.'

'It's owned by a doctor's widow, Eleanor Royce. Every real estate developer in town has been bidding on that property.'

'Have we been out-bid?'

'It isn't that. The old lady isn't interested in money. She's loaded.'

'What *is* she interested in?'

'She wants some kind of monument to her husband. Apparently she thinks she was married to Albert Schweitzer. She wants to keep his flame burning. She doesn't want her property turned into anything crass or commercial. I hear Steve Murchison has been trying to talk her into selling.'

'Oh?'

Lara sat there quietly for a full minute. When she spoke, she said, 'Who's your doctor, Howard?'

'What?'

'Who's your doctor?'

'Seymour Bennett. He's Chief of Staff at Midtown Hospital.'

The following morning Lara's attorney, Terry Hill, was sitting in the office of Dr Seymour Bennett.

'My secretary told me that you wanted to see me urgently, and that it has nothing to do with a medical problem.'

'In a sense,' Terry Hill said, 'it does concern a medical problem, Dr Bennett. I represent an investment group that wants to put up a non-profit clinic. We want to be able to take care of those unfortunate people who can't afford regular medical care.'

'That's a splendid idea,' Dr Bennett said. 'What can I do to help you?'

Terry Hill told him.

*

The following day, Dr Bennett was having tea in the home of Eleanor Royce.

'They've asked me to approach you on behalf of this group, Mrs Royce. They want to build a beautiful clinic, and they want to name it after your late husband. They visualize it as sort of a shrine to him.'

Mrs Royce's face lit up. 'They do?'

They discussed the group's plans for an hour, and at the end of that time, Mrs Royce said, 'George would have loved this. You tell them that they have a deal.'

Construction began six months later. When it was completed, it was gigantic. The entire square block was filled with huge apartment buildings, an enormous shopping mall, and a theatre complex. In a remote corner of the property was a small one-storey brick building. A simple sign over the door read:

GEORGE ROYCE
MEDICAL CLINIC.

On Christmas Day, Lara stayed at home. She had been invited to a dozen parties, but Paul Martin was going to drop by. 'I have to be with Nina and the kids today,' he had explained, 'but I want to come by and see you.'

She wondered what Philip Adler was doing on this Christmas Day.

It was a Currier and Ives postcard kind of day. New York was blanketed in a beautiful white snowfall, wrapped in silence. When Paul Martin arrived, he had a shopping bag full of gifts for Lara.

'I had to stop at the office to pick these up,' he said. *So his wife wouldn't know.*

'You give me so much, Paul. You don't have to bring anything.'

'I wanted to. Open them up now.'

Lara was touched by his eagerness to see her reaction.

The gifts were thoughtful and expensive. A necklace from Cartier's, scarves from Hermes, books from Rizzoli, an antique carriage clock, and a small white envelope. Lara opened it. It read: *Cameron Reno Hotel & Casino* in large block letters. She looked up at him in surprise. 'I have the hotel?'

He nodded confidently. 'You will have. The

bidding starts next week. You're going to have fun with it,' Paul Martin predicted.

'I don't know anything about running a casino.'

'Don't worry. I'll put some professionals in to manage it for you. The hotel, you can handle yourself.'

'I don't know how to thank you. You do so much for me.'

He took her hands in his. 'There isn't anything in the world that I wouldn't do for you. Remember that.'

'I will,' she said solemnly.

He was looking at his watch. 'I have to get back home. I wish . . .' He hesitated.

'Yes?'

'Never mind. Merry Christmas, Lara.'

'Merry Christmas, Paul.'

She went to the window and looked out. The sky had become a delicate curtain of dancing snowflakes. Restless, Lara walked to the radio and turned it on. An announcer was saying, '. . . and now, for its holiday programme, the Boston Symphony Orchestra presents Beethoven's Piano Concerto No. 5 in E flat, with Philip Adler, soloist.'

Lara listened with her eyes, seeing him at the piano, handsome and elegant. When the music ended, she thought, *I've got to see him again.*

Bill Whitman was one of the best construction supervisors in the business. He had risen through the ranks and was in great demand. He worked steadily and earned good money, but he was dissatisfied. For years he had watched builders reaping enormous for-

246

tunes while he got nothing but a salary. *In a way*, he thought, *they're making their money off of me. The owner gets the cake; I get the crumbs.* But the day Lara Cameron had gone before the Zoning Commission, everything changed. She had lied to get the Board's permission, and that lie could destroy her. *If I went to the Board and told them the truth, she'd be out of business.*

But Bill Whitman had no intention of doing that. He had a better plan. He intended to use what had happened as leverage. The boss lady was going to give him anything he asked for. He could sense from their meeting at which he had asked for promotion and a raise that she was going to give in. She had no choice. *I'll start small*, Bill Whitman thought happily, *and then I'll really begin squeezing.*

Two days after Christmas, work began again on the Eastside Plaza project. Whitman looked around at the huge site and thought, *This one's going to be a real money-maker. Only this time, I'm going to cash in on it, too.*

The site was crowded with heavy equipment. Cranes were digging into the earth and lifting tons of it into waiting trucks. A crane wielding a giant saw-toothed scoop bucket seemed to be stuck. The huge arm hung suspended high in mid air. Whitman strode toward the cab, under the huge metal bucket.

'Hey, Jesse,' he called. 'What's the matter up there?'

The man in the cab mumbled something that Whitman could not hear.

Whitman moved closer. 'What?'

Everything happened in a split second. A chain slipped and the huge metal bucket came crashing down on Whitman, smashing him to the ground. Men came running toward the body, but there was nothing to be done.

'The safety brake slipped,' the operator explained later. 'Gee, I feel really awful. I liked Bill a lot.'

When she heard the news, Lara immediately telephoned Paul Martin. 'Did you hear about Bill Whitman?'

'Yes. It was on television.'

'Paul, you didn't . . . ?'

He laughed. 'Don't go getting any crazy ideas. You've been seeing too many movies. Remember, the good guys always win in the end.'

And Lara wondered, *Am I one of the good guys?*

There were more than a dozen bidders for the Reno hotel.

'When do I bid?' Lara asked Paul.

'You don't. Not until I tell you. Let the others jump in first.'

The bidding was secret and the bids were sealed, to be opened on the following Friday. By Wednesday, Lara still had not made a bid. She telephoned Paul Martin.

'Sit tight,' he said. 'I'll tell you when.'

They stayed in touch by phone several times a day.

At 5 p.m., one hour before the bidding was to close, Lara received a phone call.

'Now! The high bid is a hundred and twenty million. I want you to go five million over it.'

Lara gasped. 'But if I do that, I'll lose money on the deal.'

'Trust me,' Paul said. 'After you get the hotel and start redoing it, you can cut corners on the changes. They'll all be endorsed by the supervising engineer. You'll make up the five million and then some.'

The following day, Lara was notified that hers was the winning bid.

Now Lara and Keller were on their way to Reno.

The hotel was called the Reno Palace. It was large and sumptuous, with 1,500 rooms, and a huge, glittering casino that was empty. Lara and Howard Keller were being escorted through the casino by a man named Tony Wilkie.

'The people who owned this got a bum deal,' Wilkie said.

'What kind of bum deal?' Keller asked.

'Well, it seems that a couple of the boys were pocketing a little money from the cash cage . . .'

'Skimming,' Keller interjected.

'Yeah. Of course, the owners didn't know anything about it.'

'Of course not.'

'But someone blew the whistle and the Gaming Commission pulled out the rug. It's too bad. It was a very profitable operation.'

'I know.' Keller had already studied the books.

When the tour of inspection was completed, and Lara and Howard were alone, she said, 'Paul was right. This is a gold mine.' She saw the expression on Howard's face. 'What's the matter?'

He shrugged. 'I don't know. I just don't like us getting involved in anything like this.'

'What's "anything like this"? It's a cash cow, Howard.'

'Who's going to run the casino?'

'We'll find people,' Lara said evasively.

'Where from? The Girl Scouts? It takes gamblers to run an operation like this. I don't know any, do you?

Lara was silent.

'I'll bet Paul Martin does.'

'Leave him out of this,' Lara said.

'I'd like to, and I'd like to leave you out of it. I don't think this is such a great idea.'

'You didn't think the Queens project was a great idea either, did you? Or the shopping centre on Houston Street. But they're making money, aren't they?'

'Lara, I never said they weren't good deals. All I said was that I think we're moving too fast. You're swallowing up everything in sight, but you haven't digested anything yet.'

Lara patted his cheek. 'Relax.'

The members of the Gaming Commission received Lara with elaborate courtesy.

'We don't often meet a beautiful young woman in here,' the Chairman said. 'It brightens up our day.'

Lara did look beautiful. She was wearing a Donna Karan beige wool suit, with a cream-coloured silk blouse, and, for good luck, one of the scarves Paul had given her for Christmas. She smiled. 'Thank you.'

'What can we do for you?' one of the Gaming Commissioners asked. They all knew perfectly well what they could do for her.

'I'm here because I would like to do something for Reno,' Lara said earnestly. 'I would like to give it the biggest, most beautiful hotel in Nevada. I'd like to add five storeys to the Reno Palace, and put up a large convention centre to attract more tourists here to gamble.'

The members of the board glanced at one another. The Chairman said, 'I think something like that would have a very beneficial effect on the city. Of course, our job is to make sure that an operation like this would be run completely above board.'

'I'm not exactly an escaped convict,' Lara smiled.

They chuckled at her little joke. 'We know your record, Miss Cameron, and it is admirable. However, you've had no experience in running a casino.'

'That's true,' Lara admitted. 'On the other hand, I'm sure it will be easy to find fine, qualified employees who will meet the approval of this board. I would certainly welcome your guidance.'

One of the members of the board spoke up. 'As far as the financing is concerned, can you guarantee . . . ?'

The Chairman interrupted. 'That's all right, Tom, Miss Cameron has submitted the financials on it. I'll see that you each get a copy.'

Lara sat there, waiting.

The Chairman said, 'I can't promise anything at this moment, Miss Cameron, but I think I'm safe in saying that I don't see any obstacles to your being granted a licence.'

Lara beamed. 'That's wonderful. I'd like to get moving as quickly as possible.'

'I'm afraid things don't move quite that fast here. There will be a one month waiting period before we can give you a definite answer.'

Lara was dismayed. 'A month?'

'Yes. We have a bit of checking to do.'

'I understand,' Lara said. 'That will be fine.'

There was a music store in the hotel's shopping complex. In the window was a large poster of Philip Adler, advertising his new compact disc.

Lara was not interested in the music. She bought the CD for Philip's photograph on the back of the case.

On their way back to New York, Lara said, 'Howard, what do you know about Philip Adler?'

'Just what everybody else knows. He's probably the top concert pianist in the world today. He plays with the finest symphony orchestras. I read somewhere that he just set up a foundation for scholarships for minority musicians in inner cities.'

'What's it called?'

'The Philip Adler Foundation, I think.'

'I'd like to make a contribution,' Lara said. 'Send them a cheque for ten thousand dollars in my name.'

Keller looked at her in surprise. 'I thought you didn't care for classical music.'

'I'm starting to get interested in it,' Lara said.

*

The headline read:

DISTRICT ATTORNEY PROBE OF PAUL MARTIN –
ATTORNEY REPUTED TO HAVE MAFIA TIES

Lara read the story with dismay, and telephoned Paul immediately.

'What's going on?' Lara asked.

He chuckled. 'The DA is on another fishing expedition. They've been trying to tie me in with the boys for years, and they haven't had any luck. Every time an election comes up, they try to use me as their whipping boy. Don't worry about it. What about dinner tonight?'

'Fine,' Lara said.

'I know a little place on Mulberry Street where no one will bother us.'

Over dinner, Paul Martin said, 'I hear that the meeting with the Gaming Commission went well.'

'I think it did. They seemed friendly, but I've never done anything like this before.'

'I don't think you'll have any problem. I'll get you some good boys for the casino. The man who owned the licence got greedy.' He changed the subject. 'How are all the construction jobs going?'

'Fine. I have three projects in the works, Paul.'

'You're not getting in over your head, are you, Lara?'

He sounded like Howard Keller. 'No. Every job is on budget and on schedule.'

'That's good, baby. I wouldn't want anything to ever go wrong for you.'

'Nothing will.' She put her hand on his. 'You're my safety net.'

'I'll always be there.' He squeezed her hand.

Two weeks went by and Lara had not heard from Philip Adler. She sent for Keller. 'Did you make that $10,000 contribution to the Adler Foundation?'

'Yes, the day you mentioned it.'

'Strange. I would have thought he would have called me.'

Keller shrugged. 'He's probably travelling somewhere.'

'Probably.' She tried to conceal her disappointment. 'Let's talk about the building in Queens.'

'That's going to take a big financial bite out of us,' Keller said.

'I know how to protect us. I'd like to lock the deal in with one tenant.'

'Do you have anyone in mind?'

'Yes. Mutual Security Insurance. The president is a man named Horace Guttman. I've heard they're looking for a new location. I'd like it to be our building.'

'I'll check it out,' Keller said.

Lara noticed that he made no notes. 'You constantly amaze me. You remember everything, don't you?'

Keller grinned. 'I have a photographic memory. It used to be for baseball statistics.' *It all seems so long ago*, Howard thought. *The kid with the magic arm, the star of the Chicago Cubs minor league. Someone else and another time.* 'Sometimes it's a cúrse. There are a few things in my life I'd like to forget.'

'Howard, have the architect go ahead and draw up the plans for the Queens building. Find out how many floors Mutual Security will need, and how much floor space.'

Two days later, Keller walked into Lara's office. 'I'm afraid I have some bad news.'

'What's the problem?'

'I did a little snooping around. You were right about Mutual Security Insurance. They *are* looking for a new headquarters, but Guttman is thinking about a building in Union Square. It's your old friend, Steve Murchison's building.'

Murchison again! She was sure that the box of dirt had been sent by him. *I'm not going to let him bluff me.*

'Has Guttman committed to it?' Lara asked.

'Not yet.'

'All right. I'll handle it.'

That afternoon, Lara made a dozen phone calls. She hit the jackpot on the last call. Barbara Roswell.

'Horace Guttman? Sure, I know him, Lara. What's your interest in him?'

'I'd like to meet him. I'm a big fan of his. I want you to do me a favour. Could you please invite him to dinner next Saturday night, Barbara?'

'You've got it.'

The dinner party was simple but elegant. There were fourteen people at the Roswell residence. Alice Guttman wasn't feeling well that evening, so Horace Guttman had come to the party alone. Lara had been seated next to him. He was in his sixties, but he seemed much older. He had a stern, worn face and a stubborn chin. Lara looked enchanting, provocative. She was wearing a low-cut, black Halston gown and simple but stunning jewellery. They had had their cocktails and were seated at the dining table.

'I've been wanting to meet you,' Lara confessed. 'I've heard so much about you.'

'I've heard a lot about you, young lady. You've made quite a splash in this town.'

'I hope I'm making a contribution,' Lara said modestly. 'It's such a wonderful town.'

'Where are you from?'

'Gary, Indiana.'

'Really?' He looked at her in surprise. 'That's where I was born. So, you're a Hoosier, eh?'

Lara smiled. 'That's right. I have such fond memories of Gary. My father worked for the *Post Tribune*. I went to Roosevelt High. On weekends, we'd go to Gleason Park for picnics and outdoor concerts, or we'd go bowling at the Twelve and Twenty. I hated having to leave.'

'You've done well for yourself, Miss Cameron.'

'Lara.'

'Lara. What are you up to these days?'

'The project I'm most excited about,' Lara told him, 'is a new building I'm putting up in Queens. It's going to have thirty storeys, and 200,000 square feet of floor space.'

'That's interesting,' Guttman said, thoughtfully.

'Oh,' Lara said innocently. 'Why?'

'It happens that we're looking for a building just about that size for our new headquarters.'

'Really? Have you chosen one yet?'

'Not exactly, but . . .'

'If you'd like, I can show you the plans for our new building. They've already been drawn up.'

He studied her a moment. 'Yes, I'd like to see them.'

'I can bring them to your office Monday morning.'

'I'll look forward to it.'

The rest of the evening went well.

When Horace Guttman reached home that night, he walked into his wife's bedroom.

'How are you feeling?' he asked.

'Better, darling. How was the party?'

He sat down on the bed. 'Well, they all missed you, but I had an interesting time. Have you ever heard of Lara Cameron?'

'Certainly. Everyone has heard of Lara Cameron.'

'She's quite a woman. A little strange. Says she was born in Gary, Indiana, same as me. Knew all about Gary – Gleason Park and the Twelve and Twenty.'

'What's strange about that?'

Guttman looked at his wife and grinned. 'The little lady comes from Nova Scotia.'

Early Monday morning, Lara appeared at Horace Guttman's office, carrying the blueprints for the Queens project. She was ushered in immediately.

'Nice to see you, Lara. Sit down.'

She laid the blueprints on his desk and sat across from him.

'Before you look at these,' Lara said, 'I have something to confess, Horace.'

Guttman leaned back in his chair. 'Yes?'

'That story I told on Saturday about Gary, Indiana . . .'

'What about it?'

'I've never even been to Gary, Indiana. I was trying to impress you.'

He laughed. 'Now you've succeeded in confusing me. I'm not sure I'm going to be able to keep up with you, young lady. Let's look at these blueprints.'

Half an hour later, he was through examining them.

'You know,' he said reflectively, 'I was pretty well set on another location.'

'Were you?'

'Why should I change my mind and move into your building?'

'Because you're going to be happier there. I'll see that you have everything you need.' She smiled. 'Besides, it's going to cost your company ten per cent less.'

'Really? You don't know what my deal is for the other building.'

'It doesn't matter. I'll take your word for it.'

'You *could* have come from Gary, Indiana,' Guttman said. 'You've got a deal.'

When Lara returned to her office there was a message that Philip Adler had telephoned.

The ballroom at the Waldorf Astoria was crowded with patrons of Carnegie Hall. Lara moved through the crowd, looking for Philip. She recalled the telephone conversation they had had a few days earlier.

'Miss Cameron, this is Philip Adler.'

Her throat went suddenly dry.

'I'm sorry I wasn't able to thank you earlier for the donation you made to the Foundation. I've just returned from Europe and learned about it.'

'It was my pleasure,' Lara said. She had to keep him talking. 'As . . . as a matter of fact, I'm interested in knowing more about the Foundation. Perhaps we could get together and discuss it.'

There was a pause. 'There's going to be a charity dinner at the Waldorf on Saturday evening. We could meet there. Are you free?'

Lara quickly glanced at her schedule. She had a dinner meeting that evening with a banker from Texas.

She made a quick decision. 'Yes. I'd be delighted to go.'

'Wonderful. There will be a ticket at the door for you.'

When Lara replaced the receiver, she was beaming.

Philip Adler was nowhere in sight. Lara moved through the huge ballroom, listening to the conversations around her.

'. . . So the leading tenor said, "Dr Klemperer, I have only two high Cs left. Do you want to hear them now, or tonight at the performance?" . . .'

'. . . Oh, I admit that he has a good stick. His dynamics and tonal shadings are excellent . . . but the *tempi! Tempi!* Spare me! . . .'

'. . . you're insane! Stravinsky is too structured. His music could have been written by a robot. He holds back his feelings. Bartok, on the other hand, lets loose the floodgates, and we're bathed in emotions . . .'

'I simply can't stand her playing. Her Chopin is an exercise in tortured *rubato*, butchered textures, and purple passion . . .'

It was an arcane language that was beyond Lara's comprehension. And then she saw Philip, surrounded by an admiring coterie. Lara pushed her way through the crowd. An attractive young woman was saying, 'When you played the B-flat minor sonata, I felt that Rachmaninoff was smiling. Your tone and voicing, and the soft-grained readings . . . Wonderful!'

Philip smiled. 'Thank you.'

A middle-aged dowager was gushing, 'I keep listening to your recording of the *Hammerklavier* over and over. My God! The vitality is irresistible! I think you must be the only pianist left in this world who really understands that Beethoven sonata . . .'

Philip saw Lara. 'Ah. Excuse me,' he said.

He made his way over to where she was standing, and took her hand. His touch aroused her. 'Hello. I'm glad you could come, Miss Cameron.'

'Thank you.' She looked around. 'This is quite a crowd.'

He nodded. 'Yes. I assume that you're a lover of classical music?'

Lara thought of the music she had grown up with. *'Annie Laurie', 'Comin' Through the Rye', 'The Hills of Home'* . . .

'Oh, yes,' Lara said. 'My father brought me up on classical music.'

'I want to thank you again for your contribution. That was really very generous.'

'Your foundation sounds so interesting. I would love to hear more about it. If . . .'

'Philip, darling! There are no words! Magnificent!' He was surrounded again.

Lara managed to make herself heard. 'If you're free one evening next week . . .'

Philip shook his head. 'I'm sorry, I leave for Rome tomorrow.'

Lara felt a sudden sense of loss. 'Oh.'

'But I'll be back in three weeks. Perhaps then we could . . .'

'Wonderful!' Lara said.

'. . . spend an evening discussing music.'

Lara smiled. 'Yes. I'll look forward to that.'

At that moment, they were interrupted by two middle-aged men. One wore his hair in a ponytail, the other had on a single earring.

'Philip! You must settle an argument for us. When you're playing Liszt, which do you think is more important – a piano with heavy action that gives you a colourful sound, or light action where you can do a colourful manipulation?'

Lara had no idea what they were talking about. They went off into a discussion about neutral sonority and long sounds and transparency. Lara watched the animation in Philip's face as he talked, and she thought, *This is his world. I've got to find a way to get into it.*

The following morning, Lara appeared at the Manhattan School of Music. She said to the woman at the reception desk, 'I'd like to see one of the music professors, please.'

'Anyone in particular?'

'No.'

'Just a moment, please.' She disappeared into another room.

A few minutes later, a small, grey-haired man appeared at Lara's side.

'Good morning. I'm Leonard Meyers. How may I help you?'

'I'm interested in classical music.'

'Ah, you wish to enroll here. What instrument do you play?'

'I don't play any instrument. I just want to learn about classical music.'

'I'm afraid you've come to the wrong place. This school is not for beginners.'

'I'll pay you five thousand dollars for two weeks of your time.'

Professor Meyers blinked. 'I'm sorry, Miss . . . I didn't get your name.'

'Cameron. Lara Cameron.'

'You wish to pay me five thousand dollars for a two-week *discussion* of classical music?' He had trouble getting the words out.

'That's right. You can use the money for a scholarship fund if you wish.'

Professor Meyers lowered his voice. 'That will not be necessary. This can just be between you and me.'

'That's fine.'

'When . . . er . . . would you like to begin?'

'Now.'

'I have a class at the moment, but give me five minutes . . .'

Lara and Professor Meyers were seated in a classroom alone.

'Let us start at the beginning. Do you know anything about classical music?'

'Very little.'

'I see. Well, there are two ways to understand music,' the professor began. 'Intellectually and emotionally. Someone once said that music reveals to man his hidden soul. Every great composer was able to accomplish that.'

Lara was listening intently.

'Are you familiar with *any* composers, Miss Cameron?'

She smiled. 'Not too many.'

The professor frowned. 'I don't really understand your interest in . . .'

'I want to get enough of a background so that I can talk intelligently to a professional musician about the classics. I'm . . . I'm particularly interested in piano music.'

'I see.' Meyers thought for a moment. 'I'll tell you how we're going to begin. I'm going to give you some CDs to play.'

Lara watched him walk over to a shelf and pull down some compact discs.

'We'll start with these. I want you to listen carefully to the *allegro* in Mozart's Piano Concerto No. 21 in C, K.467, and the *adagio* in Brahms' Piano Concerto No. 1, and the *moderato* in Rachmaninoff's Piano Concerto No. 2 in C minor, Op. 18, and finally, the *romanze* in Chopin's Piano Concerto No. 1. They're all marked.'

'Right.'

'If you would like to play these and come back in a few days . . .'

'I'll be back tomorrow.'

The following day, when Lara came in, she was carrying half a dozen CDs of Philip Adler's concerts and recitals.

'Ah, splendid!' Professor Meyers said. 'Maestro Adler is the best. You are particularly interested in his playing?'

'Yes.'

'The maestro has recorded many beautiful sonatas.'

'Sonatas?'

He sighed. 'You don't know what a sonata is?'

'I'm afraid I don't.'

'A sonata is a piece, usually in several movements, that has a certain basic musical form. And when that form is used in a piece for a solo instrument, like a

264

piano or violin, the piece is called a sonata. A symphony is a sonata for orchestra.'

'I understand.' *That shouldn't be difficult to work into a conversation.*

'The piano was originally known as the piano-*forte*. That is Italian for "soft-loud" . . .'

They spent the next few days discussing tapes that Philip had recorded – Beethoven, Liszt, Bartok, Mozart, Chopin.

Lara listened, and absorbed, and remembered.

'He likes Liszt. Tell me about him.'

'Franz Liszt was a boy genius. Everyone admired him. He was brilliant. He was treated like a pet by the aristocracy, and he finally complained that he had become on par with a juggler or a performing dog . . .'

'Tell me about Beethoven.'

'A difficult man. He was such an unhappy person that in the middle of his great success he decided he didn't like the work that he had done, and he changed to longer and more emotional compositions, like the *Eroica* and the *Pastoral* . . .'

'Chopin?'

'Chopin was criticized for writing music only for the piano; the critics of his day called him limited . . .'

Later: 'Liszt could play Chopin better than Chopin could . . .'

Another day: 'There's a difference between French pianists and American pianists. The French like clarity and elegance. Traditionally, their technical schooling is grounded in *jeu perlé* – perfectly pearly evenness of articulation with a steady wrist . . .'

Each day they played one of Philip's recordings and discussed it.

At the end of the two weeks, Professor Meyers said, 'I must confess that I'm impressed, Miss Cameron. You are a truly dedicated pupil. Perhaps you should take up an instrument.'

Lara laughed. 'Let's not get carried away.' She handed him a cheque. 'Here you are.'

She could not wait for Philip to return to New York.

The day started with good news. Terry Hill called.

'Lara?'

'Yes?'

'We just heard from the Gaming Commission. You've got your licence.'

'That's wonderful, Terry!'

'I'll go over the details when I see you, but it's a green light. Apparently you impressed the hell out of them.'

'I'll get everything started right away,' Lara said. 'Thanks.'

Lara told Keller what had happened.

'That's great. We can sure use the cash flow. That will take care of a lot of our problems . . .'

Lara looked at her calendar. 'We can fly down there on Tuesday and get things moving.'

Kathy buzzed her. 'There's a Mr Adler on line two. Shall I tell him . . . ?'

Lara was suddenly nervous. 'I'll take it.' She picked up the telephone. 'Philip?'

'Hello. I'm back.'

'I'm glad.' *I missed you.*

'I know it's short notice, but I wondered whether you might be free for dinner this evening.'

She had a dinner engagement with Paul Martin. 'Yes. I'm free.'

'Wonderful. Where would you like to dine?'

'It doesn't matter.'

'Le Côte Basque?'

'Fine.'

'Why don't we meet there? Eight o'clock?'

'Yes.'

'See you tonight.'

When Lara hung up, she was smiling.

'Was that *Philip* Adler?' Keller asked.

'Uh huh. I'm going to marry him.'

Keller was looking at her, stunned. 'Are you serious?'

'Yes.'

It was a jolt. *I'm going to lose her*, Keller thought. And then: *Who am I kidding? I could never have her*.

'Lara . . . you hardly know him!'

I've known him all my life.

'I don't want you to make a mistake.'

'I'm not. I . . .' Her private telephone rang. The one she had had installed for Paul Martin. Lara picked it up. 'Hello, Paul.'

'Hi, Lara. What time would you like to make dinner tonight? Eight?'

She felt a sudden sense of guilt. 'Paul . . . I'm afraid I can't make it tonight. Something came up. I was going to call you.'

'Oh? Is everything all right?'

'Yes. Some people just flew in from Rome' – that part at least was true – 'and I have to meet with them.'

'My bad luck. Another night, then.'

'Of course.'

'I hear the licence came through for the Reno hotel.'

'Yes.'

'We're going to have fun with that place.'

'I'm looking forward to it. I'm sorry about tonight. I'll talk to you tomorrow.'

The line went dead.

Lara replaced the receiver slowly.

Keller was watching her. She could see the disapproval on his face.

'Is something bothering you?'

'Yeah. It's all this modern equipment.'

'What are you talking about?'

'I think you have too many phones in your office. He's bad news, Lara.'

Lara stiffened. 'Mr Bad News has saved our hides a few times, Howard. Anything else?'

Keller shook his head. 'No.'

'Right. Let's get back to work.'

Philip was waiting for her when she arrived at Le Côte Basque. People turned to stare at Lara as she walked into the restaurant. Philip stood up to greet her, and Lara's heart skipped a beat.

'I hope I'm not late,' she said.

'Not at all.' He was looking at her admiringly. His eyes were warm. 'You look lovely.'

She had changed clothes half a dozen times. *Should I wear something simple or elegant or sexy?* Finally, she had decided on a simple Dior. 'Thank you.'

When they were seated, Philip said, 'I feel like an idiot.'

'Oh? Why?'

'I never connected the name. You're *that* Cameron.'

She laughed. 'Guilty.'

'My God! You're a hotel chain, you're apartment buildings, office buildings. When I travel, I see your name all over the country.'

'Good,' Lara smiled. 'It will remind you of me.'

He was studying her. 'I don't think I need any reminding. Do you get tired of people telling you that you're very beautiful?'

She started to say, 'I'm glad you think I'm beautiful.' What came out was, 'Are you married?' She wanted to bite her tongue.

He smiled. 'No. It would be impossible for me to get married.'

'Why?' For an instant she held her breath. *Surely he's not . . .*

'Because I'm on tour most of the year. One night I'm in Budapest, the next night in London or Paris or Tokyo.'

There was a sweeping sense of relief. 'Ah. Philip, tell me about yourself.'

'What do you want to know?'

'Everything.'

Philip laughed. 'That would take at least five minutes.'

'No, I'm serious. I really want to know about you.'

He took a deep breath. 'Well, my parents were Viennese. My father was a musical conductor and my mother was a piano teacher. They left Vienna to escape Hitler and settled in Boston. I was born there.'

'Did you always know you wanted to be a pianist?'

'Yes.'

He was six years old. He was practising the piano and his father came storming into the room. 'No, no, no! Don't you know a major chord from a minor?' His hairy finger slashed at the sheet music. 'That's a minor chord. Minor. Do you understand?'

'Father, please, can I go? My friends are waiting for me outside.'

'No. You will sit here until you get it right.'

He was eight years old. He had practised for four hours that morning, and had had a terrible fight with his parents. 'I hate the piano,' he cried. 'I never want to touch it again.'

His mother said, 'Fine. Now, let me hear the Andante once more.'

He was ten years old. The apartment was filled with guests, most of them old friends of his parents from Vienna. All of them were musicians.

'Philip is going to play something for us now,' his mother announced.

'We'd love to hear little Philip play,' they said in patronizing voices.

'Play the Mozart, Philip.'

Philip looked into their bored faces and sat down at the piano, angry. They went on chatting among themselves.

He began to play, his fingers flashing across the keyboard. The talking suddenly stopped. He played a Mozart sonata, and the music was alive. And at that moment he was Mozart, filling the room with the magic of the master.

As Philip's fingers struck the last chord, there was an awed silence. His parents' friends rushed over to the piano, talking excitedly, effusive with their *praise. He listened to their applause and adulation, and that was the moment of his epiphany, when he knew who he was and what he wanted to do with his life.*

'Yes, I always knew I wanted to be a pianist,' Philip told Lara.

'Where did you study piano?'

'My mother taught me until I was fourteen, and then they sent me to study at the Curtis Institute in Philadelphia.'

'Did you enjoy that?'

'Very much.'

He was fourteen years old, alone in the city with no friends. The Curtis Institute of Music was located in four turn-of-the-century mansions near Philadelphia's Rittenhouse Square. It was the closest American equivalent to the Moscow Conservatory of Viardo, Egorov and Toradze. Its graduates included Samuel Barber, Leonard Bernstein, Gian Carlo Menotti, Peter Serkin, and dozens of other brilliant musicians.

'Weren't you lonely there?'

'No.'

He was miserable. He had never been away from home before. He had auditioned for the Curtis Institute, and when they accepted him, the realization struck him that he was about to begin a new life, that he would never go home again. The teachers recognized the young boy's talent immediately. His piano teachers were Isabelle Vengerova and Rudolf Serkin, and Philip studied piano, theory, harmony, orchestration and flute. When he was not in class, he played chamber music with the other students. The piano, which he had been forced to practise from the time he was three years old, was now the focus of his life. To him, it had become a magical instrument out of which his fingers could draw romance and passion and thunder. It spoke a universal language.

'I gave my first concert when I was eighteen with the Detroit Symphony.'

'Were you frightened?'

·He was terrified. He found that it was one thing to play before a group of friends. It was another to face a huge auditorium filled with people who had paid money to hear him. He was nervously pacing backstage when the stage manager grabbed his arm and said, 'Go. You're on.' He had never forgotten the feeling he had when he walked out onto the stage and the audience began to applaud him. He sat down at the piano and his nervousness vanished in an instant. After that, his life became a marathon of concerts. He toured all over Europe and Asia, and after each tour his reputation grew. William Ellerbee, an important artists' manager, agreed to represent him. Within two years, Philip Adler was in demand everywhere.

Philip looked at Lara and smiled. 'Yes. I still get frightened before a concert.'

'What's it like to go on tour?'

'It's never dull. Once I was on a tour with the Philadelphia Symphony. We were in Brussels, on our way to give a concert in London. The airport was closed because of fog, so they took us by bus to Schiphol Airport in Amsterdam. The man in charge explained that the plane they had chartered for us was small, and that the musicians could take either their instruments or their luggage. Naturally, they chose their instruments. We arrived in London just in time to begin the concert. We played it in jeans, sneakers, and unshaven.'

Lara laughed. 'And I'll bet the audience loved it.'

'They did. Another time I was giving a concert in Indiana, and the piano was locked away in a closet and no one had a key. We had to break the door down.'

Lara giggled.

'Last year I was scheduled to do a Beethoven concerto in Rome, and one of the music critics wrote: "Adler gave a ponderous performance, with his phrasing in the finale completely missing the point. The tempo was too broad, rupturing the pulse of the piece."'

'That's awful!' Lara said sympathetically.

'The awful part was that I never even gave that concert. I had missed my plane!'

Lara leaned forward, eagerly. 'Tell me more.'

'Well, one time in São Paulo the pedals fell off the piano in the middle of a Chopin concert.'

'What did you do?'

'I finished the sonata without pedals. Another time, the piano slid clear across the stage.'

When Philip talked about his work, his voice was filled with enthusiasm.

'I'm very lucky. It's wonderful to be able to touch people and transport them into another world. The music gives each of them a dream. Sometimes I think music is the only sanity left in an insane world.' He laughed self-consciously. 'I didn't mean to sound pompous.'

'No. You make millions of people so happy. I love to hear you play.' She took a deep breath. 'When I hear you play Debussy's *Voiles*, I'm on a lonely beach, and I see the mast of a ship sailing in the distance . . .'

He smiled. 'Yes, so do I.'

'And when I listen to your Scarlatti, I'm in Naples, and I can hear the horses and the carriages, and see the people walking through the streets . . .' She could see the pleasure in his face as he listened to her.

She was dredging up every memory of her sessions with Professor Meyers.

'With Bartok, you take me to the villages of Central Europe, to the peasants of Hungary. You're painting pictures, and I lose myself in them.'

'You're very flattering,' Philip said.

'No. I mean every word of it.'

Dinner arrived. It consisted of a Chateaubriand with pommes frites, a Waldorf salad, fresh asparagus, and a fruit torte for dessert. There was a wine for each course. Over dinner, Philip said, 'Lara, we keep talking about me. Tell me about you. What is it like to put up enormous buildings all over the country?'

Lara was silent for a moment. 'It's difficult to describe. *You* create with your hands. *I* create with my mind. I don't physically put up a building, but I make it possible. I dream a dream of bricks and concrete and steel, and make it come true. I create jobs for hundreds of people; architects and bricklayers and designers and carpenters and plumbers. Because of me, they're able to support their families. I give people beautiful surroundings to live in and make them comfortable. I build attractive stores where people can shop and buy things they need. I build monuments to the future.' She smiled, sheepishly. 'I didn't mean to make a speech.'

'You're quite remarkable, do you know that?'

'I want you to think so.'

It was an enchanted evening, and by the time it was over, Lara knew that for the first time in her life she was in love. She had been so afraid that she might be disappointed, that no man could live up to the image in her imagination. But here was Lochinvar in the flesh, and she was stirred.

When Lara got home, she was so excited she was unable to go to sleep. She went over the evening in her mind, replaying the conversation again and again and again. Philip Adler was the most fascinating man she had ever met. The telephone rang. Lara smiled and picked it up. She started to say, 'Philip . . .' when Paul Martin said, 'Just checking to make sure you got home safely.'

'Yes,' Lara said.

'How did your meeting go?'

'Fine.'

'Good. Let's have dinner tomorrow night.'

Lara hesitated. 'All right.' *I wonder if there's going to be a problem.*

The following morning, a dozen red roses were delivered to Lara's apartment. *So, he enjoyed the evening, too,* Lara thought happily. She hurriedly tore open the card attached to the flowers. It read:

'Baby, looking forward to our dinner tonight. Paul.'

Lara felt a sharp sense of disappointment. She waited all morning for a call from Philip. She had a busy schedule, but she was unable to keep her mind on her work.

At ten o'clock Kathy said, 'The new secretaries are here for you to interview.'

'Start sending them in.'

There were half a dozen of them, all highly qualified. Gertrude Meeks was the choice of the day. She was in her thirties, bright and up-beat, and obviously in awe of Lara.

Lara looked over her résumé. It was impressive. 'You've worked in the real estate development field before.'

'Yes, ma'am. But I've never worked for anyone like you. To tell you the truth, I'd take this job for no salary!'

Lara smiled. 'That won't be necessary. These are good references. All right, we'll give you a try.'

'Thank you so much.' She was almost blushing.

'You'll have to sign a form agreeing not to give any interviews or ever to discuss anything that happens at this firm. Is that agreeable?'

'Of course.'

'Kathy will show you to your desk.'

There was an eleven o'clock publicity meeting with Jerry Townsend.

'How's your father?' Lara asked.

'He's in Switzerland. The doctor says he may have a chance.' His voice grew husky. 'If he has, it's because of you.'

'Everyone deserves a chance, Jerry. I hope he gets well.'

'Thanks.' He cleared his throat. 'I . . . I don't know how to tell you how grateful I . . .'

Lara stood up. 'I'm late for a meeting.'

And she walked out, leaving him standing there, looking after her.

The meeting was with the architects on a New Jersey development. 'You've done a good job,' Lara said, 'but I'd like some changes. I want an elliptical arcade with lobbies on three sides and marble walls. Change the roof to the shape of a copper pyramid, with a beacon to light up at night. Any problem with that?'

'I don't see any, Miss Cameron.'

When the meeting was over, the intercom buzzed.

'Miss Cameron, Raymond Duffy, one of the construction foremen, is on the line for you. He says it's urgent.'

Lara picked up the telephone. 'Hello, Raymond.'

'We have a problem, Miss Cameron.'

'Go on.'

'They just delivered a load of cement blocks. They won't pass inspection. There are cracks in them. I'm going to send them back, but I wanted to tell you first.'

Lara was thoughtful for a moment. 'How bad is it?'

'Bad enough. The point is, they don't meet our specifications, and . . .'

'Can they be fixed?'

'I guess they could, but it would be expensive.'

'Fix them,' Lara said.

There was a silence at the other end of the line.

'Right. You're the boss.'

Lara replaced the receiver. There were only two cement suppliers in the city, and it would be suicide to antagonize them.

By five o'clock, Philip still had not called. Lara dialled the number at his foundation. 'Philip Adler, please.'

'Mr Adler is out of town on tour. Can I help you?'

He hadn't mentioned that he was leaving town. 'No, thank you.'

That's that, Lara thought. *For now*.

The day ended with a visit from Steve Murchison. He was a huge man, built like a stack of bricks. He stormed into Lara's office.

'What can I do for you, Mr Murchison?' Lara asked.

279

'You can keep your nose out of my fucking business,' Murchison said.

Lara looked at him calmly. 'What's your problem?'

'You. I don't like people horning in on my deals.'

'If you're talking about Mr Guttman . . .'

'You're damn right I am.'

'. . . he preferred my building to yours.'

'You suckered him into it, lady. You've been getting in my hair long enough. I warned you once. I'm not going to warn you again. There's not room enough for both of us in this town. I don't know where you keep your balls, but hide 'em, because if you ever do that to me again, I'm going to cut them off.'

And he stormed out.

The dinner at her apartment that evening with Paul was strained.

'You seem preoccupied, baby,' Paul said. 'Any problems?'

Lara managed a smile. 'No. Everything's fine.' *Why didn't Philip tell me he was going away?*

'When does the Reno project start?'

'Howard and I are going to fly down again next week. We should be able to open in about nine months.'

'You could have a baby in nine months.'

Lara looked at him in surprise. 'What?'

Paul Martin took her hand in his. 'You know I'm crazy about you, Lara. You've changed my whole life. I wish things could have turned out differently. I would have loved for us to have had kids together.'

There was nothing Lara could say to that.

'I have a little surprise for you.' He reached into his pocket and pulled out a jewellery box. 'Open it.'

'Paul, you've already given me so much . . .'

'Open it.'

Inside the box was an exquisite diamond necklace. 'It's lovely.'

He stood up and she felt his hands on her as he put the necklace around her neck. His hands slid down, caressing her breasts, and he said huskily, 'Let's check it out.'

Paul was leading her into the bedroom. Lara's mind was spinning. She had never been in love with him, and going to bed with him had been easy – the payment for all he had done for her – but now there was a difference. She was in love. *I'm a fool*, Lara thought. *I'll probably never see Philip again*.

She undressed slowly, reluctantly, and then they were in bed, and Paul Martin was on top of her, inside her, moaning, 'Baby, I'm nuts about you.' And she looked up and it was Philip's face she saw.

Everything was progressing smoothly. The renovations on the Reno hotel were proceeding rapidly, Cameron Towers was going to be finished on schedule, and Lara's reputation kept growing. She had called Philip Adler several times over the past few months, but he was always away on tour.

'Mr Adler is in Beijing . . .'

'Mr Adler is in Paris . . .'

'Mr Adler is in Sydney . . .'

To hell with him, Lara thought.

*

During the next six months, Lara managed to outbid Steve Murchison on three properties he was after.

Keller came to Lara, worried. 'The word around town is that Murchison is making threats against you. Maybe we should cool it with him. He's a dangerous enemy, Lara.'

'So am I,' Lara said. 'Maybe he should get into another business.'

'It's not a joking matter, Lara. He . . .'

'Forget about him, Howard. I just got a tip about a property in Los Angeles. It's not on the market yet. If we move fast, I think we can get it. We'll fly out in the morning.'

The property was on the site of the old Biltmore Hotel and consisted of five acres. A real estate agent was showing Lara and Howard around the grounds.

'Prime property,' he was saying. 'Yes, sir. You can't go wrong with this. You can build a beautiful little city in this area . . . apartment buildings, shopping centres, theatres, malls . . .'

'No.'

He looked at Lara in surprise. 'I beg your pardon?'

'I'm not interested.'

'You're not? Why?'

'The neighbourhood,' Lara said. 'I don't think people are going to move into this area. Los Angeles is moving west. People are like lemmings. You aren't going to get them to reverse direction.'

'But . . .'

'I'll tell you what I *am* interested in. Condos. Find me a good location.'

Lara turned to Howard, 'I'm sorry I wasted our time. We'll fly back this afternoon.'

When they returned to their hotel, Keller bought a newspaper at the newsstand. 'Let's see what the market is doing today.'

They looked through the paper. In the entertainment section was a large advertisement that read: TONIGHT AT THE HOLLYWOOD BOWL – PHILIP ADLER. Lara's heart gave a little jump.

'Let's go back tomorrow,' Lara said.

Keller studied her a moment. 'Are you interested in the music or the musician?'

'Get us two tickets.'

Lara had never been to the Hollywood Bowl before. The largest natural amphitheatre in the world, it is surrounded by the hills of Hollywood, the grounds a park, open year round for visitors to enjoy. The Bowl itself seats 18,000 people. It was filled to capacity, and Lara could sense the anticipation of the crowd. The musicians began to come onto the stage, and they were greeted with expectant applause. André Previn appeared and the applause grew more enthusiastic. There was a hush, then loud applause from the audience as Philip Adler walked out on the stage, elegant in white tie and tails.

Lara squeezed Keller's arm. 'Isn't he handsome?' she whispered.

Keller did not answer.

Philip sat down at the piano, and the programme began. His magic took over instantly, enveloping the audience. There was a mysticism about the night.

The stars were shining down, lighting the dark hills surrounding the Bowl. Thousands of people sat there silently, moved by the majesty of the music. When the last notes of the concerto died away, there was a roar from the audience, as the people leaped to their feet, applauding and cheering. Philip stood there, taking bow after bow.

'Let's go backstage,' Lara said.

Keller turned to look at her. Her voice was trembling with excitement.

The backstage entrance was at the side of the orchestra shell. A guard stood at the door, keeping the crowd out. Keller said, 'Miss Cameron is here to see Mr Adler.'

'Is he expecting you?' the guard asked.

'Yes,' Lara said.

'Wait here, please.' A moment later the guard returned. 'You can go in, Miss Cameron.'

Lara and Keller walked into the green room. Philip was in the centre of a crowd that was congratulating him.

'Darling, I've never heard Beethoven played so exquisitely. You were unbelievable . . .'

Philip was saying, 'Thank you . . .'

'. . . thank you . . . with music like that, it's easy to be inspired . . .'

'. . . thank you . . . André is such a brilliant conductor . . .'

'. . . thank you . . . I always enjoy playing at the Bowl . . .'

He looked up and saw Lara and again there was that smile. 'Excuse me,' he said. He made his way through the crowd, toward her. 'I had no idea you were in town.'

'We just flew in this morning. This is Howard Keller, my associate.'

'Hello,' Keller said curtly.

Philip turned to a short, heavy-set man, standing behind him. 'This is my manager, William Ellerbee.' They exchanged hellos.

Philip was looking at Lara. 'There's a party tonight at the Beverly Hilton. I was wondering . . .'

'We'd love to,' Lara said.

When Lara and Keller arrived at the Beverly Hilton's International Ballroom, it was filled with musicians and music lovers, talking music.

'. . . Have you ever noticed that the closer you get to the equator, the more demonstrative and hot-blooded the fans are . . . ?'

'. . . When Franz Liszt played, his piano became an orchestra . . .'

'. . . I disagree with you. DeGroote's talent is not for Liszt or Paganini études, but more for Beethoven . . .'

'. . . You have to dominate the concerto's emotional landscape . . .'

Musicians speaking in tongues, Lara thought.

Philip was surrounded, as usual, by adoring fans. Just watching him gave Lara a warm glow.

When Philip saw her arrive, he greeted her with a broad smile. 'You made it. I'm so glad.'

'I wouldn't have missed it.'

Howard Keller watched the two of them talking, and he thought, *Maybe I should have learned to play the piano. Or maybe I should just wake up to reality.* It seemed so long ago when he had first met the bright, eager, ambitious, young girl. Time had been good to her, and it had stood still for him.

Lara was saying, 'I have to go back to New York tomorrow, but perhaps we could have breakfast.'

'I wish I could. I'm leaving for Tokyo early in the morning.'

She felt a sharp pang of disappointment. 'Why?'

He laughed. 'That's what I do, Lara. I give a hundred and fifty concerts a year. Sometimes two hundred.'

'How long will you be gone this time?'

'Eight weeks.'

'I'll miss you,' Lara said quietly. *You have no idea how much*.

During the next few weeks Lara and Keller flew to Atlanta to investigate two sites at Ansley Park and one at Dunwoody.

'Get me some prices on Dunwoody,' Lara said. 'We might put up some condos there.'

From Atlanta, they flew to New Orleans. They spent two days exploring the Central Business District, and a day at Lake Pontchartrain. Lara found two sites she liked.

A day after they returned, Keller walked into Lara's office. 'We had some bad luck on the Atlanta project,' he said.

'What do you mean?'

'Someone beat us to it.'

Lara looked at him, surprised. 'How could they? Those properties weren't even on the market.'

'I know. Word must have leaked out.'

Lara shrugged. 'I guess you can't win them all.'

That afternoon Keller had more bad news. 'We lost the Lake Pontchartrain deal.'

The following week they flew to Seattle and explored Mercer Island and Kirkland. There was one site that interested Lara, and when they returned to New York, she said to Keller, 'Let's go after it. I think it could be a money-maker.'

'Right.'

At a meeting the next day, Lara asked, 'Did you put in the bid on Kirkland?'

Keller shook his head. 'Someone got there ahead of us.'

Lara was thoughtful. 'Oh. Howard, see if you can find out who's jumping the gun on us.'

It took him less than twenty-four hours. 'Steve Murchison.'

'Did he get all those deals?'

'Yes.'

'So someone in this office has a big mouth.'

'It looks that way.'

Her face was grim. The next morning she hired a detective agency to find the culprit. They had no success.

'As far as we can tell, all your employees are clean, Miss Cameron. None of the offices is bugged, and your phones haven't been tapped.'

They had reached a dead end.

Maybe they were just coincidences, Lara thought. She did not believe it.

The 68-storey residential tower in Queens was half completed, and Lara had invited the bankers to come and inspect its progress. The higher the number of floors, the more expensive the unit. Lara's 68 storeys had only 57 actual floors. It was a trick she had learned from Paul Martin.

·'Everybody does it,' Paul had laughed. 'All you do is change the floor numbers.'

'How do you do that?'

'It's very simple. Your first bank of elevators is from the lobby to the 24th floor. The second bank of elevators is from the 35th floor to the 68th. It's done all the time.'

Because of the unions, the construction jobs had half a dozen phantoms on salary – people who did not exist. There was a Director of Safety Practices, the Coordinator of Construction, the Supervisor of Materials, and others with impressive-sounding titles. In the beginning, Lara had questioned it.

'Don't worry about it,' Paul had told her. 'It's all part of the CDB – the cost of doing business.'

Howard Keller had been living in a small apartment in Washington Square, and when Lara had visited him one evening, she had looked around the tiny apartment and said, 'This is a rat trap. You've got to move out of here.' At Lara's urging, he had moved into a condominium uptown.

One night, Lara and Keller were working late, and when they finally finished, Lara said, 'You look exhausted. Why don't you go home and get some sleep, Howard?'

'Good idea,' Keller yawned. 'See you in the morning.'

'Come in late,' Lara told him.

Keller got into his car and started driving home. He was thinking about a deal they had just closed and how well Lara had handled it. It was exciting working with her. Exciting and frustrating. Somehow, in the back of his mind, he kept hoping that a miracle would happen. *I was blind not to have seen it before,*

Howard darling. I'm not interested in Paul Martin or Philip Adler. It's you I've loved all along.

Fat chance.

When Keller reached his apartment, he took out his key and put it in the lock. It did not fit. Puzzled, he tried again. Suddenly the door flew open from the inside, and a stranger was standing there. 'What the hell do you think you're doing?' the man asked.

Keller looked at him, bewildered. 'I live here.'

'The hell you do.'

'But I . . .' Realization suddenly hit him. 'I . . . I'm sorry,' he stammered, red-faced. 'I *used* to live here. I . . .'

The door was slammed in his face. Keller stood there, disconcerted. *How could I have forgotten that I moved? I've been working too hard.*

Lara was in the middle of a conference when her private phone rang. 'You've been pretty busy lately, baby. I've missed you.'

'I've been travelling a lot, Paul.' She couldn't bring herself to say that she had missed him.

'Let's have lunch today.'

Lara thought about all he had done for her.

'I'd like that,' she said. The last thing in the world she wanted to do was to hurt him.

They had lunch at Mr Chow's.

'You're looking great,' Paul said. 'Whatever

you've been doing agrees with you. How's the Reno hotel coming?'

'It's coming along beautifully,' Lara said enthusiastically. She spent the next fifteen minutes describing how the work was progressing. 'We should be ready to open in two months.'

A man and woman across the room were just leaving. The man's back was to Lara, but he looked familiar. When he turned for an instant, she caught a glimpse of his face. Steve Murchison. The woman with him looked familiar, also. She stooped to pick up her purse and Lara's heart skipped a beat. *Gertrude Meeks, my secretary.* 'Bingo,' Lara said softly.

'Is anything wrong?' Paul asked.

'No. Everything's fine.'

Lara went on describing the hotel.

When Lara returned from lunch, she sent for Keller.

'Do you remember the property in Phoenix we looked at a few months ago?'

'Yeah, we turned it down. You said it was a dog.'

'I've changed my mind.' She pressed down the intercom. 'Gertrude, would you come in here, please?'

'Yes, Miss Cameron.'

Gertrude Meeks came into the office.

'I want to dictate a memo,' Lara said. 'To the Baron Brothers in Phoenix.'

Gertrude started writing.

'Gentlemen, I have reconsidered the Scottsdale property and have decided to go ahead with it immediately. I think in time it is going to be my most valuable asset.' Keller was staring at her. 'I'll be in touch with you regarding price in the next few days. Best regards. I'll sign it.'

'Yes, Miss Cameron. Is that all?'

'That's all.'

Keller watched Gertrude leave the room. He turned to Lara. 'Lara, what are you doing? We had that property analysed. It's worthless! If you . . .'

'Calm down. We're not making a deal for it.'

'Then why . . . ?'

'Unless I miss my guess, Steve Murchison will. I saw Gertrude having lunch with him today.'

Keller was staring at Lara. 'I'll be damned.'

'I want you to wait a couple of days and then call Baron and ask about the property.'

Two days later, Keller came into Lara's office, grinning. 'You were right,' he said. 'Murchison took the bait – hook, line and sinker. He's now the proud owner of fifty acres of worthless land.'

Lara sent for Gertrude Meeks.

'Yes, Miss Cameron?'

'You're fired,' Lara said.

Gertrude looked at her in surprise. 'Fired? Why?'

'I don't like the company you keep. Go back to Steve Murchison and tell him I said so.'

Gertrude's face lost its colour. 'But I . . .'

'That's all. I'll have you escorted out of here.'

At midnight, Lara buzzed Max, her chauffeur. 'Bring the car around to the front,' Lara said.

'Yes, Miss Cameron.'

The car was there waiting for her.

'Where would you like to go, Miss Cameron?' Max asked.

'Drive around Manhattan. I want to see what I've done.'

He was staring at her. 'I beg your pardon?'

'I want to look at my buildings.'

They drove around the city, and stopped at the shopping mall, the housing centre, and the sky-scraper. There was Cameron Square, Cameron Plaza, Cameron Center and the skeleton of Cameron Towers. Lara sat in the car, staring at each building, thinking about the people living there and working there. She had touched all their lives. *I've made this city better*, Lara thought. *I've done everything I wanted to do. Then why am I restless? What is missing?* But she knew.

The following morning, Lara telephoned William Ellerbee, Philip's concert manager.

'Good morning, Mr Ellerbee.'

'Good morning, Miss Cameron. What can I do for you?'

'I was wondering where Philip Adler is playing this week.'

'Philip has a pretty heavy schedule. Tomorrow night he'll be in Amsterdam, then he goes on to Milan, Venice and . . . do you want to know the rest of his . . . ?'

'No, no. That's fine. I was just curious. Thank you.'

'No problem.'

Lara walked into Keller's office. 'Howard, I have to go to Amsterdam.'

He looked at her in surprise. 'What do we have going on there?'

'It's just an idea,' Lara said evasively. 'I'll let you know if it checks out. Have them get the jet ready for me, will you?'

'You sent Bert to London on it, remember? I'll tell them to have it back here tomorrow, and . . .'

'I want to leave today.' There was an urgency in her that took her completely by surprise. 'I'll fly commercial.' She returned to her office and said to Kathy, 'Get me a seat on the first flight to Amsterdam on KLM.'

'Yes, Miss Cameron.'

'Are you going to be gone long?' Keller asked. 'We have some meetings coming up that . . .'

'I'll be back in a day or two.'

'Do you want me to come with you?'

'Thanks, Howard. Not this time.'

'I talked to a senator friend of mine in Washington. He thinks there's a chance they're going to pass a bill that will remove most of the tax incentives for building. If it passes, it's going to kill capital gains taxes and stop accelerated depreciation.'

'That would be stupid,' Lara said. 'It would cripple the real estate industry.'

'I know. He's against the bill.'

'A lot of people will be against it. It will never pass,' Lara predicted. 'In the first place . . .'

The private phone on the desk rang. Lara stared at it. It rang again.

'Aren't you going to answer it?' Keller asked.

Lara's mouth was dry. 'No.'

Paul Martin listened to the hollow ring a dozen times before he replaced the receiver. He sat there a long time thinking about Lara. It seemed to him that lately she had been less accessible, a little cooler. *Could there be someone else? No*, Paul Martin thought. *She belongs to me. She'll always belong to me.*

The flight on KLM was pleasant. The first class seats in the wide-bodied 747 were spacious and comfortable, and the cabin attendants were attentive.

Lara was too nervous to eat or drink anything. *What am I doing?* she wondered. *I'm going to Amsterdam uninvited, and he'll probably be too busy to even see me. Running after him is going to ruin whatever chance I might have had. Too late.*

She checked in at the Grand Hotel on Oudezijds Voorburgwal 197, one of the most beautiful hotels in Amsterdam.

'We have a lovely suite for you, Miss Cameron,' the clerk said.

'Thank you. I understand that Philip Adler is giving a recital this evening. Do you know where he would be playing?'

'Of course, Miss Cameron. At the *Concertgebouw*.'

'Could you arrange a ticket for me?'

'It will be my pleasure.'

As Lara entered her suite, the telephone was ringing. It was Howard Keller.

'Did you have a nice flight?'

'Yes, thanks.'

'I thought you'd like to know that I've spoken to the two banks about the Seventh Avenue deal.'

'And?'

His voice was vibrant. 'They're jumping at it.'

Lara was elated. 'I told you! This is going to be a big one. I want you to start assembling a team of architects, builders – our construction group – the works.'

'Right. I'll talk to you tomorrow.' She replaced the receiver and thought about Howard Keller. He was so dear. *I'm so lucky. He's always there for me. I have to find someone wonderful for him.*

Philip Adler was always nervous before playing. He had rehearsed with the orchestra in the morning, and had a light lunch, and then, to take his mind off the concert, had gone to see an English movie. As he watched the picture, his mind was filled with the music he was going to play that evening. He was unaware that he was drumming his fingers on the arm of his seat until the person next to him said, 'Would you mind stopping that awful sound?'

'I beg your pardon,' Philip said politely.

He got up and left the cinema, and roamed the streets of Amsterdam. He visited the Rijksmuseum, and he strolled through the Botanical Gardens of the Free University, and window shopped along P.C. Hooftstraat. At four o'clock he went back to his hotel to take a nap. He was unaware that Lara Cameron was in the suite directly above him.

At 7 p.m., Philip arrived at the Artists' Entrance of the *Concertgebouw*, the lovely old hall in the heart of Amsterdam. The lobby was already crowded with early arrivals.

Backstage, Philip was in his dressing room, changing into tails. The director of the *Concertgebouw* bustled into the room.

'We're completely sold out, Mr Adler! And we had to turn away so many people. If it were possible for you to stay another day or two, I would . . . I know you are fully booked . . . I will talk to Mr Ellerbee about your return here next year and perhaps . . .'

Philip was not listening. His mind was focused on the recital that lay ahead. The director finally shrugged apologetically and bowed his way out. Philip played the music over and over in his mind. A page knocked at the dressing room door.

'They're ready for you on stage, Mr Adler.'

'Thank you.'

It was time. Philip rose to his feet. He held out his hands. They were trembling slightly. The nervousness before playing never went away. It was true of all the great pianists – Horowitz, Rubenstein, Serkin. Philip's stomach was churning and his heart was pounding. *Why do I put myself through this agony?* he asked himself. But he knew the answer. He took one last look in the mirror, then stepped out of the dressing room, and walked through the long corridor, and started to descend the thirty-three steps that led onto the stage. There was a spotlight on him as he moved toward the piano. The applause grew thunderous. He sat down at the piano and, as if by magic, his nervousness disappeared. It was as though another person were taking his place, someone calm, and poised, and completely in charge. He began to play.

Lara, seated in the audience, felt a thrill as she watched Philip walk out on the stage. There was a presence about him that was mesmerizing. *I am going to marry him*, Lara thought. *I know it.* She sat back in her seat, and let his playing wash over her.

The recital was a triumph, and afterward, the green room was packed. Philip had long ago learned to divide the crowd invited to the green room into two groups: the fans and other musicians. The fans were always enthusiastic. If the performance was a success, the congratulations of the other musicians were cordial. If it was a failure, their congratulations were *very* cordial.

Philip had many avid fans in Amsterdam, and on this particular evening, the green room was crowded with them. He stood in the centre of the room, smiling, signing autographs, and being patiently polite to a hundred strangers. Invariably someone would say, 'Do you remember me?' And Philip would pretend to. 'Your face looks so familiar . . .'

He remembered the story of Sir Thomas Beecham, who had hit upon a device to conceal his bad memory. When someone asked, 'Do you remember me?', the great conductor would reply, 'Of course, I do! How are you, and how is your father, and what is he doing?' The device worked well until a concert in London when a young woman in the green room said, 'Your performance was wonderful, Maestro. Do you remember me?' and Beecham gallantly replied, 'Of course, I do, my dear. How is your father, and what is he doing?' The young woman said, 'Father is fine, thank you. And he's still King of England.'

Philip was busily signing autographs, listening to the familiar phrases: 'You made Brahms come alive for me!' . . . 'I can't tell you how moved I was!' . . . 'I have all your albums' . . . 'Would you sign an autograph for my mother, too? She's your biggest fan . . .' – when something made him look up. Lara was standing in the doorway, watching. His eyes widened in surprise. 'Excuse me.'

He made his way over to her and took her hand. 'What a wonderful surprise! What are you doing in Amsterdam?'

Careful, Lara. 'I had some business to attend to here, and when I heard you were playing, I had to come.' *That was innocent enough.* 'You were wonderful, Philip.'

'Thank you . . . I . . .' He stopped to sign another autograph. 'Look, if you're free for supper . . .'

'I'm free,' Lara said quickly.

They had supper at the Bali restaurant on Leidsestraat. As they entered the restaurant, the patrons rose and applauded. *In the United States*, Lara thought, *the excitement would have been for me.* But she felt a warm glow, simply being at Philip's side.

'It's a great honour to have you with us, Mr Adler,' the maître d' said as he led them to their table.

'Thank you.'

As they were being seated, Lara looked around at all the people staring admiringly at Philip. 'They really love you, don't they?'

He shook his head. 'It's the music they love. I'm just the messenger. I learned that a long time ago. When I was very young and perhaps a little arrogant, I gave a concert, and when I had finished my solo, there was tremendous applause, and I was bowing to the audience and smugly smiling at them, and the conductor turned to the audience and held up the score over his head to remind everyone that they were really applauding Mozart. It's a lesson I've never forgotten.'

'Don't you ever get tired of playing the same music over and over, night after night?'

'No, because no two recitals are the same. The music may be the same, but the conductor is different, and the orchestra is different.'

They ordered a *rijsttafel* dinner, and Philip said, 'We try to make each recital perfect, but there's no such thing as a completely successful one because we're dealing with music that is always better than we are. We have to re-think the music each time in order to recreate the sound of the composer.'

'You're never satisfied?'

'Never. Each composer has his own distinctive sound. Whether it's Debussy, Brahms, Haydn, Beethoven . . . Our goal is to capture that particular sound.'

Supper arrived. The *rijsttafel* was an Indonesian feast, consisting of twenty-one courses, including a variety of meats, fish, chicken, noodles and two desserts.

'How can anyone eat all this?' Lara laughed.

'The Dutch have hearty appetites.'

Philip found it difficult to take his eyes off Lara. He found himself ridiculously pleased that she was there. He had been involved with more than his share of beautiful women, but Lara was like no one he had ever known. She was strong and yet very feminine, and totally unselfconscious about her beauty. He liked her throaty, sexy voice. *In fact, I like everything about her*, Philip admitted to himself.

'Where do you go from here?' Lara was asking.

'Tomorrow I'll be in Milan. Then Venice and Vienna, Paris and London, and finally New York.'

'It sounds so romantic.'

Philip laughed. 'I'm not sure romantic is the word I would choose. We're talking about iffy airline schedules, strange hotels, and eating out in restaurants every night. I don't really mind because the act of playing is so wonderful. It's the "say cheese" syndrome that I hate.'

'What's that?'

'Being put on exhibit all the time, smiling at people you care nothing about, living your life in a world of strangers.'

'I know what that's like,' Lara said slowly.

As they were finishing supper, Philip said, 'Look, I'm always keyed up after a concert. Would you care to take a ride on the canal?'

'I'd love to.'

They boarded a canal bus that cruised the Amstel. There was no moon, but the city was alive with thousands of sparkling lights. The canal trip was an enchantment. A loudspeaker poured out information in four languages:

'We are now passing centuries-old merchants'

301

houses with their richly decorated gables. Ahead are ancient church towers. There are 1,200 bridges on the canals, all in the shade of magnificent avenues of elm trees . . .'

They passed the Smalste Huis – the narrowest house in Amsterdam – which was only as wide as the front door, and the 'Westerkerk' with the Crown of the Hapsburg Emperor Maximilian, and they went under the wooden lift bridge over the Amstel, and the Magere Brug – the skinny bridge – and passed scores of houseboats that served as home for hundreds of families.

'This is such a beautiful city,' Lara said.

'You've never been here before?'

'No.'

'And you're here on business.'

Lara took a deep breath. 'No.'

He looked at her, puzzled. 'I thought you said . . .'

'I came to Amsterdam to see you.'

He felt a sudden frisson of pleasure. 'I . . . I'm very flattered.'

'And I have another confession to make. I told you I was interested in classical music. That's not true.'

A smile touched the corner of Philip's lips. 'I know.'

Lara looked at him in surprise. 'You know?'

'Professor Meyers is an old friend of mine,' he said gently. 'He called to tell me that he was giving you a crash course on Philip Adler. He was concerned that you might have designs on me.'

Lara said softly, 'He was right. Are you involved with anyone?'

'You mean seriously?'

Lara was suddenly embarrassed. 'If you're not interested I'll leave and . . .'

He took her hand in his. 'Let's get off at the next stop.'

When they arrived back at the hotel, there were a dozen messages from Howard Keller. Lara put them in her purse, unread. At this moment, nothing else in her life seemed important.

'Your room or mine?' Philip asked lightly.

'Yours.'

There was a burning urgency in her.

It seemed to Lara that she had waited all her life for this moment. This was what she had been missing. She had found the stranger she was in love with. They reached Philip's room and there was an urgency in both of them. Philip took her in his arms and kissed her softly and tenderly, exploring, and Lara murmured, 'Oh, my God,' and they began to undress each other.

The silence of the room was broken by a sudden clap of thunder outside. Slowly, grey clouds in the sky spread their skirts open, wider and wider, and soft rain began to fall. It started quietly and gently, caressing the warm air erotically, licking at the sides of buildings, sucking at the soft grass, kissing all the dark corners of the night. It was a hot rain, wanton and sensuous, sliding down slowly, slowly, until the tempo began to increase and it changed to a driving, pounding storm, fierce and demanding, an orgiastic beat in a steady, savage rhythm, plunging down harder and harder, moving faster and faster until it finally exploded in a burst of thunder. Suddenly, as quickly as it had started, it was over.

Lara and Philip lay in each other's arms, spent. Philip held Lara close, and he could feel the beating of her heart. He thought of a line he had once heard in a movie. *Did the earth move for you? By God, it did*, Philip thought. *If she were music, she would be Chopin's Barcarolle or Schumann's Fantasy*.

He could feel the soft contours of her body pressed against him, and he began to get aroused again.

'Philip . . .' Her voice was husky.

'Yes?'

'Would you like me to go with you to Milan?'

He found himself grinning. 'Oh, my God, yes!'

'Good,' Lara murmured. She leaned over him and her soft hair started to trail down his lean, hard body.

It began to rain again.

When Lara finally returned to her room, she telephoned Keller. 'Did I wake you up, Howard?'

'No.' His voice was groggy. 'I'm always up at four in the morning. What's going on there?'

Lara was bursting to tell him, but she said. 'Nothing. I'm leaving tomorrow for Milan.'

'What? We aren't doing anything in Milan.'

Oh yes we are, Lara thought happily.

'Did you see my messages?'

She had forgotten to look at them. Guiltily, she said, 'Not yet.'

'I've been hearing rumours about the casino.'

'What's the problem?'

'There have been some complaints about the bidding.'

'Don't worry about it. If there's any problem, Paul Martin will take care of it.'

'You're the boss.'

'I want you to send the plane to Milan. Have the pilots wait for me there. I'll get in touch with them at the airport.'

'All right, but . . .'

'Go back to sleep.'

At four o'clock in the morning, Paul Martin was wide awake. He had left several messages on Lara's private answering machine at her apartment, but none of his calls had been returned. In the past, she had always let him know when she was going to be away. Something was happening. What was she up to? *Be careful, my darling*, he whispered. *Be very careful*.

In Milan, Lara and Philip Adler checked into the Antica Locanda Solferino, a charming hotel with only twelve rooms, and they spent the morning making passionate love. Afterward, they took the drive to Cernobia and had lunch at Lake Como, at the beautiful Villa d'Este.

The concert that night was a triumph, and the green room at La Scala Opera House was packed with well-wishers.

Lara stood to one side, watching as Philip's fans surrounded him, touching him, adoring him, asking for autographs, handing him little gifts. Lara felt a sharp pang of jealousy. Some of the women were young and beautiful, and it seemed to Lara that all of them were obvious. An American woman in an elegant Fendi gown was saying, coyly, 'If you're free tomorrow, Mr Adler, I'm having an intimate little dinner at my villa. *Very* intimate.'

Lara wanted to strangle the bitch.

Philip smiled. 'Er . . . thank you, but I'm afraid I'm not free.'

Another woman tried to slip Philip her hotel key. He shook his head.

Philip looked over at Lara and grinned. Women kept crowding around him.

'*Lei era magnifico, Maestro!*'

'*Moito gentile da parte sua,*' Philip replied.

'*L'ho sentita suonare il anno scorso. Bravo!*'

'*Grazie,*' Philip smiled.

A woman was clutching his arm, '*Sarebbe possibile cenare insieme?*'

Philip shook his head. '*Ma non credo che sarai impossibile.*'

To Lara, it seemed to go on for ever. Finally, Philip made his way over to Lara and whispered, 'Let's get out of here.'

'Si!' Lara grinned.

They went to Biffy, the restaurant in the opera house, and the moment they walked in, the patrons, dressed in black-tie for the concert, rose to their feet and began applauding. The maître d' led Philip and Lara toward a table in the centre of the room. 'It's such an honour to have you with us, Mr Adler.'

A complimentary bottle of champagne arrived and they drank a toast.

'To us,' Philip said warmly.

'To us.'

Philip ordered two of the specialities of the house, *Osso Buco* and *Penne all' Arrabbiata*. All during supper they talked, and it was as though they had known each other for ever.

They were constantly interrupted by people coming up to the table to compliment Philip, and to ask for autographs.

It's always like this, isn't it?' Lara asked.

Philip shrugged. 'It goes with the territory. For every two hours you spend on stage, you spend countless more signing autographs or giving interviews.'

As if to punctuate what he was saying, he stopped to sign another autograph.

'You've made this tour wonderful for me.' Philip sighed. 'The bad news is that I have to leave for Venice tomorrow. I'm going to miss you a lot.'

'I've never been to Venice,' Lara said.

Lara's jet was waiting for them at Linate Airport. When they arrived there, Philip looked at the huge jet in astonishment.

'This is *your* plane?'

'Yes. It's going to take us to Venice.'

'You're going to spoil me, lady.'

Lara said softly, 'I intend to.'

They landed at Marco Polo Airport in Venice thirty-five minutes later, where a limousine waited to drive them the short distance to the dock. From the dock they would take a motorboat to the island of Giudecca, where the Cipriani Hotel was located.

'I arranged for two suites for us,' Lara said. 'I thought it would be more discreet that way.'

In the motorboat on the way to the hotel, Lara asked, 'How long will we be here?'

'Only one night, I'm afraid. I'm giving a recital at La Fenice, and then we head for Vienna.'

The 'we' gave Lara a little thrill. They had discussed it the night before. 'I'd like you to stay with me as long as you can,' Philip had said, 'but are you sure I'm not keeping you from something more important?'

'There *is* nothing more important.'

'Are you going to be all right by yourself this afternoon? I'm going to be busy rehearsing.'

'I'll be fine,' Lara assured him.

After they had checked into their suites, Philip took Lara in his arms. 'I have to go to the theatre now, but there's a lot to see here. Enjoy Venice. I'll see you later this afternoon.' They kissed. It was meant to be a brief one, but it turned into a long, lingering kiss. 'I'd better get out of here while I can,' Philip murmured, 'or I'll never be able to make it through the lobby.'

'Happy rehearsal,' Lara grinned.

And Philip was gone.

Lara telephoned Howard Keller.

'Where are you?' Keller demanded. 'I've been trying to reach you.'

'I'm in Venice.'

There was a pause. 'Are we buying a canal?'

'I'm checking it out,' Lara laughed.

'You really should be back here,' Keller said. 'There's a lot going on. Young Frank Rose brought in some new plans. I like them, but I need your approval so we can get . . .'

'If you like them,' Lara interrupted, 'go ahead.'

'You don't want to see them?' Keller's voice was filled with surprise.

'Not now, Howard.'

'All right. And on the negotiations for the West Side property, I need your okay to . . .'

'You have it.'

'Lara . . . are you feeling all right?'

'I've never felt better in my life.'

'When are you coming home?'

'I don't know. I'll stay in touch. Goodbye, Howard.'

Venice was the kind of magical city that Prospero might have created. Lara spent the rest of the morning and all afternoon exploring. She roamed through San Marco Square, and visited the Doges' Palace and the Bell Tower, and wandered along the crowded Riva degli Schiavoni, and everywhere she went she thought of Philip. She walked through the winding little side streets, crammed with jewellery shops and leather goods and restaurants, and stopped to buy expensive sweaters and scarves and lingerie for the secretaries at the office, and wallets and ties for Keller and some of the other men. She stopped in at a jeweller's to buy Philip a Piaget watch with a gold band.

'Would you please inscribe it "To Philip with Love from Lara"?' Just saying his name made her miss him.

When Philip returned to the hotel, they had coffee in the verdant garden of the Cipriani.

Lara looked across at Philip and thought, *What a perfect place this would be for a honeymoon.*

'I have a present for you,' Lara said. She handed him the box with the watch in it.

He opened it, and stared. 'My God! This must have cost a fortune. You shouldn't have, Lara.'

'Don't you like it?'

'Of course I do. It's beautiful, but . . .'

'Ssh! Wear it and think of me.'

310

'I don't need this to think of you, but thank you.'

'What time do we have to leave for the theatre?' Lara asked.

'Seven o'clock.'

Lara glanced at Philip's new watch, and said innocently, 'That gives us two hours.'

The theatre was packed. The audience was volatile, applauding and cheering each number.

When the concert was over, Lara went back to the green room to join Philip. It was London and Amsterdam and Milan all over again, and the women seemed even more nubile and eager. There were at least half a dozen beautiful women in the room, and Lara wondered which one Philip would have spent the night with if she were not there.

They had supper at the storied Harry's Bar and were warmly greeted by the affable owner, Arrigo Cipriano.

'What a pleasure to see you, *signore*. And *signorina*. Please!'

He led them to a corner table. They ordered *Bellinis*, the speciality of the house. Philip said to Lara, 'I recommend starting with the *Pasta Fagiole*. It's the best in the world.'

Later, Philip had no memory of what he had eaten for dinner. He was mesmerized by Lara. He knew he was falling in love with her and it terrified him. *I can't make a commitment*, he thought. *It's impossible. I'm a nomad*. He hated to think about the moment when she would leave him to go back to New York. He wanted to prolong their evening as long as possible.

When they had finished supper, Philip said, 'There's a casino out on the Lido. Do you gamble?'

Lara laughed aloud.

'What's so funny?'

Lara thought about the hundreds of millions of dollars she gambled on her buildings. 'Nothing,' she said. 'I'd love to go.'

They took a motorboat to Lido Island. They walked past the Excelsior Hotel and went over to the huge white building that housed the casino. It was filled with eager gamblers.

'Dreamers,' Philip said.

Philip played roulette, and within half an hour, had won two thousand dollars. He turned to Lara. 'I've never won before. You're my good luck charm.'

They played until 3 a.m., and by that time they were hungry again.

A motorboat took them back to San Marco Square, and they wandered through the side streets until they came to the Cantina Do Mori.

'This is one of the best *Bacaros* in Venice,' Philip said.

Lara said, 'I believe you. What's a *Bacaro*?'

'It's a wine bar where they serve *Cicchetti Tapas* – little nibbles of local delicacies.'

Bottle-glass doors led to a dark, narrow space where copper pots hung from the ceiling and dishes gleamed on a long banquette.

It was dawn before they got back to their hotel. They got undressed and Lara said, 'Speaking of nibbles . . .'

*

Early the following morning, Lara and Philip flew to Vienna.

'Going to Vienna is like going into another century,' Philip explained. 'There's a legend that airline pilots say, "Ladies and gentlemen, we're on our final approach to Vienna Airport. Please make sure your seatbacks and table trays are in the upright position, refrain from smoking until inside the terminal, and set your watches back one hundred years."'

Lara laughed.

'My parents were born here. They used to talk about the old days, and it made me envious.'

They were driving along the Ringstrasse and Philip was filled with excitement, like a small boy eager to share his treasures with her.

'Vienna is the city of Mozart, Haydn, Beethoven, Brahms.' He looked at Lara and grinned. 'Oh, I forgot – you're an expert on classical music.'

They checked into the Imperial Hotel.

'I have to go to the concert hall,' Philip told Lara, 'but I've decided that tomorrow we're going to take the whole day off. I'm going to show you Vienna.'

'I'd like that, Philip.'

He held Lara in his arms. 'I wish we had more time now,' he said ruefully.

'So do I.'

He kissed her lightly on the forehead. 'We'll make up for it tonight.'

She held him close. 'Promises, promises.'

The concert that evening took place at the *Musikverein*. The recital consisted of compositions by Chopin,

Schumann and Prokofiev, and it was another triumph for Philip.

The green room was packed again, but this time the language was German.

'Sie waren wunderbar, Herr Adler!'

Philip smiled. *'Das ist sehr nett von ihnen. Danke.'*

'Ich bin ein grosser Anhänger von ihner.'

Philip smiled again. *'Sie sind sehr freundlich.'*

He was talking to them, but he could not take his eyes off Lara.

After the recital, Lara and Philip had a late supper in the hotel. They were greeted by the maître.

'What an honour!' he exclaimed. 'I was at the concert tonight. You were magnificent! Magnificent!'

'You're very kind,' Philip said modestly.

The dinner was delicious, but they were both too excited by each other to eat. When the waiter asked, 'Would you like some dessert?' Philip said quickly, 'Yes.' And he was looking at Lara.

His instincts told him that something was wrong. She had never been gone this long without telling him where she was. Was she deliberately avoiding him? If she was, there could be only one reason. *And I can't allow that*, Paul Martin thought.

A beam of pale moonlight streamed through the window, making soft shadows on the ceiling. Lara and Philip lay in bed, naked, watching their shadows move above their heads. The ripple of the curtains made the shadows dance, in a soft swaying motion. The shadows came slowly together and separated and came together again, until the two became entwined, became one, and the movement of the dance became faster, and faster, a wild, savage pounding, and suddenly it stopped, and there was only the gentle ripple of the curtains.

Early the following morning, Philip said, 'We have a whole day and an evening here. I have a lot to show you.'

They had breakfast downstairs in the hotel dining room, then walked over to the Kärtner Strasse, where no cars were permitted. The shops there were filled with beautiful clothes and jewellery and antiques.

Philip hired a horse-drawn *Fiaker*, and they rode through the wide streets of the city along the Ring Road. They visited Schönbrunn Palace, and looked at the colourful Imperial Coach collection. In the afternoon they got tickets for the Spanish Riding School, and saw the Lipizzaner stallions. They rode the huge ferris wheel at the Prater, and afterward Philip said, 'Now we're going to sin!'

'Ooh!'

'No,' Philip laughed. 'I had something else in mind.'

He took Lara to Demel's for their incomparable pastry and coffee.

Lara was fascinated by the mix of architecture in Vienna: Beautiful Baroque buildings centuries old, that faced neo-modern buildings.

Philip was interested in the composers. 'Did you

know that Franz Schubert started as a singer here, Lara? He was in the Imperial Chapel choir, and when his voice changed at seventeen, he was thrown out. That's when he decided to compose music.'

They had a leisurely dinner at a small bistro, and stopped at a wine tavern in Grinzing. Afterward, Philip said, 'Would you like to go for a cruise on the Danube?'

'I'd love to.'

It was a perfect night, with a bright full moon and a soft summer breeze. The stars were shining down.

They're shining down on us, Lara thought, *because we're so happy*. Lara and Philip boarded one of the cruise ships, and from the ship's loudspeaker system came the soft strains of 'The Blue Danube'. In the distance, they saw a falling star.

'Quick! Make a wish,' Philip said.

Lara closed her eyes and was silent for a moment.

'Did you make your wish?'

'Yes.'

'What did you wish for?'

Lara looked up at him and said seriously. 'I can't tell you, or it won't come true.' *I'm going to make it come true*, Lara thought.

Philip leaned back and smiled at Lara. 'This is perfect, isn't it?'

'It can always be this way, Philip.'

'What do you mean?'

'We could get married.'

And there it was, out in the open. He had been thinking of nothing else for the past few days. He was deeply in love with Lara, but he knew he could not make a commitment to her.

316

'Lara, that's impossible.'

'Is it? Why?'

'I've explained it to you, darling. I'm almost always on tour like this. You couldn't travel with me all the time, could you?'

'No,' Lara said, 'but . . .'

'There you are. It would never work. Tomorrow in Paris, I'll show you . . .'

'I'm not going to Paris with you, Philip.'

He thought he had misunderstood her. 'What?'

Lara took a deep breath. 'I'm not going to see you again.'

It was like a blow to the stomach. 'Why? I love you, Lara. I . . .'

'And I love you. But I'm not a groupie. I don't want to be just another one of your fans, chasing you around. You can have all of those you want.'

'Lara, I don't want anyone but you. But don't you see, darling, our marriage could never work. We have separate lives that are important to both of us. I would want us to be together all the time, and we couldn't be.'

'That's it then, isn't it?' Lara said tightly. 'I won't see you again, Philip.'

'Wait. Please! Let's talk about this. Let's go to your room, and . . .'

'No, Philip. I love you very much, but I won't go on like this. It's over.'

'I don't want it to be over,' Philip insisted. 'Change your mind.'

'I can't. I'm sorry. It's all or nothing.'

They were silent the rest of the way back to their hotel. When they reached the lobby, Philip said,

'Why don't I come up to your room? We can talk about this and . . .'

'No, my darling. There's nothing more to talk about.'

He watched Lara get into the elevator and disappear.

When Lara reached her suite, the telephone was ringing. She hurried to pick it up. 'Philip . . .'

'It's Howard. I've been trying to reach you all day.'

She managed to hide her disappointment. 'Is anything wrong?'

'No. Just checking in. There's a lot going on around here. When do you think you'll be coming back?'

'Tomorrow,' Lara said. 'I'll be back in New York tomorrow.' Slowly, Lara replaced the receiver.

She sat there, staring at the telephone, willing it to ring. Two hours later, it was still silent. *I made a mistake*, Lara thought miserably. *I gave him an ultimatum, and I lost him. If I had only waited . . . If only I had gone to Paris with him . . . if . . . if . . .* She tried to visualize her life without Philip. It was too painful to think about. *But we can't go on this way*, Lara thought. *I want us to belong to each other.* Tomorrow she would have to return to New York.

Lara lay down on the couch, fully dressed, the telephone by her side. She felt drained. She knew it would be impossible to get any sleep.

She slept.

In his room, Philip was pacing back and forth like a caged animal. He was furious with Lara, furious with himself. He could not bear the thought of not seeing her again, not holding her in his arms. *Damn all women!* he thought. His parents had warned him. *Your life is music. If you want to be the best, there's no room for anything else.* And until he met Lara, he had believed it. But now, everything had changed. *Damn it! What we had was wonderful. Why did she have to destroy it?* He loved her, but he knew he could never marry her.

Lara was awakened by the ringing of the telephone. She sat up on the couch, groggy, and looked at the clock on the wall. It was five o'clock in the morning. Sleepily, Lara picked up the telephone.

'Howard?'

It was Philip's voice. 'How would you like to get married in Paris?'

The marriage of Lara Cameron to Philip Adler made headlines around the world. When Howard Keller heard the news, he went out and got drunk for the first time in his life. He had kept telling himself that Lara's infatuation with Philip Adler would pass. *Lara and I are a team. We belong together. No one can come between us.* He stayed drunk for two days and when he sobered up, he telephoned Lara in Paris.

'If it's true,' he said, 'tell Philip I said he's the luckiest man who ever lived.'

'It's true,' Lara assured him brightly.

'You sound happy.'

'I've never been happier in my life!'

'I . . . I'm pleased for you, Lara. When are you coming home?'

'Philip is giving a concert in London tomorrow, and then we'll be back in New York.'

'Did you talk to Paul Martin before the wedding?'

She hesitated. 'No.'

'Don't you think you should do it now?'

'Yes, of course.' She had been more concerned about that than she wanted to admit to herself. She was not sure how he was going to take the news of her marriage. 'I'll talk to him when I get back.'

'I'll sure be glad to see you. I miss you.'

'I miss you, too, Howard.' And it was true. He was very dear. He had always been a good and loyal friend. *I don't know what I would have done without him*, Lara thought.

When the 727 taxied up to the Butler Aviation terminal at New York's La Guardia airport, the press was there in full force. There were newspaper reporters and television cameras.

The airport manager led Lara and Philip into the reception office. 'I can sneak you out of here,' he said, 'or . . .'

Lara turned to Philip. 'Let's get this over with, darling. Otherwise, they'll never let us have any peace.'

'You're probably right.'

The press conference lasted for two hours. 'Where did you two meet . . . ?'

'Have you always been interested in classical music, Mrs Adler . . . ?'

'How long have you known each other . . . ?'

'Are you going to live in New York . . . ?'

'Will you give up your touring, Mr Adler . . . ?'

Finally, it was over.

There were two limousines waiting for them. The second one was for luggage.

'I'm not used to travelling in this kind of style,' Philip said.

Lara laughed. 'You'll get used to it.'

When they were in the limousine, Philip asked, 'Where are we going? I have an apartment on Fifty-Seventh Street . . .'

'I think you might be more comfortable at my

place, darling. Look it over, and if you like it, we'll have your things moved in.'

They arrived at the Cameron Plaza. Philip looked up at the huge building.

'You *own* this?'

'A few banks and I.'

'I'm impressed.'

Lara squeezed his arm. 'Good. I want you to be.'

The lobby had been freshly decorated with flowers. Half a dozen employees were waiting to greet them.

'Welcome home, Mrs Adler, Mr Adler.'

Philip looked around, and said, 'My God! All this is yours?'

'*Ours*, sweetheart.'

The elevator took them up to the penthouse. It covered the whole forty-fifth floor. The door was opened by the butler.

'Welcome home, Mrs Adler.'

'Thank you, Simms.'

Lara introduced Philip to the rest of the staff and showed him through the duplex penthouse. There was a large white drawing room, filled with antiques, a large enclosed terrace, a dining room, four master bedrooms and three staff bedrooms, six bathrooms, a kitchen, a library, and an office.

'Do you think you could be comfortable here, darling?' Lara asked.

Philip grinned. 'It's a little small – but I'll manage.'

In the middle of the drawing room was a beautiful new Bechstein piano. Philip walked over to it and ran his fingers over the keys.

'It's wonderful!' he said.

322

Lara moved to his side. 'It's your wedding present.'

'Really?' He was touched. He sat down at the piano, and began to play.

'I just had it tuned for you.' Lara listened as the cascade of notes filled the room. 'Do you like it?'

'I love it! Thank you, Lara.'

'You can play here to your heart's content.'

Philip rose from the piano bench. 'I'd better give Ellerbee a call,' Philip said. 'He's been trying to reach me.'

'There's a telephone in the library, darling.'

Lara went into her office and turned on the answering machine. There were half a dozen messages from Paul Martin. 'Lara, where are you? I miss you, darling' . . . 'Lara, I assume you're out of the country, or I would have heard from you' . . . 'I'm worried about you, Lara. Call me . . .' Then the tone changed. 'I just heard about your marriage. Is it true? Let's talk.'

Philip had walked into the room. 'Who's the mysterious caller?' he asked.

Lara turned. 'An . . . an old friend of mine.'

Philip walked up to her, and put his arms around her. 'Is he someone I should be jealous of?'

Lara said, softly, 'You don't have to be jealous of anyone in the world. You're the only man I've ever loved.' *And it's true*.

Philip held her closely. 'You're the only woman I've ever loved.'

Later that afternoon, while Philip sat at the piano, Lara went back into her office and returned Paul Martin's telephone calls.

He came on the line almost immediately. 'You're back.' His voice was tight.

'Yes.' She had been dreading this conversation.

'I don't mind telling you that the news was quite a shock, Lara.'

'I'm sorry, Paul . . . I . . . it happened rather suddenly.'

'It must have.'

'Yes.' She tried to read his mood.

'I thought we had something pretty good going for us. I thought it was something special.'

'It was, Paul, but . . .'

'We'd better talk about it.'

'Well, I . . .'

'Let's make it lunch tomorrow. Vitello's. One o'clock.' It was an order.

Lara hesitated. It would be foolish to antagonize him any further. 'All right, Paul. I'll be there.'

The line went dead. Lara sat there worried. How angry was Paul, and was he going to do anything about it?

The following morning when Lara arrived at Cameron Center, the entire staff was waiting to congratulate her.

'It's wonderful news!'

'It was such a big surprise to all of us!'

'I'm sure you'll be very happy . . .'

And on it went.

Howard Keller was waiting in Lara's office for her. He gave her a big hug. 'For a lady who doesn't like classical music, you sure went and did it!'

Lara smiled. 'I did, didn't I?'

'I'll have to get used to calling you Mrs Adler.'

Lara's smile faded. 'I think it might be better, for business reasons, if I keep using Cameron, don't you?'

'Whatever you say. I'm sure glad you're back. Everything is piling up here.'

Lara settled in a chair opposite Howard. 'Okay, tell me what's been happening.'

'Well, the West Side hotel is going to be a money losing proposition. We have a buyer lined up from Texas who's interested in it, but I went over to the hotel yesterday. It's in terrible shape. It needs a complete refurbishing, and that's going to run into five or six million dollars.'

'Has the buyer seen it yet?'

'No. I told him I'd show it to him tomorrow.'

'Show it to him next week. Get some painters in there. Make it look squeaky clean. Arrange for a crowd to be in the lobby when he's there.'

He grinned. 'Right. Frank Rose is here with some new sketches. He's waiting in my office.'

'I'll take a look at them.'

'The Midland Insurance Company that was going into the new building?'

'Yes.'

'They haven't signed the deal yet. They're a little shaky.'

Lara made a note. 'I'll talk to them about it. Next?'

'Gotham Bank's seventy-five million loan on the new project?'

'Yes?'

'They're pulling back. They think you're getting over-extended.'

'How much interest were they going to charge us?'

'Seventeen per cent.'

'Set up a meeting with them. We're going to offer to pay twenty per cent.'

He was looking at her, aghast. 'Twenty per cent? My God, Lara! No one pays twenty per cent.'

'I would rather be alive at twenty per cent than dead at seventeen per cent. Do it, Howard.'

'All right.'

The morning went by swiftly. At twelve thirty, Lara said, 'I'm going to meet Paul Martin for lunch.'

Howard looked worried. 'Make sure you aren't lunch.'

'What do you mean?'

'I mean he's Sicilian. They don't forgive and they don't forget.'

326

'You're being melodramatic. Paul would never do anything to harm me.'

'I hope you're right.'

Paul Martin was waiting for Lara at the restaurant when she arrived. He looked thin and haggard, and there were circles under his eyes, as though he had not been sleeping well.

'Hello, Lara.' He did not get up.

'Paul.' She sat down across from him.

'I left some stupid messages on your answering machine. I'm sorry. I had no idea . . .' He shrugged.

'I should have let you know, Paul, but it all happened so fast.'

'Yeah.' He was studying her face. 'You're looking great.'

'Thank you.'

'Where did you meet Adler?'

'In London.'

'And you fell in love with him just like that?' There was a bitter undertone to his words.

'Paul, what you and I had was wonderful, but it wasn't enough for me. I needed something more than that. I needed someone to come home to every night.'

He was listening, watching her.

'I would never do anything in the world to hurt you, but this just . . . just happened.'

More silence.

'Please understand.'

'Yeah.' A wintry smile crossed his face. 'I guess I have no choice, have I? What's done is done. It was just kind of a shock to read about it in the newspapers and see it on television. I thought we were closer than that.'

'You're right,' Lara said again. 'I should have told you.'

His hand reached out and caressed her chin. 'I was crazy about you, Lara. I guess I still am. You were my *miracolo*. I could have given you anything in the world you wanted except what he could give you – a wedding ring. I love you enough to want you to be happy.'

Lara felt a wave of relief sweep through her. 'Thank you, Paul.'

'When am I going to meet your husband?'

'We're giving a party next week for our friends. Will you come?'

'I'll be there. You tell him that he had better treat you right, or he'll have to answer to me.'

Lara smiled. 'I'll tell him.'

When Lara returned to her office, Howard Keller was waiting for her. 'How did the luncheon go?' he asked nervously.

'Fine. You were wrong about Paul. He behaved beautifully.'

'Good. I'm glad I was wrong. Tomorrow morning I've set up some meetings for you with . . .'

'Cancel them,' Lara said. 'I'm staying home with my husband tomorrow. We're honeymooning for the next few days.'

'I'm glad you're so happy,' Howard said.

'Howard, I'm so happy it scares me. I'm afraid that I'll wake up and find this is all a dream. I never knew anyone could be this happy.'

He smiled. 'All right, I'll handle the meetings.'

'Thank you.' She kissed him on the cheek. 'Philip and I are giving a party next week. We expect you there.'

The party took place the following Saturday at the penthouse. There was a lavish buffet, and more than a hundred guests. Lara had invited the men and women she worked with: Bankers, builders, architects, construction chiefs, city officials, the zoning commissioner, and the heads of unions. Philip had invited his musician friends and music patrons and benefactors. The combination proved to be disastrous.

It wasn't that the two groups did not *try* to mix. The problem was that most of them had nothing in common. The builders were interested in construction and architecture, and the musicians were interested in music and composers.

Lara introduced the zoning commissioner to a group of musicians. The commissioner stood there, trying to follow the discussion.

'Do you know what Rossini felt about Wagner's music? One day, he sat his ass on the piano keys and said, "That's what Wagner sounds like to me."'

'Wagner deserved it. When a fire broke out at the Ring Theatre in Vienna during a performance of *The Tales of Hoffmann*, four hundred people burned to death. When Wagner heard about it he said, "That's what they get for listening to an Offenbach operetta."'

The commissioner hastily moved on.

Lara introduced some of Philip's friends to a group of real estate men.

'The problem,' one of the men said, 'is that you need thirty-five per cent of the tenants signed up before you can go co-op.'

'If you want my opinion, that's a pretty stupid rule.'

'I agree. I'm switching to hotels. Do you know the hotels in Manhattan now are averaging two hundred dollars a room per night? Next year . . .'

The musicians moved on.

Conversations seemed to be going on in two different languages.

'The trouble with the Viennese is that they love dead composers . . .'

'There's a new hotel going up on two parcels, between Forty-Seventh and Forty-Eighth Streets. Chase Manhattan is financing it . . .'

'He might not be the greatest conductor in the world, but his stick technique is *genau* . . .'

'. . . I remember a lot of the mavens said that the 1929 stock market crash wasn't a bad thing. It would teach people to put their money in real estate . . .'

'. . . and Horowitz wouldn't play for years because he thought his fingers were made of glass . . .'

'. . . I've seen the plans. There's going to be a classic base rising from three floors from Eighth Avenue, and inside an elliptical arcade with lobbies on three sides . . .'

'. . . Einstein loved the piano. He used to play with Rubenstein, but Einstein kept playing off beat. Finally, Rubenstein couldn't stand it any more and he yelled, "Albert, can't you count?"'

'. . . Congress must have been drunk to pass the Tax Reform Act. It's going to cripple the building industry . . .'

'. . . And at the end of the evening when Brahms left the party he said, "If there's anyone here I've forgotten to insult, I apologize."'

The Tower of Babel.

Paul Martin arrived alone and Lara hurried over to the door to greet him. 'I'm so glad you could come, Paul.'

'I wouldn't have missed it.' He looked around the room. 'I want to meet Philip.'

Lara took him over to where Philip was standing with a group. 'Philip, this is an old friend of mine, Paul Martin.'

Philip held out his hand. 'I'm pleased to meet you.'

The two men shook hands.

'You're a lucky man, Mr Adler. Lara's a remarkable woman.'

'That's what I keep telling him,' Lara smiled.

'She doesn't have to tell me,' Philip said. 'I know how lucky I am.'

Paul was studying him. 'Do you?'

Lara could feel the sudden tension in the air. 'Let me get you a cocktail,' she said to Paul.

'No, thanks. Remember? I don't drink.'

Lara bit her lip. 'Of course. Let me introduce you to some people.' She escorted him around the room, introducing him to some of the guests.

One of the musicians was saying, 'Leon Fleisher is giving a recital tomorrow night. I wouldn't miss it for the world.' He turned to Paul Martin, who was standing next to Howard Keller. 'Have you heard him play?'

'No.'

'He's remarkable. He plays only with his left hand, of course.'

Paul Martin was puzzled. 'Why would he do that?'

'Fleisher developed carpal-tunnel syndrome in his right hand about ten years ago.'

'But how can he give a recital with one hand?'

'Half a dozen composers wrote concertos for the left hand. There's one by Demuth, Franz Schmidt, Korngold, and a beautiful concerto by Ravel.'

Some of the guests were asking Philip to play for them.

'All right. This is for my bride.' He sat down at the piano and began to play a theme from a Rachmaninoff piano concerto. The room was hushed. Everyone seemed mesmerized by the lovely strains that filled the penthouse. When Philip rose, there was loud applause.

An hour later, the party began to break up. When they had seen the last guest to the door, Philip said, 'That was quite a party.'

'You hate big parties, don't you?' Lara said.

Philip took her in his arms and grinned. 'Did it show?'

'We'll only do this every ten years,' Lara promised. 'Philip, did you have a feeling that our guests were from two different planets?'

He put his lips to her cheek. 'It doesn't matter. We have our own planet. Let's make it spin . . .'

In order to spend more time with Philip, Lara decided to work at home in the mornings.

'I want us to be together as much as possible,' she told Philip.

Lara asked Kathy to arrange for some secretaries to be interviewed at the penthouse. Lara talked to half a dozen before Marian Bell appeared. She was in her middle twenties with soft, blonde hair, attractive features, and a warm personality.

'Sit down,' Lara said.

'Thank you.'

Lara was looking over her résumé. 'You were graduated from Wellesley College?'

'Yes.'

'And you have a BA. Why do you want a job as a secretary?'

'I think I can learn a lot working for you. Whether I get this job or not, I'm a big fan of yours, Miss Cameron.'

'Really? Why?'

'You're my role model. You've accomplished a lot, and you've done it on your own.'

Lara was studying the girl. 'This job would mean long hours. I get up early. You'd be working at my apartment. You'd start at six in the morning.'

'That wouldn't be a problem. I'm a hard worker.'

Lara smiled. She liked the girl. 'I'll give you a one-week trial,' she said.

By the end of the week, Lara knew that she had found a jewel. Marian was capable and intelligent and pleasant. Gradually, a routine was established. Unless there was an emergency, Lara spent the mornings working at the apartment. In the afternoon, she would go to the office.

Each morning, Lara and Philip had breakfast together and afterward Philip would go to the piano and sit in a sleeveless athletic shirt and jeans and practise for two or three hours while Lara went into her office and dictated to Marian. Sometimes Philip would play old Scottish tunes for Lara: 'Annie Laurie', and 'Comin' through the Rye'. She was touched. They would have lunch together.

'Tell me what your life was like in Glace Bay,' Philip said.

'It would take at least five minutes,' Lara smiled.

'No, I'm serious. I really want to know.'

She talked about the boarding house, but she could not bring herself to talk about her father. She told Philip the story of Charles Cohn, and Philip said, 'Good for him. I'd like to meet him one day.'

'I'm sure you will.'

Lara told him about her experience with Sean MacAllister, and Philip said, 'That bastard! I'd like to kill him!' He held Lara close and said, 'No one is ever going to hurt you again.'

*

Philip was working on a concerto. She would hear him play three notes at a time, over and over and then move on, practising slowly and picking up the tempo until the different phrases finally flowed into one.

In the beginning, Lara would walk into the drawing room while Philip was playing and interrupt him.

'Darling, we're invited to Long Island for the weekend. Would you like to go?'

Or, 'I have theatre tickets for the new Neil Simon play.'

Or, 'Howard Keller would like to take us out to dinner Saturday night.'

Philip had tried to be patient. Finally he said, 'Lara, please don't interrupt me while I'm at the piano. It breaks my concentration.'

'I'm sorry,' Lara said. 'But I don't understand why you practise every day. You're not giving a concert now.'

'I practise every day so I *can* give a concert. You see, my darling, when you put up a building and a mistake is made, it can be corrected. You can change the plans or you can redo the plumbing or the lighting or whatever. But at a recital, there is no second chance. You're live in front of an audience and every note has to be perfect.'

'I'm sorry,' Lara apologized. 'I understand.'

Philip took her in his arms. 'There's the old joke about a man in New York carrying a violin case. He was lost. He stopped a stranger and said, "How do you get to Carnegie Hall?" "Practise," the stranger said, "practise."'

Lara laughed. 'Go back to your piano. I'll leave you alone.'

She sat in her office listening to the faint strains of Philip playing and she thought, *I'm so lucky. Thousands of women would envy me sitting here listening to Philip Adler play.*

She just wished he did not have to practise so often.

They both enjoyed playing backgammon, and in the evening, after dinner, they would sit in front of the fireplace and have mock-fierce contests. Lara treasured those moments of being alone with him.

The Reno casino was getting ready to open. Six months earlier, Lara had had a meeting with Jerry Townsend. 'I want them to read about this opening in Timbuktu,' Lara said. 'I'm flying in the chef from Maxim's for the opening. I want you to get me the hottest talent available. Start with Frank Sinatra and work your way down. I want the invitation list to include the top names in Hollywood, New York and Washington. I want people fighting to get on that list.'

Now, as Lara looked it over, she said, 'You've done a good job. How many turn-downs have we had?'

'A couple dozen,' Townsend said. 'That's not bad from a list of six hundred.'

'Not bad at all,' Lara agreed.

*

Keller telephoned Lara in the morning. 'Good news,' he said. 'I got a call from the Swiss bankers. They're flying in to meet with you tomorrow to discuss the joint venture.'

'Great,' Lara said. 'Nine o'clock, my office.'

'I'll set it up.'

At dinner that evening, Philip said, 'Lara, I'm doing a recording session tomorrow. You've never been to one, have you?'

'No.'

'Would you like to come and watch?'

Lara hesitated, thinking about the meeting with the Swiss. 'Of course,' she said.

Lara telephoned Keller. 'Start the meeting without me. I'll get there as soon as I can.'

The recording studio was located on West 34th Street, in a large warehouse filled with electronic equipment. There were a hundred and thirty musicians seated in the room and a glass-enclosed control booth where the sound engineers worked. It seemed to Lara that the recording was going very slowly. They kept stopping and starting again. During one of the breaks she telephoned Keller.

'Where are you?' he demanded. 'I'm stalling, but they want to talk to you.'

'I'll be there in an hour or two,' she said. 'Keep them talking.'

Two hours later, the recording session was still going on.

Lara telephoned Keller again.

'I'm sorry, Howard, I can't leave. Have them come back tomorrow.'

'What's so important?' Keller demanded.

'My husband,' Lara said. And she replaced the receiver.

When they returned to the apartment, Lara said, 'We're going to Reno next week.'

'What's in Reno?'

'It's the opening of the hotel and casino. We'll fly down on Wednesday.'

Philip's voice was filled with distress. 'Damn!'

'What's the matter?'

'I'm sorry, darling, I can't.'

She was staring at him. 'What do you mean?'

'I thought I had mentioned it. I'm leaving on a tour on Monday.'

'What are you talking about?'

'Ellerbee has booked me on a six-week tour. I'm going to Australia and . . .'

'*Australia?*'

'Yes. Then Japan and Hong Kong.'

'You can't, Philip. I mean . . . why are you doing this? You don't have to. I want to be with you.'

'Well, come with me, Lara. I'd love that.'

'You know I can't. Not now. There's too much happening here,' Lara said miserably, 'I don't want you to leave me.'

'I don't want to. But darling, I warned you before we were married that this is what my life is about.'

'I know,' Lara said, 'but that was before. Now it's different. Everything has changed.'

'Nothing has changed,' Philip said gently, 'except

338

that I'm absolutely crazy about you and when I go away I'll miss you like the devil.'

There was nothing Lara could say to that.

Philip was gone, and Lara had never known such loneliness. In the middle of a meeting, she would suddenly think about Philip and her heart would melt.

She wanted him to go on with his career, but she needed him with her. She thought of the wonderful times they had had together, and of his arms around her, and his warmth and gentleness. She had never known she could love anyone so much. Philip telephoned her every day, but somehow it made the loneliness worse.

'Where are you, darling?'

'I'm still in Tokyo.'

'How's the tour going?'

'Beautifully. I miss you.'

'I miss you, too.' Lara could not tell him how much she missed him.

'I leave for Hong Kong tomorrow and then . . .'

'I wish you'd come home.' She regretted it the moment she said it.

'You know I can't.'

There was a silence. 'Of course not.'

They talked for half an hour and when Lara put the receiver down she was lonelier than ever. The time differences were maddening. Sometimes her Tuesday would be his Wednesday, and he would call in the middle of the night or in the early hours of the morning.

'How's Philip?' Keller asked.

'Fine. Why does he do it, Howard?'

'Why does he do what?'

'This tour of his. He doesn't have to do it. I mean, he certainly doesn't need the money.'

'Whoa. I'm sure he's not doing it for the money. It's what he *does*, Lara.'

The same words that Philip had used. She understood it intellectually, but not emotionally.

'Lara,' Keller said, 'you only married the man – you don't own him.'

'I don't want to own him. I was just hoping that I was more important to him than . . .' She stopped herself in mid-sentence. 'Never mind. I know I'm being silly.'

Lara telephoned William Ellerbee.

'Are you free for lunch today?' Lara asked.

'I can make myself free,' Ellerbee said. 'Is anything wrong?'

'No, no. I just thought we should have a talk.'

They met at Le Cirque.

'Have you talked to Philip lately?' Ellerbee asked.

'I talk to him every day.'

'He's having a successful tour.'

'Yes.'

Ellerbee said, 'Frankly, I never thought Philip would get married. He's like a priest – dedicated to what he does.'

'I know . . .' Lara hesitated, '. . . but don't you think he's travelling too much?'

'I don't understand.'

'Philip has a home now. There's no reason for

him to be running all over the world.' She saw the expression on Ellerbee's face. 'Oh, I don't mean he should just stay in New York. I'm sure you could arrange concerts for him in Boston, Chicago, Los Angeles. You know . . . where he wouldn't have to travel so far from home.'

Ellerbee said carefully, 'Have you discussed this with Philip?'

'No. I wanted to talk to you first. It *would* be possible, wouldn't it? I mean, Philip doesn't need the money, not any more.'

'Mrs Adler, Philip makes thirty-five thousand dollars a performance. Last year he was on tour for forty weeks.'

'I understand, but . . .'

'Do you have any idea how few pianists make it to the top, or how hard they have to struggle to get there? There are thousands of pianists out there, playing their fingers to the bone, and there are only about four or five superstars. Your husband is one of them. You don't know much about the concert world. The competition is murderous. You can go to a recital and see a soloist on the stage dressed in tails, looking prosperous and glamorous, but when he gets off that stage, he can barely afford to pay his rent or buy a decent meal. It took Philip a long time to become a world class pianist. Now you're asking me to take that away from him.'

'No, I'm not. I'm merely suggesting . . .'

'What you're suggesting would destroy his career. You don't really want to do that, do you?'

'Of course not,' Lara said. She hesitated. 'I understand that you get fifteen per cent of what Philip earns.'

341

'That's right.'

'I wouldn't want you to lose anything if Philip gave fewer concerts,' Lara said carefully. 'I'd be glad to make up the difference and . . .'

'Mrs Adler, I think this is something you should discuss with Philip. Shall we order?'

27

Liz Smith's column read:

IRON BUTTERFLY ABOUT TO GET HER WINGS CLIPPED

What beautiful real estate tycoon is about to hit her penthouse roof when she learns that a book about her, written by a former employee, is going to be published by Candlelight Press? The word is that it's going to be hot! Hot! Hot!

Lara slammed the newspaper down. It had to be Gertrude Meeks, the secretary she had fired! Lara sent for Jerry Townsend. 'Have you seen Liz Smith's column this morning?'

'Yes, I just read it. There isn't much we can do about it, boss. If you . . .'

'There's a lot we can do. All my employees sign an agreement that they will not write anything about me during or after their employment here. Gertrude Meeks has no right to do this. I'm going to sue the publisher for all he's worth.'

Jerry Townsend shook his head. 'I wouldn't do that.'

'Why not?'

'Because it will create a lot of unfavourable

publicity. If you let it ride, it becomes a small wind that will blow over. If you try to stop it, it will become a hurricane.'

She listened, unimpressed. 'Find out who owns the company,' Lara ordered.

One hour later, Lara was speaking on the phone to Lawrence Seinfeld, the owner and publisher of Candlelight Press.

'This is Lara Cameron. I understand you intend to publish a book about me.'

'You read the Liz Smith item, huh? Yes, it's true, Miss Cameron.'

'I want to warn you that if you publish the book, I'm going to sue you for invasion of privacy.'

The voice at the other end of the phone said, 'I think perhaps you should check with your attorney. You're a public figure, Miss Cameron. You have no right of privacy. And according to Gertrude Meeks' manuscript, you're quite a colourful character.'

'Gertrude Meeks signed a paper forbidding her to write anything about me.'

'Well, that's between you and Gertrude. You can sue her . . .'

But by then, of course, the book would be out.

'I don't want it published. If I can make it worth your while not to publish it . . .'

'Hold on. I think you're treading on dangerous ground. I would suggest that we terminate this conversation. Goodbye.' The line went dead.

Damn him! Lara sat there thinking. She sent for Howard Keller.

'What do you know about Candlelight Press?'

He shrugged. 'They're a small outfit. They do

exploitation books. They did a hatchet job on Cher, Madonna . . .'

'Thanks. That's all.'

Howard Keller had a headache. It seemed to him that he was getting a lot of headaches lately. Not enough sleep. He was under pressure and he felt that things were moving too rapidly. He had to find a way to slow Lara down. *Maybe this was a hunger headache*. He buzzed his secretary.

'Bess, order some lunch in for me, would you?'

There was a silence.

'Bess?'

'Are you joking, Mr Keller?'

'Joking? No, why?'

'You just had your lunch.'

Keller felt a chill go through him.

'But if you're still hungry . . .'

'No, no.' He remembered now. He had had a salad and a roast beef sandwich and . . . *My God*, he thought, *what's happening to me?*

'Just kidding, Bess,' he said. *Who am I kidding?*

The opening of the Cameron Palace in Reno was a smash. The hotel was fully booked, and the casino was crowded with players. Lara had spared no expense to see that the invited celebrities were well taken care of. Everyone was there. *There's only one person missing*, Lara thought. Philip. He had sent an enormous bouquet of flowers with a note: 'You're the music in my life. I adore you and miss you. Hub.'

Paul Martin arrived. He came up to Lara. 'Congratulations. You've outdone yourself.'

'Thanks to you, Paul. I couldn't have done it without you.'

He was looking around. 'Where's Philip?'

'He couldn't be here. He's on tour.'

'He's out playing piano somewhere? This is a big night for you, Lara. He should be at your side.'

Lara smiled. 'He really wanted to be.'

The manager of the hotel came up to Lara. 'This is quite a night, isn't it? The hotel is fully booked for the next three months.'

'Let's keep it that way, Donald.'

Lara had hired a Japanese and a Brazilian agent to bring in big players from abroad. She had spent a million dollars on each of the luxury suites, but it was going to pay off.

'You've got a gold mine here, Miss Cameron,' the manager said. He looked around. 'By the way, where's your husband? I've been looking forward to meeting him.'

'He couldn't be here,' Lara said. *He's out playing the piano somewhere*.

The entertainment was brilliant, but Lara was the star of the evening. Sammy Cahn had written special lyrics for *My Kind of Town*. It went, 'My Kind of Gal, Lara is . . .' She got up to make a speech, and there was enthusiastic applause. Everyone wanted to meet her, to touch her. The press was there in full force, and Lara gave interviews for television, radio and the press. It all went well until the interviewers asked, 'Where's your husband tonight?' And Lara found herself getting more and more upset. *He should have been at my side. The concert could have waited.* But she smiled sweetly and said, 'Philip was so disappointed he couldn't be here.'

When the entertainment was over, there was dancing. Paul Martin walked up to Lara's table. 'Shall we?'

Lara rose and stepped into his arms.

'How does it feel owning all this?' Paul asked.

'It feels wonderful. Thanks for all your help.'

'What are friends for? I notice that you have some heavyweight gamblers here. Be careful with them, Lara. Some of them are going to lose big, and you have to make them feel like they're winners. Get them a new car or girls or anything that will make them feel important.'

'I'll remember,' Lara said.

'It's good to hold you again,' Paul said.

'Paul . . .'

'I know. Do you remember what I said about your husband taking good care of you?'

'Yes.'

'He doesn't seem to be doing a very good job.'

'Philip wanted to be here,' Lara said defensively. And even as she said it she thought, *Did he really?*

He telephoned her late that night, and the sound of his voice made her twice as lonely.

'Lara, I've been thinking about you all day, darling. How did the opening go?'

'Wonderfully. I wish you could have been here, Philip.'

'So do I. I miss you like crazy.'

Then why aren't you here with me? 'I miss you, too. Hurry home.'

*

Howard Keller walked into Lara's office carrying a thick manila envelope.

'You're not going to like this,' Keller said.

'What's up?'

Keller laid the envelope on Lara's desk. 'This is a copy of Gertrude Meeks' manuscript. Don't ask me how I got hold of it. We could both go to jail.'

'Have you read it?'

He nodded. 'Yes.'

'And?'

'I think you'd better read it yourself. She wasn't even working here when some of these things happened. She must have done a lot of digging.'

'Thanks, Howard.'

Lara waited until he left the office, then she pressed down the key on the intercom. 'No calls.'

She opened the manuscript and began to read.

It was devastating. It was a portrait of a scheming, domineering woman who had clawed her way to the top. It depicted her temper tantrums and her imperious manner with her employees. It was mean spirited, filled with nasty little anecdotes. What the manuscript left out was Lara's independence and courage, her talent and vision and generosity. She went on reading.

'. . . One of the Iron Butterfly's tricks was to schedule her business meetings early on the first morning of negotiations so that the others were jet-lagged and Cameron was fresh.

'. . . At a meeting with the Japanese, they were served tea with Valium in it, while Lara Cameron drank coffee with Ritalin, a stimulant that speeds up the thought process.

'. . . At a meeting with some German bankers,

they were served coffee with Valium, while she drank tea with Ritalin.

'. . . When Lara Cameron was negotiating for the Queens property and the zoning commission turned her down, she got them to change their mind by making up a story that she had a young daughter who was going to live in one of the buildings . . .

'. . . When tenants refused to leave the building at the Dorchester Apartments, Lara Cameron filled it with homeless people . . .'

Nothing had been left out. When Lara finished reading it, she sat at her desk for a long time, motionless. She sent for Howard Keller.

'I want you to run a Dun and Bradstreet on Henry Seinfeld. He owns Candlelight Press.'

'Right.'

He was back fifteen minutes later. 'Seinfeld has a D-C rating.'

'Which means?'

'That's the lowest rating there is. A fourth line credit rating is poor, and he's four notches below that. A good stiff wind would blow him over. He lives from book to book. One flop and he's out of business.'

'Thanks, Howard.' She telephoned Terry Hill, her attorney.

'Terry, how would you like to be a book publisher?'

'What did you have in mind?'

'I want you to buy Candlelight Press in your name. It's owned by Henry Seinfeld.'

'That should be no problem. How much do you want to pay?'

'Try to buy him out for five hundred thousand. If

you have to, go to a million. Make sure that the deal includes all the literary properties he owns. Keep my name out of it.'

The offices of Candlelight Press were downtown in an old building on 34th Street. Henry Seinfeld's quarters consisted of a small secretarial office and a slightly larger office for himself.

Seinfeld's secretary said, 'There's a Mr Hill to see you, Mr Seinfeld.'

'Send him in.'

Terry Hill had called earlier that morning.

He walked into the shabby little office. Seinfeld was sitting behind the desk.

'What can I do for you, Mr Hill?'

'I'm representing a German publishing company that might be interested in buying your company.'

Seinfeld took his time lighting a cigar. 'My company's not for sale,' he said.

'Oh, that's too bad. We're trying to break into the American market, and we like your operation.'

'I've built this company up from scratch,' Seinfeld said. 'It's like my baby. I'd hate to part with it.'

'I understand how you feel,' the lawyer said sympathetically. 'We'd be willing to give you five hundred thousand dollars for it.'

Seinfeld almost choked on his cigar. 'Five hundred? Hell, I've got one book coming out that's going to be worth a million dollars alone. No, sir. Your offer's an insult.'

'My offer's a gift. You have no assets and you're over a hundred thousand dollars in debt. I checked.

Tell you what I'll do. I'll go up to six hundred thousand. That's my final offer.'

'I'd never forgive myself. Now, if you could see your way clear to going to seven . . .'

Terry Hill rose to his feet. 'Goodbye, Mr Seinfeld. I'll find another company.'

He started toward the door.

'Wait a minute,' Seinfeld said. 'Let's not be hasty. The fact is, my wife's been after me to retire. Maybe this would be a good time.'

Terry Hill walked over to the desk and pulled a contract out of his pocket. 'I have a cheque here for six hundred thousand dollars. Just sign where the "x" is.'

Lara sent for Keller.

'We just bought Candlelight Press.'

'Great. What do you want to do with it?'

'First of all, kill Gertrude Meeks' book. See that it doesn't get published. There are plenty of ways to keep stalling. If she sues to get her rights back, we can tie her up in court for a year.'

'Do you want to fold the company?'

'Of course not. Put someone in to run it. We'll keep it as a tax loss.'

When Keller returned to his office, he said to his secretary, 'I want to give you a letter. Jack Hellman, Hellman Realty. Dear Jack, I discussed your offer with Miss Cameron and we feel that it would be unwise to go into your venture at this time. However, we want you to know that we would be interested in any future . . .'

His secretary had stopped taking notes.

Keller looked up. 'Do you have that?'

She was staring at him. 'Mr Keller?'

'Yes.'

'You dictated this letter yesterday.'

Keller swallowed. 'What?'

'It's already gone out in the mail.'

Howard Keller tried to smile. 'I guess I'm on overload.'

At four o'clock that afternoon, Keller was being examined by Dr Seymour Bennett.

'You seem to be in excellent shape,' Dr Bennett said. 'Physically, there's nothing wrong with you at all.'

'What about these lapses of memory?'

'How long since you've had a vacation, Howard?'

Keller tried to think. 'I guess it's been quite a few years,' he said. 'We've been pretty busy.'

Dr Bennett smiled. 'There you are. You're on overload.' *That word again.* 'This is more common than you think. Go somewhere where you can relax for a week or two. Get business off your mind. When you come back, you'll feel like a new man.'

Keller stood up, relieved.

Keller went to see Lara in her office. 'Could you spare me for a week?'

'About as easily as I can spare my right arm. What did you have in mind?'

352

'The doctor thinks I should take a little vacation, Lara. To tell you the truth, I've been having some problems with my memory.'

She was watching him, concerned. 'Anything serious?'

'No, not really. It's just annoying. I thought I might go to Hawaii for a few days.'

'Take the jet.'

'No, no, you'll be using it. I'll fly commercial.'

'Charge everything to the company.'

'Thanks. I'll check in every . . .'

'No, you won't. I want you to forget about the office. Just take care of yourself. I don't want anything to happen to you.'

I hope he's all right, Lara thought. *He's got to be all right.*

Philip telephoned the next day. When Marian Bell said, 'Mr Adler is calling from Taipei,' Lara hurriedly picked up the telephone.

'Philip . . . ?'

'Hello, darling. There's been a phone strike. I've been trying to reach you for hours. How do you feel?'

Lonely. 'Wonderful. How is the tour going?'

'It's the usual. I miss you.'

In the background, Lara could hear music and voices.

'Where are you?'

'Oh, they're giving a little party for me. You know how it is.'

Lara could hear the sound of a woman laughing.

'Yes, I know how it is.'

'I'll be home Wednesday.'

'Philip?'

'Yes?'

'Nothing, darling. Hurry home.'

'I will. Goodbye.'

She replaced the receiver. What was he going to do after the party? Who was the woman? She was filled with a sense of jealousy so strong that it almost smothered her. She had never been jealous of anyone in her life.

Everything is so perfect, Lara thought. *I don't want to lose it. I can't lose it.*

She lay awake thinking about Philip and what he was doing.

Howard Keller was stretched out on Kona Beach at a small hotel on the big island of Hawaii. The weather had been ideal. He had gone swimming every day. He had gotten a tan, played some golf, and had daily massages. He was completely relaxed, and had never felt better. *Dr Bennett was right*, he thought. *Overload. I'm going to have to slow down a little when I get back.* The truth was that the episodes of memory loss had frightened him more than he wanted to admit.

Finally, it was time to return to New York. He took a midnight flight back, and was in Manhattan at four o'clock in the afternoon. He went directly to the office. His secretary was there, smiling. 'Welcome back, Mr Keller. You look great.'

'Thank you . . .' He stood there, and his face drained of colour.

He could not remember her name.

354

28

Philip arrived home on Wednesday afternoon, and Lara took the limousine to the airport to meet him. Philip stepped off the plane and the image of Lochinvar instantly sprang to Lara's mind.

My God, but he's handsome! She ran into his arms.

'I've missed you,' she said, hugging him.

'I've missed you too, darling.'

'How much?'

He held his thumb and forefinger half an inch apart. 'This much.'

'You beast,' she said. 'Where's your luggage?'

'It's coming.'

One hour later, they were back at the apartment. Marian Bell opened the door for them. 'Welcome back, Mr Adler.'

'Thanks, Marian.' He looked around. 'I feel as though I've been away for a year.'

'Two years,' Lara said. She started to add, 'Don't ever leave me again' and bit her lip.

'Can I do anything for you, Mrs Adler?' Marian asked.

'No. We're fine. You can run along now. I'll dictate some letters in the morning. I won't be going into the office today.'

'Very well. Goodbye.' Marian left.

'Sweet girl,' Philip said.

'Yes, isn't she?' Lara moved into Philip's arms. 'Now show me how much you missed me.'

Lara stayed away from the office for the next three days. She wanted to be with Philip, to talk to him, touch him, assure herself that he was real. They had breakfast in the morning and while Lara dictated to Marian, Philip was at the piano practising.

At lunch on the third day, Lara told Philip about the casino opening. 'I wish you could have been there, darling. It was fantastic.'

'I'm so sorry I missed it.'

He's out playing the piano somewhere. 'Well, you'll have your chance next month. The mayor is giving me the keys to the city.'

Philip said unhappily, 'Darling, I'm afraid I'm going to have to miss that, too.'

Lara froze. 'What do you mean?'

'Ellerbee's booked me for another tour. I leave for Germany in three weeks.'

'You can't!' Lara said.

'The contracts have already been signed. There's nothing I can do about it.'

'You just got back. How can you go away again so soon?'

'It's an important tour, darling.'

'And our marriage isn't important?'

'Lara . . .'

'You don't have to go,' Lara said angrily. 'I want a husband, not a part-time . . .'

Marian Bell came into the room carrying some letters. 'Oh, I'm sorry. I didn't mean to interrupt. I have these letters ready for you to sign.'

'Thank you,' Lara said stiffly. 'I'll call you when I need you.'

'Yes, Miss Cameron.'

They watched Marian retreat to her office.

'I know you have to give concerts,' Lara said, 'but you don't have to give them this often. It's not as though you were some kind of travelling salesman.'

'No, it isn't, is it?' His tone was cool.

'Why don't you stay here for the ceremony and then go on your tour?'

'Lara, I know that it's important to you, but you must understand that my concert tours are important to me. I'm very proud of you and what you're doing, but I want you to be proud of me.'

'I am,' Lara said. 'Forgive me, Philip, I just . . .' She was trying hard not to cry.

'I know, darling.' He took her in his arms. 'We'll work it out. When I come back we'll take a long vacation together.'

A vacation's impossible, Lara thought. *There are too many projects in the works.*

'Where are you going this time, Philip?'

'I'll be going to Germany, Norway, Denmark, England, and then back here.'

Lara took a deep breath. 'I see.'

'I wish you could come with me, Lara. It's very lonely out there without you.'

She thought of the laughing lady. 'Is it?' She shook herself out of her mood and managed to smile. 'I'll tell you what. Why don't you take the jet? It will make it more comfortable for you.'

'Are you sure you're . . . ?'

'Absolutely. I'll manage without it until you're back.'

357

'There's no one in the world like you,' Philip said.

Lara rubbed a finger slowly along his cheek. 'Remember that.'

Philip's tour was a huge success. In Berlin the audiences went wild and the reviews were ecstatic.

Afterward, the green rooms were always crowded with eager fans, most of them female:

'I've travelled three hundred miles to hear you play . . .'

'I have a little castle not far from here, and I was wondering . . .'

'I've prepared a midnight supper just for the two of us . . .'

Some of them were rich and beautiful, and most of them were very willing. But Philip was in love. He called Lara after the concert in Denmark. 'I miss you.'

'I miss you, too, Philip. How did the concert go?'

'Well, no one walked out while I was playing.'

Lara laughed. 'That's a good sign. I'm right in the middle of a meeting now, darling. I'll call you at your hotel in an hour.'

Philip said, 'I won't be going right to the hotel, Lara. The manager of the concert hall is giving a dinner party for me and . . .'

'Oh? Really? Does he have a beautiful daughter?' She regretted it the moment the words were out.

'What?'

'Nothing. I have to go now. I'll talk to you later.'

She hung up and turned to the men in the office. Keller was watching her. 'Is everything all right?'

'Fine,' Lara said lightly. She found it difficult to

concentrate on the meeting. She visualized Philip at the party, beautiful women handing him their hotel keys. She was consumed with jealousy, and she hated herself for it.

The mayor's ceremony honouring Lara was standing-room only. The press was out in force.

'Could we get a shot of you and your husband together?'

And Lara was forced to say, 'He wanted so much to be here . . .'

Paul Martin was there.

'He's gone again, huh?'

'He really wanted to be here, Paul.'

'Bullshit! This is a big honour for you. He should be at your side. What the hell kind of husband is he? Someone should have a talk with him!'

That night she lay in bed alone, unable to sleep. Philip was 10,000 miles away. The conversation with Paul Martin ran through Lara's mind. *What the hell kind of husband is he? Someone should have a talk with him!*

When Philip returned from Europe, he seemed happy to be home. He brought Lara an armload of gifts. There was an exquisite porcelain figurine from Denmark, lovely dolls from Germany, silk blouses and a gold purse from England. In the purse was a diamond bracelet.

'It's lovely,' Lara said. 'Thank you, darling.'

The next morning Lara said to Marian Bell, 'I'm going to work at home all day.'

Lara sat in her office dictating to Marian, and from the drawing room she could hear the sounds of Philip at the piano. *Our life is so perfect like this*, Lara thought. *Why does Philip want to spoil it?*

William Ellerbee telephoned Philip. 'Congratulations,' he said. 'I hear the tour went wonderfully.'

'It did. The Europeans are great audiences.'

'I got a call from the management at Carnegie Hall. They have an unexpected opening a week from Friday, on the seventeenth. They would like to book you for a recital. Are you interested?'

'Very much.'

'Good. I'll work out the arrangements. By the way,' Ellerbee said, 'are you thinking of cutting back on your concerts?'

Philip was taken aback. 'Cutting back? No. Why?'

'I had a talk with Lara and she indicated that you might want to just tour the United States. Perhaps it would be best if you talked to her and . . .'

Philip said, 'I will. Thank you.'

Philip replaced the receiver and walked into Lara's office. She was dictating to Marian.

'Would you excuse us?' Philip asked.

Marian smiled. 'Certainly.' She left the room.

Philip turned to Lara. 'I just had a call from William Ellerbee. Did you talk to him about my cutting down on foreign tours?'

'I might have mentioned something like that, Philip. I thought it might be better for both of us if . . .'

'Please, don't do that again.' Philip said. 'You know how much I love you. But apart from our lives

360

together, you have a career and I have a career. Let's make a rule. I won't interfere in yours, and you won't interfere in mine. Is that fair enough?'

'Of course it is,' Lara said. 'I'm sorry, Philip. It's just that I miss you so much when you're away.' She went into his arms. 'Forgive me?'

'It's forgiven and forgotten.'

Howard Keller came to the penthouse to bring Lara contracts to sign. 'How's everything going?'

'Beautifully,' Lara said.

'The wandering minstrel is home?'

'Yes.'

'So music is your life now, huh?'

'The musician is my life. You have no idea how wonderful he is, Howard.'

'When are you coming into the office? We need you.'

'I'll come in a few days.'

Keller nodded. 'Okay.'

They began to examine the papers he had brought.

The following morning, Terry Hill telephoned. 'Lara, I just received a call from the Gaming Commission in Reno,' the attorney said. 'There's going to be a hearing on your casino licence.'

'Why?' Lara asked.

'There have been some allegations that the bidding was rigged. They want you to go there and testify on the seventeenth.'

'How serious is this?' Lara asked.

The lawyer hesitated. 'Are you aware of any irregularities in the bidding?'

361

'No, of course not.'

'Then you have nothing to worry about. I'll fly down to Reno with you.'

'What happens if I don't go?'

'They'll subpoena you. It would look better if you went on your own.'

'All right.'

Lara telephoned Paul Martin's private number at the office. He picked up the phone immediately.

'Lara?'

'Yes, Paul.'

'You haven't used this number in a long time.'

'I know. I'm calling about Reno . . .'

'I heard.'

'Is there a real problem?'

He laughed. 'No. The losers are upset that you beat them to it.'

'Are you sure it's all right, Paul?' She hesitated. 'We did discuss the other bids.'

'Believe me, it's done all the time. Anyway, they have no way of proving that. Don't worry about a thing.'

'All right. I won't.'

She replaced the receiver and sat there, worried.

At lunch Philip said, 'By the way, they offered me a concert at Carnegie Hall. I'm going to do it.'

'Wonderful,' Lara smiled. 'I'll buy a new dress. When is it?'

'The seventeenth.'

Lara's smile faded. 'Oh.'

'What's the matter?'

'I'm afraid I won't be able to be there, darling. I have to be in Reno. I'm so sorry.'

Philip put his hands over hers. 'Our timing seems to be off, doesn't it? Oh, well. Don't worry. There will be plenty more recitals.'

Lara was in her office at Cameron Center. Howard Keller had called her at home that morning.

'I think you'd better get down here,' he had said. 'We have a few problems.'

'I'll be there in an hour.'

They were in the middle of a meeting. 'A couple of deals have gone sour,' Keller told her. 'The insurance company that was moving into our building in Houston has gone bankrupt. They were our only tenant.'

'We'll find someone else,' Lara said.

'It's not going to be that simple. The Tax Reform Act is hurting us. Hell, it's hurting everybody. Congress has wiped out corporate tax shelters, and eliminated most deductions. I think we're heading for a goddamned recession. The savings and loan companies we're dealing with are in trouble. Drexel, Burnham, Lambert may go out of business. Junk bonds are turning into land mines. We're having problems with half a dozen of our buildings. Two of them are only half finished. Without financing, those costs will eat us up.'

Lara sat there, thinking. 'We can handle it. Sell whatever properties we have to to keep up our mortgage payments.'

'The bright side of it,' Keller said, 'is that we have

a cash flow from Reno that's bringing us in close to fifty million a year.'

Lara said nothing.

On Friday the seventeenth, Lara left for Reno. Philip rode with her to the airport. Terry Hill was waiting at the plane.

'When will you be back?' Philip asked.

'Probably tomorrow. This shouldn't take long.'

'I'll miss you,' Philip said.

'I'll miss you, too, darling.'

He stood there watching the plane taking off. *I am going to miss her*, Philip thought. *She's the most fantastic woman in the world.*

In the offices of the Nevada Gaming Commission, Lara was facing the same group of men she had met during the application for a casino licence. This time, however, they were not as friendly.

Lara was sworn in, and a court reporter took down her testimony.

The chairman said, 'Miss Cameron, some rather disturbing allegations have been made concerning the licensing of your casino.'

'What kind of allegations?' Terry Hill demanded.

'We'll come to those in due course.' The chairman turned his attention back to Lara. 'We understood that this was your first experience in acquiring a gambling casino.'

'That's right. I told you that at the first hearing.'

'How did you arrive at the bid you put in? I mean . . . how did you come to that precise figure?'

Terry Hill interrupted. 'I'd like to know the reason for the question.'

'In a moment, Mr Hill. Will you permit your client to answer the question?'

Terry Hill looked at Lara and nodded.

Lara said, 'I had my comptroller and accountants give me an estimate on how much we could afford to bid, and we figured in a small profit we could add to that, and that became my bid.'

The chairman scanned the paper in front of him. 'Your bid was five million dollars more than the next highest bid.'

'Was it?'

'You weren't aware of that at the time you made your bid?'

'No. Of course not.'

'Miss Cameron, are you acquainted with Paul Martin?'

Terry Hill interrupted. 'I don't see the relevance of this line of questioning.'

'We'll come to that in a moment. Meanwhile, I'd like Miss Cameron to answer the question.'

'I have no objection,' Lara said. 'Yes. I know Paul Martin.'

'Have you ever had any business dealings with him?'

Lara hesitated. 'No. He's just a friend.'

'Miss Cameron, are you aware that Paul Martin is reputed to be involved with the Mafia, that . . .'

'Objection. It's hearsay and it has no place in this record.'

'Very well, Mr Hill. I'll withdraw that. Miss Cameron, when was the last time you saw or talked to Paul Martin?'

Lara hesitated. 'I'm not sure, exactly. To be perfectly candid, since I got married, I've seen very little of Mr Martin. We run into each other at parties occasionally, that's all.'

'But it wasn't your habit to speak regularly with him on the telephone?'

'Not after my marriage, no.'

'Did you ever have any discussions with Paul Martin regarding this casino?'

Lara looked over at Terry Hill. He nodded. 'Yes, I believe that after I won the bid for it, he called to congratulate me. And then once again after I got the licence to operate the casino.'

'But you did not talk to him at any other time?'

'No.'

'I'll remind you that you're under oath, Miss Cameron.'

'Yes.'

'You're aware of the penalty for perjury?'

'Yes.'

He held up a sheet of paper. 'I have here a list of fifteen telephone calls between you and Paul Martin, made during the time sealed bids were being submitted for the casino.'

29

Most soloists are dwarfed by the huge twenty-eight
hundred seat space at Carnegie Hall. There are not
many musicians who can fill the prestigious hall, but
on Friday night, it was packed. Philip Adler walked
out onto the vast stage to the thunderous applause
of the audience. He sat down at the piano, paused a
moment, then began to play. The programme consisted of Beethoven sonatas. Over the years he had
disciplined himself to concentrate only on the music.
But on this night, Philip's thoughts drifted away to
Lara and their problems, and for a split second, his
fingers started to fumble, and he broke out in a cold
sweat. It happened so swiftly that the audience did
not notice.

There was loud applause at the end of the first part
of the recital. At the intermission Philip went to his
dressing room.

The concert manager said, 'Wonderful, Philip.
You held them spellbound. Can I get anything for
you?'

'No, thanks.' Philip closed the door. He wished
the recital were over. He was deeply disturbed by
the situation with Lara. He loved her a great deal,
and he knew she loved him, but they seemed to have
come to an impasse. There had been a lot of tension
between them before Lara had left for Reno. *I've*

got to do something about it, Philip thought. *But what? How do we compromise?* He was still thinking about it when there was a knock at the door, and the stage manager's voice said, 'Five minutes, Mr Adler.'

'Thank you.'

The second half of the programme consisted of the *Hammerklavier* sonata. It was a stirring, emotional piece, and when the last notes had thundered out through the vast hall, the audience rose to its feet with wild applause. Philip stood on the stage bowing, but his mind was elsewhere. *I've got to go home and talk to Lara.* And then he remembered that she was away. *We'll have to settle this now*, Philip thought. *We can't go on like this.*

The applause continued. The audience was shouting 'bravo' and 'encore'. Ordinarily, Philip would have played another selection, but on this evening he was too upset. He returned to his dressing room and changed into his street clothes. From outside, he could hear the distant rumble of thunder. The papers had said rain, but that had not kept the crowd away. The green room was filled with well-wishers waiting for him. It was always exciting to feel and hear the approval of his fans, but tonight he was in no mood for them. He stayed in his dressing room until he was sure the crowd had gone. When he came out, it was almost midnight. He walked through the empty back-stage corridors and went out the stage door. The limousine was not there. *I'll find a taxi*, Philip decided.

He stepped outside into a pouring rain. There was a cold wind blowing, and Fifty-Seventh street was dark. As Philip moved toward Sixth Avenue, a large man in a raincoat approached from the shadows.

'Excuse me,' he said, 'how do you get to Carnegie Hall?'

Philip thought of the old joke he had told Lara, and was tempted to say 'practise', but he pointed to the building behind him. 'It's right there.'

As Philip turned, the man shoved him hard against the building. In his hand was a deadly-looking switchblade knife. 'Give me your wallet.'

Philip's heart was pounding. He looked around for help. The rain-swept street was deserted. 'All right,' Philip said. 'Don't get excited. You can have it.'

The knife was pressing against his throat.

'Look, there's no need to . . .'

'Shut up! Just give it to me.'

Philip reached into his pocket and pulled out his wallet. The man grabbed it with his free hand and put it in his pocket. He was looking at Philip's watch. He reached down and tore it from Philip's wrist. As he took the watch, he grabbed Philip's left hand, held it tightly, and slashed the razor-sharp knife across Philip's wrist, slicing it to the bone. Philip screamed aloud with pain. Blood began to gush out. The man fled.

Philip stood there in shock, watching his blood mingling with the rain, dripping onto the street.

He fainted.

Book Four

30

Lara received the news about Philip in Reno.

Marian Bell was on the phone, near hysteria.

'Is he badly hurt?' Lara demanded.

'We don't have any details yet. He's at New York Hospital in the emergency room.'

'I'll come back immediately.'

When Lara arrived at the hospital six hours later, Howard Keller was waiting there for her. He looked shaken.

'What happened?' Lara asked.

'Apparently, Philip was mugged after he left Carnegie Hall. They found him in the street, unconscious.'

'How bad is it?'

'His wrist was slashed. He's heavily sedated, but he's conscious.'

They went into the hospital room. Philip was lying on a bed with IV tubes feeding liquid into his body.

'Philip . . . Philip.' It was Lara's voice calling to him from a long way off. He opened his eyes. Lara and Howard Keller were there. There seemed to be two of each. His mouth was dry, and he felt groggy.

'What happened?' Philip mumbled.

'You were hurt,' Lara said. 'But you're going to be all right.'

Philip looked down and saw that his left wrist was heavily bandaged. Memory came flooding back. 'I was . . . I was held up. A man took my wallet and watch . . . and then he . . . cut my hand.' It was an effort to talk.

Keller said, 'The stage doorman found you lying in the street. You lost a lot of blood.'

Clarity was beginning to return. Philip looked at his hand again. 'My wrist . . . he slashed my wrist . . . how bad is it?'

'I don't know, darling,' Lara said. 'I'm sure it will be fine. The doctor is coming in to see you.'

Keller said reassuringly, 'Doctors can do anything these days.'

Philip was drifting back to sleep. 'I told him to take what he wanted. He shouldn't have hurt my wrist,' he mumbled. 'He shouldn't have hurt my wrist . . .'

Two hours later, Dr Dennis Stanton walked into Philip's room and the moment Philip saw the expression on his face he knew what he was going to say.

Philip took a deep breath. 'Tell me.'

Dr Stanton sighed. 'I'm afraid I don't have very good news for you, Mr Adler.'

'How bad is it?'

'The flexor tendons have been severed, so you'll have no motion in your hand, and there will be a permanent numbness. In addition to that, there's median and ulnar nerve damage.' He illustrated on his hand. 'The median nerve affects the thumb and first three fingers. The ulnar nerve goes to all the fingers.'

Philip closed his eyes tightly against the wave of sudden despair that engulfed him. After a moment, he spoke. 'Are you saying that I'll . . . I'll never have the use of my left hand again?'

'That's right. The fact is that you're lucky to be alive. Whoever did this, cut the artery. It's a wonder you didn't bleed to death. It took sixty stitches to sew your wrist together again.'

Philip said in desperation, 'My God, isn't there *anything* you can do?'

'Yes. We could put in an implant in your left hand so you would have some motion, but it would be very limited.'

He might as well have killed me, Philip thought despairingly.

'As your hand starts to heal, there's going to be a great deal of pain. We'll give you medication to control it, but I can assure you that in time the pain will go away.'

Not the real pain, Philip thought. *Not the real pain.* He was caught up in a nightmare. And there was no escape.

A detective came to see Philip at the hospital. He stood by the side of Philip's bed. He was one of the old breed, in his late fifties and tired, with eyes that had already seen it all twice.

'I'm Lieutenant Mancini. I'm sorry about what happened, Mr Adler,' he said. 'It's too bad they couldn't have broken your leg instead. I mean . . . if it had to happen . . .'

'I know what you mean,' Philip said curtly.

Howard Keller came into the room. 'I was looking for Lara.' He saw the stranger. 'Oh, sorry.'

'She's around here somewhere,' Philip said. 'This is Lieutenant Mancini. Howard Keller.'

Mancini was staring at him. 'You look familiar. Have we met before?'

'I don't think so.'

Mancini's face lit up. 'Keller! My God, you used to play baseball in Chicago.'

'That's right. How do you . . . ?'

'I was a scout for the White Sox one summer. I still remember your sliders and your change-ups. You could have had a big career.'

'Yeah. Well, if you'll excuse me . . .' He looked at Philip. 'I'll wait for Lara outside.' He left.

Mancini turned to Philip. 'Did you get a look at the man who attacked you?'

'He was a male Caucasian. A large man. About six foot two. Maybe fifty or so.'

'Could you identify him if you saw him again?'

'Yes.' It was a face he would never forget.

'Mr Adler, I could ask you to look through a lot of mug shots, but frankly, I think it would be a waste of your time. I mean, this isn't exactly a high-tech crime. There are hundreds of muggers all over the city. Unless someone nabs them on the spot, they usually get away with it.' He took out his notebook. 'What was taken from you?'

'My wallet and my wristwatch.'

'What kind of watch was it?'

'A Piaget.'

'Was there anything distinctive about it? Did it have an inscription, for example?'

It was the watch Lara had given him. 'Yes. On the

back of the case, it read "To Philip with Love from Lara."'

He made a note. 'Mr Adler . . . I have to ask you this. Had you ever seen this man before?'

Philip looked up at him in surprise. 'Seen him before? No. Why?'

'I just wondered.' Mancini put the notebook away. 'Well, we'll see what we can do. You're a lucky man, Mr Adler.'

'Really?' Philip's voice was filled with bitterness.

'Yeah. We have thousands of muggings a year in this city and we can't afford to spend much time on them, but our Captain happens to be a fan of yours. He collects all your records. He's going to do everything he can to catch the SOB who did this to you. We'll send out a description of your watch to pawn shops around the country.'

'If you catch him, do you think he can give me my hand back?' Philip asked bitterly.

'What?'

'Nothing.'

'You'll be hearing from us. Have a nice day.'

Lara and Keller were waiting in the corridor for the detective.

'You said you wanted to see me?' Lara asked.

'Yes. I'd like to ask you a couple of questions,' Lieutenant Mancini said. 'Mrs Adler, does your husband have any enemies that you know of?'

Lara frowned. 'Enemies? No. Why?'

'No one who might be jealous of him? Another musician maybe? Someone who wants to hurt him?'

377

'What are you getting at? It was a simple street mugging, wasn't it?'

'To be perfectly frank, this doesn't fit the pattern of an ordinary mugging. He slashed your husband's wrist *after* he took his wallet and watch.'

'I don't see what difference . . .'

'That was a pretty senseless thing to do, unless it was deliberate. Your husband didn't put up any resistance. Now, a kid on dope might do a thing like that, but . . .' He shrugged. 'I'll be in touch.'

They watched him walk away.

'Jesus!' Keller said. 'He thinks it was a set-up.'

Lara had turned pale.

Keller looked at her and said slowly, 'My God! One of Paul Martin's hoods! But why would he do this?'

Lara found it difficult to speak. 'He . . . he might have thought he was doing it for me. Philip has . . . has been away a lot, and Paul kept saying that it . . . it wasn't right, that someone should have a talk with him. Oh, Howard!' She buried her head in his shoulder, fighting back the tears.

'That sonofabitch! I warned you to stay away from that man.'

Lara took a deep breath. 'Philip is going to be all right. He *has* to be.'

Three days later, Lara brought Philip home from the hospital. He looked pale and shaken. Marian Bell was at the door, waiting for them. She had gone to the hospital every day to see Philip, and to bring him his messages. There had been an outpouring of sympathy from all around the world – cards and

378

letters, and telephone calls from distraught fans. The newspapers had played the story up, condemning the violence on the streets of New York.

Lara was in the library when the telephone rang.

'It's for you,' Marian Bell said. 'A Mr Paul Martin.'

'I . . . I can't talk to him,' Lara told her. And she stood there, fighting to keep her body from trembling.

31

Overnight their lives together changed.

Lara said to Keller, 'I'm going to be working at home from now on. Philip needs me.'

'Sure. I understand.'

The calls and get well cards kept pouring in, and Marian Bell proved to be a blessing. She was self-effacing and never got in the way. 'Don't worry about them, Mrs Adler. I'll handle them, if you like.'

'Thank you, Marian.'

William Ellerbee called several times, but Philip refused to take his calls. 'I don't want to talk to anyone,' he told Lara.

Dr Stanton had been right about the pain. It was excruciating. Philip tried to avoid taking pain pills until he could no longer stand it.

Lara was always at his side. 'We're going to get you the best doctors in the world, darling. There must be *someone* who can fix your hand. I heard about a doctor in Switzerland . . .'

Philip shook his head. 'It's no use.' He looked at his bandaged hand. 'I'm a cripple.'

'Don't talk like that,' Lara said fiercely. 'There are a thousand things you can still do. I blame myself. If I hadn't gone to Reno that day, if I had been with you at the concert, this never would have happened. If . . .'

Philip smiled wryly. 'You wanted me to stay home more. Well, now I have nowhere else to go.'

Lara said huskily, 'Someone said, "Be careful what you wish for, because you might get it." I did want you to stay home, but not like this. I can't stand to see you in pain.'

'Don't worry about me,' Philip said. 'I just have to work a few things out in my mind. It's all happened so suddenly. I . . . I don't think I've quite realized it, yet.'

Howard Keller came to the penthouse with some contracts. 'Hello Philip. How do you feel?'

'Wonderful,' Philip snapped. 'I feel just wonderful.'

'It was a stupid question. I'm sorry.'

'Don't mind me,' Philip apologized. 'I haven't been myself lately.' He pounded his right hand against the chair. 'If the bastards had only cut my *right* hand. There are a dozen left-handed concertos I could have played.'

And Keller remembered the conversation at the party. *Oh, there are a lot of concertos written for the left hand. Half a dozen composers wrote concertos for the left hand. There's one by Demuth, Franz Schmidt. Korngold, and a beautiful concerto by Ravel.*

And Paul Martin had been there and heard it.

Dr Stanton came to the penthouse to see Philip. Carefully, he removed the bandage, exposing a long angry scar.

'Can you flex your hand at all?'

Philip tried.

It was impossible.

'How's the pain?' Dr Stanton asked.

'It's bad, but I don't want to take any more of those damned pain pills.'

'I'll leave another prescription anyway. You can take them when you have to. Believe me, the pain will stop in the next few weeks.' He rose to leave. 'I really am sorry. I happen to be a big fan of yours.'

'Buy my records,' Philip said curtly.

Marian Bell made a suggestion to Lara. 'Do you think it might help Mr Adler if a therapist came to work on his hand?'

Lara thought about it. 'We can try. Let's see what happens.'

When Lara suggested it to Philip, he shook his head. 'No. What's the point? The doctor said . . .'

'Doctor can be wrong,' Lara said firmly. 'We're going to try everything.'

The next day a young therapist appeared at the apartment. Lara brought him in to Philip. 'This is Mr Rossman. He works at Columbia Hospital. He's going to try to help you, Philip.'

'Good luck,' Philip said bitterly.

'Let's take a look at that hand, Mr Adler.'

Philip held out his hand. Rossman examined it carefully. 'Looks as though there's been quite a bit of muscle damage, but we'll see what we can do. Can you move your fingers?'

Philip tried.

'There's not much motion, is there? Let's try to exercise it.'

382

It was unbelievably painful.

They worked for half an hour and at the end of that time, Rossman said, 'I'll come back tomorrow.'

'No,' Philip said. 'Don't bother.'

Lara had come into the room. 'Philip, won't you try?'

'I tried,' he snarled. 'Don't you understand? My hand is dead. Nothing's going to bring it back to life.'

'Philip . . .' Her eyes filled with tears.

'I'm sorry,' Philip said. 'I just . . . give me time.'

That night, Lara was awakened by the sound of the piano. She got out of bed and quietly walked over to the entrance of the drawing room. Philip was in his robe, seated at the piano, his right hand softly playing. He looked up when he saw Lara.

'Sorry if I woke you up.'

Lara moved toward him. 'Darling . . .'

'It's a big joke, isn't it? You married a concert pianist and you wound up with a cripple.'

She put her arms around him and held him close. 'You're not a cripple. There are so many things you can do.'

'Stop being a goddamn Pollyanna!'

'I'm sorry. I just meant . . .'

'I know. Forgive me, I . . .' He held up his mutilated hand. '. . . I just can't get used to this.'

'Come back to bed.'

'No. You go ahead. I'll be all right.'

He sat up all night, thinking about his future, and he wondered angrily, *What future?*

*

Lara and Philip had dinner together every evening, and after dinner they read or watched television, and then went to sleep.

Philip said apologetically, 'I know I'm not being much of a husband, Lara. I just . . . I just don't feel like sex. Believe me, it has nothing to do with you.'

Lara sat up in bed, her voice trembling. 'I didn't marry you for your body. I married you because I was wildly head over heels in love with you. I still am. If we never make love again, it will be fine with me. All I want is for you to hold me and love me.'

'I do love you,' Philip said.

Invitations to dinner parties and charity events came in constantly, but Philip refused them all. He did not want to leave the apartment. 'You go,' he would tell Lara. 'It's important to your business.'

'Nothing is more important to me than you. We'll have a nice quiet dinner at home.'

Lara saw to it that their chef prepared all of Philip's favourite dishes. He had no appetite. Lara arranged to hold her meetings at the penthouse. When it was necessary for her to go out during the day, she would say to Marian, 'I'll be gone for a few hours. Keep an eye on Mr Adler.'

'I will,' Marian promised.

One morning Lara said, 'Darling, I hate to leave you, but I have to go to Cleveland for a day. Will you be all right?'

'Of course,' Philip said. 'I'm not helpless. Please go. Don't worry about me.'

Marian brought in some letters she had finished answering for Philip. 'Would you like to sign these, Mr Adler?'

Philip said, 'Sure. It's a good thing I'm right-handed, isn't it?' There was a bitter edge to his voice. He looked at Marian and said, 'I'm sorry. I didn't mean to take it out on you.'

Marian said quietly, 'I know that, Mr Adler. Don't you think it would be a good idea for you to go outside and see some friends?'

'My friends are all working,' Philip snapped. 'They're musicians. They're busy playing concerts. How can you be so stupid?'

He stormed out of the room.

Marian stood there looking after him.

An hour later, Philip walked back into the office. Marian was at the typewriter. 'Marian?'

She looked up. 'Yes, Mr Adler?'

'Please forgive me. I'm not myself. I didn't mean to be rude.'

'I understand,' she said quietly.

He sat down opposite her. 'The reason I'm not going out,' Philip said, 'is because I feel like a freak. I'm sure that everybody's going to be staring at my hand. I don't want anyone's pity.'

She was watching him, saying nothing.

'You've been very kind, and I appreciate it, I really do. But there's nothing anyone can do. You know the expression, "the bigger they are, the harder they fall"? Well, I was big, Marian – really big. Everybody came to hear me play . . . kings and queens and . . .' he broke off. 'People all over the world heard my music. I've given recitals in China and Russia and India and Germany.' His voice choked up and tears began rolling down his cheeks. 'Have you noticed I cry a lot lately?' he said. He was fighting to control himself.

Marian said softly, 'Please don't. Everything's going to be all right.'

'No! Nothing's going to be all right. Nothing! I'm a goddamn cripple.'

'Don't say that. Mrs Adler is right, you know. There are a hundred things you can do. When you get over this pain, you'll begin to do them.'

Philip took out a handkerchief and wiped his eyes. 'Jesus Christ, I'm becoming a damn cry baby.'

'If it helps you,' Marian said, 'do it.'

He looked up at her and smiled. 'How old are you?'

'Twenty-six.'

'You're a pretty wise twenty-six, aren't you?'

'No. I just know what you're going through, and I'd give anything if it hadn't happened. But it has happened, and I know that you're going to figure out the best way to deal with it.'

'You're wasting your time here,' Philip said. 'You should have been a shrink.'

'Would you like me to make a drink for you?'

'No, thanks. Are you interested in a game of backgammon?' Philip asked.

'I'd love it, Mr Adler.'

'If you're going to be my backgammon partner, you'd better start calling me Philip.'

'Philip.'

From that time on, they played backgammon every day.

*

Lara received a telephone call from Terry Hill.

'Lara, I'm afraid I have some bad news for you.'

Lara readied herself. 'Yes?'

'The Nevada Gaming Commission has voted to suspend your gambling licence until further investigation. You may be facing criminal charges.'

It was a shock. She thought of Paul Martin's words, *Don't worry. They can't prove anything.* 'Isn't there something we can do about it, Terry?'

'Not for the present. Just sit tight. I'm working on it.'

When Lara told Keller the news, he said, 'My God! We're counting on the cash flow from the casino to pay off the mortgages on three buildings. Are they going to reinstate your licence?'

'I don't know.'

Keller was thoughtful. 'All right. We'll sell the Chicago hotel and use the equity to pay the mortgage on the Houston property. The real estate market has gone to hell. A lot of banks and savings and loans are in deep trouble. Drexel, Burnham Lambert has folded. It's the end of Milken honey.'

'It will turn around,' Lara said.

'It had better turn around *fast*. I've been getting calls from the banks about our loans.'

'Don't worry,' Lara said confidently. 'If you owe a bank a million dollars, they own you. If you owe a bank a hundred million dollars, you own them. They can't afford to let anything happen to me.'

The following day, an article appeared in *Businessweek*. It was headlined: 'Cameron Empire Shaky – Lara Cameron Facing Possible Criminal Indictment In Reno. Can The Iron Butterfly Keep Her Empire Together?'

Lara slammed her fist against the magazine. 'How dare they print that. I'm going to sue them.'

Keller said, 'Not a great idea.'

Lara said earnestly, 'Howard, Cameron Towers is almost fully rented, right?'

'Seventy per cent, so far, and climbing. Southern Insurance has taken twenty floors and International Investment Banking has taken ten floors.'

'When the building is finished it will throw off enough money to take care of all our problems. How far away are we from completion?'

'Six months.'

Lara's voice was filled with excitement. 'Look what we'll have then. The biggest skyscraper in the world! It's going to be beautiful.'

She turned to the framed sketch of it behind her desk. It showed a towering glass-sheathed monolith, whose facets reflected the other buildings around it. On the lower floors were a promenade and atrium, with expensive shops. Above were apartments and Lara's offices.

'We'll have a big publicity promotion,' Lara said.

'Good idea.' He frowned.

'What's the matter?'

'Nothing. I was just thinking about Steve Murchison. He wanted that site pretty bad.'

'Well, we beat him to it, didn't we?'

'Yes,' Keller said slowly. 'We beat him to it.'

Lara sent for Jerry Townsend.

'Jerry, I want to do something special for the opening of Cameron Towers. Any ideas?'

'I have a great idea. The opening is September 10th?'

'Yes.'

'Doesn't that ring a bell?'

'Well, it's my birthday . . .'

'Right.' A smile lit up Jerry Townsend's face. 'Why don't we give you a big birthday party to celebrate the completion of the skyscraper?'

Lara was thoughtful for a moment. 'I like it. It's a wonderful idea. We'll invite everybody! We'll make a noise that will be heard around the world. Jerry, I want you to make up a guest list. Two hundred people. I want you to handle it personally.'

Townsend grinned. 'You've got it. I'll give you the guest list to approve.'

Lara slammed her fist down on the magazine again. 'We're going to show them!'

'Excuse me, Mrs Adler,' Marian said. 'I have the secretary of the National Builders Association on line three. You haven't responded to their invitation for the dinner Friday night.'

'Tell them I can't make it,' Lara said. 'Give them my apologies.'

'Yes, ma'am.' Marian left the room.

Philip said, 'Lara, you can't turn yourself into a hermit because of me. It's important for you to go to those things.'

'Nothing is more important than my being here with you. That funny little man who married us in Paris said, "For better or for worse."' She frowned. 'At least I *think* that's what he said. I don't speak French.'

Philip smiled. 'I want you to know how much I appreciate you. I feel like I'm putting you through hell.'

Lara moved closer to him. 'Wrong word,' she said. 'Heaven.'

Philip was getting dressed. Lara was helping him with the buttons on his shirt. Philip looked in the mirror. 'I look like a damned hippie,' Philip said. 'I need a haircut.'

'Do you want me to have Marian make an appointment with your barber?'

He shook his head. 'No. I'm sorry, Lara. I'm just not ready to go out.'

The following morning, Philip's barber and a manicurist appeared at the apartment. Philip was taken aback. 'What's all this?'

'If Mohammed won't go to the mountain, the mountain comes to Mohammed. They'll be here every week for you.'

'You're a wonder,' Philip said.

'You ain't seen nothin' yet,' Lara grinned.

The following day, a tailor arrived with some sample swatches for suits and shirts.

'What's going on?' Philip asked.

Lara said, 'You're the only man I know who has six pairs of tails, four dinner jackets, and two suits. I think it's time we got you a proper wardrobe.'

'Why?' Philip protested. 'I'm not going anywhere.'

But he allowed himself to be fitted for the suits and shirts.

A few days later, a custom shoe maker arrived.

'Now what?' Philip asked.

'It's time you had some new shoes.'

'I told you, I'm not going out.'

'I know, baby. But when you do, your shoes will be ready.'

Philip held her close. 'I don't deserve you.'

'That's what I keep telling you.'

They were in a meeting at the office. Howard Keller was saying, 'We're losing the shopping mall in Los Angeles. The banks have decided to call in the loans.'

'They can't do that.'

'They're doing it,' Keller said. 'We're over-leveraged.'

'We can pay the loans off by borrowing on one of the other buildings.'

Keller said, patiently, 'Lara, you're already leveraged to the hilt. You have a sixty-million-dollar payment coming up on the skyscraper.'

'I know that, but completion is only four months away now. We can roll the loan over. The building's on schedule, isn't it?'

'Yes.' Keller was studying her thoughtfully. It was a question she never would have asked one year ago. Then she would have known exactly where everything stood. 'I think it might be better if you spent more time here in the office,' Keller told her. 'Too many things are becoming unravelled. There are some decisions that only you can make.'

Lara nodded. 'All right,' she said reluctantly. 'I'll be in tomorrow morning.'

'William Ellerbee is on the telephone for you,' Marian announced.

'Tell him I can't talk to him.' Philip watched her as she returned to the phone.

'I'm sorry, Mr Ellerbee. Mr Adler is not available just now. Can I take a message?' She listened a moment. 'I'll tell him. Thank you.' She replaced the receiver and looked up at Philip. 'He's really anxious to have lunch with you.'

'He probably wants to talk about the commissions he's not getting any more.'

'You're probably right,' Marian said mildly. 'I'm sure he must hate you because you were attacked.'

Philip said quietly, 'Sorry. Is that the way I sounded?'

'Yes.'

'How do you put up with me?'

Marian smiled. 'It's not that difficult.'

The following day, William Ellerbee called again. Philip was out of the room. Marian spoke to Ellerbee for a few minutes then went to find Philip.

'That was Mr Ellerbee,' Marian said.

'Next time, tell him to stop calling.'

'Maybe you should tell him yourself,' Marian said. 'You're having lunch with him Thursday at one o'clock.'

'*I'm what?*'

'He suggested Le Cirque, but I thought a smaller restaurant might be better.' She looked at the pad in her hand. 'He's going to meet you at Fu's at one o'clock. I'll arrange for Max to drive you there.'

Philip was staring at her, furious. 'You made a lunch date for me without asking me?'

392

She said calmly, 'If I had asked you, you wouldn't have gone. You can fire me if you want to.'

He glared at her for a long moment and then he broke into a slow smile. 'You know something? I haven't had Chinese food in a long time.'

When Lara arrived home from the office, Philip said, 'I'm going out for lunch on Thursday with Ellerbee.'

'That's wonderful, darling! When did you decide that?'

'Marian decided it for me. She thought it would be a good idea for me to get out.'

'Oh, really?' *But you wouldn't go out when I suggested it.* 'That was very thoughtful of her.'

'Yes. She's quite a woman.'

I've been stupid, Lara thought. *I shouldn't have thrown them together like this. And Philip is so vulnerable right now.*

That was the moment when Lara knew she had to get rid of Marian.

When Lara arrived home the following day, Philip and Marian were playing backgammon in the game room.

Our game, Lara thought.

'How can I beat you if you keep rolling doubles?' Philip was saying, laughing.

Lara stood in the doorway watching. She had not heard Philip laugh in a long time.

Marian looked up and saw her. 'Good evening, Mrs Adler.'

Philip sprang to his feet. 'Hello, darling.' He kissed her. 'She's beating the pants off me.'

Not if I can help it, Lara thought.

'Will you need me tonight, Mrs Adler?'

'No, Marian. You can run along. I'll see you in the morning.'

'Thank you. Goodnight.'

'Good night, Marian.'

They watched her leave.

'She's good company,' Philip said.

Lara stroked his cheek. 'I'm glad, darling.'

'How's everything at the office?'

'Fine.' She had no intention of burdening Philip with her problems. She would have to fly to Reno and talk to the gaming commission again. If she was forced to, she would find a way to survive their cutting off the gambling at the hotel, but it would make it a lot easier if she could dissuade them.

'Philip, I'm afraid I'm going to have to start spending more time at the office. Howard can't make all the decisions himself.'

'No problem. I'll be fine.'

'I'm going to Reno in the next day or two,' Lara said. 'Why don't you come with me?'

Philip shook his head. 'I'm not ready yet.' He looked at his crippled left hand. 'Not yet.'

'All right, darling. I shouldn't be gone more than two or three days.'

Early the following morning when Marian Bell arrived for work, Lara was waiting for her. Philip was still asleep.

'Marian . . . you know the diamond bracelet that Mr Adler gave me for my birthday?'

'Yes, Mrs Adler?'

'When did you see it last?'

She stopped to think. 'It was on the dressing table in your bedroom.'

'So you did see it?'

'Why, yes. Is something wrong?'

'I'm afraid there is. The bracelet is missing.'

Marian was staring at her. 'Missing? Who could have . . . ?'

'I've questioned the staff here. They don't know anything about it.'

'Shall I call the police and . . . ?'

'That won't be necessary. I don't want to do anything that might embarrass you.'

'I don't understand.'

'Don't you? For your sake, I think it would be best if we dropped the whole matter.'

Marian was staring at Lara in shock. 'You know I didn't take that bracelet, Mrs Adler.'

'I don't know anything of the kind. You'll have to leave.' And she hated herself for what she was doing.

But no one is going to take Philip away from me. No one.

When Philip came down to breakfast, Lara said, 'By the way, I'm getting a new secretary to work here at the apartment.'

Philip looked at her in surprise. 'What happened to Marian?'

'She quit. She was offered a . . . a job in San Francisco.'

He looked at Lara in surprise. 'Oh. That's too bad. I thought she liked it here.'

'I'm sure she did, but we wouldn't want to stand in her way, would we?' *Forgive me*, Lara thought.

'No, of course not,' Philip said. 'I'd like to wish her luck. Is she . . . ?'

'She's gone.'

Philip said, 'I guess I'll have to find a new back-gammon partner.'

'When things settle down a bit, I'll be here for you.'

Philip and William Ellerbee were seated in a corner table at Fu's restaurant.

Ellerbee said, 'It's so good to see you, Philip. I've been calling you, but . . .'

'I know, I'm sorry. I haven't felt like talking to anyone, Bill.'

'I hope they catch the bastard who did this to you.'

'The police have been good enough to explain to me that muggings are not a high priority in their lives. They equate them just below lost cats. They'll never catch him.'

Ellerbee said hesitantly, 'I understand that you're not going to be able to play again.'

'You understand right.' Philip held up his crippled hand. 'It's dead.'

Ellerbee leaned forward and said earnestly, 'But *you're* not, Philip. You still have your whole life ahead of you.'

'Doing what?'

'Teaching.'

There was a wry smile on Philip's lips. 'It's ironic,

isn't it? I had thought about doing that one day when I was through giving concerts.'

Ellerbee said quietly, 'Well, that day is here, isn't it? I took the liberty of talking to the head of the Eastman School of Music in Rochester. They would give anything to have you teach there.'

Philip frowned. 'That would mean my moving up there. Lara's headquarters are in New York.' He shook his head. 'I couldn't do that to her. You don't know how wonderful she's been to me, Bill.'

'I'm sure she has.'

'She's practically given up her business to take care of me. She's the most thoughtful, considerate woman I've ever known. I'm crazy about her.'

'Philip, would you at least think about the offer from Eastman?'

'Tell them I appreciate it, but I'm afraid the answer is no.'

'If you change your mind, will you let me know?'

Philip nodded. 'You'll be the first.'

When Philip returned to the penthouse, Lara had gone to the office. He wandered around the apartment, restless. He thought about his conversation with Ellerbee. *I would love to teach*, Philip thought, *but I can't ask Lara to move to Rochester, and I can't go there without her.*

He heard the front door open. 'Lara?'

It was Marian. 'Oh, I'm sorry, Philip. I didn't know anyone was here. I came to return my key.'

'I thought you'd be in San Francisco by now.'

She looked at him, puzzled. 'San Francisco? Why?'

'Isn't that where your new job is?'

'I have no new job.'

'But Lara said . . .'

Marian suddenly understood. 'I see. She didn't tell you why she fired me?'

'Fired you? She told me that you quit . . . that you had a better offer.'

'That's not true.'

Philip said slowly, 'I think you'd better sit down.'

They sat across from each other. 'What's going on here?' Philip asked.

Marian took a deep breath. 'I think your wife believes that I . . . that I had designs on you.'

'What are you talking about?'

'She accused me of stealing the diamond bracelet you gave her, as an excuse to fire me. I'm sure she has it put away somewhere.'

'I can't believe this,' Philip protested. 'Lara would never do anything like that.'

'She would do anything to hold on to you.'

He was studying her, bewildered. 'I . . . I don't know what to say. Let me talk to Lara and . . .'

'No. Please don't. It might be better if you didn't let her know I was here.' She rose.

'What are you going to do now?'

'Don't worry. I'll find another job.'

'Marian, if there's anything I can do . . .'

'There is nothing.'

'Are you sure?'

'I'm sure. Take care of yourself, Philip.' And she was gone.

Philip watched her leave, disturbed. He couldn't believe that Lara could be guilty of such a deception, and he wondered why she hadn't told him about it. Perhaps, he thought, Marian *did* steal the bracelet, and Lara had not wanted to upset him. Marian was lying.

32

The pawnshop was on South State Street in the heart of the Loop. When Jesse Shaw walked through the door, the old man behind the counter looked up.

'Good morning. Can I help you?'

Shaw laid a wristwatch on the counter. 'How much will you give me for this?'

The pawnbroker picked up the watch and studied it. 'A Piaget. Nice watch.'

'Yeah. I hate like hell to part with it, but I've run into a little bad luck. You understand what I mean?'

The pawnbroker shrugged. 'It's my business to understand. You wouldn't believe the hard luck stories I hear.'

'I'll redeem it in a few days. I'm starting a new job Monday. Meanwhile, I need to get as much cash as I can for it.'

The pawnbroker was looking at the watch more closely. On the back of the case, some writing had been scratched off. He looked up at the customer. 'If you'll excuse me a minute, I'll take a look at the movement. Sometimes these watches are made in Bangkok, and they forget to put anything inside.'

He took the watch into the back room. He put a loupe to his eye and studied the scratch marks. He could faintly make out the letters 'T Phi p wi h L v fro L ra.'

The old man opened a drawer and took out a police flyer. It had a description of the watch and the engraving on the back, 'To Philip with Love from Lara.' He started to pick up the telephone, when the customer yelled, 'Hey, I'm in a hurry. Do you want the watch or don't you?'

'I'm coming,' the pawnbroker said. He walked back into the next room, 'I can loan you five hundred dollars on it.'

'Five hundred? This watch is worth . . .'

'Take it or leave it.'

'All right,' Shaw said grudgingly. 'I'll take it.'

'You'll have to fill out this form,' the pawnbroker said.

'Sure.' He wrote down *John Jones, 21 Hunt Street*. As far as he knew, there was no Hunt Street in Chicago, and he sure as hell was not John Jones. He pocketed the cash. 'Much obliged. I'll be back in a few days for it.'

'Right.'

The pawnbroker picked up the telephone and made a call.

A detective arrived at the pawnshop twenty minutes later.

'Why didn't you call while he was here?' he demanded.

'I tried. He was in a hurry, and he was jumpy.'

The detective studied the form the customer had filled out.

'That won't do you no good,' the pawnbroker said. 'It's probably a false name and address.'

The detective grunted. 'No kidding. Did he fill this out himself?'

'Yes.'

'Then we'll nail him.'

At police headquarters, it took the computer less than three minutes to identify the thumbprint on the form. *Jesse Shaw.*

The butler came into the drawing room. 'Excuse me, Mr Adler, there's a gentleman on the telephone for you. A Lieutenant Mancini. Shall I . . . ?'

'I'll take it.' Philip picked up the telephone. 'Hello?'

'Philip Adler?'

'Yes . . . ?'

'This is Lieutenant Mancini. I came to see you in the hospital.'

'I remember.'

'I wanted to bring you up to date on what's happening. We had a bit of luck. I told you that our Chief was going to send out flyers to pawnshops with a description of your watch?'

'Yes.'

'They found it. The watch was pawned in Chicago. They're tracking down the person who pawned it. You did say that you could identify your assailant, didn't you?'

'That's right.'

'Good. We'll be in touch.'

*

Jerry Townsend came into Lara's office. He was excited. 'I've worked out the party list we talked about. The more I think about the idea, the better I like it. We'll celebrate your fortieth birthday on the day the tallest skyscraper in the world opens.' He handed Lara the list. 'I've included the Vice President. He's a big admirer of yours.'

Lara scanned it. It read like a *Who's Who* from Washington, Hollywood, New York and London. There were government officials, motion picture celebrities, rock stars . . . it was impressive.

'I like it,' Lara said. 'Let's go with it.'

Townsend put the list in his pocket. 'Right. I'll have the invitations printed up and sent out. I've already called Carlos and told him to reserve the Grand Ballroom and arrange your favourite menu. We're setting up for two hundred people. We can always add or subtract a few if we have to. By the way, is there any more news on the Reno situation?'

Lara had talked to Terry Hill that morning. *'A Grand Jury is investigating, Lara. There's a possibility that they'll hand down a criminal indictment.'*

'How can they? The fact that I had some conversations with Paul Martin doesn't prove anything. We could have been talking about the state of the world, or his ulcers, or a dozen other damned things.'

'Lara, don't get angry with me. I'm on your side.'

Then do something. You're my lawyer. Get me the hell out of this.'

'No. Everything's fine,' Lara told Townsend.

'Good. I understand that you and Philip are going to the Mayor's dinner Saturday night.'

'Yes.' She had wanted to turn down the invitation at first, but Philip had insisted.

'You need these people. You can't afford to offend them. I want you to go.'

'Not without you, darling.'

He had taken a deep breath. 'All right. I'll go with you. I guess it's time I stopped being a hermit.'

On Saturday evening Lara helped Philip get dressed. She put his studs and cufflinks in his shirt, and tied his tie for him. He stood there, silently, cursing his helplessness.

'It's like Ken and Barbie, isn't it?'

'What?'

'Nothing.'

'There you are, darling. You'll be the most handsome man there.'

'Thanks.'

'I'd better get dressed,' Lara said. 'The Mayor doesn't like to be kept waiting.'

'I'll be in the library,' Philip told her.

Thirty minutes later, Lara walked into the library. She looked ravishing. She was dressed in a beautiful white Oscar de la Renta gown. On her wrist was the diamond bracelet Philip had given her.

Philip had difficulty sleeping on Saturday night. He looked across the bed at Lara, and wondered how she could have falsely accused Marian of stealing the bracelet. He knew he had to confront her with it, but he wanted to speak with Marian first.

Early on Sunday morning, while Lara was still asleep, Philip quietly got dressed and left the penthouse. He took a taxi to Marian's apartment. He rang the bell and waited.

A sleepy voice said, 'Who is it?'

'It's Philip. I have to talk to you.'

The door opened and Marian stood there.

'Philip? Is something wrong?'

'We have to talk.'

'Come in.'

He entered the apartment. 'I'm sorry if I woke you up,' Philip said, 'but this is important.'

'What's happened?'

He took a deep breath. 'You were right about the bracelet. Lara wore it last night. I owe you an apology, I thought . . . perhaps that you . . . I just wanted to say I'm sorry.'

Marian said quietly, 'Of course you would have believed her. She's your wife.'

'I'm going to confront Lara with it this morning, but I wanted to talk to you first.'

Marian turned to him. 'I'm glad you did. I don't want you to discuss it with her.'

'Why not?' Philip demanded. 'And why would she do such a thing?'

'You don't know, do you?'

'Frankly, no. It makes no sense.'

'I think I understand her better than you do. Lara is madly in love with you. She would do anything to hold on to you. You're probably the only person she has ever really loved in her life. She needs you. And I think you need her. You love her very much, don't you, Philip?'

'Yes.'

'Then let's forget all this. If you bring it up with her, it won't do any good, and it will only make things worse between the two of you. I can easily find another job.'

'But it's unfair to you, Marian.'

She smiled wryly. 'Life isn't always fair, is it?' *If it were, I would be Mrs Philip Adler.* 'Don't worry. I'll be fine.'

'At least let me do something for you. Let me give you some money to make up for . . .'

'Thank you, but no.'

There was so much she wanted to say, but she knew that it was hopeless. He was a man in love. What she said was, 'Go back to her, Philip.'

The construction site was on Chicago's Wabash Avenue, south of the Loop. It was a twenty-five-storey office building, and it was half finished. An unmarked police car pulled up to the corner, and two detectives got out. They walked over to the site, and stopped one of the workers passing by. 'Where's the foreman?'

He pointed to a huge, burly man cursing out a workman. 'Over there.'

The detectives went over to him. 'Are you in charge here?'

He turned and said impatiently, 'I'm not only in charge, I'm very busy. What do you want?'

'Do you have a man in your crew named Jesse Shaw?'

'Shaw? Sure. He's up there.' The foreman pointed to a man working on a steel girder a dozen storeys up.

'Would you ask him to come down, please?'

'Hell, no. He has work to . . .'

One of the detectives pulled out a badge. 'Get him down here.'

'What's the problem? Is Jesse in some kind of trouble?'

'No, we just want to talk to him.'

'Okay.' The foreman turned to one of the men working nearby, 'Go up top and tell Jesse to come down here.'

'Right.'

A few minutes later, Jesse Shaw was approaching the two detectives.

'These men want to talk to you,' the foreman said, and walked away.

Jesse grinned at the two men. 'Thanks. I can use a break. What can I do for you?'

One of the detectives pulled out a wristwatch. 'Is this your watch?'

Shaw's grin faded. 'No.'

'Are you sure?'

'Yeah.' He pointed to his wrist. 'I wear a Seiko.'

'But you pawned this watch.'

Shaw hesitated. 'Oh, yeah. I did. The bastard only gave me five hundred for it. It's worth at least . . .'

'You said it wasn't your watch.'

'That's right. It's not.'

'Where did you get it?'

'I found it.'

'Really? Where?'

'On the sidewalk near my apartment building.' He was warming up to his story. 'It was in the grass, and I got out of my car, and there it was. The sun hit the band and made it sparkle. That's how I happened to see it.'

'Lucky it wasn't a cloudy day.'

'Yeah.'

'Mr Shaw, do you like to travel?'

'No.'

'That's too bad. You're going to take a little trip to New York. We'll help you pack.'

When they got to Shaw's apartment, the two detectives began looking around.

'Hold it!' Shaw said. 'You guys got a search warrant?'

'We don't need one. We're just helping you pack your things.'

One of the men was looking in a clothes closet. There was a shoe box high up on a shelf. He took it down and opened it. 'Jesus!' he said. 'Look what Santa Claus left.'

Lara was in her office when Kathy's voice came over the intercom. 'Mr Tilly is on line four, Miss Cameron.'

Tilly was the project manager on Cameron Towers.

Lara picked up the phone. 'Hello?'

'We had a little problem this morning, Miss Cameron.'

'Yes?'

'We had a fire. It's out now.'

'What happened?'

'There was an explosion in the air conditioning unit. A transformer blew. There was a short circuit. It looks like someone wired it up wrong.'

'How bad is it?'

'Well, it looks like we'll lose a day or two. We

should be able to clean everything up and rewire it by then.'

'Stay on it. Keep me informed.'

Lara came home late each evening, worried and exhausted.

'I'm concerned about you,' Philip told her. 'Is there anything I can do?'

'Nothing, darling. Thank you.' She managed a smile. 'Just a few problems at the office.'

He took her in his arms. 'Did I ever tell you that I'm mad about you?'

She looked up at him and smiled. 'Tell me again.'

'I'm mad about you.'

She held him close and thought. *This is what I want. This is what I need.* 'Darling, when my little problems are over, let's go away somewhere. Just the two of us.'

'It's a deal.'

Someday, Lara thought, *I must tell him what I did to Marian. I know it was wrong. But I would die if I lost him.*

The following day, Tilly called again. 'Did you cancel the order for the marble for the lobby floors?'

Lara said slowly, 'Why would I do that?'

'I don't know. Somebody did. The marble was supposed to have been delivered today. When I called, they said it was cancelled two months ago by your order.'

Lara sat there fuming. 'I see. How badly are we delayed?'

'I'm not sure yet.'

'Tell them to put a rush on it.'

Keller came into Lara's office.

'I'm afraid the banks are getting nervous, Lara. I don't know how much longer I can hold them off.'

'Just until Cameron Towers is finished. We're almost there, Howard. We're only three months away from completion.'

'I told them that,' he sighed. 'All right. I'll talk to them again.'

Kathy's voice came over the intercom. 'Mr Tilly's on line one.'

Lara looked at Keller. 'Don't go.' She picked up the phone. 'Yes?' Lara said.

'We're having another problem here, Miss Cameron.'

'I'm listening,' Lara said.

'The elevators are malfunctioning. The pro-grammes are out of sync, and the signals are all screwed up. You press the button for down and it goes up. Press the eighteenth floor and it will take you to the basement. I've never seen anything like this before.'

'Do you think it was done deliberately?'

'It's hard to say. Could have been carelessness.'

'How long will it take to straighten it out?'

'I have some people on the way over now.'

'Get back to me.' She replaced the receiver.

'Is everything all right?' Keller asked.

Lara evaded the question. 'Howard, have you heard anything about Steve Murchison lately?'

He looked at her, surprised. 'No. Why?'

'I just wondered.'

The consortium of bankers financing Cameron Enterprises had good reason to be concerned. It was not only Cameron Enterprises that was in trouble – a majority of their corporate clients had serious problems. The decline in junk bonds had become a full-fledged disaster, and it was a crippling blow to the corporations that had depended on them.

There were six bankers in the room with Howard Keller, and the atmosphere was grim.

'We're holding overdue notes for almost a hundred million dollars,' their spokesman said. 'I'm afraid we can't accommodate Cameron Enterprises any longer.'

'You're forgetting a couple of things,' Keller reminded them. 'Number one, we expect the casino gambling licence in Reno to be renewed any day now. That cash flow will more than take care of any deficit. Number two, Cameron Towers is right on schedule. It's going to be finished in ninety days. We already have a seventy per cent tenancy, and you can be assured that the day it's finished everybody is going to be clamouring to get in. Gentlemen, your money couldn't be more secure. You're dealing with the Lara Cameron magic.'

The men looked at one another.

The spokesman said. 'Why don't we discuss this among ourselves and we'll get back to you.'

'Fine. I'll tell Miss Cameron.'

*

Keller reported back to Lara.

'I think they'll go along with us,' he told her. 'But in the meantime, we're going to have to sell off a few more assets to stay afloat.'

'Do it.'

Lara was getting to the office early in the morning and leaving late at night, fighting desperately to save her empire. She and Philip saw very little of each other. Lara did not want him to know how much trouble she was facing. *He has enough problems*, Lara thought. *I can't burden him with any more.*

At six o'clock on Monday morning, Tilly was on the phone. 'I think you'd better get over here, Miss Cameron.'

Lara felt a sharp sense of apprehension. 'What's wrong?'

'I'd rather you saw it for yourself.'

'I'm on my way.'

Lara telephoned Keller. 'Howard, there's another problem at Cameron Towers. I'll pick you up.'

Half an hour later they were on their way to the construction site.

'Did Tilly say what the trouble was?' Keller asked.

'No, but I don't believe in accidents any more. I've been thinking about what you said. Steve Murchison wanted that property badly. I took it away from him.'

When they arrived at the site, they saw large sheets of crated tinted glass lying on the ground, and more glass being delivered by trucks. Tilly hurried over to Lara and Keller.

'I'm glad you're here.'

'What's the problem?'

412

'This isn't the glass we ordered. It's the wrong tint and the wrong cut. There's no way it will fit the sides of our building.'

Lara and Keller looked at each other. 'Can we re-cut it here?' Keller asked.

Tilly shook his head. 'Not a chance. You'd wind up with a mountain of silicate.'

Lara said, 'Who did we order this from?'

'The New Jersey Panel and Glass Company.'

'I'll call them,' Lara said. 'What's our deadline on this?'

Tilly stood there calculating. 'If it got here in two weeks, we could be back on schedule. It would be a push, but we'd be okay.'

Lara turned to Keller, 'Let's go.'

Otto Karp was the manager of the New Jersey Panel and Glass Company. He came on the phone almost immediately. 'Yes, Miss Cameron? I understand you have a problem.'

'No,' Lara snapped. '*You* have a problem. You shipped us the wrong glass. If I don't get the right order in the next two weeks, I'm going to sue your company out of business. You're holding up a three-hundred-million-dollar project.'

'I don't understand. Will you hold on, please?'

He was gone almost five minutes. When he came back on the line, he said, 'I'm terribly sorry, Miss Cameron, the order was written up wrong. What happened is . . .'

'I don't care what happened,' Lara interrupted. 'All I want you to do is to get our order filled and ship it out.'

'I'll be happy to do that.'

Lara felt a sharp sense of relief. 'How soon can we have it?'

'In two to three months.'

'Two to three months! That's impossible! We need it *now*.'

'I'd be happy to accommodate you,' Karp said, 'but unfortunately we're way behind in our orders.'

'You don't understand,' Lara said. 'This is an emergency and . . .'

'I certainly appreciate that. And we'll do the best we can. You'll have the order in two to three months. I'm sorry we can't do better . . .'

Lara slammed down the receiver. 'I don't believe this,' Lara said. She looked over at Tilly. 'Is there another company we can deal with?'

Tilly rubbed his hand across his forehead. 'Not at this late date. If we went to anyone else, they'd be starting from scratch, and their other customers would be ahead of us.'

Keller said, 'Lara, could I talk to you for a minute?' He took her aside. 'I hate to suggest this, but . . .'

'Go ahead.'

'. . . your friend Paul Martin might have some connections over there. Or he might know someone who knows someone.'

Lara nodded. 'Good idea, Howard. I'll find out.'

Two hours later, Lara was seated in Paul Martin's office.

'You don't know how happy I am that you called,'

the lawyer said. 'It's been too long. God, you look beautiful, Lara.'

'Thank you, Paul.'

'What can I do for you?'

Lara said hesitantly, 'I seem to come to you whenever I'm in trouble.'

'I've always been there for you, haven't I?'

'Yes. You're a good friend.' She sighed. 'Right now I need a good friend.'

'What's the problem? Another strike?'

'No. It's about Cameron Towers.'

He frowned. 'I heard that was on schedule.'

'It is. Or it was. I think Steve Murchison is out to sabotage the project. He has a vendetta against me. Things have suddenly started to go wrong at the building. Up to now, we've been able to handle them. Now . . . We have a big problem. It could put us past our completion date. Our two biggest tenants would pull out. I can't afford to let that happen.'

She took a deep breath, trying to control her anger.

'Six months ago we ordered tinted glass from the New Jersey Panel and Glass Company. We received our delivery this morning. It wasn't our glass.'

'Did you call them?'

'Yes, but they're talking about two or three months. I need that glass in two weeks. Until it's in, there's nothing for the men to do. They've stopped working. If that building isn't completed on schedule, I'll lose everything I have.'

Paul Martin looked at her and said quietly, 'No, you won't. Let me see what I can do.'

Lara felt an overwhelming sense of relief. 'Paul, I . . .' It was difficult to put into words. 'Thank you.'

He took her hand in his and smiled. 'The dinosaur isn't dead yet,' he said. 'I should have some word for you by tomorrow.'

The following morning, Lara's private phone rang for the first time in months. She picked it up eagerly. 'Paul?'

'Hello, Lara. I had a little talk with some of my friends. It's not going to be easy, but it can be done. They promised a delivery a week from Monday.'

On the day the glass shipment was scheduled to arrive, Lara telephoned Paul Martin again.

'The glass hasn't come yet, Paul,' Lara said.

'Oh?' There was a silence. 'I'll look into it.' His voice softened. 'You know, the only good thing about this, baby, is that I get to talk to you again.'

'Yes. I . . . Paul . . . if I don't get that glass on time . . .'

'You'll have it. Don't give up.'

By the end of the week, there was still no word.

Keller came into Lara's office. 'I just talked to Tilly. Our deadline is Friday. If the glass arrives by then, we'll be okay. Otherwise, we're dead.'

By Thursday, nothing had changed.

Lara went to visit Cameron Towers. There were no workmen there. The skyscraper rose majestically into the sky, overshadowing everything around it. It

416

was going to be a beautiful building. Her monument. *I'm not going to let it fail*, Lara thought fiercely.

Lara telephoned Paul Martin again.

'I'm sorry,' his secretary said. 'Mr Martin is out of the office. Is there any message?'

'Please ask him to call me,' Lara said. She turned to Keller, 'I have a hunch I'd like you to check out. See if the owner of that glass factory happens to be Steve Murchison.'

Thirty minutes later, Keller returned to Lara's office. His face was pale.

'Well? Did you find out who owns the glass company?'

'Yes,' he said slowly. 'It's registered in Delaware. It's owned by Etna Enterprises.'

'Etna Enterprises?'

'Right. They bought it a year ago. Etna Enterprises is Paul Martin.'

33

The bad publicity about Cameron Enterprises continued. The reporters who had been so eager to praise Lara before now turned on her.

Jerry Townsend went in to see Howard Keller.

'I'm worried,' Townsend said.

'What's the problem?'

'Have you been reading the press?'

'Yeah. They're having a field day.'

'I'm worried about the birthday party, Howard. I've sent out the invitations. Since all this bad publicity, I've been getting nothing but turn-downs. The bastards are afraid they might be contaminated. It's a fiasco.'

'What do you suggest?'

'That we cancel the party. I'll make up some excuse.'

'I think you're right. I don't want anything to embarrass her.'

'Good. I'll go ahead and cancel it. Will you tell Lara?'

'Yes.'

Terry Hill called.

'I just received notice that you're being subpoenaed to testify before the Grand Jury in Reno, day after tomorrow. I'll go with you.'

Transcript of Interrogation of Jesse Shaw by Detective Lieutenant Sal Mancini.

M: Good morning, Mr Shaw. I'm Lieutenant Mancini. You're aware that a stenographer is taking down our conversation?

S: Sure.

M: And you've waived the right to an attorney?

S: I don't need no attorney. All I did was find a watch, for Christ's sake, and they drag me all the way up here like I'm some kind of animal.

M: Mr Shaw, do you know who Philip Adler is?

S: No. Should I?

M: No one paid you to attack him?

S: I told you – I never heard of him.

M: The police in Chicago found fifty thousand dollars in cash in your apartment. Where did that money come from?

S: [No response]

M: Mr Shaw . . . ?

S: I won it gambling.

M: Where?

S: At the track . . . football bets . . . you know.

M: You're a lucky man, aren't you?

S: Yeah. I guess so.

M: At present, you have a job in Chicago. Is that right?

S: Yes.

M: Did you ever work in New York?

S: Well, one time, yeah.

M: I have a police report here that says you were operating a crane at a development in Queens that killed a construction foreman named Bill Whitman. Is that correct?

S: Yeah. It was an accident.

M: How long had you been on that job?

S: I don't remember.

M: Let me refresh your memory. You were on that job seventy-two hours. You flew in from Chicago the day before the accident with the crane, and flew back to Chicago two days later. Is that correct?

S: I guess so.

M: According to American Airlines' records, you flew from Chicago to New York again two days before Philip Adler was attacked, and you returned to Chicago the following day. What was the purpose of such a short trip?

S: I wanted to see some plays.

M: Do you remember the names of the plays you saw?

S: No. That was a while ago.

M: At the time of the accident with the crane, who was your employer?

S: Cameron Enterprises.

M: And who is your employer on the

construction job you're working on in Chicago?

S: Cameron Enterprises.

Howard Keller was in a meeting with Lara. For the past hour, they had been talking about damage control to offset the bad publicity the company was receiving. As the meeting was about to break up, Lara said, 'Anything else?'

Howard frowned. Someone had told him to tell Lara something, but he could not remember what it was. *Oh, well, it's probably not important.*

Simms, the butler, said, 'There's a telephone call for you, Mr Adler. A Lieutenant Mancini.'

Philip picked up the telephone. 'Lieutenant. What can I do for you?'

'I have some news for you, Mr Adler.'

'What is it? Did you find the man?'

'I'd prefer to come up and discuss it with you in person. Would that be all right?'

'Of course.'

'I'll be there in half an hour.'

Philip replaced the receiver, wondering what it was that the detective did not want to talk about on the telephone.

When Mancini arrived, Simms showed him into the library.

'Afternoon, Mr Adler.'

'Good afternoon. What's going on?'

'We caught the man who attacked you.'

'You did? I'm surprised,' Philip said. 'I thought you said it was impossible to catch muggers.'

'He's not an ordinary mugger.'

Philip frowned. 'I don't understand.'

'He's a construction worker. He works out of Chicago and New York. He has a police record – assault, breaking and entering. He pawned your watch and we got his prints.' Mancini held up a wrist-watch. 'This is your watch, isn't it?'

Philip stared at it, not wanting to touch it. The sight of it brought back the horrible moment when the man had grabbed his wrist and slashed it. Reluctantly, he reached out and took the watch. He looked at the back of the case where some of the letters had been scratched off. 'Yes. It's mine.'

Lieutenant Mancini took the watch back. 'We'll keep this for the moment, as evidence. I'd like you to come downtown tomorrow morning to identify the man in a police line-up.'

The thought of seeing his attacker again, face to face, filled Philip with a sudden fury. 'I'll be there.'

'The address is One Police Plaza, Room 212. Ten o'clock?'

'Fine.' He frowned. 'What did you mean when you said he wasn't an ordinary mugger?'

Lieutenant Mancini hesitated. 'He was paid to attack you.'

Philip was staring at him, bewildered. '*What?*'

'What happened to you wasn't an accident. He got paid fifty thousand dollars to cut you up.'

'I don't believe it,' Philip said slowly. 'Who would pay anyone fifty thousand dollars to cripple me?'

'He was hired by your wife.'

34

He was hired by your wife!

Philip was stunned. *Lara?* Could Lara have done such a terrible thing? What reason would she have?

I don't understand why you practise every day. You're not giving a concert now . . .

You don't have to go. I want a husband. Not a part-time . . . It's not as though you were some kind of travelling salesman . . .

She accused me of stealing the diamond bracelet you gave her. She would do anything to hold on to you . . .

And Ellerbee: *I had a talk with Lara. Are you thinking of cutting back on your concerts? . . .*

Lara.

At One Police Plaza, a meeting was in progress with the District Attorney, the Police Commissioner, and Lieutenant Mancini.

The District Attorney was saying, 'We're not dealing here with Jane Doe. The lady has a lot of clout. How much solid evidence do you have, Lieutenant?'

Mancini said, 'I checked with personnel at Cameron Enterprises. Jesse Shaw was hired at the request of Lara Cameron. I asked them if she had ever personally hired anyone on the construction crew before. The answer was "no".'

'What else?'

'There was a rumour that a construction boss named Bill Whitman was bragging to his buddies that he had something on Lara Cameron that was going to make him a rich man. Shortly after that, he was killed by a crane operated by Jesse Shaw. Shaw had been pulled off his job in Chicago to go to New York. After the accident he went right back to Chicago. There's no question but that it was a hit. Incidentally, his airline ticket was paid for by Cameron Enterprises.'

'What about the attack on Adler?'

'Same MO. Shaw flew in from Chicago two days before the attack, and left the next day. If he hadn't got greedy and decided to pick up a little extra money by pawning the watch, instead of throwing it away, we would never have caught him.'

The Police Commissioner asked, 'What about motive? Why would she do that to her husband?'

'I talked to some of the servants. Lara Cameron was crazy about her husband. The only thing they ever quarrelled about was his going away on concert tours. She wanted him to stay home.'

'And now he's staying home.'

'Exactly.'

The District Attorney asked, 'What's her story? Does she deny it?'

'We haven't confronted her yet. We wanted to talk to you first to see if we have a case.'

'You say that Philip Adler can identify Shaw?'

'Yes.'

'Good.'

'Why don't you send one of your men over to question Lara Cameron? See what she has to say.'

Lara was in a meeting with Howard Keller when the intercom buzzed. 'There's a Lieutenant Mancini here to see you.'

Lara frowned. 'What about?'

'He didn't say.'

'Send him in.'

Lieutenant Mancini was treading on delicate ground. Without hard evidence, it was going to be difficult to get anything out of Lara Cameron. *But I've got to give it a try*, he thought. He had not expected to see Howard Keller there.

'Good afternoon, Lieutenant.'

'Afternoon.'

'You've met Howard Keller.'

'I certainly have. Best pitching arm in Chicago.'

'What can I do for you?' Lara asked.

This was the tricky part. *First establish that she knew Jesse Shaw and then lead her on from there.*

'We've arrested the man who attacked your husband.' He was watching her face.

'You have? What . . . ?'

Howard Keller interrupted. 'How did you catch him?'

'He pawned a watch that Miss Cameron gave her husband.' Mancini looked at Lara again. 'The man's name is Jesse Shaw.'

There was not the faintest change of expression. *She's good*, Mancini thought. *The lady is really good.*

'Do you know him?'

Lara frowned. 'No. Should I?'

That's her first slip, Mancini thought. *I've got her*.

'He worked on the construction crew of one of your buildings in Chicago. He also worked for you on a project in Queens. He was operating a crane that killed a man.' He pretended to consult his notebook. 'A Bill Whitman. The Coroner's inquest put it down as an accident.'

Lara swallowed. 'Yes . . .'

Before she could go on, Keller spoke up. 'Look, Lieutenant, we have hundreds of people working for this company. You can't expect us to know them all.'

'You don't know Jesse Shaw?'

'No. And I'm sure Miss Cameron . . .'

'I'd rather hear it from her, if you don't mind.'

Lara said, 'I've never heard of the man.'

'He was paid fifty thousand dollars to attack your husband.'

'I . . . I can't believe it!' Her face was suddenly drained of colour.

Now I'm getting to her, Mancini thought. 'You don't know anything about it?'

Lara was staring at him, her eyes suddenly blazing. 'Are you suggesting . . . ? How dare you! If someone put him up to that, I want to know who it was!'

'So does your husband, Miss Cameron.'

'You discussed this with Philip?'

'Yes. I . . .'

A moment later, Lara was flying out of the office.

*

When Lara reached the penthouse, Philip was in the bedroom packing, clumsily because of his crippled hand.

'Philip . . . what are you doing?'

He turned to face her, and it was as though he was seeing her for the first time. 'I'm leaving.'

'Why? You can't believe that . . . that terrible story?'

'No more lies, Lara.'

'But I'm *not* lying. You've got to listen to me. I had nothing to do with what happened to you. I wouldn't hurt you for anything in the world. I love you, Philip.'

He turned to face her. 'The police say that the man worked for you. That he was paid fifty thousand dollars to . . . to do what he did.'

She shook her head. 'I don't know anything about it. I only know that I had nothing to do with it. Do you believe me?'

He stared at her, silent.

Lara stood there for a long moment, then turned and blindly walked out of the room.

Philip spent a sleepless night at a downtown hotel. Visions of Lara kept coming to his mind. *I'm interested in knowing more about the foundation. Perhaps we could get together and discuss it . . .*

Are you married? Tell me about yourself . . .

When I listen to your Scarlatti, I'm in Naples . . .

I dream a dream of bricks and concrete and steel, and make it come true . . .

I came to Amsterdam to see you . . .

Would you like me to go with you to Milan . . . ?

427

You're going to spoil me, lady . . . I intend to . . .

And Lara's warmth, compassion, and caring. Could I have been that wrong about her?

When Philip arrived at police headquarters, Lieutenant Mancini was waiting for him. He led Philip into a small auditorium with a raised platform at the far end.

'All we need is for you to identify him in the line-up.'

So they can tie him in with Lara, Philip thought.

There were six men in the line-up, all roughly the same build and age. Jesse Shaw was in the middle. When Philip saw him, his head began to pound suddenly. He could hear his voice saying, '*Give me your wallet.*' He could feel the terrible pain of the knife slashing across his wrist. *Could Lara have done that to me?* '*You're the only man I've ever loved.*'

Lieutenant Mancini was speaking. 'Take a good look, Mr Adler.'

'*I'm going to be working at home from now on. Philip needs me . . .*'

'Mr Adler . . .'

'*We're going to get you the best doctors in the world.*' She had been there for him every moment, nurturing him, caring for him. '*If Mohammed won't go to the mountain . . .*'

'Would you point him out to me?'

'*I married you because I was wildly head over heels in love with you. I still am. If we never make love again it will be fine with me. All I want is for you to hold me and love me . . .*' And she had meant it.

And then the last scene in the apartment. '*I had*

*nothing to do with what happened to you. I wouldn't
hurt you for anything in the world . . .'*

'Mr Adler . . .'

The police must have made a mistake, Philip
thought. *By God, I believe her. She couldn't have
done it!*

Mancini was speaking again. 'Which one is he?'

And Philip turned to him and said, 'I don't know.'

'What?'

'I don't see him.'

'You told us you got a good look at him.'

'That's right.'

'Then tell me which one he is.'

'I can't,' Philip said. 'He's not up there.'

Lieutenant Mancini's face was grim. 'You're sure
about that?'

Philip stood up. 'I'm positive.'

'Then I guess that's all, Mr Adler. Thanks a lot
for your cooperation.'

I've got to find Lara, Philip thought. *I've got to
find Lara.*

She was seated at her desk, staring out of the
window. Philip had not believed her. That was what
hurt so terribly. And Paul Martin. *Of course he was
behind it. But why did he do it?* 'Do you remember
what I said about your husband taking care of you?
He doesn't seem to be doing a very good job. Someone should have a talk with him!' Was it because he
loved her? Or was it an act of vengeance because he
hated her?

Howard Keller walked in. His face looked white
and drawn. 'I just got off the phone. We lost

429

Cameron Towers, Lara. Both Southern Insurance and International Investment Banking are pulling out because we can't meet our completion date. There's no way we can handle our mortgage payments. We almost made it, didn't we? The biggest skyscraper in the world. I'm . . . I'm sorry. I know how much it meant to you.'

Lara turned to face him, and Keller was shocked by her appearance. Her face was pale, and there were black circles under her eyes. She seemed dazed, as though the energy had been drained from her.

'Lara . . . did you hear what I said? We've lost Cameron Towers.'

When she spoke, her voice was unnaturally calm. 'I heard you. Don't worry, Howard. We'll borrow on some of the other buildings and pay everything off.'

She was frightening him. 'Lara, there's nothing more to borrow on. You're going to have to file for bankruptcy and . . .'

'Howard . . . ?'

'Yes?'

'Can a woman love a man too much?'

'What?'

Her voice was dead. 'Philip has left me.'

It suddenly explained a lot. 'I . . . I'm sorry, Lara.'

She had a strange smile on her face. 'It's funny, isn't it? I'm losing everything at once. First Philip, now my buildings. Do you know what it is, Howard? It's the Fates. They're against me. You can't fight the Fates, can you?'

He had never seen her in such pain. It tore at him. 'Lara . . .'

'They're not through with me yet. I have to fly to

430

Reno this afternoon. There's a Grand Jury hearing. If . . .'

The intercom buzzed. 'There's a Lieutenant Mancini here.'

'Send him in.'

Howard Keller looked at Lara quizzically. 'Mancini? What does he want?'

Lara took a deep breath. 'He's here to arrest me, Howard.'

'*Arrest* you? What are you talking about?'

Her voice was very quiet. 'They think I arranged the attack on Philip.'

'That's ridiculous! They can't . . .'

The door opened and Lieutenant Mancini walked in. He stood there, looking at the two of them for a moment, then moved forward.

'I have a warrant here for your arrest.'

Howard Keller's face was pale. He said hoarsely, 'You can't arrest her. She hasn't done anything.'

'You're right, Mr Keller. I'm not arresting her. The warrant is for you.'

35

Transcript of Interrogation of Howard Keller by Detective Lieutenant Sal Mancini.

M: You have been read your rights, Mr Keller?

K: Yes.

M: And you have waived the right to have an attorney present?

K: I don't need an attorney. I was going to come in anyway. I couldn't let anything happen to Lara.

M: You paid Jesse Shaw $50,000 to attack Philip Adler?

K: Yes.

M: Why?

K: He was making her miserable. She begged him to stay home with her, but he kept leaving her.

M: So you arranged to have him crippled.

K: It wasn't like that. I never meant for Jesse to go so far. He got carried away.

M: Tell me about Bill Whitman.

K: He was a bastard. He was trying to blackmail Lara. I couldn't let him do that. He could have ruined her.

M: So you had him killed?

K: For Lara's sake, yes.

M: Was she aware of what you were doing?

K: Of course not. She never would have
    allowed it. No. I was there to protect
    her, you see. Anything I did, I did for
    her. I would die for her.
    Can I ask you a question? How did you
    know I was involved in this?

End of Interrogation.

At One Police Plaza, Captain Bronson said to Mancini, 'How *did* you know he was behind it?'

'He left a loose thread and I unravelled it. I almost missed it. In Jesse Shaw's rap sheet, it mentioned that he took a fall when he was seventeen for stealing some baseball equipment from a Chicago Cubs American Legion League team. I remembered that Howard Keller had played for that team. I checked it out and sure enough, they were team-mates. That's where Keller slipped up. When I asked him, he told me he had never heard of Jesse Shaw. I called a friend of mine who used to be a sports editor for the *Chicago Sun Times*. He remembered them both. They were buddies. I figured it was Keller who got Shaw the job with Cameron Enterprises. Lara Cameron hired Jesse Shaw because Howard Keller asked her to. She probably never even saw Shaw.'

'Nice work, Sal.'

Mancini shook his head. 'You know something? In the end, it really didn't matter. If I hadn't caught him, and if we had gone after Lara Cameron, Howard Keller would have come in and confessed.'

*

Her world was collapsing. It was unbelievable to Lara that Howard Keller, of all people, could have been responsible for the terrible things that had happened. *He did it for me*, Lara thought. *I have to try to help him.*

Kathy buzzed her. 'The car is here, Miss Cameron. Are you ready?'

'Yes.' She was on her way to Reno to testify before the Grand Jury.

Five minutes after Lara left, Philip telephoned the office.

'I'm sorry, Mr Adler. You just missed her. She's on her way to Reno.'

He felt a sharp pang of disappointment. He was desperately eager to see her, to ask her forgiveness. 'When you speak to her, tell her I'll be waiting for her.'

'I'll tell her.'

He made a second phone call, spoke for ten minutes, and then telephoned William Ellerbee.

'Bill . . . I'm going to stay in New York. I'm going to teach at Juilliard.'

'What can they do to me?' Lara asked.

Terry Hill said, 'That depends. They'll listen to your testimony. They can either decide that you're innocent, in which case you'll get your casino back, or they can recommend that there's enough evidence against you to indict you. If that's their verdict, you'll be tried on criminal charges and face prison.'

Lara mumbled something.

'I'm sorry?'

'I said Papa was right. It's the Fates.'

The Grand Jury hearing lasted for four hours. Lara was questioned about the acquisition of the Cameron Palace Hotel and Casino. When they came out of the hearing room, Terry Hill squeezed Lara's hand. 'You did very well, Lara. I think you really impressed them. They have no hard evidence against you, so there's a good chance that . . .' He broke off, stunned. Lara turned. Paul Martin had come into the anteroom. He was dressed in an old fashioned double breasted suit and his white hair was combed in the same style as when Lara had first met him.

Terry Hill said, 'Oh, God! He's here to testify.' He turned to Lara. 'How much does he hate you?'

'What do you mean?'

'Lara, if they've offered him leniency to testify against you, you're finished. You'll go to prison.'

Lara was looking across the room at Paul Martin. 'But . . . then he would destroy himself, too.'

'That's why I asked you how much he hates you. Would he do that to himself to destroy you?'

Lara said numbly, 'I don't know.'

Paul Martin was walking toward them. 'Hello, Lara. I hear things have been going badly for you.' His eyes revealed nothing. 'I'm so sorry.'

Lara remembered Howard Keller's words. *'He's Sicilian. They never forgive and they never forget.'* He had been carrying this burning thirst for vengeance inside him and she had had no idea.

Paul Martin started to move away.

'Paul . . .'

He stopped. 'Yes?'

'I need to talk to you.'

He hesitated a moment. 'All right.'

He nodded toward an empty office down the corridor. 'We can talk in there.'

Terry Hill watched as the two of them went into the office. The door closed behind them. He would have given anything to have heard their conversation.

She did not know how to begin.

'What is it you want, Lara?'

It was much more difficult than she had anticipated. When she spoke, her voice was hoarse. 'I want you to let me go.'

His eyebrows were raised. 'How can I? I don't have you.' He was mocking her.

She was finding it hard to breathe.

'Don't you think you've punished me enough?'

Paul Martin stood there, stone, his expression unreadable.

'The time we had together was wonderful, Paul. Outside of Philip, you've meant more to me than anyone in my life. I owe you more than I could ever repay. I never meant to hurt you. You must believe that.'

It was difficult to go on.

'You have the power to destroy me. Is that really what you want? Will sending me to prison make you happy?' She was fighting to hold back her tears. 'I'm begging you, Paul. Give me back my life. Please, stop treating me like an enemy . . .'

Paul Martin stood there, his black eyes giving away nothing.

'I'm asking for your forgiveness. I . . . I'm too tired to fight any more, Paul. You've won . . .' Her voice broke.

There was a knock on the door, and the bailiff peered into the room. 'The Grand Jury is ready for you, Mr Martin.'

He stood there, looking at Lara for a long time, then he turned and left without a word.

It's all over, Lara thought. *It's finished.*

Terry Hill came hurrying into the office. 'I wish to God I knew how he was going to testify in there. There's nothing to do now but wait.'

They waited. It seemed an eternity. When Paul Martin finally emerged from the Hearing Room, he looked tired and drawn. *He's become old*, Lara thought. *He blames me for that.* He was watching her. He hesitated a moment, then walked over to her.

'I can never forgive you. You made a fool of me. But you were the best thing that ever happened to me. I guess I owe you something for that. I didn't tell them anything in there, Lara.'

Her eyes filled with tears. 'Oh, Paul. I don't know how to . . .'

'Call it my birthday present to you. Happy Birthday, baby.'

She watched him walk away and his words suddenly hit her. *It was her birthday!* So many events had been piling on top of one another that she had completely forgotten about it. And the party. Two hundred guests were going to be waiting for her at the Manhattan Cameron Plaza!

Lara turned to Terry Hill. 'I've got to get back to New York tonight. There's a big party for me. Will they let me go?'

'Just a minute,' Terry Hill said. He disappeared inside the hearing room, and when he came out five minutes later, he said, 'You can go to New York. The Grand Jury will give its verdict in the morning, but it's just a formality now. You can return here tonight. By the way, your friend told you the truth. He didn't talk in there.'

Thirty minutes later, Lara was headed for New York.

'Are you going to be all right?' Terry Hill asked.

She looked at him and said, 'Of course I am.' There would be hundreds of important people at the party to honour her that night. She would hold her head high. She was Lara Cameron . . .

She stood in the centre of the deserted Grand Ballroom and looked around. *I created this. I created monuments that towered into the sky, that changed the lives of thousands of people all over America. And now it's all going to belong to the faceless bankers.* She could hear her father's voice so clearly. '*It's the Fates. They've always been agin' me.*' She thought of Glace Bay and the little boarding house where she had grown up. She remembered how terrified she had been on her first day at school: '*Can anyone think of a word beginning with F?*' She remembered the boarders. Bill Rogers . . . '*The first*

*rule in real estate is other people's money. Never for-
get that.'* And Charles Cohn: *'I eat only kosher food,
and I'm afraid Glace Bay doesn't have any.'* . . .

*'If I could acquire this land, would you give me a
five-year lease?'* . . .

*'No, Lara, it would have to be a ten-year
lease.'* . . .

And Sean MacAllister . . . *'I would need a very
special reason to make this loan to you. Have you
ever had a lover?'* . . .

And Howard Keller: *'You're going about this all
wrong.'* . . .

'I want you to come and work for me.' . . .

And then the successes. The wonderful, brilliant
successes. And Philip. Her Lochinvar. The man she
adored. That was the greatest loss of all.

A voice called, 'Lara . . .'

She turned.

It was Jerry Townsend. 'Carlos told me you were
here.' He walked up to her. 'I'm sorry about the
birthday party.'

She looked at him. 'What . . . what happened?'

He was staring at her. 'Didn't Howard tell you?'

'Tell me what?'

'There were so many cancellations because of the
bad publicity that we decided it would be best to call
it off. I asked Howard to tell you.'

*To tell you the truth, I've been having some prob-
lems with my memory.*

Lara said softly, 'It doesn't matter.' She took one
last look at the beautiful room. 'I had my fifteen
minutes, didn't I?'

'What?'

'Nothing.' She started to walk toward the door.

'Lara, let's go up to the office. There are some things that have to be wound up.'

'All right.' *I'll probably never be in this building again*, Lara thought.

In the elevator on the way up to the Executive Offices, Jerry said, 'I heard about Keller. It's hard to believe he was responsible for what happened.'

Lara shook her head. 'I was responsible, Jerry. I'll never forgive myself.'

'It's not your fault.'

She felt a sudden wave of loneliness. 'Jerry, if you haven't had your dinner yet . . .'

'I'm sorry, Lara. I'm busy tonight.'

'Oh. That's all right.'

The elevator door opened and the two of them stepped out.

'The papers that you have to sign are on the Conference Room table,' Jerry said.

'Fine.'

The door to the Conference Room was closed. He let Lara open the door and as she did, forty voices started to sing out, 'Happy Birthday to you, Happy Birthday to you . . .'

Lara stood there, stunned. The room was filled with people she had worked with over the years – the architects, contractors and construction managers. Charles Cohn was there and Professor Meyers. Horace Guttman and Kathy and Jerry Townsend's father. But the only one that Lara saw was Philip. He was moving toward her, his arms outstretched, and she suddenly found it difficult to breathe.

'Lara . . .' It was a caress.

440

And she was in his arms, fighting to hold back the tears, and she thought, *I'm home. This is where I belong* and it was a healing, a blessed feeling of peace. Lara felt a warm glow as she held him. *This is all that matters*, Lara thought.

People were crowding around her and everyone seemed to be talking at once.

'Happy birthday, Lara . . .'

'You look wonderful . . .'

'Were you surprised . . . ?'

Lara turned to Jerry Townsend. 'Jerry, how did you . . . ?'

He shook his head. 'Philip arranged it.'

'Oh, darling!'

Waiters were coming in now with hors d'oeuvres and drinks.

Charles Cohn said, 'No matter what happens, I'm proud of you, Lara. You said you wanted to make a difference, and you did.'

Jerry Townsend's father was saying, 'I owe my life to this woman.'

'So do I,' Kathy smiled.

'Let's drink a toast,' Jerry Townsend said, 'to the best boss I ever had, or ever will have!'

Charles Cohn raised his glass. 'To a wonderful little girl who became a wonderful woman!'

The toasts went on, and finally it was Philip's turn. There was too much to say, and he put it in five words: 'To the woman I love.'

Lara's eyes were brimming with tears. She found it difficult to speak. 'I . . . I owe so much to all of you,' Lara said. 'There's no way I can ever repay you. I just want to say . . .' She choked up, unable to go on. '. . . thank you.'

Lara turned to Philip. 'Thank you for this, darling. It's the nicest birthday I've ever had.' She suddenly remembered. 'I have to fly back to Reno tonight!'

Philip looked at her and grinned. 'I've never been to Reno . . .'

Half an hour later they were in the limousine on their way to the airport. Lara was holding Philip's hand and thinking, *I haven't lost everything after all. I'll spend the rest of my life making it up to him. Nothing else matters. The only important thing is being with him and taking care of him. I don't need anything else.*

'Lara . . . ?'

She was looking out of the window. 'Stop, Max!'

The limousine braked to a quick stop.

Philip looked at her, puzzled. They had stopped in front of a huge empty lot, covered with weeds. Lara was staring at it.

'Lara . . .'

'Look, Philip!'

He turned to look. 'What?'

'Don't you see it?'

'See what?'

'Oh, it's beautiful! A shopping mall over there, in the far corner! In the middle we'll put up luxury apartment houses. There's room enough for four buildings. You see it now, don't you?'

He was staring at Lara, mesmerized.

She turned to him, her voice charged with excitement. 'Now, here's my plan . . .'

THE
BEST LAID
PLANS

*This book is dedicated to you
with my appreciation*

One

The first entry in Leslie Stewart's diary read:

> *Dear Diary: This morning I met the man I am going to marry.*

It was a simple, optimistic statement, with not the slightest portent of the dramatic chain of events that was about to occur.

It was one of those rare, serendipitous days when nothing could go wrong, when nothing would dare go wrong. Leslie Stewart had no interest in astrology, but that morning, as she was leafing through the *Lexington Herald-Leader*, a horoscope in an astrology column by Zoltaire caught her eye. It read:

> For Leo (July 23rd to August 22nd). The new moon illuminates your love life. You are in your lunar cycle high now, and must pay close attention to an

1

EXCITING NEW EVENT IN YOUR LIFE. YOUR
COMPATIBLE SIGN IS VIRGO. TODAY WILL
BE A RED-LETTER DAY. BE PREPARED TO
ENJOY IT.

Be prepared to enjoy what? Leslie thought wryly. Today
was going to be like every other day. Astrology was
nonsense, mind candy for fools.

Leslie Stewart was a public relations and advertising
executive at the Lexington, Kentucky, firm of Bailey &
Tomkins. She had three meetings scheduled for that
afternoon, the first with the Kentucky Fertilizer Company, whose executives were excited about the new
campaign she was working up for them. They especially
liked its beginning: 'If you want to smell the roses
. . .' The second meeting was with the Breeders Stud
Farm, and the third with the Lexington Coal Company.
Red-letter day?

In her late twenties, with a slim, provocative figure, Leslie
Stewart had an exciting, exotic look; gray, sloe eyes, high
cheek-bones, and soft, honey-colored hair, which she
wore long and elegantly simple. A friend of Leslie's had
once told her, 'If you're beautiful and have a brain and
a vagina, you can own the world.'

Leslie Stewart was beautiful and had an IQ of 170, and
nature had taken care of the rest. But she found her looks
a disadvantage. Men were constantly propositioning her

2

or proposing, but few of them bothered to try really to get to know her.

Aside from the two secretaries who worked at Bailey & Tomkins, Leslie was the only woman there. There were fifteen male employees. It had taken Leslie less than a week to learn that she was more intelligent than any of them. It was a discovery she decided to keep to herself.

In the beginning, both partners, Jim Bailey, an overweight, soft-spoken man in his forties, and Al Tomkins, anorexic and hyper, ten years younger than Bailey, individually tried to talk Leslie into going to bed with them.

She had stopped them very simply. 'Ask me once more, and I'll quit.'

That had put an end to that. Leslie was too valuable an employee to lose.

Her first week on the job, during a coffee break, Leslie had told her fellow employees a joke.

'Three men came across a female genie who promised to grant each one a wish. The first man said, "I wish I were twenty-five percent smarter." The genie blinked, and the man said, "Hey, I feel smarter already."

'The second man said, "I wish I were fifty percent smarter." The genie blinked, and the man exclaimed, "That's wonderful! I think I know things now that I didn't know before."

'The third man said, "I'd like to be one hundred percent smarter."

'So the genie blinked, and the man changed into a woman.'

Leslie looked expectantly at the men at the table. They were all staring at her, unamused.

Point taken.

The red-letter day that the astrologer had promised began at eleven o'clock that morning. Jim Bailey walked into Leslie's tiny, cramped office.

'We have a new client,' he announced. 'I want you to take charge.'

She was already handling more accounts than anyone else at the firm, but she knew better than to protest.

'Fine,' she said. 'What is it?'

'It's not a what, it's a who. You've heard of Oliver Russell, of course?'

Everyone had heard of Oliver Russell. A local attorney and candidate for governor, he had his face on billboards all over Kentucky. With his brilliant legal record, he was considered, at thirty-five, the most eligible bachelor in the state. He was on all the talk shows on the major television stations in Lexington – WDKY, WTVQ, WKYT – and on the popular local radio stations, WKQQ and WLRO. Strikingly handsome, with black, unruly hair, dark eyes, an athletic build, and a warm smile, he had the reputation of having slept with most of the ladies in Lexington.

'Yes, I've heard of him. What are we going to do for him?'

4

'We're going to try to help turn him into the governor of Kentucky. He's on his way here now.'

Oliver Russell arrived a few minutes later. He was even more attractive in person than in his photographs.

When he was introduced to Leslie, he smiled warmly. 'I've heard a lot about you. I'm so glad you're going to handle my campaign.'

He was not at all what Leslie had expected. There was a completely disarming sincerity about the man. For a moment, Leslie was at a loss for words.

'I – thank you. Please sit down.'

Oliver Russell took a seat.

'Let's start at the beginning,' Leslie suggested. 'Why are you running for governor?'

'It's very simple. Kentucky's a wonderful state. We know it is, because we live here, and we're able to enjoy its magic – but much of the country thinks of us as a bunch of hillbillies. I want to change that image. Kentucky has more to offer than a dozen other states combined. The history of this country began here. We have one of the oldest capitol buildings in America. Kentucky gave this country two presidents. It's the land of Daniel Boone and Kit Carson and Judge Roy Bean. We have the most beautiful scenery in the world – exciting caves, rivers, bluegrass fields – everything. I want to open all that up to the rest of the world.'

He spoke with a deep conviction, and Leslie found herself strongly drawn to him. She thought of the astrology column. *'The new moon illuminates your love life. Today will be a red-letter day. Be prepared to enjoy it.'*

Oliver Russell was saying, 'The campaign won't work unless you believe in this as strongly as I do.'

'I do,' Leslie said quickly. Too quickly? 'I'm really looking forward to this.' She hesitated a moment. 'May I ask you a question?'

'Certainly.'

'What's your birth sign?'

'Virgo.'

After Oliver Russell left, Leslie went into Jim Bailey's office. 'I like him,' she said. 'He's sincere. He really cares. I think he'd make a fine governor.'

Jim looked at her thoughtfully. 'It's not going to be easy.'

She looked at him, puzzled. 'Oh? Why?'

Bailey shrugged. 'I'm not sure. There's something going on that I can't explain. You've seen Russell on all the billboards and on television?'

'Yes.'

'Well, that's stopped.'

'I don't understand. Why?'

'No one knows for certain, but there are a lot of strange rumors. One of the rumors is that someone was backing Russell, putting up all the money for his campaign, and then for some reason suddenly dropped him.'

'In the middle of a campaign he was winning? That doesn't make sense, Jim.'

'I know.'

'Why did he come to us?'

'He really wants this. I think he's ambitious. And he feels he can make a difference. He would like us to figure out a campaign that won't cost him a lot of money. He can't afford to buy any more airtime or do much advertising. All we can really do for him is to arrange interviews, plant newspaper articles, that sort of thing.' He shook his head. 'Governor Addison is spending a fortune on his campaign. In the last two weeks, Russell's gone way down in the polls. It's a shame. He's a good lawyer. Does a lot of pro bono work. I think he'd make a good governor, too.'

That night Leslie made her first note in her new diary.

Dear Diary: This morning I met the man I am going to marry.

Leslie Stewart's early childhood was idyllic. She was an extraordinarily intelligent child. Her father was an English professor at Lexington Community College and her mother was a housewife. Leslie's father was a handsome man, patrician and intellectual. He was a caring father, and he saw to it that the family took their vacations together and traveled together. Her father adored her. 'You're Daddy's girl,' he would say. He would tell her how beautiful she looked and compliment her on her grades, her behavior, her friends. Leslie could do no wrong in his eyes. For her ninth birthday, her father bought her a beautiful brown velvet dress with lace cuffs. He would have her put the dress on, and he would show her off to his friends when they came to dinner. 'Isn't she a beauty?' he would say.

Leslie worshiped him.

One morning, a year later, in a split second, Leslie's wonderful life vanished. Her mother, face stained with tears, sat her down. 'Darling, your father has ... left us.'

Leslie did not understand at first. 'When will he be back?'

'He's not coming back.'

And each word was a sharp knife.

My mother has driven him away, Leslie thought. She felt sorry for her mother because now there would be a divorce and a custody fight. Her father would never let her go. Never. *He'll come for me,* Leslie told herself.

But weeks passed, and her father never called. *They won't let him come and see me,* Leslie decided. *Mother's punishing him.*

It was Leslie's elderly aunt who explained to the child that there would be no custody battle. Leslie's father had fallen in love with a widow who taught at the university and had moved in with her, in her house on Limestone Street.

One day when they were out shopping, Leslie's mother

pointed out the house. 'That's where they live,' she said bitterly.

Leslie resolved to visit her father. *When he sees me*, she thought, *he'll want to come home.*

On a Friday, after school, Leslie went to the house on Limestone Street and rang the doorbell. The door was opened by a girl Leslie's age. She was wearing a brown velvet dress with lace cuffs. Leslie stared at her, in shock.

The little girl was looking at her curiously. 'Who are you?'

Leslie fled.

Over the next year, Leslie watched her mother retire into herself. She had lost all interest in life. Leslie had believed that 'dying of a broken heart' was an empty phrase, but Leslie helplessly watched her mother fade away and die, and when people asked her what her mother had died of, Leslie answered, 'She died of a broken heart.'

And Leslie resolved that no man would ever do that to her.

After her mother's death, Leslie moved in with her aunt. Leslie attended Bryan Station High School and was graduated from the University of Kentucky summa cum laude. In her final year in college, she was voted beauty queen, and turned down numerous offers from modeling agencies.

Leslie had two brief affairs, one with a college football hero, and the other with her economics professor. They quickly bored her. The fact was that she was brighter than both of them.

Just before Leslie was graduated, her aunt died. Leslie finished school and applied for a job at the advertising and public relations agency of Bailey & Tomkins. Its offices were on Vine Street in a U-shaped brick building with a copper roof and a fountain in the courtyard.

Jim Bailey, the senior partner, had examined Leslie's résumé, and nodded. 'Very impressive. You're in luck. We need a secretary.'

'A secretary? I hoped –'

'Yes?'

'Nothing.'

Leslie started as a secretary, taking notes at all the meetings, her mind all the while judging and thinking of ways to improve the advertising campaigns that were being suggested. One morning, an account executive was saying, 'I've thought of the perfect logo for the Rancho Beef Chili account. On the label of the can, we show a picture of a cowboy roping a cow. It suggests that the beef is fresh, and –'

That's a terrible idea, Leslie thought. They were all staring at her, and to her horror, Leslie realized she had spoken aloud.

'Would you mind explaining that, young lady?'

'I . . .' She wished she were somewhere else. Anywhere. They were all waiting. Leslie took a deep breath. 'When people eat meat, they don't want to be reminded that they're eating a dead animal.'

There was a heavy silence. Jim Bailey cleared his throat. 'Maybe we should give this a little more thought.'

The following week, during a meeting on how to publicize a new beauty soap account, one of the executives said, 'We'll use beauty contest winners.'

'Excuse me,' Leslie said diffidently. 'I believe that's been done. Why couldn't we use lovely flight attendants from around the world to show that our beauty soap is universal?'

In the meetings after that, the men found themselves turning to Leslie for her opinion.

A year later, she was a junior copywriter, and two years after that, she became an account executive, handling both advertising and publicity.

Oliver Russell was the first real challenge that Leslie had had at the agency. Two weeks after Oliver Russell came to them, Bailey suggested to Leslie that it might be better to drop him, because he could not afford to pay their usual agency fee, but Leslie persuaded him to keep the account.

11

'Call it pro bono,' she said.

Bailey studied her a moment. 'Right.'

Leslie and Oliver Russell were seated on a bench in Triangle Park. It was a cool fall day, with a soft breeze coming from the lake. 'I hate politics,' Oliver Russell said.

Leslie looked at him in surprise. 'Then why in the world are you —?'

'Because I want to change the system, Leslie. It's been taken over by lobbyists and corporations that help put the wrong people in power and then control them. There are a lot of things I want to do.' His voice was filled with passion. 'The people who are running the country have turned it into an old boys' club. They care more about themselves than they do about the people. It's not right, and I'm going to try to correct that.'

Leslie listened as Oliver went on, and she was thinking, *He could do it.* There was such a compelling excitement about him. The truth was that she found everything about him exciting. She had never felt this way about a man before, and it was an exhilarating experience. She had no way of knowing how he felt about her. *He is always the perfect gentleman, damn him.* It seemed to Leslie that every few minutes people were coming up to the park bench to shake Oliver's hand and to wish him well. The women were visually throwing daggers at Leslie. *They've probably all been out with him*, Leslie thought. *They've probably all been to bed with him. Well, that's none of my business.*

She had heard that until recently he had been dating the daughter of a senator. She wondered what had happened. *That's none of my business, either.*

There was no way to avoid the fact that Oliver's campaign was going badly. Without money to pay his staff, and no television, radio, or newspaper ads, it was impossible to compete·with Governor Cary Addison, whose image seemed to be everywhere. Leslie arranged for Oliver to appear at company picnics, at factories, and at dozens of social events, but she knew these appearances were all minor-league, and it frustrated her.

'Have you seen the latest polls?' Jim Bailey asked Leslie. 'Your boy is going down the tubes.'

Not if I can help it, Leslie thought.

Leslie and Oliver were having dinner at Cheznous. 'It's not working, is it?' Oliver asked quietly.

'There's still plenty of time,' Leslie said reassuringly. 'When the voters get to know you –'

Oliver shook his head. 'I read the polls, too. I want you to know I appreciate everything you've tried to do for me, Leslie. You've been great.'

She sat there looking at him across the table, thinking, *He's the most wonderful man I've ever met, and I can't help him.* She wanted to take him in her arms and hold him and console him. *Console him? Who am I kidding?*

As they got up to leave, a man, a woman, and two small girls approached the table.

'Oliver! How are you?' The speaker was in his forties, an attractive-looking man with a black eye patch that gave him the raffish look of an amiable pirate.

Oliver rose and held out his hand. 'Hello, Peter. I'd like you to meet Leslie Stewart. Peter Tager.'

'Hello, Leslie.' Tager nodded toward his family. 'This is my wife, Betsy, and this is Elizabeth and this is Rebecca.' There was enormous pride in his voice.

Peter Tager turned to Oliver. 'I'm awfully sorry about what happened. It's a damned shame. I hated to do it, but I had no choice.'

'I understand, Peter.'

'If there was anything I could have done –'

'It doesn't matter. I'm fine.'

'You know I wish you only the best of luck.'

On the way home, Leslie asked, 'What was that all about?'

Oliver started to say something, then stopped. 'It's not important.'

Leslie lived in a neat one-bedroom apartment in the Brandywine section of Lexington. As they approached the building, Oliver said hesitantly, 'Leslie, I know that your agency is handling me for almost nothing, but

14

frankly, I think you're wasting your time. It might be better if I just quit now.'

'No,' she said, and the intensity of her voice surprised her. 'You can't quit. We'll find a way to make it work.'

Oliver turned to look at her. 'You really care, don't you?'

Am I reading too much into that question? 'Yes,' she said quietly. 'I really care.'

When they arrived at her apartment, Leslie took a deep breath. 'Would you like to come in?'

He looked at her a long time. 'Yes.'

Afterward, she never knew who made the first move. All she remembered was that they were undressing each other and she was in his arms and there was a wild, feral haste in their lovemaking, and after that, a slow and easy melting, in a rhythm that was timeless and ecstatic. It was the most wonderful feeling Leslie had ever experienced.

They were together the whole night, and it was magical. Oliver was insatiable, giving and demanding at the same time, and he went on forever. He was an animal. And Leslie thought, *Oh, my God, I'm one, too.*

In the morning, over a breakfast of orange juice, scrambled eggs, toast, and bacon, Leslie said, 'There's going to be a picnic at Green River Lake on Friday, Oliver. There will be a lot of people there. I'll arrange for you to make a

15

speech. We'll buy radio time to let everyone know you're going to be there. Then we'll –'

'Leslie,' he protested, 'I haven't the money to do that.'

'Oh, don't worry about that,' she said airily. 'The agency will pay for it.'

She knew that there was not the remotest chance that the agency would pay for it. She intended to do that herself. She would tell Jim Bailey that the money had been donated by a Russell supporter. And it would be the truth. *I'll do anything in the world to help him*, she thought.

There were two hundred people at the picnic at Green River Lake, and when Oliver addressed the crowd, he was brilliant.

'Half the people in this country don't vote,' he told them. 'We have the lowest voting record of any industrial country in the world – less than fifty percent. If you want things to change, it's your responsibility to make sure they do change. It's more than a responsibility, it's a privilege. There's an election coming up soon. Whether you vote for me or my opponent, vote. Be there.'

They cheered him.

Leslie arranged for Oliver to appear at as many functions as possible. He presided at the opening of a children's

16

clinic, dedicated a bridge, talked to women's groups, labor groups, at charity events, and retirement homes. Still, he kept slipping in the polls. Whenever Oliver was not campaigning, he and Leslie found some time to be together. They went riding in a horse-drawn carriage through Triangle Park, spent a Saturday afternoon at the Antique Market, and had dinner at À la Lucie. Oliver gave Leslie flowers for Groundhog Day and on the anniversary of the Battle of Bull Run, and left loving messages on her answering machine: 'Darling – where are you? I miss you, miss you, miss you.'

'I'm madly in love with your answering machine. Do you have any idea how sexy it sounds?'

'I think it must be illegal to be this happy. I love you.'

It didn't matter to Leslie where she and Oliver went: She just wanted to be with him.

One of the most exciting things they did was to go whitewater rafting on the Russell Fork River one Sunday. The trip started innocently, gently, until the river began to pound its way around the base of the mountains in a giant loop that began a series of deafening, breathtaking vertical drops in the rapids: five feet . . . eight feet . . . nine feet . . . only a terrifying raft length apart. The trip took three and a half hours, and when Leslie and Oliver got off the raft, they were soaking wet and glad to be alive. They could not keep their hands off each other. They made love in their cabin, in the back of his automobile, in the woods.

One early fall evening, Oliver prepared dinner at his home, a charming house in Versailles, a small town near Lexington. There were grilled flank steaks marinated in soy sauce, garlic, and herbs, served with baked potato, salad, and a perfect red wine.

'You're a wonderful cook,' Leslie told him. She snuggled up to him. 'In fact, you're a wonderful everything, sweetheart.'

'Thank you, my love.' He remembered something. 'I have a little surprise for you that I want you to try.' He disappeared into the bedroom for a moment and came out carrying a small bottle with a clear liquid inside.

'Here it is,' he said.

'What is it?'

'Have you heard of Ecstasy?'

'Heard of it? I'm in it.'

'I mean the drug Ecstasy. This is liquid Ecstasy. It's supposed to be a great aphrodisiac.'

Leslie frowned. 'Darling – you don't need that. We don't need it. It could be dangerous.' She hesitated. 'Do you use it often?'

Oliver laughed. 'As a matter of fact, I don't. Take that look off your face. A friend of mine gave me this and told me to try it. This would have been the first time.'

'Let's not have a first time,' Leslie said. 'Will you throw it away?'

'You're right. Of course I will.' He went into the bathroom, and a moment later Leslie heard the toilet flush. Oliver reappeared.

'All gone.' He grinned. 'Who needs Ecstasy in a bottle? I have it in a better package.'

And he took her in his arms.

Leslie had read the love stories and had heard the love songs, but nothing had prepared her for the incredible reality. She had always thought that romantic lyrics were sentimental nonsense, wishful dreaming. She knew better now. The world suddenly seemed brighter, more beautiful. Everything was touched with magic, and the magic was Oliver Russell.

One Saturday morning, Oliver and Leslie were hiking in the Breaks Interstate Park, enjoying the spectacular scenery that surrounded them.

'I've never been on this trail before,' Leslie said.

'I think you're going to enjoy it.'

They were approaching a sharp curve in the path. As they rounded it, Leslie stopped, stunned. In the middle of the path was a hand-painted wooden sign: LESLIE, WILL YOU MARRY ME?

Leslie's heart began to beat faster. She turned to Oliver, speechless.

He took her in his arms. 'Will you?'

How did I get so lucky? Leslie wondered. She hugged him tightly and whispered, 'Yes, darling. Of course I will.'

'I'm afraid I can't promise you that you're going to marry a governor, but I'm a pretty good attorney.'

She snuggled up to him and whispered, 'That will do nicely.'

A few nights later, Leslie was getting dressed to meet Oliver for dinner when he telephoned.

'Darling, I'm terribly sorry, but I've bad news. I have to go to a meeting tonight, and I'll have to cancel our dinner. Will you forgive me?'

Leslie smiled and said softly, 'You're forgiven.'

The following day, Leslie picked up a copy of the *State Journal*. The headline read: WOMAN'S BODY FOUND IN KENTUCKY RIVER. The story went on: 'Early this morning, the body of a nude woman who appeared to be in her early twenties was found by police in the Kentucky River ten miles east of Lexington. An autopsy is being performed to determine the cause of death . . .'

Leslie shuddered as she read the story. *To die so young. Did she have a lover? A husband? How thankful I am to be alive and so happy and so loved.*

*   *   *

It seemed that all of Lexington was talking about the forthcoming wedding. Lexington was a small town, and Oliver Russell was a popular figure. They were a spectacular-looking couple, Oliver dark and handsome, and Leslie with her lovely face and figure and honey-blond hair. The news had spread like wildfire.

'I hope he knows how lucky he is,' Jim Bailey said.

Leslie smiled. 'We're both lucky.'

'Are you going to elope?'

'No. Oliver wants to have a formal wedding. We're getting married at the Calvary Chapel church.'

'When does the happy event take place?'

'In six weeks.'

A few days later, a story on the front page of the *State Journal* read: 'An autopsy has revealed that the woman found in the Kentucky River, identified as Lisa Burnette, a legal secretary, died of an overdose of a dangerous illegal drug known on the streets as liquid Ecstasy . . .'

Liquid Ecstasy. Leslie recalled the evening with Oliver. And she thought, *How lucky it was that he threw that bottle away.*

The next few weeks were filled with frantic preparations for the wedding. There was so much to do. Invitations

21

went out to two hundred people. Leslie chose a maid of honor and selected her outfit, a ballerina-length dress with matching shoes and gloves to complement the length of the sleeves. For herself, Leslie shopped at Fayette Mall on Nicholasville Road and selected a floor-length gown with a full skirt and a sweep train, shoes to match the gown, and long gloves.

Oliver ordered a black cutaway coat with striped trousers, gray waistcoat, a wing-collared white shirt, and a striped ascot. His best man was a lawyer in his firm.

'Everything is set,' Oliver told Leslie. 'I've made all the arrangements for the reception afterward. Almost everyone has accepted.'

Leslie felt a small shiver go through her. 'I can't wait, my darling.'

On a Thursday night one week before the wedding, Oliver came to Leslie's apartment.

'I'm afraid something has come up, Leslie. A client of mine is in trouble. I'm going to have to fly to Paris to straighten things out.'

'Paris? How long will you be gone?'

'It shouldn't take more than two or three days, four days at the most. I'll be back in plenty of time.'

'Tell the pilot to fly safely.'

'I promise.'

When Oliver left, Leslie picked up the newspaper

on the table. Idly, she turned to the horoscope by Zoltaire. It read:

FOR LEO (JULY 23RD TO AUGUST 22ND). THIS IS NOT A GOOD DAY TO CHANGE PLANS. TAKING RISKS CAN LEAD TO SERIOUS PROBLEMS.

Leslie read the horoscope again, disturbed. She was almost tempted to telephone Oliver and tell him not to leave. *But that's ridiculous,* she thought. *It's just a stupid horoscope.*

By Monday, Leslie had not heard from Oliver. She telephoned his office, but the staff had no information. There was no word from him Tuesday. Leslie was beginning to panic. At four o'clock on Wednesday morning, she was awakened by the insistent ringing of the telephone. She sat up in bed and thought: *It's Oliver! Thank God.* She knew that she should be angry with him for not calling her sooner, but that was unimportant now.

She picked up the receiver. 'Oliver . . .'

A male voice said, 'Is this Leslie Stewart?'

She felt a sudden cold chill. 'Who – who is this?'

'Al Towers, Associated Press. We have a story going out on our wires, Miss Stewart, and we wanted to get your reaction.'

Something terrible had happened. Oliver was dead.

'Miss Stewart?'

23

'Yes.' Her voice was a strangled whisper.

'Could we get a quote from you?'

'A quote?'

'About Oliver Russell marrying Senator Todd Davis's daughter in Paris.'

For an instant the room seemed to spin.

'You and Mr Russell were engaged, weren't you? If we could get a quote . . .'

She sat there, frozen.

'Miss Stewart.'

She found her voice. 'Yes. I – I wish them both well.' She replaced the receiver, numb. It was a nightmare. She would awaken in a few minutes and find that she had been dreaming.

But this was no dream. She had been abandoned again. *'Your father's not coming back.'* She walked into the bathroom and stared at her pale image in the mirror. *'We have a story going out on our wires.'* Oliver had married someone else. *Why? What have I done wrong? How have I failed him?* But deep down she knew that it was Oliver who had failed her. He was gone. How could she face the future?

When Leslie walked into the agency that morning, everyone was trying hard not to stare at her. She went into Jim Bailey's office.

He took one look at her pale face and said, 'You shouldn't have come in today, Leslie. Why don't you go home and –'

24

She took a deep breath. 'No, thank you. I'll be fine.'

The radio and television newscasts and afternoon news-papers were filled with details of the Paris wedding. Senator Todd Davis was without doubt Kentucky's most influential citizen, and the story of his daughter's marriage and of the groom's jilting Leslie was big news.

The phones in Leslie's office never stopped ringing.

'This is the *Courier-Journal*, Miss Stewart. Could you give us a statement about the wedding?'

'Yes. The only thing I care about is Oliver Russell's happiness.'

'But you and he were going to be –'

'It would have been a mistake for us to marry. Senator Davis's daughter was in his life first. Obviously, he never got over her. I wish them both well.'

'This is the *State Journal* in Frankfort . . .'

And so it went.

It seemed to Leslie that half of Lexington pitied her, and the other half rejoiced at what had happened to her. Wherever Leslie went, there were whispers and hastily broken-off conversations. She was fiercely determined not to show her feelings.

'How could you let him do this to –?'

'When you truly love someone,' Leslie said firmly, 'you want him to be happy. Oliver Russell is the finest human being I've ever known. I wish them both every happiness.'

She sent notes of apology to all those who had been invited to the wedding and returned their gifts.

Leslie had been half hoping for and half dreading the call from Oliver. Still, when it came, she was unprepared. She was shaken by the familiar sound of his voice.

'Leslie . . . I don't know what to say.'

'It's true, isn't it?'

'Yes.'

'Then there isn't anything to say.'

'I just wanted to explain to you how it happened. Before I met you, Jan and I were almost engaged. And when I saw her again – I – I knew that I still loved her.'

'I understand, Oliver. Goodbye.'

Five minutes later, Leslie's secretary buzzed her. 'There's a telephone call for you on line one, Miss Stewart.'

'I don't want to talk to –'

'It's Senator Davis.'

The father of the bride. *What does he want with me?* Leslie wondered. She picked up the telephone.

A deep southern voice said, 'Miss Stewart?'

'Yes.'

'This is Todd Davis. I think you and I should have a little talk.'

She hesitated. 'Senator, I don't know what we –'

'I'll pick you up in one hour.' The line went dead.

*   *   *

Exactly one hour later, a limousine pulled up in front of the office building where Leslie worked. A chauffeur opened the car door for Leslie. Senator Davis was in the backseat. He was a distinguished-looking man with flowing white hair and a small, neat mustache. He had the face of a patriarch. Even in the fall he was dressed in his trademark white suit and white broad-brimmed leghorn hat. He was a classic figure from an earlier century, an old-fashioned southern gentleman.

As Leslie got into the car, Senator Davis said, 'You're a beautiful young woman.'

'Thank you,' she said stiffly.

The limousine started off.

'I didn't mean just physically, Miss Stewart. I've been hearing about the manner in which you've been handling this whole sordid matter. It must be very distressing for you. I couldn't believe the news when I heard it.' His voice filled with anger. 'Whatever happened to good old-fashioned morality? To tell you the truth, I'm disgusted with Oliver for treating you so shabbily. And I'm furious with Jan for marrying him. In a way, I feel guilty, because she's my daughter. They deserve each other.' His voice was choked with emotion.

They rode in silence for a while. When Leslie finally spoke, she said, 'I know Oliver. I'm sure he didn't mean to hurt me. What happened . . . just happened. I want only the best for him. He deserves that, and I wouldn't do anything to stand in his way.'

'That's very gracious of you.' He studied her a moment. 'You really are a remarkable young lady.'

The limousine had come to a stop. Leslie looked out the window. They had reached Paris Pike, at the Kentucky Horse Center. There were more than a hundred horse farms in and around Lexington, and the largest of them was owned by Senator Davis. As far as the eye could see were white plank fences, white paddocks with red trim, and rolling Kentucky bluegrass.

Leslie and Senator Davis stepped out of the car and walked over to the fence surrounding the racetrack. They stood there a few moments, watching the beautiful animals working out.

Senator Davis turned to Leslie. 'I'm a simple man,' he said quietly. 'Oh, I know how that must sound to you, but it's the truth. I was born here, and I could spend the rest of my life here. There's no place in the world like it. Just look around you, Miss Stewart. This is as close as we may ever come to heaven. Can you blame me for not wanting to leave all this? Mark Twain said that when the world came to an end, he wanted to be in Kentucky, because it's always a good twenty years behind. I have to spend half my life in Washington, and I loathe it.'

'Then why do you do it?'

'Because I have a sense of obligation. Our people voted me into the Senate, and until they vote me out, I'll be there trying to do the best job I can.' He abruptly changed the subject. 'I want you to know how much I admire your sentiments and the way you've behaved. If you had been nasty about this, I suppose it could have created quite a scandal. As it is, well – I'd like to show my appreciation.'

Leslie looked at him.

'I thought that perhaps you would like to get away for a while, take a little trip abroad, spend some time traveling. Naturally, I'd pick up all the –'

'Please don't do this.'

'I was only –'

'I know. I haven't met your daughter, Senator Davis, but if Oliver loves her, she must be very special. I hope they'll be happy.'

He said awkwardly, 'I think you should know they're coming back here to get married again. In Paris, it was a civil ceremony, but Jan wants a church wedding here.'

It was a stab in the heart. 'I see. All right. They have nothing to worry about.'

'Thank you.'

The wedding took place two weeks later, in the Calvary Chapel church where Leslie and Oliver were to have been married. The church was packed.

Oliver Russell, Jan and Senator Todd Davis were standing before the minister at the altar. Jan Davis was an attractive brunette, with an imposing figure and an aristocratic air.

The minister was nearing the end of the ceremony. 'God meant for man and woman to be united in holy matrimony, and as you go through life together . . .'

The church door opened, and Leslie Stewart walked in. She stood at the back for a moment, listening, then moved to the last pew, where she remained standing.

The minister was saying, '. . . so if anyone knows why this couple should not be united in holy matrimony, let him speak now or forever hold his . . .' He glanced up and saw Leslie. '. . . hold his peace.'

Almost involuntarily, heads began to turn in Leslie's direction. Whispers began to sweep through the crowd. People sensed that they were about to witness a dramatic scene, and the church filled with sudden tension.

The minister waited a moment, then nervously cleared his throat. 'Then, by the power vested in me, I now pronounce you man and wife.' There was a note of deep relief in his voice. 'You may kiss the bride.'

When the minister looked up again, Leslie was gone.

The final note in Leslie Stewart's diary read:

> *Dear Diary: It was a beautiful wedding. Oliver's bride is very pretty. She wore a lovely white lace-and-satin wedding gown with a halter top and a bolero jacket. Oliver looked more handsome than ever. He seemed very happy. I'm pleased.*
>
> *Because before I'm finished with him, I'm going to make him wish he had never been born.*

30

Two

It was Senator Todd Davis who had arranged the reconciliation of Oliver Russell and his daughter.

Todd Davis was a widower. A multibillionaire, the senator owned tobacco plantations, coal mines, oil fields in Oklahoma and Alaska, and a world-class racing stable. As Senate majority leader, he was one of the most powerful men in Washington, and was serving his fifth term. He was a man with a simple philosophy: Never forget a favor, never forgive a slight. He prided himself on picking winners, both at the track and in politics, and early on he had spotted Oliver Russell as a comer. The fact that Oliver might marry his daughter was an unexpected plus, until, of course, Jan foolishly called it off. When the senator heard the news of the impending wedding between Oliver Russell and Leslie Stewart, he found it disturbing. Very disturbing.

Senator Davis had first met Oliver Russell when Oliver handled a legal matter for him. Senator Davis was impressed. Oliver was intelligent, handsome, and articulate, with a boyish charm that drew people to him. The senator arranged to have lunch with Oliver on a regular basis, and Oliver had no idea how carefully he was being assessed.

A month after meeting Oliver, Senator Davis sent for Peter Tager. 'I think we've found our next governor.'

Tager was an earnest man who had grown up in a religious family. His father was a history teacher and his mother was a housewife, and they were devout churchgoers. When Peter Tager was eleven, he had been traveling in a car with his parents and younger brother when the brakes of the car failed. There had been a deadly accident. The only one who survived was Peter, who lost an eye.

Peter believed that God had spared him so that he could spread His word.

Peter Tager understood the dynamics of politics better than anyone Senator Davis had ever met. Tager knew where the votes were and how to get them. He had an uncanny sense of what the public wanted to hear and what it had gotten tired of hearing. But even more important to Senator Davis was the fact that Peter Tager was a man he could trust, a man of integrity. People liked him. The black eye patch he wore gave him a dashing look. What mattered to Tager more than anything in the world was his family. The senator had never met a man so deeply proud of his wife and children.

When Senator Davis first met him, Peter Tager had been contemplating going into the ministry.

'So many people need help, Senator. I want to do what I can.'

But Senator Davis had talked him out of the idea. 'Think of how many more people you can help by working for me in the Senate of the United States.' It had been a felicitous choice. Tager knew how to get things done.

'The man I have in mind to run for governor is Oliver Russell.'

'The attorney?'

'Yes. He's a natural. I have a hunch if we get behind him, he can't miss.'

'Sounds interesting, Senator.'

The two of them began to discuss it.

Senator Davis spoke to Jan about Oliver Russell. 'The boy has a hot future, honey.'

'He has a hot past, too, Father. He's the biggest wolf in town.'

'Now, darling, you mustn't listen to gossip. I've invited Oliver to dinner here Friday.'

The dinner Friday evening went well. Oliver was charming, and in spite of herself, Jan found herself warming to him. The senator sat at his place watching them, asking questions that brought out the best in Oliver.

At the end of the evening, Jan invited Oliver to a dinner party the following Saturday. 'I'd be delighted.'

From that night on, they started seeing only each other.

'They'll be getting married soon,' the senator predicted to Peter Tager. 'It's time we got Oliver's campaign rolling.'

Oliver was summoned to a meeting at Senator Davis's office.

'I want to ask you a question,' the senator said. 'How would you like to be the governor of Kentucky?'

Oliver looked at him in surprise. 'I – I haven't thought about it.'

'Well, Peter Tager and I have. There's an election coming up next year. That gives us more than enough time to build you up, let people know who you are. With us behind you, you can't lose.'

And Oliver knew it was true. Senator Davis was a powerful man, in control of a well-oiled political machine, a machine that could create myths or destroy anyone who got in its way.

'You'd have to be totally committed,' the senator warned.

'I would be.'

'I have some even better news for you, son. As far as I'm concerned, this is only the first step. You serve a term or two as governor, and I promise you we'll move you into the White House.'

Oliver swallowed. 'Are – are you serious?'

'I don't joke about things like this. I don't have to tell you that this is the age of television. You have something that money can't buy – charisma. People are drawn to you. You genuinely like people, and it shows. It's the same quality Jack Kennedy had.'

'I – I don't know what to say, Todd.'

'You don't have to say anything. I have to return to Washington tomorrow, but when I get back, we'll go to work.'

A few weeks later, the campaign for the office of governor began. Billboards with Oliver's picture flooded the state. He appeared on television and at rallies and political seminars. Peter Tager had his own private polls that showed Oliver's popularity increasing each week.

'He's up another five points,' he told the senator. 'He's only ten points behind the governor, and we've still got plenty of time left. In another few weeks, they should be neck and neck.'

Senator Davis nodded. 'Oliver's going to win. No question about it.'

*   *   *

Todd Davis and Jan were having breakfast. 'Has our boy proposed to you yet?'

Jan smiled. 'He hasn't come right out and asked me, but he's been hinting around.'

'Well, don't let him hint too long. I want you to be married before he becomes governor. It will play better if the governor has a wife.'

Jan put her arms around her father. 'I'm so glad you brought him into my life. I'm mad about him.'

The senator beamed. 'As long as he makes you happy, I'm happy.'

Everything was going perfectly.

The following evening, when Senator Davis came home, Jan was in her room, packing, her face stained with tears.

He looked at her, concerned. 'What's going on, baby?'

'I'm getting out of here. I never want to see Oliver again as long as I live!'

'Whoa! Hold on there. What are you talking about?'

She turned to him. 'I'm talking about Oliver.' Her tone was bitter. 'He spent last night in a motel with my best friend. She couldn't wait to call and tell me what a wonderful lover he was.'

The senator stood there in shock. 'Couldn't she have been just –?'

'No. I called Oliver. He – he couldn't deny it. I've decided to leave. I'm going to Paris.'

36

'Are you sure you're doing –?'

'I'm positive.'

And the next morning Jan was gone.

The senator sent for Oliver. 'I'm disappointed in you, son.'

Oliver took a deep breath. 'I'm sorry about what happened, Todd. It was – it was just one of those things. I had a few drinks and this woman came on to me and – well, it was hard to say no.'

'I can understand that,' the senator said sympathetically. 'After all, you're a man, right?'

Oliver smiled in relief. 'Right. It won't happen again, I can assure –'

'It's too bad, though. You would have made a fine governor.'

The blood drained from Oliver's face. 'What – what are you saying, Todd?'

'Well, Oliver, it wouldn't look right if I supported you now, would it? I mean, when you think about Jan's feelings –'

'What does the governorship have to do with Jan?'

'I've been telling everybody that there was a good chance that the next governor was going to be my son-in-law. But since you're not going to be my son-in-law, well, I'll just have to make new plans, won't I?'

'Be reasonable, Todd. You can't –'

Senator Davis's smile faded. 'Never tell me what I can

or can't do, Oliver. I can make you and I can break you!' He smiled again. "But don't misunderstand me. No hard feelings. I wish you only the best.'

Oliver sat there, silent for a moment. 'I see.' He rose to his feet. 'I – I'm sorry about all this.'

'I am, too, Oliver. I really am.'

When Oliver left, the senator called in Peter Tager. 'We're dropping the campaign.'

'Dropping it? Why? It's in the bag. The latest polls –'

'Just do as I tell you. Cancel all of Oliver's appearances. As far as we're concerned, he's out of the race.'

Two weeks later, the polls began to show a drop in Oliver Russell's ratings. The billboards started to disappear, and the radio and television ads had been canceled.

'Governor Addison is beginning to pick up ratings in the polls. If we're going to find a new candidate, we'd better hurry,' Peter Tager said.

The senator was thoughtful. 'We have plenty of time. Let's play this out.'

It was a few days later that Oliver Russell went to the Bailey & Tomkins agency to ask them to handle his campaign. Jim Bailey introduced him to Leslie, and Oliver was immediately taken with her. She was not only beautiful, she was intelligent and sympathetic and believed in him. He had sometimes felt a certain aloofness in Jan, but he had overlooked it. With Leslie, it was completely different. She was warm and sensitive, and it had been natural to fall in love with her. From time to time, Oliver thought about what he had lost. '... *this is only the first step. You serve a term or two as governor, and I promise you we'll move you into the White House.*'

The hell with it. I can be happy without any of that, Oliver persuaded himself. But occasionally, he could not help thinking about the good things he might have accomplished.

With Oliver's wedding imminent, Senator Davis had sent for Tager.

'Peter, we have a problem. We can't let Oliver Russell throw away his career by marrying a nobody.'

Peter Tager frowned. 'I don't know what you can do about it now, Senator. The wedding is all set.'

Senator Davis was thoughtful for a moment. 'The race hasn't been run yet, has it?'

He telephoned his daughter in Paris. 'Jan, I have some terrible news for you. Oliver is getting married.'

There was a long silence. 'I – I heard.'

'The sad part is that he doesn't love this woman. He told me he's marrying her on the rebound because you left him. He's still in love with you.'

'Did Oliver say that?'

'Absolutely. It's a terrible thing he's doing to himself. And, in a way, you're forcing him to do it, baby. When you ran out on him, he just fell apart.'

'Father, I – I had no idea.'

'I've never seen a more unhappy man.'

'I don't know what to say.'

'Do you still love him?'

'I'll always love him. I made a terrible mistake.'

'Well, then, maybe it's not too late.'

'But he's getting married.'

'Honey, why don't we just wait and see what happens? Maybe he'll come to his senses.'

When Senator Davis hung up, Peter Tager said, 'What are you up to, Senator?'

'Me?' Senator Davis said innocently. 'Nothing. Just putting a few pieces back together, where they belong. I think I'll have a little talk with Oliver.'

That afternoon, Oliver Russell was in Senator Davis's office.

'It's good to see you, Oliver. Thank you for dropping by. You're looking very well.'

'Thank you, Todd. So are you.'

'Well, I'm getting on, but I do the best I can.'

'You asked to see me, Todd?'

'Yes, Oliver. Sit down.'

Oliver took a chair.

'I want you to help me out with a legal problem I'm

having in Paris. One of my companies over there is in trouble. There's a stockholders' meeting coming up. I'd like you to be there for it.'

'I'll be glad to. When is the meeting? I'll check my calendar and –'

'I'm afraid you'd have to leave this afternoon.'

Oliver stared at him. 'This afternoon?'

'I hate to give you such short notice, but I just heard about it. My plane's waiting at the airport. Can you manage it? It's important to me.'

Oliver was thoughtful. 'I'll try to work it out, somehow.'

'I appreciate that, Oliver. I knew I could count on you.' He leaned forward. 'I'm real unhappy about what's been happening to you. Have you seen the latest polls?' He sighed. 'I'm afraid you're way down.'

'I know.'

'I wouldn't mind so much, but . . .' He stopped.

'But –?'

'You'd have made a fine governor. In fact, your future couldn't have been brighter. You would have had money . . . power. Let me tell you something about money and power, Oliver. Money doesn't care who owns it. A bum can win it in a lottery, or a dunce can inherit it, or someone can get it by holding up a bank. But power – that's something different. To have power is to own the world. If you were governor of this state, you could affect the lives of everybody living here. You could get bills passed that would help the people, and you'd have the power to veto bills that could harm them. I once promised you that someday you could be President of the United States. Well, I meant it, and you could have been. And think about that power, Oliver, to be the most important man in the world, running the most powerful country in the world. That's something worth dreaming about, isn't it? Just think about it.' He repeated slowly, 'The most powerful man in the world.'

Oliver was listening, wondering where the conversation was leading.

As though in answer to Oliver's unspoken question, the senator said, 'And you let all that get away, for a piece of pussy. I thought you were smarter than that, son.'

Oliver waited.

Senator Davis said casually, 'I talked to Jan this morning. She's in Paris, at the Ritz. When I told her you were getting married – well, she just broke down and sobbed.'

'I – I'm sorry, Todd. I really am.'

The senator sighed. 'It's just a shame that you two couldn't get together again.'

'Todd, I'm getting married next week.'

'I know. And I wouldn't interfere with that for anything in the world. I suppose I'm just an old sentimentalist, but to me marriage is the most sacred thing on earth. You have my blessing, Oliver.'

'I appreciate that.'

'I know you do.' The senator looked at his watch. 'Well, you'll want to go home and pack. The background and details of the meeting will be faxed to you in Paris.'

Oliver rose. 'Right. And don't worry. I'll take care of things over there.'

'I'm sure you will. By the way, I've booked you in at the Ritz.'

On Senator Davis's luxurious Challenger, flying to Paris, Oliver thought about his conversation with the senator. *'You'd have made a fine governor. In fact, your future couldn't have been brighter ... Let me tell you something about money and power, Oliver ... To have power is to own the world. If you were governor of this state, you could affect the lives of everybody living here. You could get bills passed that would help the people, and you could veto bills that might harm them.'*

But I don't need that power, Oliver reassured himself. *No. I'm getting married to a wonderful woman. We'll make each other happy. Very happy.*

When Oliver arrived at the TransAir ExecuJet base at Le Bourget Airport in Paris, there was a limousine waiting for him.

'Where to, Mr Russell?' the chauffeur asked.

'By the way, I've booked you in at the Ritz.' Jan was at the Ritz.

It would be smarter, Oliver thought, *if I stayed at a different hotel – the Plaza-Athénée or the Meurice.*

43

The chauffeur was looking at him expectantly.

'The Ritz,' Oliver said. The least he could do was to apologize to Jan.

He telephoned her from the lobby. 'It's Oliver. I'm in Paris.'

'I know,' Jan said. 'Father called me.'

'I'm downstairs. I'd like to say hello if you –'

'Come up.'

When Oliver walked into Jan's suite, he was still not sure what he was going to say.

Jan was waiting for him at the door. She stood there a moment, smiling, then threw her arms around him and held him close. 'Father told me you were coming here. I'm so glad!'

Oliver stood there, at a loss. He was going to have to tell her about Leslie, but he had to find the right words. *I'm sorry about what happened with us . . . I never meant to hurt you . . . I've fallen in love with someone else . . . but I'll always . . .*

'I – I have to tell you something,' he said awkwardly. 'The fact is . . .' And as he looked at Jan, he thought of her father's words. *'I once promised you that some day you could be President of the United States. Well, I meant it . . . And think about that power, Oliver, to be the most important man in the world, running the most powerful country in the world. That's something worth dreaming about, isn't it?'*

44

'Yes, darling?'

And the words poured out as though they had a life of their own. 'I made a terrible mistake, Jan. I was a bloody fool. I love you. I want to marry you.'

'Oliver!'

'Will you marry me?'

There was no hesitation. 'Yes. Oh, yes, my love!'

He picked her up and carried her into the bedroom, and moments later they were in bed, naked, and Jan was saying, 'You don't know how much I've missed you, darling.'

'I must have been out of my mind . . .'

Jan pressed close to his naked body and moaned. 'Oh! This feels so wonderful.'

'It's because we belong together.' Oliver sat up. 'Let's tell your father the news.'

She looked at him, surprised. 'Now?'

'Yes.'

And I'm going to have to tell Leslie.

Fifteen minutes later Jan was speaking to her father. 'Oliver and I are going to be married.'

'That's wonderful news, Jan. I couldn't be more surprised or delighted. By the way, the mayor of Paris is an old friend of mine. He's expecting your call. He'll marry you there. I'll make sure everything's arranged.'

'But —'

'Put Oliver on.'

'Just a minute, Father.' Jan held out the phone to Oliver. 'He wants to talk to you.'

Oliver picked up the phone. 'Todd?'

'Well, my boy, you've made me very happy. You've done the right thing.'

'Thank you. I feel the same way.'

'I'm arranging for you and Jan to be married in Paris. And when you come home, you'll have a big church wedding here. At the Calvary Chapel.'

Oliver frowned. 'The Calvary Chapel? I – I don't think that's a good idea, Todd. That's where Leslie and I . . . Why don't we –?'

Senator Davis's voice was cold. 'You embarrassed my daughter, Oliver, and I'm sure you want to make up for that. Am I right?'

There was a long pause. 'Yes, Todd. Of course.'

'Thank you, Oliver. I look forward to seeing you in a few days. We have a lot to talk about . . . governor . . .'

The Paris wedding was a brief civil ceremony in the mayor's office. When it was over, Jan looked at Oliver and said, 'Father wants to give us a church wedding at the Calvary Chapel.'

Oliver hesitated, thinking about Leslie and what it would do to her. But he had come too far to back down now. 'Whatever he wants.'

Oliver could not get Leslie out of his mind. She had done nothing to deserve what he had done to her. *I'll call her*

46

and explain. But each time he picked up the telephone, he thought: *How can I explain? What can I tell her?* And he had no answer. He had finally gotten up the nerve to call her, but the press had gotten to her first, and he had felt worse afterward.

The day after Oliver and Jan returned to Lexington, Oliver's election campaign went back into high gear. Peter Tager had set all the wheels in motion, and Oliver became ubiquitous again on television and radio and in the newspapers. He spoke to a large crowd at the Kentucky Kingdom Thrill Park and headed a rally at the Toyota Motor Plant in Georgetown. He spoke at the twenty-thousand-square-foot mall in Lancaster. And that was only the beginning.

Peter Tager arranged for a campaign bus to take Oliver around the state. The bus toured from Georgetown down to Stanford and stopped at Frankfort . . . Versailles . . . Winchester . . . Louisville. Oliver spoke at the Kentucky Fairground and at the Exposition Center. In Oliver's honor, they served burgoo, the traditional Kentucky stew made of chicken, veal, beef, lamb, pork, and a variety of fresh vegetables cooked in a big kettle over an open fire.

Oliver's ratings kept going up. The only interruption in the campaign had been Oliver's wedding. He had seen

Leslie at the back of the church, and he had had an uneasy feeling. He talked about it with Peter Tager.

'You don't think Leslie would try to do anything to hurt me, do you?'

'Of course not. And even if she wanted to, what could she do? Forget her.'

Oliver knew that Tager was right. Things were moving along beautifully. There was no reason to worry. Nothing could stop him now. Nothing.

On election night, Leslie Stewart sat alone in her apartment in front of her television set, watching the returns. Precinct by precinct, Oliver's lead kept mounting. Finally, at five minutes before midnight, Governor Addison appeared on television to make his concession speech. Leslie turned off the set. She stood up and took a deep breath.

> *Weep no more, my lady,*
> *Oh, weep no more today!*
> *We will sing one song for the old Kentucky home,*
> *For the old Kentucky home far away.*

It was time.

Three

Senator Todd Davis was having a busy morning. He had flown into Louisville from the capital for the day, to attend a sale of Thoroughbreds.

'You have to keep up the bloodlines,' he told Peter Tager, as they sat watching the splendid-looking horses being led in and out of the large arena. 'That's what counts, Peter.'

A beautiful mare was being led into the center of the ring. 'That's Sail Away,' Senator Davis said. 'I want her.'

The bidding was spirited, but ten minutes later, when it was over, Sail Away belonged to Senator Davis.

The cellular phone rang. Peter Tager answered it. 'Yes?' He listened a moment, then turned to the senator. 'Do you want to talk to Leslie Stewart?'

Senator Davis frowned. He hesitated a moment, then took the phone from Tager.

'Miss Stewart?'

'I'm sorry to bother you, Senator Davis, but I wonder if I could see you? I need a favor.'

'Well, I'm flying back to Washington tonight, so –'

'I could come and meet you. It's really important.'

Senator Davis hesitated a moment. 'Well, if it's that important, I can certainly accommodate you, young lady. I'll be leaving for my farm in a few minutes. Do you want to meet me there?'

'That will be fine.'

'I'll see you in an hour.'

'Thank you.'

Davis pressed the END button and turned to Tager. 'I was wrong about her. I thought she was smarter than that. She should have asked me for money *before* Jan and Oliver got married.' He was thoughtful for a moment, then his face broke into a slow grin. 'I'll be a son of a bitch.'

'What is it, Senator?'

'I just figured out what this urgency is all about. Miss Stewart has discovered that she's pregnant with Oliver's baby and she's going to need a little financial help. It's the oldest con game in the world.'

One hour later, Leslie was driving onto the grounds of Dutch Hill, the senator's farm. A guard was waiting outside the main house. 'Miss Stewart?'

'Yes.'

'Senator Davis is expecting you. This way, please.'

He showed Leslie inside, along a wide corridor that led to a large paneled library crammed with books. Senator

Davis was at his desk, thumbing through a volume. He looked up and rose as Leslie entered.

'It's good to see you, my dear. Sit down, please.'

Leslie took a seat.

The senator held up his book. 'This is fascinating. It lists the name of every Kentucky Derby winner from the first derby to the latest. Do you know who the first Kentucky Derby winner was?'

'No.'

'Aristides, in 1875. But I'm sure you didn't come here to discuss horses.' He put the book down. 'You said you wanted a favor.'

He wondered how she was going to phrase it. *I just found out I'm going to have Oliver's baby, and I don't know what to do ... I don't want to cause a scandal, but ... I'm willing to raise the baby, but I don't have enough money ...*

'Do you know Henry Chambers?' Leslie asked.

Senator Davis blinked, caught completely off guard. 'Do I – Henry? Yes, I do. Why?'

'I would appreciate it very much if you would give me an introduction to him.'

Senator Davis looked at her, hastily reorganizing his thoughts. 'Is that the favor? You want to meet Henry Chambers?'

'Yes.'

'I'm afraid he's not here anymore, Miss Stewart. He's living in Phoenix, Arizona.'

'I know. I'm leaving for Phoenix in the morning. I thought it would be nice if I knew someone there.'

Senator Davis studied her a moment. His instinct told him that there was something going on that he did not understand.

He phrased his next question cautiously. 'Do you know anything about Henry Chambers?'

'No. Only that he comes from Kentucky.'

He sat there, making up his mind. *She's a beautiful lady*, he thought. *Henry will owe me a favor.* 'I'll make a call.'

Five minutes later, he was speaking to Henry Chambers.

'Henry, it's Todd. You'll be sorry to know that I bought Sail Away this morning. I know you had your eye on her.' He listened a moment, then laughed. 'I'll bet you did. I hear you just got another divorce. Too bad. I liked Jessica.'

Leslie listened as the conversation went on for a few more minutes. Then Senator Davis said, 'Henry, I'm going to do you a good turn. A friend of mine is arriving in Phoenix tomorrow, and she doesn't know a soul there. I would appreciate it if you would keep an eye on her ... What does she look like?' He looked over at Leslie and smiled. 'She's not too bad-looking. Just don't get any ideas.'

He listened a moment, then turned back to Leslie. 'What time does your plane get in?'

'At two-fifty. Delta flight 159.'

The senator repeated the information into the phone. 'Her name is Leslie Stewart. You'll thank me for this. You take care now, Henry. I'll be in touch.' He replaced the receiver.

'Thank you,' Leslie said.

'Is there anything else I can do for you?'

'No. That's all I need.'

Why? What the hell does Leslie Stewart want with Henry Chambers?

The public fiasco with Oliver Russell had been a hundred times worse than anything Leslie could have imagined. It was a never-ending nightmare. Everywhere Leslie went there were the whispers:

'She's the one. He practically jilted her at the altar . . .'

'I'm saving my wedding invitation as a souvenir . . .'

'I wonder what she's going to do with her wedding gown? . . .'

The public gossip fueled Leslie's pain, and the humiliation was unbearable. She would never trust a man again. Never. Her only consolation was that somehow, someday, she was going to make Oliver Russell pay for the unforgivable thing he had done to her. She had no idea how. With Senator Davis behind him, Oliver would have money and power. *Then I have to find a way to have more money and more power*, Leslie thought. *But how? How?*

The inauguration took place in the garden of the state capitol in Frankfort, near the exquisite thirty-four-foot floral clock.

Jan stood at Oliver's side, proudly watching her handsome husband being sworn in as governor of Kentucky.

If Oliver behaved himself, the next stop was the White House, her father had assured her. And Jan intended to do everything in her power to see that nothing went wrong. Nothing.

After the ceremony, Oliver and his father-in-law were seated in the palatial library of the Executive Mansion, a beautiful building modeled after the Petit Trianon, Marie Antoinette's villa near the palace of Versailles.

Senator Todd Davis looked around the luxurious room and nodded in satisfaction. 'You're going to do fine here, son. Just fine.'

'I owe it all to you,' Oliver said warmly. 'I won't forget that.'

Senator Davis waved a hand in dismissal. 'Don't give it a thought, Oliver. You're here because you deserve to be. Oh, maybe I helped push things along a wee bit. But this is just the beginning. I've been in politics a long time, son, and there are a few things I've learned.'

He looked over at Oliver, waiting, and Oliver said dutifully, 'I'd love to hear them, Todd.'

'You see, people have got it wrong. It's not who you know,' Senator Davis explained, 'it's what you know about who you know. Everybody's got a little skeleton buried somewhere. All you have to do is dig it up, and you'll be surprised how glad they'll be to help you with whatever you need. I happen to know that there's a congressman in Washington who once spent a year in a mental institution. A representative from up North served time in a reform school for stealing. Well, you can see what it would do to their careers if word ever got out. But it's grist for our mills.'

The senator opened an expensive leather briefcase and took out a sheaf of papers and handed them to Oliver. 'These are the people you'll be dealing with here in Kentucky. They're powerful men and women, but they all have Achilles' heels.' He grinned. 'The mayor has an Achilles' high heel. He's a transvestite.'

Oliver was scanning the papers, wide-eyed.

'You keep those locked up, you hear? That's pure gold.'

'Don't worry, Todd. I'll be careful.'

'And, son – don't put too much pressure on those people when you need something from them. Don't break them – just bend them a little.' He studied Oliver a moment. 'How are you and Jan getting along?'

'Great,' Oliver said quickly. It was true, in a sense. As far as Oliver was concerned, it was a marriage of convenience, and he was careful to see that he did nothing to disrupt it. He would never forget what his earlier indiscretion had almost cost him.

'That's fine. Jan's happiness is very important to me.' It was a warning.

'For me, as well,' Oliver said.

'By the way, how do you like Peter Tager?'

Oliver said enthusiastically, 'I like him a lot. He's been a tremendous help to me.'

Senator Davis nodded. 'I'm glad to hear that. You won't find anyone better. I'm going to lend him to you, Oliver. He can smooth a lot of paths for you.'

Oliver grinned. 'Great. I really appreciate that.'

Senator Davis rose. 'Well, I have to get back to Washington. You let me know if you need anything.'

'Thanks, Todd. I will.'

On the Sunday after his meeting with Senator Davis, Oliver tried to find Peter Tager.

'He's in church, Governor.'

'Right. I forgot. I'll see him tomorrow.'

Peter Tager went to church every Sunday with his family, and attended a two-hour prayer meeting three times a week. In a way, Oliver envied him. *He's probably the only truly happy man I've ever known*, he thought.

On Monday morning, Tager came into Oliver's office. 'You wanted to see me, Oliver?'

'I need a favor. It's personal.'

Peter nodded. 'Anything I can do.'

'I need an apartment.'

Tager glanced around the large room in mock disbelief. 'This place is too small for you, Governor?'

'No.' Oliver looked into Tager's one good eye. 'Sometimes I have private meetings at night. They have to be discreet. You know what I mean?'

There was an uncomfortable pause. 'Yes.'

'I want someplace away from the center of town. Can you handle that for me?'

'I guess so.'

'This is just between us, of course.'

Peter Tager nodded, unhappily.

One hour later, Tager telephoned Senator Davis in Washington.

'Oliver asked me to rent an apartment for him, Senator. Something discreet.'

'Did he now? Well, he's learning, Peter. He's learning. Do it. Just make damned sure Jan never hears about it.' The senator was thoughtful for a moment. 'Find him a place out in Indian Hills. Someplace with a private entrance.'

'But it's not right for him to –'

'Peter – just do it.'

Four

The solution to Leslie's problem had come in two disparate items in the *Lexington Herald-Leader*. The first was a long, flattering editorial praising Governor Oliver Russell. The last line read, 'None of us here in Kentucky who knows him will be surprised when one day Oliver Russell becomes President of the United States.'

The item on the next page read: 'Henry Chambers, a former Lexington resident, whose horse Lightning won the Kentucky Derby five years ago, and Jessica, his third wife, have divorced. Chambers, who now lives in Phoenix, is the owner and publisher of the *Phoenix Star*.'

The power of the press. That was real power. Katharine Graham and her *Washington Post* had destroyed a president.

And that was when the idea jelled.

Leslie had spent the next two days doing research on Henry Chambers. The Internet had some interesting information on him. Chambers was a fifty-five-year-old philanthropist who had inherited a tobacco fortune and had devoted most of his life to giving it away. But it was not his money that interested Leslie.

It was the fact that he owned a newspaper and that he had just gotten a divorce.

Half an hour after her meeting with Senator Davis, Leslie walked into Jim Bailey's office. 'I'm leaving, Jim.'

He looked at her sympathetically. 'Of course. You need a vacation. When you come back, we can –'

'I'm not coming back.'

'What? I – I don't want you to go, Leslie. Running away won't solve –'

'I'm not running away.'

'You've made up your mind?'

'Yes.'

'We're going to hate to lose you. When do you want to leave?'

'I've already left.'

Leslie Stewart had given a lot of thought to the various ways in which she could meet Henry Chambers. There were endless possibilities, but she discarded them one by one. What she had in mind had to be planned very carefully. And then she had thought of Senator Davis. Davis and Chambers had the same background, traveled in the same circles. The two men would certainly know each other. That was when Leslie had decided to call the senator.

When Leslie arrived at Sky Harbor Airport in Phoenix, on an impulse, she walked over to the newsstand in the terminal. She bought a copy of the *Phoenix Star* and scanned it. No luck. She bought the *Arizona Republic*, and then the *Phoenix Gazette*, and there it was, the astrological column by Zoltaire. *Not that I believe in astrology. I'm much too intelligent for that nonsense. But . . .*

> FOR LEO (JULY 23rd to AUGUST 22nd).
> JUPITER IS JOINING YOUR SUN. ROMAN-
> TIC PLANS MADE NOW WILL BE FULFILLED.
> EXCELLENT PROSPECTS FOR THE FUTURE.
> PROCEED CAUTIOUSLY.

There was a chauffeur and limousine waiting for her at the curb. 'Miss Stewart?'

'Yes.'

'Mr Chambers sends his regards and asked me to take you to your hotel.'

'That's very kind of him.' Leslie was disappointed. She had hoped that he would come to meet her himself.

'Mr Chambers would like to know whether you are free to join him for dinner this evening.'

60

Better. Much better.

'Please tell him I would be delighted.'

At eight o'clock that evening, Leslie was dining with Henry Chambers. Chambers was a pleasant-looking man, with an aristocratic face, graying brown hair, and an endearing enthusiasm.

He was studying Leslie admiringly. 'Todd really meant it when he said he was doing me a favor.'

Leslie smiled. 'Thank you.'

'What made you decide to come to Phoenix, Leslie?'

You don't really want to know. 'I've heard so much about it, I thought I might enjoy living here.'

'It's a great place. You'll love it. Arizona has everything – the Grand Canyon, desert, mountains. You can find anything you want here.'

And I have, Leslie thought.

'You'll need a place to live. I'm sure I can help you locate something.'

Leslie knew the money she had would last for no more than three months. As it turned out, her plan took no more than two months.

Bookstores were filled with how-to books for women on how to get a man. The various pop psychologies ranged from 'Play hard to get' to 'Get them hooked in bed.' Leslie followed none of that advice. She had her own

61

method: She teased Henry Chambers. Not physically, but mentally. Henry had never met anyone like her. He was of the old school that believed if a blonde was beautiful, she must be dumb. It never occurred to him that he had always been attracted to women who were beautiful and not overly bright. Leslie was a revelation to him. She was intelligent and articulate and knowledgeable about an amazing range of subjects.

They talked about philosophy and religion and history, and Henry confided to a friend, 'I think she's reading up on a lot of things so she can keep up with me.'

Henry Chambers enjoyed Leslie's company tremendously. He showed her off to his friends and wore her on his arm like a trophy. He took her to the Carefree Wine and Fine Art Festival and to the Actors Theater. They watched the Phoenix Suns play at the America West Arena. They visited the Lyon Gallery in Scottsdale, the Symphony Hall, and the little town of Chandler to see the Doo-dah Parade. One evening, they went to see the Phoenix Roadrunners play hockey.

After the hockey game, Henry said, 'I really like you a lot, Leslie. I think we'd be great together. I'd like to make love with you.'

She took his hand in hers and said softly, 'I like you, too, Henry, but the answer is no.'

* * *

The following day they had a luncheon date. Henry telephoned Leslie. 'Why don't you pick me up at the *Star*? I want you to see the place.'

'I'd love to,' Leslie said. That was what she had been waiting for. There were two other newspapers in Phoenix, the *Arizona Republic* and the *Phoenix Gazette*. Henry's paper, the *Star*, was the only one losing money.

The offices and production plant of the *Phoenix Star* were smaller than Leslie had anticipated. Henry took her on a tour, and as Leslie looked around, she thought, *This isn't going to bring down a governor or a president*. But it was a stepping-stone. She had plans for it.

Leslie was interested in everything she saw. She kept asking Henry questions, and he kept referring them to Lyle Bannister, the managing editor. Leslie was amazed at how little Henry seemed to know about the newspaper business and how little he cared. It made her all the more determined to learn everything she could.

It happened at the Borgata, a restaurant in a castlelike old Italian village setting. The dinner was superb. They had enjoyed a lobster bisque, medallions of veal with a sauce béarnaise, white asparagus vinaigrette, and a Grand Marnier soufflé. Henry Chambers was charming and easy to be with, and it had been a beautiful evening.

'I love Phoenix,' Henry was saying. 'It's hard to believe

that only fifty years ago the population here was just sixty-five thousand. Now it's over a million.'

Leslie was curious about something. 'What made you decide to leave Kentucky and move here, Henry?'

He shrugged. 'It wasn't my decision, really. It was my damned lungs. The doctors didn't know how long I had to live. They told me Arizona would be the best climate for me. So I decided to spend the rest of my life – whatever that means – living it up.' He smiled at her. 'And here we are.' He took her hand in his. 'When they told me how good it would be for me, they had no idea. You don't think I'm too old for you, do you?' he asked anxiously.

Leslie smiled. 'Too young. Much too young.'

Henry looked at her for a long moment. 'I'm serious. Will you marry me?'

Leslie closed her eyes for a moment. She could see the hand-painted wooden sign on the Breaks Interstate Park trail: LESLIE, WILL YOU MARRY ME? ... *'I'm afraid I can't promise you that you're going to marry a governor, but I'm a pretty good attorney.'*

Leslie opened her eyes and looked up at Henry. 'Yes, I want to marry you.' *More than anything in the world.*

They were married two weeks later.

When the wedding announcement appeared in the *Lexington Herald-Leader*, Senator Todd Davis studied it for a long time. *'I'm sorry to bother you, Senator, but I wonder if I could see you? I need a favor ... Do you know Henry Chambers? ... I'd appreciate it if you'd introduce me to him.'*

If that's all she was up to, there would be no problem.

If that's all she was up to.

Leslie and Henry honeymooned in Paris, and wherever they went, Leslie wondered whether Oliver and Jan had visited those same places, walked those streets, dined there, shopped there. She pictured the two of them together, making love, Oliver whispering the same lies into Jan's ears that he had whispered into hers. Lies that he was going to pay dearly for.

Henry sincerely loved her and went out of his way to make her happy. Under other circumstances, Leslie might have fallen in love with him, but something deep within her had died. *I can never trust any man again.*

A few days after they returned to Phoenix, Leslie surprised Henry by saying, 'Henry, I'd like to work at the paper.'

He laughed. 'Why?'

'I think it would be interesting. I was an executive at an advertising agency. I could probably help with that part.'

He protested, but in the end, he gave in.

* * *

Henry noticed that Leslie read the *Lexington Herald-Leader* every day.

'Keeping up with the hometown folks?' he teased her.

'In a way,' Leslie smiled. She avidly read every word that was written about Oliver. She wanted him to be happy and successful. *The bigger they are . . .*

When Leslie pointed out to Henry that the *Star* was losing money, he laughed. 'Honey, it's a drop in the bucket. I've got money coming in from places you never even heard of. It doesn't matter.'

But it mattered to Leslie. It mattered a great deal. As she began to get more and more involved in the running of the newspaper, it seemed to her that the biggest reason it was losing money was the unions. The *Phoenix Star*'s presses were outdated, but the unions refused to let the newspaper put in new equipment, because they said it would cost union members their jobs. They were currently negotiating a new contract with the *Star*.

When Leslie discussed the situation with Henry, he said, 'Why do you want to bother with stuff like that? Let's just have fun.'

'I'm having fun,' Leslie assured him.

Leslie had a meeting with Craig McAllister, the *Star*'s attorney.

'How are the negotiations going?'

'I wish I had better news, Mrs Chambers, but I'm afraid the situation doesn't look good.'

'We're still in negotiation, aren't we?'

'Ostensibly. But Joe Riley, the head of the printers' union, is a stubborn son of a – a stubborn man. He won't give an inch. The pressmen's contract is up in ten days, and Riley says if the union doesn't have a new contract by then, they're going to walk.'

'Do you believe him?'

'Yes. I don't like to give in to the unions, but the reality is that without them, we have no newspaper. They can shut us down. More than one publication has collapsed because it tried to buck the unions.'

'What are they asking?'

'The usual. Shorter hours, raises, protection against future automation . . .'

'They're squeezing us, Craig. I don't like it.'

'This is not an emotional issue, Mrs Chambers. This is a practical issue.'

'So your advice is to give in?'

'I don't think we have a choice.'

'Why don't I have a talk with Joe Riley?'

The meeting was set for two o'clock, and Leslie was late coming back from lunch. When she walked into the reception office, Riley was waiting, chatting with Leslie's secretary, Amy, a pretty, dark-haired young woman.

Joe Riley was a rugged-looking Irishman in his middle forties. He had been a pressman for more than fifteen years. Three years earlier he had been appointed head of his union and had earned the reputation of being the toughest negotiator in the business. Leslie stood there for a moment, watching him flirting with Amy.

Riley was saying, '. . . and then the man turned to her and said, "That's easy for you to say, but how will I get back?"'

Amy laughed. 'Where do you hear those, Joe?'

'I get around, darlin'. How about dinner tonight?'

'I'd love it.'

Riley looked up and saw Leslie. 'Afternoon, Mrs Chambers.'

'Good afternoon, Mr Riley. Come in, won't you?'

Riley and Leslie were seated in the newspaper's conference room. 'Would you like some coffee?' Leslie offered.

'No, thanks.'

'Anything stronger?'

He grinned. 'You know it's against the rules to drink during company hours, Mrs Chambers.'

Leslie took a deep breath. 'I wanted the two of us to have a talk because I've heard that you're a very fair man.'

'I try to be,' Riley said.

'I want you to know that I'm sympathetic to the union. I think your men are entitled to something, but what you're asking for is unreasonable. Some of their habits are costing us millions of dollars a year.'

'Could you be more specific?'

'I'll be glad to. They're working fewer hours of straight time and finding ways to get on the shifts that pay overtime. Some of them put in three shifts back to back, working the whole weekend. I believe they call it "going to the whips." We can't afford that anymore. We're losing money because our equipment is outdated. If we could put in new cold-type production –'

'Absolutely not! The new equipment you want to put in would put my men out of work, and I have no intention of letting machinery throw my men out into the street. Your goddam machines don't have to eat, my men do.' Riley rose to his feet. 'Our contract is up next week. We either get what we want, or we walk.'

When Leslie mentioned the meeting to Henry that evening, he said, 'Why do you want to get involved in all that? The unions are something we all have to live with. Let me give you a piece of advice, sweetheart. You're new to all this, and you're a woman. Let the men handle it. Let's not –' He stopped, out of breath.

'Are you all right?'

He nodded. 'I saw my stupid doctor today, and he thinks I should get an oxygen tank.'

'I'll arrange it,' Leslie said. 'And I'm going to get you a nurse so that when I'm not here –'

'No! I don't need a nurse. I'm – I'm just a little tired.'

'Come on, Henry. Let's get you into bed.'

Three days later, when Leslie called an emergency board meeting, Henry said, 'You go, baby. I'll just stay here and take it easy.' The oxygen tank had helped, but he was feeling weak and depressed.

Leslie telephoned Henry's doctor. 'He's losing too much weight and he's in pain. There must be something you can do.'

'Mrs Chambers, we're doing everything we can. Just see that he gets plenty of rest and stays on the medication.'

Leslie sat there, watching Henry lying in bed, coughing.

'Sorry about the meeting,' Henry said. 'You handle the board. There's nothing anyone can do, anyway.'

She only smiled.

Five

The members of the board were gathered around the table in the conference room, sipping coffee and helping themselves to bagels and cream cheese, waiting for Leslie.

When she arrived, she said, 'Sorry to keep you waiting, ladies and gentlemen. Henry sends his regards.'

Things had changed since the first board meeting Leslie had attended. The board had snubbed her then, and treated her as an interloper. But gradually, as Leslie had learned enough about the business to make valuable suggestions, she had won their respect. Now, as the meeting was about to begin, Leslie turned to Amy, who was serving coffee. 'Amy, I would like you to stay for the meeting.'

Amy looked at her in surprise. 'I'm afraid my shorthand isn't very good, Mrs Chambers. Cynthia can do a better job of –'

'I don't want you to take minutes of the meeting. Just make a note of whatever resolutions we pass at the end.'

'Yes, ma'am.' Amy picked up a notebook and pen and

sat in a chair against the wall.

Leslie turned to face the board. 'We have a problem. Our contract with the pressmen's union is almost up. We've been negotiating for three months now, and we haven't been able to reach an agreement. We have to make a decision, and we have to make it fast. You've all seen the reports I sent you. I'd like to have your opinions.'

She looked at Gene Osborne, a partner in a local law firm.

'If you ask me, Leslie, I think they're getting too damn much already. Give them what they want now, and tomorrow they'll want more.'

Leslie nodded and looked at Aaron Drexel, the owner of a local department store. 'Aaron?'

'I have to agree. There's a hell of a lot of featherbedding going on. If we give them something, we should get something in return. In my opinion, we can afford a strike, and they can't.'

The comments from the others were similar.

Leslie said, 'I have to disagree with all of you.' They looked at her in surprise. 'I think we should let them have what they want.'

'That's crazy.'

'They'll wind up owning the newspaper.'

'There won't be any stopping them.'

'You can't give in to them.'

Leslie let them speak. When they had finished, she said, 'Joe Riley is a fair man. He believes in what he's asking for.'

Seated against the wall, Amy was following the discussion, astonished.

One of the women spoke up. 'I'm surprised you're taking his side, Leslie.'

'I'm not taking anyone's side. I just think we have to be reasonable about this. Anyway, it's not my decision. Let's take a vote.' She turned to look at Amy. 'This is what I want you to put in the record.'

'Yes, ma'am.'

Leslie turned back to the group. 'All those opposed to the union demands, raise your hands.' Eleven hands went into the air. 'Let the record show that I voted yes and that the rest of the committee has voted not to accept the union demands.'

Amy was writing in her notebook, a thoughtful expression on her face.

Leslie said, 'Well, that's it then.' She rose. 'If there's no further business . . .'

The others got to their feet.

'Thank you all for coming.' She watched them leave, then turned to Amy. 'Would you type that up, please?'

'Right away, Mrs Chambers.'

Leslie headed for her office.

The telephone call came a short time later.

'Mr Riley is on line one,' Amy said.

Leslie picked up the telephone. 'Hello.'

'Joe Riley. I just wanted to thank you for what you

73

tried to do.'

Leslie said, 'I don't understand . . .'

'The board meeting. I heard what happened.'

Leslie said, 'I'm surprised, Mr Riley. That was a private meeting.'

Joe Riley chuckled. 'Let's just say I have friends in low places. Anyway, I thought what you tried to do was great. Too bad it didn't work.'

There was a brief silence, then Leslie said slowly, 'Mr Riley . . . what if I could make it work?'

'What do you mean?'

'I have an idea. I'd rather not discuss it on the phone. Could we meet somewhere . . . discreetly?'

There was a pause. 'Sure. Where did you have in mind?'

'Someplace where neither of us will be recognized.'

'What about meeting at the Golden Cup?'

'Right. I'll be there in an hour.'

'I'll see you.'

The Golden Cup was an infamous café in the seedier section of Phoenix, near the railroad tracks, an area police warned tourists to stay away from. Joe Riley was seated at a corner booth when Leslie walked in. He rose as she approached him.

'Thank you for being here,' Leslie said. They sat down.

'I came because you said there might be a way for me to get my contract.'

'There is. I think the board is being stupid and short-sighted. I tried to talk to them, but they wouldn't listen.'

He nodded, 'I know. You advised them to give us the new contract.'

'That's right. They don't realize how important you pressmen are to our newspaper.'

He was studying her, puzzled. 'But if they voted you down, how can we . . . ?'

'The only reason they voted me down is that they're not taking your union seriously. If you want to avoid a long strike, and maybe the death of the paper, you have to show them you mean business.'

'How do you mean?'

Leslie said nervously, 'What I'm telling you is very confidential, but it's the only way that you're going to get what you want. The problem is simple. They think you're bluffing. They don't believe you mean business. You have to show them that you do. Your contract is up this Friday at midnight.'

'Yes . . .'

'They'll expect you just to quietly walk out.' She leaned forward. 'Don't!' He was listening intently. 'Show them that they can't run the *Star* without you. Don't just go out like lambs. Do some damage.'

His eyes widened.

'I don't mean anything serious,' Leslie said quickly. 'Just enough to show them that you mean business. Cut a few cables, put a press or two out of commission. Let them learn that they need you to operate them. Everything can be repaired in a day or two, but meanwhile, you'll have scared them into their senses. They'll finally know what they're dealing with.'

Joe Riley sat there for a long time, studying Leslie. 'You're a remarkable lady.'

'Not really. I thought it over, and I have a very simple choice. You can cause a little damage that can be easily corrected, and force the board to deal with you, or you can walk out quietly and resign yourself to a long strike that the paper may never recover from. All I care about is protecting the paper.'

A slow smile lit Riley's face. 'Let me buy you a cup of coffee, Mrs Chambers.'

'We're striking!'

Friday night, at one minute past midnight, under Joe Riley's direction, the pressmen attacked. They stripped parts from the machines, overturned tables full of equipment, and set two printing presses on fire. A guard who tried to stop them was badly beaten. The pressmen, who had started out merely to disable a few presses, got caught up in the fever of the excitement, and they became more and more destructive.

'Let's show the bastards that they can't shove us around!' one of the men cried.

'There's no paper without us!'

'We're the *Star*!'

Cheers went up. The men attacked harder. The press-room was turning into a shambles.

In the midst of the wild excitement, floodlights suddenly flashed on from the four corners of the room. The men stopped, looking around in bewilderment. Near the doors, television cameras were recording the fiery scene and the destruction. Next to them were reporters from the *Arizona Republic*, the *Phoenix Gazette*, and several news services, covering the havoc. There were at least a dozen policemen and firemen.

Joe Riley was looking around in shock. *How the hell had they all gotten here so fast?* As the police started to close in and the firemen turned on their hoses, the answer suddenly came to Riley, and he felt as though someone had kicked him in the stomach. Leslie Chambers had set him up! When these pictures of the destruction the union had caused got out, there would be no sympathy for them. Public opinion would turn against them. *The bitch had planned this all along . . .*

The television pictures were aired within the hour, and the radio waves were filled with details of the wanton destruction. News services around the world printed the story, and they all carried the theme of the vicious employees who had turned on the hand that fed them. It was a public relations triumph for the *Phoenix Star*.

*   *   *

Leslie had prepared well. Earlier, she had secretly sent some of the *Star*'s executives to Kansas to learn how to run the giant presses, and to teach nonunion employees cold-type production. Immediately after the sabotage incident, two other striking unions, the mailers and photoengravers, came to terms with the *Star*.

With the unions defeated, and the way open to modernize the paper's technology, profits began to soar. Overnight, productivity jumped 20 percent.

The morning after the strike, Amy was fired.

On a late Friday afternoon, two years from the date of their wedding, Henry had a touch of indigestion. By Saturday morning, it had become chest pains, and Leslie called for an ambulance to rush him to the hospital. On Sunday, Henry Chambers passed away.

He left his entire estate to Leslie.

The Monday after the funeral, Craig McAllister came to see Leslie. 'I wanted to go over some legal matters with you, but if it's too soon –'

'No,' Leslie said. 'I'm all right.'

Henry's death had affected Leslie more than she had expected. He had been a dear, sweet man, and she had used him because she wanted him to help her get revenge against Oliver. And somehow, in Leslie's mind, Henry's death became another reason to destroy Oliver.

'What do you want to do with the *Star*?' McAllister asked. 'I don't imagine you'll want to spend your time running it.'

'That's exactly what I intend to do. We're going to expand.'

Leslie sent for a copy of the *Managing Editor*, the trade magazine that lists newspaper brokers all over the United States. Leslie selected Dirks, Van Essen and Associates in Santa Fe, New Mexico.

'This is Mrs Henry Chambers. I'm interested in acquiring another newspaper, and I wondered what might be available . . .'

It turned out to be the *Sun* in Hammond, Oregon.

'I'd like you to fly up there and take a look at it,' Leslie told McAllister.

Two days later, McAllister telephoned Leslie. 'You can forget about the *Sun*, Mrs Chambers.'

'What's the problem?'

'The problem is that Hammond is a two-newspaper town. The daily circulation of the *Sun* is fifteen thousand. The other newspaper, the *Hammond Chronicle*, has a circulation of twenty-eight thousand, almost double. And the owner of the *Sun* is asking five million dollars. The deal doesn't make any sense.'

Leslie was thoughtful for a moment. 'Wait for me,' she said. 'I'm on my way.'

* * *

Leslie spent the following two days examining the newspaper and studying its books.

'There's no way the *Sun* can compete with the *Chronicle*,' McAllister assured her. 'The *Chronicle* keeps growing. The *Sun*'s circulation has gone down every year for the past five years.'

'I know,' Leslie said. 'I'm going to buy it.'

He looked at her in surprise. 'You're going to what?'

'I'm going to buy it.'

The deal was completed in three days. The owner of the *Sun* was delighted to get rid of it. 'I suckered the lady into making a deal,' he crowed. 'She paid me the full five million.'

Walt Meriwether, the owner of the *Hammond Chronicle*, came to call on Leslie.

'I understand you're my new competitor,' he said genially.

Leslie nodded. 'That's right.'

'If things don't work out here for you, maybe you'd be interested in selling the *Sun* to me.'

Leslie smiled. 'And if things do work out, perhaps you'd be interested in selling the *Chronicle* to me.'

Meriwether laughed. 'Sure. Lots of luck, Mrs Chambers.'

When Meriwether got back to the *Chronicle*, he said confidently, 'In six months, we're going to own the *Sun*.'

*   *   *

Leslie returned to Phoenix and talked to Lyle Bannister, the *Star*'s managing editor. 'You're going with me to Hammond, Oregon. I want you to run the newspaper there until it gets on its feet.'

'I talked to Mr McAllister,' Bannister said. 'The paper has no feet. He said it's a disaster waiting to happen.'

She studied him a moment. 'Humor me.'

In Oregon, Leslie called a staff meeting of the employees of the *Sun*.

'We're going to operate a little differently from now on,' she informed them. 'This is a two-newspaper town, and we're going to own them both.'

Derek Zornes, the managing editor of the *Sun*, said, 'Excuse me, Mrs Chambers. I'm not sure you understand the situation. Our circulation is way below the *Chronicle*'s, and we're slipping every month. There's no way we can ever catch up to it.'

'We're not only going to catch up to it,' Leslie assured him, 'we're going to put the *Chronicle* out of business.'

The men in the room looked at one another and they all had the same thought: Females and amateurs should stay the hell out of the newspaper business.

'How do you plan to do that?' Zornes asked politely.

'Have you ever watched a bullfight?' Leslie asked.

He blinked. 'A bullfight? No . . .'

'Well, when the bull rushes into the ring, the matador

doesn't go for the kill right away. He bleeds the bull until it's weak enough to be killed.'

Zornes was trying not to laugh. 'And we're going to bleed the *Chronicle*?'

'Exactly.'

'How are we going to do that?'

'Starting Monday, we're cutting the price of the *Sun* from thirty-five cents to twenty cents. We're cutting our advertising rates by thirty percent. Next week, we're starting a giveaway contest where our readers can win free trips all over the world. We'll begin publicizing the contest immediately.'

When the employees gathered later to discuss the meeting, the consensus was that their newspaper had been bought by a crazy woman.

The bleeding began, but it was the *Sun* that was being bled.

McAllister asked Leslie, 'Do you have any idea how much money the *Sun* is losing?'

'I know exactly how much it's losing,' Leslie said.

'How long do you plan to go on with this?'

'Until we win,' Leslie said. 'Don't worry. We will.'

But Leslie was worried. The losses were getting heavier every week. Circulation continued to dwindle, and advertisers' reactions to the rate reduction had been lukewarm.

'Your theory's not working,' McAllister said. 'We've

got to cut our losses. I suppose you can keep pumping in money, but what's the point?'

The following week, the circulation stopped dropping.

It took eight weeks for the *Sun* to begin to rise.

The reduction in the price of the newspaper and in the cost of advertising was attractive, but what made the circulation of the *Sun* move up was the giveaway contest. It ran for twelve weeks, and entrants had to compete every week. The prizes were cruises to the South Seas and trips to London and Paris and Rio. As the prizes were handed out and publicized with front-page photographs of the winners, the circulation of the *Sun* began to explode.

'You took a hell of a gamble,' Craig McAllister said grudgingly, 'but it's working.'

'It wasn't a gamble,' Leslie said. 'People can't resist getting something for nothing.'

When Walt Meriwether was handed the latest circulation figures, he was furious. For the first time in years, the *Sun* was ahead of the *Chronicle*.

'All right,' Meriwether said grimly. 'Two can play that stupid game. I want you to cut our advertising rates and start some kind of contest.'

But it was too late. Eleven months after Leslie had bought the *Sun*, Walt Meriwether came to see her.

'I'm selling out,' he said curtly. 'Do you want to buy the *Chronicle*?'

'Yes.'

The day the contract for the *Chronicle* was signed, Leslie called in her staff.

'Starting Monday,' she said, 'we raise the price of the *Sun*, double our advertising rates, and stop the contest.'

One month later, Leslie said to Craig McAllister, 'The *Evening Standard* in Detroit is up for sale. It owns a television station, too. I think we should make a deal.'

McAllister protested. 'Mrs Chambers, we don't know anything about television, and –'

'Then we'll have to learn, won't we?'

The empire Leslie needed was beginning to build.

Six

Oliver's days were full, and he loved every minute of what he was doing. There were political appointments to be made, legislation to be put forward, appropriations to be approved, meetings and speeches and press interviews. The *State Journal* in Frankfort, the *Herald-Leader* in Lexington, and the *Louisville Courier-Journal* gave him glowing reports. He was earning the reputation of being a governor who got things done. Oliver was swept up in the social life of the superwealthy, and he knew that a large part of that was because he was married to the daughter of Senator Todd Davis.

Oliver enjoyed living in Frankfort. It was a lovely, historic city nestled in a scenic river valley among the rolling hills of Kentucky's fabled bluegrass region. He wondered what it would be like to live in Washington, D.C.

The busy days merged into weeks, and the weeks merged into months. Oliver began the last year of his term.

Oliver had made Peter Tager his press secretary. He was the perfect choice. Tager was always forthright with the press, and because of the decent, old-fashioned values he stood for and liked to talk about, he gave the party substance and dignity. Peter Tager and his black eye patch became almost as well recognized as Oliver.

Todd Davis made it a point to fly down to Frankfort to see Oliver at least once a month.

He said to Peter Tager, 'When you've got a Thoroughbred running, you have to keep an eye on him to make sure he doesn't lose his timing.'

On a chilly evening in October, Oliver and Senator Davis were seated in Oliver's study. The two men and Jan had gone out to dinner at Gabriel's and had returned to the Executive Mansion. Jan had left the men to talk.

'Jan seems very happy, Oliver. I'm pleased.'

'I try to make her happy, Todd.'

Senator Davis looked at Oliver and wondered how often he used the apartment. 'She loves you a lot, son.'

'And I love her.' Oliver sounded very sincere.

Senator Davis smiled. 'I'm glad to hear that. She's already redecorating the White House.'

Oliver's heart skipped a beat. 'I beg your pardon?'

'Oh, didn't I tell you? It's begun. Your name's becoming a byword in Washington. We're going to begin our campaign the first of the year.'

Oliver was almost afraid to ask the next question. 'Do you honestly think I have a chance, Todd?'

'The word "chance" implies a gamble, and I don't gamble, son. I won't get involved in anything unless I know it's a sure thing.'

Oliver took a deep breath. *You can be the most important man in the world.* 'I want you to know how very much I appreciate everything you've done for me, Todd.'

Todd patted Oliver's arm. 'It's a man's duty to help his son-in-law, isn't it?'

The emphasis on 'son-in-law' was not lost on Oliver.

The senator said casually, 'By the way, Oliver, I was very disappointed that your legislature passed that tobacco tax bill.'

'That money will take care of the shortfall in our fiscal budget, and –'

'But of course you're going to veto it.'

Oliver stared at him. 'Veto it?'

The senator gave him a small smile. 'Oliver, I want you to know that I'm not thinking about myself. But I have a lot of friends who invested their hard-earned money in tobacco plantations, and I wouldn't want to see them get hurt by oppressive new taxes, would you?'

There was a silence.

'Would you, Oliver?'

'No,' Oliver finally said. 'I guess it wouldn't be fair.'

'I appreciate that. I really do.'

Oliver said, 'I had heard that you'd sold your tobacco plantations, Todd.'

Todd Davis looked at him, surprised. 'Why would I want to do that?'

'Well, the tobacco companies are taking a beating in the courts. Sales are way down, and –'

'You're talking about the United States, son. There's a great big world out there. Wait until our advertising campaigns start rolling in China and Africa and India.' He looked at his watch and rose. 'I have to head back to Washington. I have a committee meeting.'

'Have a good flight.'

Senator Davis smiled. 'Now I will, son. Now I will.'

Oliver was upset. 'What the hell am I going to do, Peter? The tobacco tax is by far the most popular measure the legislature has passed this year. What excuse do I have for vetoing it?'

Peter Tager took several sheets of paper from his pocket. 'All the answers are right here, Oliver. I've discussed it with the senator. You won't have any problem. I've set up a press conference for four o'clock.'

Oliver studied the papers. Finally, he nodded. 'This is good.'

'It's what I do. Is there anything else you need me for?'

'No. Thank you. I'll see you at four.'

Peter Tager started to leave.

'Peter.'

Tager turned. 'Yes?'

'Tell me something. Do you think I really have a chance of becoming president?'

'What does the senator say?'

'He says I do.'

Tager walked back to the desk. 'I've known Senator Davis for many years, Oliver. In all that time, he hasn't been wrong once. Not once. The man has incredible instincts. If Todd Davis says you're going to be the next President of the United States, you can bet the farm on it.'

There was a knock at the door. 'Come in.'

The door opened, and an attractive young secretary walked in, carrying some faxes. She was in her early twenties, bright and eager.

'Oh, excuse me, Governor. I didn't know you were in a –'

'That's all right, Miriam.'

Tager smiled. 'Hi, Miriam.'

'Hello, Mr Tager.'

Oliver said, 'I don't know what I'd do without Miriam. She does everything for me.'

Miriam blushed. 'If there's nothing else –' She put the faxes on Oliver's desk and turned and hurried out of the office.

'That's a pretty woman,' Tager said. He looked over at Oliver.

'Yes.'

'Oliver, you are being careful, aren't you?'

'Of course I am. That's why I had you get that little apartment for me.'

'I mean big-time careful. The stakes have gone up. The next time you get horny, just stop and think about whether a Miriam or Alice or Karen is worth the Oval Office.'

'I know what you're saying, Peter, and I appreciate it. But you don't have to worry about me.'

'Good.' Tager looked at his watch. 'I have to go. I'm taking Betsy and the kids out to lunch.' He smiled. 'Did I tell you what Rebecca did this morning? She's my five-year-old. There was a tape of a kid's show she wanted to watch at eight o'clock this morning. Betsy said, "Darling, I'll run it for you after lunch." Rebecca looked at her and said, "Mama, I want lunch now." Pretty smart, huh?'

Oliver had to smile at the pride in Tager's voice.

At ten o'clock that evening, Oliver walked into the den where Jan was reading and said, 'Honey, I have to leave. I have a conference to go to.'

Jan looked up. 'At this time of night?'

He sighed. 'I'm afraid so. There's a budget committee meeting in the morning, and they want to brief me before the meeting.'

'You're working too hard. Try to come home early,

will you, Oliver?' She hesitated a moment. 'You've been out a lot lately.'

He wondered whether that was intended as a warning. He walked over to her, leaned down, and kissed her. 'Don't worry, honey. I'll be home as early as I can.'

Downstairs Oliver said to his chauffeur, 'I won't need you tonight. I'm taking the small car.'

'Yes, Governor.'

'You're late, darling.' Miriam was naked.

He grinned and walked over to her. 'Sorry about that. I'm glad you didn't start without me.'

She smiled. 'Hold me.'

He took her in his arms and held her close, her warm body pressed against his.

'Get undressed. Hurry.'

Afterward, he said, 'How would you like to move to Washington, D.C.?'

Miriam sat up in bed. 'Are you serious?'

'Very. I may be going there. I want you to be with me.'

'If your wife ever found out about us . . .'

'She won't.'

'Why Washington?'

'I can't tell you that now. All I can say is that it's going to be very exciting.'

'I'll go anywhere you want me to go, as long as you love me.'

'You know I love you.' The words slipped out easily, as they had so many times in the past.

'Make love to me again.'

'Just a second. I have something for you.' He got up and walked over to the jacket he had flung over a chair. He took a small bottle out of his pocket and poured the contents into a glass. It was a clear liquid.

'Try this.'

'What is it?' Miriam asked.

'You'll like it. I promise.' He lifted the glass and drank half of it.

Miriam took a sip, then swallowed the rest of it. She smiled. 'It's not bad.'

'It's going to make you feel real sexy.'

'I already feel real sexy. Come back to bed.'

They were making love again when she gasped and said, 'I – I'm not feeling well.' She began to pant. 'I can't breathe.' Her eyes were closing.

'Miriam!' There was no response. She fell back on the bed. 'Miriam!'

She lay there, unconscious.

Son of a bitch! Why are you doing this to me?

He got up and began to pace. He had given the liquid to a dozen women, and only once had it harmed anyone. He had to be careful. Unless he handled this right, it was going to be the end of everything. All his dreams, everything he had worked for. He could not let that happen. He stood at the side of the bed, looking down at her. He felt her pulse. She was still breathing, thank God. But he could not let her be discovered in this apartment. It would be traced back to him. He had to leave her somewhere where she would be found and be given medical help. He could trust her not to reveal his name.

It took him almost half an hour to get her dressed and to remove all traces of her from his apartment. He opened the door a crack to make sure that the hallway was empty, then picked her up, put her over his shoulder, and carried her downstairs and put her in the car. It was almost midnight, and the streets were deserted. It was beginning to rain. He drove to Juniper Hill Park, and when he was sure that no one was in sight, he lifted Miriam out of the car and gently laid her down on a park bench. He hated to leave her there, but he had no choice. None. His whole future was at stake.

There was a public phone booth a few feet away. He hurried over to it and dialed 911.

Jan was waiting up for Oliver when he returned home. 'It's after midnight,' she said. 'What took you –?'

'I'm sorry, darling. We got into a long, boring discussion on the budget, and – well, everyone had a different opinion.'

'You look pale,' Jan said. 'You must be exhausted.'

'I am a little tired,' he admitted.

She smiled suggestively. 'Let's go to bed.'

He kissed her on the forehead. 'I've really got to get some sleep, Jan. That meeting knocked me out.'

The story was on the front page of the *State Journal* the following morning:

GOVERNOR'S SECRETARY FOUND UNCON-
SCIOUS IN PARK.

At two o'clock this morning, police found the unconscious woman, Miriam Friedland, lying on the bench in the rain and immediately called for an ambulance. She was taken to Memorial Hospital, where her condition is said to be critical.

As Oliver was reading the story, Peter came hurrying into his office, carrying a copy of the newspaper.

'Have you seen this?'

'Yes. It's – it's terrible. The press has been calling all morning.'

'What do you suppose happened?' Tager asked.

Oliver shook his head. 'I don't know. I just talked to the hospital. She's in a coma. They're trying to learn what caused it. The hospital is going to let me know as soon as they find out.'

Tager looked at Oliver. 'I hope she's going to be all right.'

Leslie Chambers missed seeing the newspaper stories. She was in Brazil, buying a television station.

The telephone call from the hospital came the following day. 'Governor, we've just finished the laboratory tests. She's ingested a substance called methylenedioxymeth-amphetamine, commonly known as Ecstasy. She took it in liquid form, which is even more lethal.'

'What's her condition?'

'I'm afraid it's critical. She's in a coma. She could wake up or –' He hesitated. 'It could go the other way.'

'Please keep me informed.'

'Of course. You must be very concerned, Governor.'

'I am.'

Oliver Russell was in a conference when a secretary buzzed.

'Excuse me, Governor. There's a telephone call for you.'

'I told you no interruptions, Heather.'

'It's Senator Davis on line three.'

'Oh.'

Oliver turned to the men in the room. 'We'll finish this later, gentlemen. If you'll excuse me . . .'

He watched them leave the room, and when the door closed behind them, he picked up the telephone. 'Todd?'

'Oliver, what's this about a secretary of yours found drugged on a park bench?'

'Yes,' Oliver said. 'It's a terrible thing, Todd. I –'

'How terrible?' Senator Davis demanded.

'What do you mean?'

'You know damn well what I mean.'

'Todd, you don't think I – I swear I don't know anything about what happened.'

'I hope not.' The senator's voice was grim. 'You know how fast gossip gets around in Washington, Oliver. It's the smallest town in America. We don't want anything negative linked to you. We're getting ready to make our move. I'd be very, very upset if you did anything stupid.'

'I promise you, I'm clean.'

'Just make sure you keep it that way.'

'Of course I will. I –' The line went dead.

Oliver sat there thinking. *I'll have to be more careful. I can't let anything stop me now.* He glanced at his watch, then reached for the remote control that turned on the television set. The news was on. On the screen was a picture of a besieged street, with snipers shooting at random from buildings. The sound of mortar fire could be heard in the background.

An attractive young female reporter, dressed in battle fatigues and holding a microphone, was saying, 'The new treaty is supposed to take effect at midnight tonight, but regardless of whether it holds, it can never bring back the peaceful villages in this war-torn country or restore the lives of the innocents who have been swept up in the ruthless reign of terror.'

The scene shifted to a close-up of Dana Evans, a passionate, lovely young woman in a flak jacket and combat boots. 'The people here are hungry and tired. They ask for only one thing – peace. Will it come? Only time will tell. This is Dana Evans reporting from Sarajevo for WTE, Washington Tribune Enterprises.' The scene dissolved into a commercial.

Dana Evans was a foreign correspondent for the Washington Tribune Enterprises Broadcasting System. She reported the news every day, and Oliver tried not to miss her broadcasts. She was one of the best reporters on the air.

She's a great-looking woman, Oliver thought, not for the first time. *Why the hell would someone that young and attractive want to be in the middle of a shooting war?*

Seven

Dana Evans was an army brat, the daughter of a colonel who traveled from base to base as an armaments instructor. By the time Dana was eleven years old, she had lived in five American cities and in four foreign countries. She had moved with her father and mother to the Aberdeen Proving Ground in Maryland, Fort Benning in Georgia, Fort Hood in Texas, Fort Leavenworth in Kansas, and Fort Monmouth in New Jersey. She had gone to schools for officers' children at Camp Zama in Japan, Chiemsee in Germany, Camp Darby in Italy, and Fort Buchanan in Puerto Rico.

Dana was an only child, and her friends were the army personnel and their families who were stationed at the various postings. She was precocious, cheerful, and outgoing, but her mother worried about the fact that Dana was not having a normal childhood.

'I know that moving every six months must be terribly hard on you, darling,' her mother said.

Dana looked at her mother, puzzled. 'Why?'

Whenever Dana's father was assigned to a new post,

Dana was thrilled. 'We're going to move again!' she would exclaim.

Unfortunately, although Dana enjoyed the constant moving, her mother hated it.

When Dana was thirteen, her mother said, 'I can't live like a gypsy any longer. I want a divorce.'

Dana was horrified when she heard the news. Not about the divorce so much, but by the fact that she would no longer be able to travel around the world with her father.

'Where am I going to live?' Dana asked her mother.

'In Claremont, California. I grew up there. It's a beautiful little town. You'll love it.'

Dana's mother had been right about Claremont's being a beautiful little town. She was wrong about Dana's loving it. Claremont was at the base of the San Gabriel Mountains in Los Angeles County, with a population of about thirty-three thousand. Its streets were lined with lovely trees and it had the feel of a quaint college community. Dana hated it. The change from being a world traveler to settling down in a small town brought on a severe case of culture shock.

'Are we going to live here forever?' Dana asked gloomily.

'Why, darling?'

'Because it's too small for me. I need a bigger town.'

*   *   *

On Dana's first day at school, she came home depressed.

'What's the matter? Don't you like your school?'

Dana sighed. 'It's all right, but it's full of kids.'

Dana's mother laughed. 'They'll get over that, and so will you.'

Dana went on to Claremont High School and became a reporter for the *Wolfpacket*, the school newspaper. She found that she enjoyed newspaper work, but she desperately missed traveling.

'When I grow up,' Dana said, 'I'm going to go all over the world again.'

When Dana was eighteen, she enrolled in Claremont McKenna College, majored in journalism, and became a reporter for the college newspaper, the *Forum*. The following year, she was made editor of the paper.

Students were constantly coming to her for favors. 'Our sorority is having a dance next week, Dana. Would you mention it in the paper . . . ?'

'The debating club is having a meeting Tuesday . . .'

'Could you review the play the drama club is putting on . . . ?'

'We need to raise funds for the new library . . .'

It was endless, but Dana enjoyed it enormously. She was in a position to help people, and she liked that. In her senior year, Dana decided that she wanted a newspaper career.

'I'll be able to interview important people all over the world,' Dana told her mother. 'It will be like helping to make history.'

Growing up, whenever young Dana looked in a mirror, she became depressed. Too short, too thin, too flat. Every other girl was awesomely beautiful. It was some kind of California law. *I'm an ugly duckling in a land of swans,* she thought. She made it a point to avoid looking in mirrors. If Dana had looked, she would have realized that at the age of fourteen, her body was beginning to blossom. At the age of sixteen, she had become very attractive. When she was seventeen, boys began seriously to pursue her. There was something about her eager, heart-shaped face, large inquisitive eyes, and husky laugh that was both adorable and a challenge.

Dana had known since she was twelve how she wanted to lose her virginity. It would be on a beautiful, moon-lit night on some faraway tropical island, with the waves gently lapping against the shore. There would be soft music playing in the background. A handsome, sophisticated stranger would approach her and look deeply into her eyes, into her soul, and he would take her in his arms without a word and suavely carry her to a nearby palm tree. They would get undressed and make love and the music in the background would swell to a climax.

*　　　*　　　*

She actually lost her virginity in the back of an old Chevrolet, after a school dance, to a skinny eighteen-year-old redhead named Richard Dobbins, who worked on the *Forum* with her. He gave Dana his ring and a month later, moved to Milwaukee with his parents. Dana never heard from him again.

The month before she was graduated from college with a B.A. in journalism, Dana went down to the local newspaper, the *Claremont Examiner*, to see about a job as a reporter.

A man in the personnel office looked over her résumé. 'So you were the editor of the *Forum*, eh?'

Dana smiled modestly. 'That's right.'

'Okay. You're in luck. We're a little short-handed right now. We'll give you a try.'

Dana was thrilled. She had already made a list of the countries she wanted to cover: Russia ... China ... Africa ...

'I know I can't start as a foreign correspondent,' Dana said, 'but as soon as –'

'Right. You'll be working here as a gofer. You'll see that the editors have coffee in the morning. They like it strong, by the way. And you'll run copy down to the printing presses.'

Dana stared at him in shock. 'I can't –'

He leaned forward, frowning. 'You can't what?'

'I can't tell you how glad I am to have this job.'

The reporters all complimented Dana on her coffee, and she became the best runner the paper had ever had. She was at work early every day and made friends with everyone. She was always eager to help out. She knew that was the way to get ahead.

The problem was that at the end of six months, Dana was still a gofer. She went to see Bill Crowell, the managing editor.

'I really think I'm ready,' Dana said earnestly. 'If you give me an assignment, I'll –'

He did not even look up. 'There's no opening yet. My coffee's cold.'

It isn't fair, Dana thought. *They won't even give me a chance.* Dana had heard a line that she firmly believed in. 'If something can stop you, you might as well let it.' *Well, nothing's going to stop me*, Dana thought. *Nothing. But how am I going to get started?*

One morning, as Dana was walking through the deserted Teletype room, carrying cups of hot coffee, a police scanner printout was coming over the wires. Curious, Dana walked over and read it:

ASSOCIATED PRESS – CLAREMONT, CALIFORNIA. IN CLAREMONT THIS MORNING, THERE WAS AN ATTEMPTED KIDNAPPING.

Dana read the rest of the story, wide-eyed. She took a deep breath, ripped the story from the teletype, and put it in her pocket. No one else had seen it.

Dana hurried into Bill Crowell's office, breathless. 'Mr Crowell, someone tried to kidnap a little boy in Claremont this morning. He offered to take him on a pony ride. The boy wanted some candy first, and the kidnapper took him to a candy store, where the owner recognized the boy. The owner called the police and the kidnapper fled.'

Bill Crowell was excited. 'There was nothing on the wires. How did you hear about this?'

'I – I happened to be in the store, and they were talking about it and –'

'I'll get a reporter over there right away.'

'Why don't you let me cover it?' Dana said quickly. 'The owner of the candy store knows me. He'll talk to me.'

He studied Dana a moment and said reluctantly, 'All right.'

Dana interviewed the owner of the candy store, and her story appeared on the front page of the *Claremont Examiner* the next day and was well received.

'That wasn't a bad job,' Bill Crowell told her. 'Not bad at all.'

'Thank you.'

*   *   *

It was almost a week before Dana found herself alone again in the teletype room. There was a story coming in on the wire from the Associated Press:

POMONA, CALIFORNIA: FEMALE JUDO IN-STRUCTOR CAPTURES WOULD-BE RAPIST.

Perfect, Dana decided. She tore off the printout, crumpled it, stuffed it in her pocket, and hurried in to see Bill Crowell.

'My old roommate just called me,' Dana said excitedly. 'She was looking out the window and saw a woman attack a would-be rapist. I'd like to cover it.'

Crowell looked at her a moment. 'Go ahead.'

Dana drove to Pomona to get an interview with the judo instructor, and again her story made the front page.

Bill Crowell asked Dana to come into his office. 'How would you like to have a regular beat?'

Dana was thrilled. 'Great!' *It's begun,* she thought. *My career has finally begun.*

The following day, the *Claremont Examiner* was sold to the *Washington Tribune* in Washington, D.C.

When the news of the sale came out, most of the *Claremont Examiner* employees were dismayed. It was inevitable that there would be downsizing and that some of them would lose their jobs. Dana did not think of it that way. *I work for the* Washington Tribune *now,* she thought, and the next logical thought was, *Why don't I go to work at its headquarters?*

She marched into Bill Crowell's office. 'I'd like a ten-day leave.'

He looked at her curiously. 'Dana, most of the people around here won't go to the bathroom because they're scared to death that their desks won't be there when they get back. Aren't you worried?'

'Why should I be? I'm the best reporter you have,' she said confidently. 'I'm going to get a job at the *Washington Tribune*.'

'Are you serious?' He saw her expression. 'You're serious.' He sighed. 'All right. Try to see Matt Baker. He's in charge of Washington Tribune Enterprises – newspapers, TV stations, radio, everything.'

'Matt Baker. Right.'

Eight

Washington, D.C., was a much larger city than Dana had imagined. This was the power center of the world, and Dana could feel the electricity in the air. This is where I belong, she thought happily.

Her first move was to check into the Stouffer Renaissance Hotel. She looked up the address of the *Washington Tribune* and headed there. The *Tribune* was located on 6th Street and took up the entire block. It consisted of four separate buildings that seemed to reach to infinity. Dana found the main lobby and confidently walked up to the uniformed guard behind the desk.

'Can I help you, miss?'

'I work here. That is, I work for the *Tribune*. I'm here to see Matt Baker.'

'Do you have an appointment?'

Dana hesitated. 'Not yet, but –'

'Come back when you have one.' He turned his attention to several men who had come up to the desk.

'We have an appointment with the head of the circulation department,' one of the men said.

'Just a moment, please.' The guard dialed a number.

In the background, one of the elevators had arrived and people were getting out. Dana casually headed for it. She stepped inside, praying that it would go up before the guard noticed her. A woman got into the elevator and pressed the button, and they started up.

'Excuse me,' Dana said. 'What floor is Matt Baker on?'

'Third.' She looked at Dana. 'You're not wearing a pass.'

'I lost it,' Dana said.

When the elevator reached the third floor, Dana got out. She stood there, speechless at the scale of what she was seeing. She was looking at a sea of cubicles. It seemed as though there were hundreds of them, occupied by thousands of people. There were different-colored signs over each cubicle. EDITORIAL . . . ART . . . METRO . . . SPORTS . . . CALENDAR . . .

Dana stopped a man hurrying by. 'Excuse me. Where's Mr Baker's office?'

'Matt Baker?' He pointed. 'Down at the end of the hall to the right, last door.'

'Thank you.'

As Dana turned, she bumped into an unshaven, rumpled-looking man carrying some papers. The papers fell to the floor.

'Oh, I'm sorry. I was –'

'Why don't you look where the hell you're going?' the man snapped. He stooped to pick up the papers.

'It was an accident. Here. I'll help you. I –' Dana reached down, and as she started to pick up the papers, she knocked several sheets under a desk.

The man stopped to glare at her. 'Do me a favor. Don't help me anymore.'

'As you like,' Dana said icily. 'I just hope everyone in Washington isn't as rude as you.'

Haughtily, Dana rose and walked toward Mr Baker's office. The legend on the glass window read 'MATT BAKER.' The office was empty. Dana walked inside and sat down. Looking through the office window, she watched the frenetic activity going on.

It's nothing like the Claremont Examiner, she thought. There were thousands of people working here. Down the corridor, the grumpy, rumpled-looking man was heading toward the office.

No! Dana thought. *He's not coming in here. He's on his way somewhere else –*

And the man walked in the door. His eyes narrowed. 'What the hell are you doing here?'

Dana swallowed. 'You must be Mr Baker,' she said brightly. 'I'm Dana Evans.'

'I asked you what you're doing here.'

'I'm a reporter with the *Claremont Examiner*.'

'And?'

'You just bought it.'

'I did?'

'I – I mean the newspaper bought it. The newspaper bought the newspaper.' Dana felt it was not going well.

'Anyway, I'm here for a job. Of course, I already have a job here. It's more like a transfer, isn't it?'

He was staring at her.

'I can start right away.' Dana babbled on. 'That's no problem.'

Matt Baker moved toward the desk. 'Who the hell let you in here?'

'I told you. I'm a reporter for the *Claremont Examiner* and –'

'Go back to Claremont,' he snapped. 'Try not to knock anyone down on your way out.'

Dana rose and said stiffly, 'Thank you very much, Mr Baker. I appreciate your courtesy.' She stormed out of the office.

Matt Baker looked after her, shaking his head. The world was full of weirdos.

Dana retraced her steps to the huge editorial room, where dozens of reporters were typing out stories on their computers. *This is where I'm going to work*, Dana thought fiercely. *Go back to Claremont. How dare he!*

As Dana looked up, she saw Matt Baker in the distance, moving in her direction. The damned man was everywhere! Dana quickly stepped behind a cubicle so he could not see her.

Baker walked past her to a reporter seated at a desk. 'Did you get the interview, Sam?'

'No luck. I went to the Georgetown Medical Center,

and they said there's nobody registered by that name. Tripp Taylor's wife isn't a patient there.'

Matt Baker said, 'I know damn well she is. They're covering something up, dammit. I want to know why she's in the hospital.'

'If she is in there, there's no way to get to her, Matt.'

'Did you try the flower delivery routine?'

'Sure. It didn't work.'

Dana stood there watching Matt Baker and the reporter walk away. *What kind of reporter is it,* Dana wondered, *who doesn't know how to get an interview?*

Thirty minutes later, Dana was entering the Georgetown Medical Center. She went into the flower shop.

'May I help you?' a clerk asked.

'Yes. I'd like –' She hesitated a moment. '– fifty dollars' worth of flowers.' She almost choked on the word 'fifty.'

When the clerk handed her the flowers, Dana said, 'Is there a shop in the hospital that might have a little cap of some kind?'

'There's a gift shop around the corner.'

'Thank you.'

The gift shop was a cornucopia of junk, with a wide array of greeting cards, cheaply made toys, balloons and banners, junk-food racks, and gaudy items of clothing. On a shelf were some souvenir caps. Dana bought one that resembled a chauffeur's cap and put it on. She purchased a get-well card and scribbled something on the inside.

Her next stop was at the information desk in the hospital lobby. 'I have flowers here for Mrs Tripp Taylor.'

The receptionist shook her head. 'There's no Mrs Tripp Taylor registered here.'

Dana sighed. 'Really? That's too bad. These are from the Vice President of the United States.' She opened the card and showed it to the receptionist. The inscription read, 'Get well quickly.' It was signed, 'Arthur Cannon.'

Dana said, 'Guess I'll have to take these back.' She turned to leave.

The receptionist looked after her uncertainly. 'Just a moment!'

Dana stopped. 'Yes?'

'I can have those flowers delivered to her.'

'Sorry,' Dana said. 'Vice President Cannon asked that they be delivered personally.' She looked at the receptionist. 'Could I have your name, please? They'll want to tell Mr Cannon why I couldn't deliver the flowers.'

Panic. 'Oh, well. All right. I don't want to cause any problems. Take them to Room 615. But as soon as you deliver them, you'll have to leave.'

'Right,' Dana said.

Five minutes later, she was talking to the wife of the famous rock star Tripp Taylor.

Stacy Taylor was in her middle twenties. It was difficult

to tell whether she was attractive or not, because at the moment, her face was badly battered and swollen. She was trying to reach for a glass of water on a table near the bed when Dana walked in.

'Flowers for –' Dana stopped in shock as she saw the woman's face.

'Who are they from?' The words were a mumble.

Dana had removed the card. 'From – from an admirer.'

The woman was staring at Dana suspiciously. 'Can you reach that water for me?'

'Of course.' Dana put the flowers down and handed the glass of water to the woman in bed. 'Can I do anything else for you?' Dana asked.

'Sure,' she said through swollen lips. 'You can get me out of this stinking place. My husband won't let me have visitors. I'm sick of seeing all these doctors and nurses.'

Dana sat down on a chair next to the bed. 'What happened to you?'

The woman snorted. 'Don't you know? I was in an auto accident.'

'You were?'

'Yes.'

'That's awful,' Dana said skeptically. She was filled with a deep anger, for it was obvious that this woman had been beaten.

Forty-five minutes later, Dana emerged with the true story.

* * *

When Dana returned to the lobby of the *Washington Tribune*, a different guard was there. 'Can I help –?'

'It's not my fault,' Dana said breathlessly. 'Believe me, it's the darned traffic. Tell Mr Baker I'm on my way up. He's going to be furious with me for being late.' She hurried toward the elevator and pressed the button. The guard looked after her uncertainly, then began dialing. 'Hello. Tell Mr Baker there's a young woman who –'

The elevator arrived. Dana stepped in and pressed three. On the third floor, the activity seemed to have increased, if that was possible. Reporters were rushing to make their deadlines. Dana stood there, looking around frantically. Finally, she saw what she wanted. In a cubicle with a green sign that read GARDENING was an empty desk. Dana hurried over to it and sat down. She looked at the computer in front of her, then began typing. She was so engrossed in the story she was writing that she lost all track of time. When she was finished, she printed it and pages began spewing out. She was putting them together when she sensed a shadow over her shoulder.

'What the hell are you doing?' Matt Baker demanded.

'I'm looking for a job, Mr Baker. I wrote this story, and I thought –'

'You thought wrong,' Baker exploded. 'You don't just walk in here and take over someone's desk. Now get the hell out before I call security and have you arrested.'

'But –'

'Out!'

Dana rose. Summoning all her dignity, she thrust the pages in Matt Baker's hand and walked around the corner to the elevator.

Matt Baker shook his head in disbelief. *Jesus! What the hell is the world coming to?* There was a wastebasket under the desk. As Matt moved toward it, he glanced at the first sentence of Dana's story: 'Stacy Taylor, her face battered and bruised, claimed from her hospital bed today that she was there because her famous rock star husband, Tripp Taylor, beat her. "Every time I get pregnant, he beats me up. He doesn't want children."' Matt started to read further and stood there rooted. He looked up, but Dana was gone.

Clutching the pages in his hand, Matt raced toward the elevators, hoping to find her before she disappeared. As he ran around the corner, he bumped into her. She was leaning against the wall, waiting.

'How did you get this story?' he demanded.

Dana said simply, 'I told you. I'm a reporter.'

He took a deep breath. 'Come on back to my office.'

They were seated in Matt Baker's office again. 'That's a good job,' he said grudgingly.

'Thank you! I can't tell you how much I appreciate this,' Dana said excitedly. 'I'm going to be the best reporter you ever had. You'll see. What I really want is to be a foreign correspondent, but I'm willing to work my way up to that, even if it takes a year.' She saw the expression on his face. 'Or maybe two.'

'The *Tribune* has no job openings, and there's a waiting list.'

She looked at him in astonishment. 'But I assumed –'

'Hold it.'

Dana watched as he picked up a pen and wrote out the letters of the word 'assume,' ASS U ME. He pointed to the word. 'When a reporter assumes something, Miss Evans, it makes an *ass* out of *you* and *me*. Do you understand?'

'Yes, sir.'

'Good.' He was thoughtful for a moment, then came to a decision. 'Do you ever watch WTE? The Tribune Enterprises television station.'

'No, sir. I can't say that I –'

'Well, you will now. You're in luck. There's a job opening there. One of the writers just quit. You can take his place.'

'Doing what?' Dana asked tentatively.

'Writing television copy.'

Her face fell. 'Television copy? I don't know anything about –'

'It's simple. The producer of the news will give you the raw material from all the news services. You'll put it into English and put it on the TelePrompTer for the anchors to read.'

Dana sat there, silent.

'What?'

'Nothing, it's just that – I'm a reporter.'

'We have five hundred reporters here, and they've all spent years earning their stripes. Go over to Building Four. Ask for Mr Hawkins. If you have to start somewhere, television isn't bad.' Matt Baker reached for the phone. 'I'll give Hawkins a call.'

Dana sighed. 'Right. Thank you, Mr Baker. If you ever need –'

'Out.'

The WTE television studios took up the entire sixth floor of Building Four. Tom Hawkins, the producer of the nightly news, led Dana into his office.

'Have you ever worked in television?'

'No, sir. I've worked on newspapers.'

'Dinosaurs. They're the past. We're the present. And who knows what the future will be? Let me show you around.'

There were dozens of people working at desks and monitors. Wire copy from half a dozen news services was appearing on computers.

'Here's where stories and news breaks come in from all over the world,' Hawkins explained. 'I decide which ones we're going with. The assignment desk sends out crews to cover those stories. Our reporters in the field send in their stories by microwave or transmitters. Besides our wire services, we have one hundred and sixty police channels, reporters with cell phones, scanners, monitors. Every story is planned to the second. The writers work with tape editors to get the timing exact. The average news story runs between a minute and a half and a minute and forty-five seconds.'

'How many writers work here?' Dana asked.

'Six. Then you have a video coordinator, news tape editors, producers, directors, reporters, anchors . . .' He stopped. A man and woman were approaching them. 'Speaking of anchors, meet Julia Brinkman and Michael Tate.'

Julia Brinkman was a stunning woman, with chestnut-colored hair, tinted contacts that made her eyes a sultry green, and a practiced, disarming smile. Michael Tate was an athletic-looking man with a burstingly genial smile and an outgoing manner.

'Our new writer,' Hawkins said. 'Donna Evanston.'

'Dana Evans.'

'Whatever. Let's get to work.'

He took Dana back to his office. He nodded toward the assignment board on the wall. 'Those are the stories I'll choose from. They're called slugs. We're on twice a day. We do the noon news from twelve to one and the nightly news from ten to eleven. When I tell you which stories I want to run with, you'll put them together and make everything sound so exciting that the viewers can't switch channels. The tape editor will feed you video clips, and you'll work them into the scripts and indicate where the clips go.'

'Right.'

'Sometimes there's a breaking story, and then we'll cut into our regular programming with a live feed.'

'That's interesting,' Dana said.

She had no idea that one day it was going to save her life.

The first night's program was a disaster. Dana had put the news leads in the middle instead of the beginning, and Julia Brinkman found herself reading Michael Tate's stories while Michael was reading hers.

When the broadcast was over, the director said to Dana, 'Mr Hawkins would like to see you in his office. Now.'

Hawkins was sitting behind his desk, grim-faced.

'I know,' Dana said contritely. 'It was a new low in television, and it's all my fault.'

Hawkins sat there watching her.

Dana tried again. 'The good news, Tom, is that from now on it can only get better. Right?'

He kept staring at her.

'And it will never happen again because' – she saw the look on his face – 'I'm fired.'

'No,' Hawkins said curtly. 'That would be letting you off too easily. You're going to do this until you get it right. And I'm talking about the noon news tomorrow. Am I making myself clear?'

'Very.'

'Good. I want you here at eight o'clock in the morning.'

'Right, Tom.'

'And since we're going to be working together – you can call me Mr Hawkins.'

The noon news the next day went smoothly. Tom Hawkins had been right, Dana decided. It was just a matter of getting used to the rhythm. Get your assignment . . . write the story . . . work with the tape editor . . . set up the TelePrompTer for the anchors to read.

From that point on, it became routine.

Dana's break came eight months after she had started working at WTE. She had just finished putting the evening news report on the TelePrompTer at nine forty-five and was preparing to leave. When she walked into the television studio to say good night, there was chaos. Everyone was talking at once.

Rob Cline, the director, was shouting, 'Where the hell is she?'

'I don't know.'

'Hasn't anyone seen her?'

'No.'

'Did you phone her apartment?'

'I got the answering machine.'

'Wonderful. We're on the air' – he looked at his watch – 'in twelve minutes.'

'Maybe Julia was in an accident,' Michael Tate said. 'She could be dead.'

'That's no excuse. She should have phoned.'

Dana said, 'Excuse me . . .'

The director turned to her impatiently. 'Yes?'

'If Julia doesn't show up, I could do the newscast.'

'Forget it.' He turned back to his assistant. 'Call security and see if she's come into the building.'

The assistant picked up the phone and dialed. 'Has Julia Brinkman checked in yet . . . ? Well, when she does, tell her to get up here, fast.'

'Have him hold an elevator for her. We're on the air in' – he looked at his watch again – 'seven damned minutes.'

Dana stood there, watching the growing panic.

Michael Tate said, 'I could do both parts.'

'No,' the director snapped. 'We need two of you up there.' He looked at his watch again. 'Three minutes. Goddammit. How could she do this to us? We're on the air in –'

Dana spoke up. 'I know all the words. I wrote them.'

He gave her a quick glance. 'You have no makeup on. You're dressed wrong.'

A voice came from the sound engineer's booth. 'Two minutes. Take your places, please.'

Michael Tate shrugged and took his seat on the platform in front of the cameras.

'Places, please!'

Dana smiled at the director. 'Good night, Mr Cline.' She started toward the door.

'Wait a minute!' He was rubbing his hand across his forehead. 'Are you sure you can do this?'

'Try me,' Dana said.

'I don't have any choice, do I?' he moaned. 'All right. Get up there. My God! Why didn't I listen to my mother and become a doctor?'

Dana hurried up to the platform and took the seat next to Michael Tate.

'Thirty seconds . . . twenty . . . ten . . . five . . .'

The director signaled with his hand, and the red light on the camera flashed on.

'Good evening,' Dana said smoothly. 'Welcome to the WTE ten-o'clock news. We have a breaking story for you in Holland. There was an explosion at an Amsterdam school this afternoon and . . .'

The rest of the broadcast went smoothly.

The following morning, Rob Cline came into Dana's office. 'Bad news. Julia was in an automobile accident last night. Her face is' – he hesitated – 'disfigured.'

'I'm sorry,' Dana said, concerned. 'How bad is it?'

'Pretty bad.'

'But today plastic surgery can –'

He shook his head. 'Not this time. She won't be coming back.'

'I'd like to go see her. Where is she?'

'They're taking her back to her family, in Oregon.'

'I'm so sorry.'

'You win some, you lose some.' He studied Dana a moment. 'You were okay last night. We'll keep you on until we find someone permanent.'

Dana went to see Matt Baker. 'Did you see the news last night?' she asked.

'Yes,' he grunted. 'For God's sakes, try putting on some makeup and a more appropriate dress.'

Dana felt deflated. 'Right.'

As she turned to leave, Matt Baker said grudgingly, 'You weren't bad.' Coming from him, it was a high compliment.

On the fifth night of the news broadcast, the director said to Dana, 'By the way, the big brass said to keep you on.'

She wondered if the big brass was Matt Baker.

Within six months, Dana became a fixture on the Washington scene. She was young and attractive and her intelligence shone through. At the end of the year, she was given a raise and special assignments. One of her shows, *Here and Now*, interviews with celebrities, had zoomed to the top of the ratings. Her interviews were personal and sympathetic, and celebrities who hesitated to appear on other talk shows asked to be on Dana's show.

Magazines and newspapers began interviewing Dana. She was becoming a celebrity herself.

At night, Dana would watch the international news. She envied the foreign correspondents. They were doing something important. They were reporting history, informing the world about the important events that were happening around the globe. She felt frustrated.

Dana's two-year contract with WTE was nearly up. Philip Cole, the chief of correspondents, called her in.

'You're doing a great job, Dana. We're all proud of you.'

'Thank you, Philip.'

'It's time for us to be talking about your new contract. First of all –'

'I'm quitting.'

'I beg your pardon?'

'When my contract's up, I'm not doing the show anymore.'

He was looking at her incredulously. 'Why would you want to quit? Don't you like it here?'

'I like it a lot,' Dana said. 'I want to be with WTE, but I want to be a foreign correspondent.'

'That's a miserable life,' he exploded. 'Why in God's name would you want to do that?'

'Because I'm tired of hearing what celebrities want to

cook for dinner and how they met their fifth husband. There are wars going on, and people are suffering and dying. The world doesn't give a damn. I want to make them care.' She took a deep breath. 'I'm sorry. I can't stay on here.' She rose and started toward the door.

'Wait a minute! Are you sure this is what you want to do?'

'It's what I've always wanted to do,' Dana said quietly.

He was thoughtful for a moment. 'Where do you want to go?'

It took her a moment for the import of his words to sink in. When Dana found her voice, she said, 'Sarajevo.'

Nine

Being governor was even more exciting than Oliver Russell had anticipated. Power was a seductive mistress, and Oliver loved it. His decisions influenced the lives of hundreds of thousands of people. He became adept at swaying the state legislature, and his influence and reputation kept expanding. *I really am making a difference*, Oliver thought happily. He remembered Senator Davis's words: *'This is just a stepping-stone, Oliver. Walk carefully.'*

And he was careful. He had numerous affairs, but they were always handled with the greatest discretion. He knew that they had to be.

From time to time, Oliver checked with the hospital about Miriam's condition.

'She's still in a coma, Governor.'

'Keep me informed.'

*   *   *

One of Oliver's duties as governor was hosting state dinners. The guests of honor were supporters, sports figures, entertainers, people with political clout, and visiting dignitaries. Jan was a gracious hostess, and Oliver enjoyed the way people reacted to her.

One day Jan came to Oliver and said, 'I just talked to Father. He's giving a party next weekend at his home. He would like us to come. There are some people he wants you to meet.'

That Saturday, at Senator Davis's sumptuous home in Georgetown, Oliver found himself shaking hands with some of the most important wheelers and dealers in Washington. It was a beautiful party, and Oliver was enjoying himself immensely.

'Having a good time, Oliver?'

'Yes. It's a wonderful party. You couldn't wish for a better one.'

Peter Tager said, 'Speaking of wishes, that reminds me. The other day, Elizabeth, my six-year-old, was in a cranky mood and wouldn't get dressed. Betsy was getting desperate. Elizabeth looked at her and said, "Mama, what are you thinking?" Betsy said, "Honey, I was just wishing that you were in a good mood, and that you would get dressed and have your breakfast like a good girl." And Elizabeth said, "Mama, your wish is not being granted!" Isn't that great? Those kids are fantastic. See you later, Governor.'

A couple walked in the door and Senator Davis went to greet them.

The Italian ambassador, Atilio Picone, was an imposing-looking man in his sixties, with dark, Sicilian features. His wife, Sylva, was one of the most beautiful women Oliver had ever seen. She had been an actress before she married Atilio and was still popular in Italy. Oliver could see why. She had large, sensuous brown eyes, the face of a Madonna, and the voluptuous body of a Rubens nude. She was twenty-five years younger than her husband.

Senator Davis brought the couple over to Oliver and introduced them.

'I'm delighted to meet you,' Oliver said. He could not take his eyes off her.

She smiled. 'I've been hearing a great deal about you.'

'Nothing bad, I hope.'

'I –'

Her husband cut in. 'Senator Davis speaks very highly of you.'

Oliver looked at Sylva and said, 'I'm flattered.'

Senator Davis led the couple away. When he returned to Oliver, he said, 'That's off limits, Governor. Forbidden fruit. Take a bite of that, and you can kiss your future goodbye.'

'Relax, Todd. I wasn't –'

'I'm serious. You can alienate two countries at once.'

At the end of the evening, when Sylva and her husband were leaving, Atilio said, 'It was nice to meet you.'

'It was a pleasure.'

Sylva took Oliver's hand in hers and said softly, 'We look forward to seeing you again.'

Their eyes met. 'Yes.'

And Oliver thought, *I must be careful.*

Two weeks later, back in Frankfort, Oliver was working in his office when his secretary buzzed him.

'Governor, Senator Davis is here to see you.'

'Senator Davis is *here*?'

'Yes, sir.'

'Send him in.' Oliver knew that his father-in-law was fighting for an important bill in Washington, and Oliver wondered what he was doing in Frankfort. The door opened, and the senator walked in. Peter Tager was with him.

Senator Todd Davis smiled and put his arm around Oliver. 'Governor, it's good to see you.'

'It's great to see you, Todd.' He turned to Peter Tager. 'Morning, Peter.'

'Morning, Oliver.'

'Hope I'm not disturbing you,' Senator Davis said.

'No, not at all. Is – is anything wrong?'

Senator Davis looked at Tager and smiled. 'Oh, I don't think you could say anything's wrong, Oliver. In fact, I would say that everything's just fine.'

Oliver was studying the two of them, puzzled. 'I don't understand.'

129

'I have some good news for you, son. May we sit down?'

'Oh, forgive me. What would you like? Coffee? Whiskey –?'

'No. We're pretty well stimulated already.'

Again, Oliver wondered what was going on.

'I've just flown in from Washington. There's a pretty influential group there who think you're going to be our next president.'

Oliver felt a small thrill go through him. 'I – really?'

'As a matter of fact, the reason I flew down here is that it's time for us to start your campaign. The election is less than two years away.'

'It's perfect timing,' Peter Tager said enthusiastically. 'Before we're through, everyone in the world is going to know who you are.'

Senator Davis added, 'Peter is going to take charge of your campaign. He'll handle everything for you. You know you won't find anyone better.'

Oliver looked at Tager and said warmly, 'I agree.'

'It's my pleasure. We're going to have a lot of fun, Oliver.'

Oliver turned to Senator Davis. 'Isn't this going to cost a lot?'

'Don't worry about that. You'll go first-class all the way. I've convinced a lot of my good friends that you're the man to put their money on.' He leaned forward in his chair. 'Don't underestimate yourself, Oliver. The survey that came out a couple of months ago listed you as the third most effective governor in the country. Well, you have something that the other two don't have. I told you this before – charisma. That is something that money can't buy. People like you, and they're going to vote for you.'

Oliver was getting more and more excited. 'When do we get started?'

'We've already started,' Senator Davis told him. 'We're going to build a strong campaign team, and we're going to start lining up delegates around the country.'

'How realistic are my chances?'

'In the primaries, you're going to blow everyone away,' Tager replied. 'As for the general election, President Norton is riding pretty high. If you had to run against him, he'd be pretty tough to beat. The good news, of course, is that since this is his second term, he can't run again and Vice President Cannon is a pale shadow. A little sunshine will make him disappear.'

The meeting lasted for four hours. When it was over, Senator Davis said to Tager, 'Peter, would you excuse us for a minute?'

'Certainly, Senator.'

They watched him go out the door.

Senator Davis said, 'I had a talk with Jan this morning.'

Oliver felt a small frisson of alarm. 'Yes?'

Senator Davis looked at Oliver and smiled. 'She's very happy.'

Oliver breathed a sigh of relief. 'I'm glad.'

'So am I, son. So am I. Just keep the home fires burning. You know what I mean?'

'Don't worry about that, Todd. I –'

Senator Davis's smile faded. 'I do worry about it, Oliver. I can't fault you for being horny – just don't let it turn you into a toad.'

As Senator Davis and Peter Tager were walking through the corridor of the state capitol, the senator said, 'I want you to start putting a staff together. Don't spare any expense. To begin with, I want campaign offices in New York, Washington, Chicago, and San Francisco. Primaries begin in twelve months. The convention is eighteen months away. After that, we should have smooth sailing.' They had reached the car. 'Ride with me to the airport, Peter.'

'He'll make a wonderful president.'

Senator Davis nodded. *And I'll have him in my pocket,* he thought. *He's going to be my puppet. I'll pull the strings, and the President of the United States will speak.*

The senator pulled a gold cigar case from his pocket. 'Cigar?'

The primaries around the country started well. Senator Davis had been right about Peter Tager. He was one of the best political managers in the world, and the organization he created was superb. Because Tager was a strong family man and a deeply religious churchgoer, he attracted the religious right. Because he knew what made politics work, he was also able to persuade the liberals to put aside their differences and work together. Peter Tager was a brilliant campaign manager, and his raffish black eye patch became a familiar sight on all the networks.

Tager knew that if Oliver was to be successful, he would have to go into the convention with a minimum of two hundred delegate votes. He intended to see to it that Oliver got them.

The schedule Tager drew up included multiple trips to every state in the union.

Oliver looked at the program and said, 'This – this is impossible, Peter!'

'Not the way we've set it up,' Tager assured him. 'It's all been coordinated. The senator's lending you his Challenger. There will be people to guide you every step of the way, and I'll be at your side.'

Senator Davis introduced Sime Lombardo to Oliver. Lombardo was a giant of a man, tall and burly, dark both physically and emotionally, a brooding man who spoke little.

'How does he fit into the picture?' Oliver asked the senator when they were alone.

Senator Davis said, 'Sime is our problem-solver. Sometimes people need a little persuasion to go along. Sime is very convincing.'

Oliver did not pursue it any further.

When the presidential campaign began in earnest, Peter Tager gave Oliver detailed briefings on what to say, when to say it, and how to say it. He saw to it that Oliver made appearances in all the key electoral states. And wherever Oliver went, he said what people wanted to hear.

In Pennsylvania: 'Manufacturing is the lifeblood of this country. We're not going to forget that. We're going to open up the factories again and get America back on the track!'

Cheers.

In California: 'The aircraft industry is one of America's most vital assets. There's no reason for a single one of your plants to be shut down. We're going to open them up again.'

Cheers.

In Detroit: 'We invented cars, and the Japanese took the technology away from us. Well, we're going to get back our rightful place as number one. Detroit's going to be the automobile center of the world again!'

Cheers.

At college campuses, it was federally guaranteed student loans.

In speeches at army bases around the country, it was preparedness.

In the beginning, when Oliver was relatively unknown, the odds were stacked against him. As the campaign went on, the polls showed him moving up.

The first week in July, more than four thousand delegates and alternates, along with hundreds of party officials and candidates, gathered at the convention in Cleveland and turned the city upside down with parades and floats and parties. Television cameras from all over the world recorded the spectacle. Peter Tager and Sime Lombardo saw to it that Governor Oliver Russell was always in front of the lenses.

There were half a dozen possible nominees in Oliver's party, but Senator Todd Davis had worked behind the scenes to assure that, one by one, they were eliminated. He ruthlessly called in favors owed, some as old as twenty years.

'Toby, it's Todd. How are Emma and Suzy? . . . Good. I want to talk to you about your boy, Andrew. I'm worried about him, Toby. You know, in my opinion, he's too liberal. The South will never accept him. Here's what I suggest . . .'

'Alfred, it's Todd. How's Roy doing? . . . No need to thank me. I was happy to help him out. I want to talk to you about your candidate, Jerry. In my opinion, he's too right-wing. If we go with him, we'll lose the North. Now, here's what I would suggest . . .'

'Kenneth – Todd. I just wanted to tell you that I'm glad that real estate deal worked out for you. We all did pretty well, didn't we? By the way, I think we ought to have a little talk about Slater. He's weak. He's a loser. We can't afford to back a loser, can we? . . .'

And so it went, until practically the only viable candidate left to the party was Governor Oliver Russell.

The nomination process went smoothly. On the first ballot, Oliver Russell had seven hundred votes: more than two hundred from six northeastern industrial states, one hundred and fifty from six New England states, forty from four southern states, another one hundred and eighty from two farm states, and the balance from three Pacific states.

Peter Tager was working frantically to make sure the publicity train kept rolling. When the final tally was counted, Oliver Russell was the winner. And with the excitement of the circus atmosphere that had carefully been created, Oliver Russell was nominated by acclamation.

The next step was to choose a vice president. Melvin Wicks was a perfect choice. He was a politically correct Californian, a wealthy entrepreneur, and a personable congressman.

'They'll complement each other,' Tager said. 'Now the real work begins. We're going after the magic number – two hundred and seventy.' The number of electoral votes needed to win the presidency.

Tager told Oliver, 'The people want a young leader ... Good-looking, a little humor and a vision ... They want you to tell them how great they are – and they want to believe it. ... Let them know you're smart, but don't be too smart ... If you attack your opponent, keep it impersonal ... Never look down on a reporter. Treat them as friends, and they'll be your friends ... Try to avoid any show of pettiness. Remember – you're a statesman.'

The campaign was nonstop. Senator Davis's jet carried Oliver to Texas for three days, California for a day, Michigan for half a day, Massachusetts for six hours. Every minute was accounted for. Some days Oliver would visit as many as ten towns and deliver ten speeches. There was a different hotel every night, the Drake in Chicago, the St Regis in Detroit, the Carlyle in New York City, the Place d'Armes in New Orleans, until, finally, they all seemed to blend into one. Wherever Oliver went, there were police cars leading the procession, large crowds, and cheering voters.

Jan accompanied Oliver on most of the trips, and he had to admit that she was a great asset. She was attractive and intelligent, and the reporters liked her. From time to time, Oliver read about Leslie's latest acquisitions: a newspaper in Madrid, a television station in Mexico, a radio station in Kansas. He was happy for her success. It made him feel less guilty about what he had done to her.

Everywhere Oliver went, the reporters photographed him, interviewed him, and quoted him. There were more than a hundred correspondents covering his campaign, some of them from countries at the far ends of the earth. As the campaign neared its climax, the polls showed that Oliver Russell was the front-runner. But unexpectedly, his opponent, Vice President Cannon, began overtaking him.

Peter Tager became worried. 'Cannon's moving up in the polls. We've got to stop him.'

Two television debates between Vice President Cannon and Oliver had been agreed upon.

'Cannon is going to discuss the economy,' Tager told Oliver, 'and he'll do a good job. We have to fake him out. Here's my plan . . .'

The night of the first debate, in front of the television cameras, Vice President Cannon talked about the economy. 'America has never been more economically sound. Business is flourishing.' He spent the next ten minutes elaborating on his theme, proving his points with facts and figures.

When it was Oliver Russell's turn at the microphone, he said, 'That was very impressive. I'm sure we're all pleased that big business is doing so well and that corporate profits have never been higher.' He turned to his opponent. 'But you forgot to mention that one of the reasons corporations are doing so well is because of what is euphemistically termed "down-sizing." To put it bluntly, downsizing simply means that people are being fired to make way for machines. More people are out of work than ever before. It's the human side of the picture we should be examining. I don't happen to share your view that corporate financial success is more important than people . . .' And so it went.

Where Vice President Cannon had talked about business, Oliver Russell took a humanitarian approach and talked about emotions and opportunities. By the time he was through, Russell had managed to make Cannon sound like a cold-blooded politician who cared nothing about the American people.

The morning after the debate, the polls shifted, putting Oliver Russell within three points of the vice president. There was to be one more national debate.

Arthur Cannon had learned his lesson. At the final debate, he stood before the microphone and said, 'Ours is a land where all people must have equal opportunities. America has been blessed with freedom, but that alone is not enough. Our people must have the freedom to work, and earn a decent living . . .'

He stole Oliver Russell's thunder by concentrating on

all the wonderful plans he had in mind for the welfare of the people. But Peter Tager had anticipated that. When Cannon was finished, Oliver Russell stepped to the microphone.

'That was very touching. I'm sure we were all very moved by what you had to say about the plight of the unemployed, and, as you called him, the "forgotten man." What disturbs me is that you forgot to say how you are going to do all those wonderful things for those people.' And from then on, where Vice President Cannon had dealt in emotions, Oliver Russell talked about issues and his economic plans, leaving the vice president hanging high and dry.

Oliver, Jan, and Senator Davis were having dinner at the senator's mansion in Georgetown. The senator smiled at Jan. 'I've just seen the latest polls. I think you can begin redecorating the White House.'

Her face lit up. 'Do you really think we're going to win, Father?'

'I'm wrong about a lot of things, honey, but never about politics. That's my life's blood. In November, we're going to have a new president, and he's sitting right next to you.'

Ten

'Fasten your seat belts, please.'

Here we go! Dana thought excitedly. She looked over at Benn Albertson and Wally Newman. Benn Albertson, Dana's producer, was a hyperkinetic bearded man in his forties. He had produced some of the top-rated news shows in television and was highly respected. Wally Newman, the cameraman, was in his early fifties. He was talented and enthusiastic, and eagerly looking forward to his new assignment.

Dana thought about the adventure that lay ahead. They would land in Paris and then fly to Zagreb, Croatia, and finally to Sarajevo.

During her last week in Washington, Dana had been briefed by Shelley McGuire, the foreign editor. 'You'll need a truck in Sarajevo to transmit your stories to the satellite,' McGuire told her. 'We don't own one there so we'll rent a truck and buy time from the Yugoslav company that owns the satellite. If things go well, we'll get our own truck later. You'll be operating on two different levels. Some stories you'll cover live, but most of them will be taped. Benn Albertson will tell you what he wants, and you'll shoot the footage and then do a sound track in a local studio. I've given you the best producer and cameraman in the business. You shouldn't have any problem.'

Dana was to remember those optimistic words later.

The day before Dana left, Matt Baker had telephoned. 'Get over to my office.' His voice was gruff.

'I'll be right there.' Dana had hung up with a feeling of apprehension. *He's changed his mind about approving my transfer and he's not going to let me go. How could he do this to me? Well*, she thought determinedly, *I'm going to fight him.*

Ten minutes later, Dana was marching into Matt Baker's office.

'I know what you're going to say,' she began, 'but it won't do you any good. I'm going! I've dreamed about this since I was a little girl. I think I can do some good over there. You've got to give me a chance to try.' She took a deep breath. 'All right,' Dana said defiantly. 'What did you want to say?'

Matt Baker looked at her and said mildly, '*Bon voyage.*'

Dana blinked. 'What?'

'*Bon voyage*. It means "good journey."'

'I know what it means. I – didn't you send for me to –?'

'I sent for you because I've spoken to a few of our foreign correspondents. They gave me some advice to pass on to you.'

This gruff bear of a man had taken the time and trouble to talk to some foreign correspondents so that he could help her! 'I – I don't know how to –'

'Then don't,' he grunted. 'You're going into a shooting war. There's no guarantee you can protect yourself a hundred percent, because bullets don't give a damn who they kill. But when you're in the middle of action, the adrenaline starts to flow. It can make you reckless, and you do stupid things you wouldn't ordinarily do. You have to control that. Always play it safe. Don't wander around the streets alone. No news story is worth your life. Another thing . . .'

The lecture had gone on for almost an hour. Finally, he said, 'Well, that's it. Take care of yourself. If you let anything happen to you, I'm going to be damned mad.'

Dana had leaned over and kissed him on the cheek.

'Don't ever do that again,' he snapped. He stood up. 'It's going to be rough over there, Dana. If you should change your mind when you get there and want to come home, just let me know, and I'll arrange it.'

'I won't change my mind,' Dana said confidently.

As it turned out, she was wrong.

* * *

The flight to Paris was uneventful. They landed at Charles de Gaulle Airport and the trio took an airport minibus to Croatia Airlines. There was a three-hour delay.

At ten o'clock that night, the Croatia Airlines plane landed at Butmir Airport in Sarajevo. The passengers were herded into a security building, where their passports were checked by uniformed guards and they were waved on. As Dana moved toward the exit, a short, unpleasant-looking man in civilian clothes stepped in front of her, blocking her way. 'Passport.'

'I showed them my —'

'I am Colonel Gordan Divjak. Your passport.'

Dana handed her passport to him, along with her press credentials.

He flipped through it. 'A journalist?' He looked at her sharply. 'Whose side are you on?'

'I'm not on anyone's side,' Dana said evenly.

'Just be careful what you report,' Colonel Divjak warned. 'We do not treat espionage lightly.'

Welcome to Sarajevo.

A bulletproof Land Rover was at the airport to meet them. The driver was a swarthy-looking man in his early twenties. 'I am Jovan Tolj, for your pleasure. I will be your driver in Sarajevo.'

Jovan drove fast, swerving around corners and racing through deserted streets as though they were being pursued.

'Excuse me,' Dana said nervously. 'Is there any special hurry?'

'Yes, if you want to get there alive.'

'But –'

In the distance, Dana heard the sound of rumbling thunder, and it seemed to be coming closer.

What she was hearing was not thunder.

In the darkness, Dana could make out buildings with shattered fronts, apartments without roofs, stores without windows. Ahead, she could see the Holiday Inn, where they were staying. The front of the hotel was badly pockmarked, and a deep hole had been gouged in the driveway. The car sped past it.

'Wait! This is our hotel,' Dana cried. 'Where are you going?'

'The front entrance is too dangerous,' Jovan said. He turned the corner and raced into an alley. 'Everyone uses the back entrance.'

Dana's mouth was suddenly dry. 'Oh.'

The lobby of the Holiday Inn was filled with people milling about and chatting. An attractive young Frenchman approached Dana. 'Ah, we have been expecting you. You are Dana Evans?'

'Yes.'

'Jean Paul Hubert, M6, Métropole Télévision.'

'I'm happy to meet you. This is Benn Albertson and Wally Newman.' The men shook hands.

'Welcome to what's left of our rapidly disappearing city.'

145

Others were approaching the group to welcome them. One by one, they stepped up and introduced themselves.

'Steffan Mueller, Kabel Network.'

'Roderick Munn, BBC 2.'

'Marco Benelli, Italia I.'

'Akihiro Ishihara, TV Tokyo.'

'Juan Santos, Channel 6, Guadalajara.'

'Chun Qian, Shanghai Television.'

It seemed to Dana that every country in the world had a journalist there. The introductions seemed to go on forever. The last one was a burly Russian with a gleaming gold front tooth. 'Nikolai Petrovich, Gorizont 22.'

'How many reporters are here?' Dana asked Jean Paul.

'Over two hundred and fifty. We don't see many wars as colorful as this one. Is this your first?'

He made it sound as though it were some kind of tennis match. 'Yes.'

Jean Paul said, 'If I can be of any help, please let me know.'

'Thank you.' She hesitated. 'Who is Colonel Gordan Divjak?'

'You don't want to know. We all think he is with the Serbian equivalent of the Gestapo, but we're not sure. I would suggest you stay out of his way.'

'I'll remember.'

Later, as Dana got into her bed, there was a sudden loud explosion from across the street, and then another, and the room began to shake. It was terrifying, and at the same time exhilarating. It seemed unreal, something out of a movie. Dana lay awake all night, listening to the sounds of the terrible killing machines and watching the flashes of light reflected in the grimy hotel windows.

In the morning, Dana got dressed – jeans, boots, flak jacket. She felt self-conscious, and yet: *'Always play it safe. . . . No news story is worth your life.'*

Dana, Benn, and Wally were in the lobby restaurant, talking about their families.

'I forgot to tell you the good news,' Wally said. 'I'm going to have a grandson next month.'

'That's great!' And Dana thought: *Will I ever have a child and a grandchild? Que será será.*

'I have an idea,' Benn said. 'Let's do a general story first on what's happening here and how the people's lives have been affected. I'll go with Wally and scout locations. Why don't you get us some satellite time, Dana?'

'Fine.'

Jovan Tolj was in the alley, in the Land Rover. '*Dobro jutro.* Good morning.'

'Good morning, Jovan. I want to go to the place where they rent satellite time.'

As they drove, Dana was able to get a clear look at Sarajevo for the first time. It seemed to her that there

147

was not a building that had been untouched. The sound of gunfire was continuous.

'Don't they ever stop?' Dana asked.

'They will stop when they run out of ammunition,' Jovan said bitterly. 'And they will never run out of ammunition.'

The streets were deserted, except for a few pedestrians, and all the cafés were closed. Pavements were pockmarked with shell craters. They passed the *Oslobodjenje* building.

'That is our newspaper,' Jovan said proudly. 'The Serbs keep trying to destroy it, but they cannot.'

A few minutes later, they reached the satellite offices. 'I will wait for you,' Jovan said.

Behind a desk in the lobby, there was a receptionist who appeared to be in his eighties.

'Do you speak English?' Dana asked.

He looked at her wearily. 'I speak nine languages, madam. What do you wish?'

'I'm with WTE. I want to book some satellite time and arrange –'

'Third floor.'

The sign on the door read: YUGOSLAVIA SATELLITE DIVISION. The reception room was filled with men seated on wooden benches lined against the walls.

Dana introduced herself to the young woman at the

reception desk. 'I'm Dana Evans, with WTE. I want to book some satellite time.'

'Take a seat, please, and wait your turn.'

Dana looked around the room. 'Are all these people here to book satellite time?'

The woman looked up at her and said, 'Of course.'

Almost two hours later, Dana was ushered into the office of the manager, a short, squat man with a cigar in his mouth; he looked like the old cliché prototype of a Hollywood producer.

He had a heavy accent. 'How can I help you?'

'I'm Dana Evans, with WTE. I'd like to rent one of your trucks and book the satellite for half an hour. Six o'clock in Washington would be a good time. And I'll want that same time every day indefinitely.' She looked at his expression. 'Any problem?'

'One. There are no satellite trucks available. They have all been booked. I will give you a call if someone cancels.'

Dana looked at him in dismay. 'No –? But I need some satellite time,' she said. 'I'm –'

'So does everybody else, madam. Except for those who have their own trucks, of course.'

When Dana returned to the reception room, it was full. *I have to do something about this*, she thought.

* * *

When Dana left the satellite office, she said to Jovan, 'I'd like you to drive me around the city.'

He turned to look at her, then shrugged. 'As you wish.' He started the car and began to race through the streets.

'A little slower, please. I need to get a feel of this place.'

Sarajevo was a city under siege. There was no running water or electricity, and more houses were being bombed every hour. The air raid alarm went on so frequently that people ignored it. A miasma of fatalism seemed to hang over the city. If the bullet had your name on it, there was nowhere to hide.

On almost every street corner, men, women, and children were peddling the few possessions they had left.

'They are refugees from Bosnia and Croatia,' Jovan explained, 'trying to get enough money to buy food.'

Fires were raging everywhere. There were no firemen in sight.

'Isn't there a fire department?' Dana asked.

He shrugged. 'Yes, but they don't dare come. They make too good a target for Serb snipers.'

In the beginning, the war in Bosnia and Herzegovina had made little sense to Dana. It was not until she had been in Sarajevo for a week that she realized that it made no sense at all. No one could explain it. Someone had mentioned a professor from the university, who was a well-known historian. He had been wounded and was confined to his home. Dana decided to have a talk with him.

Jovan drove her to one of the old neighborhoods in the city, where the professor lived. Professor Mladic Staka was a small, gray-haired man, almost ethereal in appearance. A bullet had shattered his spine and paralyzed him.

'Thank you for coming,' he said. 'I do not get many visitors these days. You said you needed to talk to me.'

'Yes. I'm supposed to be covering this war,' Dana told him. 'But to tell the truth, I'm having trouble understanding it.'

'The reason is very simple, my dear. This war in Bosnia and Herzegovina is beyond understanding. For decades, the Serbs, Croats, Bosnians, and Muslims lived together in peace, under Tito. They were friends and neighbors. They grew up together, worked together, went to the same schools, intermarried.'

'And now?'

'These same friends are torturing and murdering one another. Their hatred has made them do things so disgusting that I cannot even speak about them.'

'I've heard some of the stories,' Dana said. The stories she had heard were almost beyond belief: a well filled with bloody human testicles, babies raped and slaughtered, innocent villagers locked in churches that were then set on fire.

'Who started this?' Dana asked.

He shook his head. 'It depends on whom you ask. During the Second World War, hundreds of thousand of Serbs, who were on the side of the Allies, were wiped out by the Croats, who were on the side of the Nazis. Now the Serbs are taking their bloody revenge. They are holding the country hostage, and they are merciless. More than two hundred thousand shells have fallen on Sarajevo alone. At least ten thousand people have been killed and more than sixty thousand injured. The Bosnians and Muslims must bear the responsibility for their share of the torture and killing. Those who do not want war are being forced into it. No one can trust anyone. The only thing they have left is hate. What we have is a conflagration that keeps feeding on itself, and what fuels the fires is the bodies of the innocent.'

When Dana returned to her hotel that afternoon, Benn Albertson was waiting there to tell her that he had received a message that a truck and satellite time would be available to them the following day at 6:00 P.M.

'I found the ideal place for us to shoot,' Wally Newman told her. 'There's a square with a Catholic church, a mosque, a Protestant church, and a synagogue, all within a block of one another. They've all been bombed out. You can write a story about equal-opportunity hatred, and what it has done to the people who live here, who don't want anything to do with the war but are forced to be a part of it.'

Dana nodded, excited. 'Great. I'll see you at dinner. I'm going to work.' She headed for her room.

* * *

At six o'clock the following evening, Dana and Wally and Benn were gathered in front of the square where the bombed-out churches and synagogue were located. Wally's television camera had been set up on a tripod, and Benn was waiting for confirmation from Washington that the satellite signal was good. Dana could hear sniper fire in the near background. She was suddenly glad she was wearing her flak jacket. *There's nothing to be afraid of. They're not shooting at us. They're shooting at one another. They need us to tell the world their story.*

Dana saw Wally signal. She took a deep breath, looked into the camera lens, and began.

'The bombed-out churches you see behind me are a symbol of what is happening in this country. There are no walls for people to hide behind anymore, no place that is safe. In earlier times, people could find sanctuary in their churches. But here, the past and the present and the future have all blended together and –'

At that second, she heard a shrill approaching whistle, looked up, and saw Wally's head explode into a red melon. *It's a trick of the light,* was Dana's first thought. And then she watched, aghast, as Wally's body slammed to the pavement. Dana stood there, frozen, unbelieving. People around her were screaming.

The sound of rapid sniper fire came closer, and Dana began to tremble uncontrollably. Hands grabbed her and rushed her down the street. She was fighting them, trying to free herself.

No! We have to go back. We haven't used up our ten

153

minutes. Waste not, want not . . . it was wrong to waste things. 'Finish your soup, darling. Children in China are starving.' You think you're some kind of God up there, sitting on a white cloud? Well, let me tell you something. You're a fake. A real God would never, never, never let Wally's head be blown off. Wally was expecting his first grandson. Are you listening to me? Are you? Are you?

She was in a state of shock, unaware that she was being led through a back street to the car.

When Dana opened her eyes, she was in her bed. Benn Albertson and Jean Paul Hubert were standing over her.

Dana looked up into their faces. 'It happened, didn't it?' She squeezed her eyes tightly shut.

'I'm so sorry,' Jean Paul said. 'It's an awful thing to see. You're lucky you weren't killed.'

The telephone jarred the stillness of the room. Benn picked it up. 'Hello.' He listened a moment. 'Yes. Hold on.' He turned to Dana. 'It's Matt Baker. Are you able to talk to him?'

'Yes.' Dana sat up. After a moment, she rose and walked over to the telephone. 'Hello.' Her throat was dry, and it was difficult to speak.

Matt Baker's voice boomed over the line. 'I want you to come home, Dana.'

Her voice was a whisper. 'Yes. I want to come home.'

'I'll arrange for you to be on the first plane out of there.'

'Thank you.' She dropped the telephone.

Jean Paul and Benn helped her back into bed.

'I'm sorry,' Jean Paul said, again. 'There's – there's nothing anyone can say.'

Tears were running down her cheeks. 'Why did they kill him? He never harmed anyone. What's happening? People are being slaughtered like animals and no one cares. No one cares!'

Benn said, 'Dana, there's nothing we can do about –'

'There has to be!' Dana's voice was filled with fury. 'We have to make them care. This war isn't about bombed-out churches or buildings or streets. It's about people – innocent people – getting their heads blown off. Those are the stories we should be doing. That's the only way to make this war real.' She turned to Benn and took a deep breath. 'I'm staying, Benn. I'm not going to let them scare me away.'

He was watching her, concerned. 'Dana, are you sure you –?'

'I'm sure. I know what I have to do now. Will you call Matt and tell him?'

He said reluctantly, 'If that's what you really want.'

Dana nodded. 'It's what I really want.' She watched Benn leave the room.

Jean Paul said, 'Well, I had better go and let you –'

'No.' For an instant, Dana's mind was filled with a vision of Wally's head exploding, and his body falling to the ground. 'No,' Dana said. She looked up at Jean Paul. 'Please stay. I need you.'

Jean Paul sat down on the bed. And Dana took him in her arms and held him close to her.

The following morning, Dana said to Benn Albertson, 'Can you get hold of a cameraman? Jean Paul told me about an orphanage in Kosovo that's just been bombed. I want to go there and cover it.'

'I'll round up someone.'

'Thanks, Benn. I'll go on ahead and meet you there.'

'Be careful.'

'Don't worry.'

Jovan was waiting for Dana in the alley.

'We're going to Kosovo,' Dana told him.

Jovan turned to look at her. 'That is dangerous, madam. The only road there is through the woods, and –'

'We've already had our share of bad luck, Jovan. We'll be all right.'

'As you wish.'

They sped through the city, and fifteen minutes later were driving through a heavily forested area.

'How much farther?' Dana asked.

'Not far. We should be there in –'

And at that moment, the Land Rover struck a land mine.

Eleven

As election day approached, the presidential race became too close to call.

'We've got to win Ohio,' Peter Tager said. 'That's twenty-one electoral votes. We're all right with Alabama – that's nine votes – and we have Florida's twenty-five votes.' He held up a chart. 'Illinois, twenty-two votes . . . New York, thirty-three, and California, forty-four. It's just too damned early to call it.'

Everyone was concerned except Senator Davis.

'I've got a nose,' he said. 'I can smell victory.'

In a Frankfort hospital, Miriam Friedland was still in a coma.

On election day, the first Tuesday in November, Leslie stayed home to watch the returns on television. Oliver Russell won by more than two million popular votes and a huge majority of electoral votes. Oliver Russell was the president now, the biggest target in the world.

No one had followed the election campaign more closely than Leslie Stewart Chambers. She had been busily expanding her empire and had acquired a chain of newspapers and television and radio stations across the United States, as well as in England, Australia, and Brazil.

'When are you going to have enough?' her chief editor, Darin Solana, asked.

'Soon,' Leslie said. 'Soon.'

There was one more step she had to take, and the last piece fell into place at a dinner party in Scottsdale.

A guest said, 'I heard confidentially that Margaret Portman is getting a divorce.' Margaret Portman was the owner of the *Washington Tribune*, in the nation's capital.

Leslie had no comment, but early the following morning, she was on the telephone with Chad Morton, one of her attorneys. 'I want you to find out if the *Washington Tribune* is for sale.'

The answer came back later that day. 'I don't know how you heard about it, Mrs Chambers, but it looks as though you could be right. Mrs Portman and her husband are quietly getting a divorce, and they're dividing up their property. I think Washington Tribune Enterprises is going up for sale.'

'I want to buy it.'

'You're talking about a megadeal. Washington Tribune Enterprises owns a newspaper chain, a magazine, a television network, and –'

'I want it.'

That afternoon, Leslie and Chad Morton were on their way to Washington, D.C.

Leslie telephoned Margaret Portman, whom she had met casually a few years earlier.

'I'm in Washington,' Leslie said, 'and I –'

'I know.'

Word gets around fast, Leslie thought. 'I heard that you might be interested in selling Tribune Enterprises.'

'Possibly.'

'I wonder if you would arrange a tour of the paper for me?'

'Are you interested in buying it, Leslie?'

'Possibly.'

Margaret Portman sent for Matt Baker. 'Do you know who Leslie Chambers is?'

'The Ice Princess. Sure.'

'She'll be here in a few minutes. I'd like you to take her on a tour of the plant.'

Everyone at the *Tribune* was aware of the impending sale.

'It would be a mistake to sell the *Tribune* to Leslie Chambers,' Matt Baker said flatly.

'What makes you say that?'

'First of all, I doubt if she really knows a damn thing about the newspaper business. Have you looked at what she's done to the other papers she bought?

She's turned respectable newspapers into cheap tabloids. She'll destroy the *Tribune*. She's –' He looked up. Leslie Chambers was standing in the doorway, listening.

Margaret Portman spoke up. 'Leslie! How nice to see you. This is Matt Baker, our editor in chief of Tribune Enterprises.'

They exchanged cool greetings.

'Matt is going to show you around.'

'I'm looking forward to it.'

Matt Baker took a deep breath. 'Right. Let's get started.'

At the beginning of the tour, Matt Baker said condescendingly, 'The structure is like this: At the top is the editor in chief –'

'That would be you, Mr Baker.'

'Right. And under me, the managing editor and the editorial staff. That includes Metro, National, Foreign, Sports, Business, Life and Style, People, Calendar, Books, Real Estate, Travel, Food … I'm probably leaving a few out.'

'Amazing. How many employees does Washington Tribune Enterprises have, Mr Baker?'

'Over five thousand.'

They passed a copy desk. 'Here's where the news editor lays out the pages. He's the one who decides where the photos are going to go and which stories appear on which pages. The copy desk writes the headlines, edits the stories, and then puts them together in the composing room.'

'Fascinating.'

'Are you interested in seeing the printing plants?'

'Oh, yes. I'd like to see everything.'

He mumbled something under his breath.

'I'm sorry?'

'I said, "Fine."'

They took the elevator down and walked over to the next building. The printing plant was four stories high and the size of four football fields. Everything in the huge space was automated. There were thirty robot carts in the building, carrying enormous rolls of paper that they dropped off at various stations.

Baker explained, 'Each roll of paper weighs about twenty-five hundred pounds. If you unrolled one, it would be eight miles long. The paper goes through the presses at twenty-one miles an hour. Some of the bigger carts can carry sixteen rolls at once.'

There were six presses, three on each side of the room. Leslie and Matt Baker stood there and watched as the newspapers were automatically assembled, cut, folded, put into bales, and delivered to the trucks waiting to carry them off.

'In the old days it took about thirty men to do what one man can do today,' Matt Baker said. 'The age of technology.'

Leslie looked at him a moment. 'The age of downsizing.'

'I don't know if you're interested in the economics of the operation?' Matt Baker asked dryly. 'Perhaps you'd prefer your lawyer or accountant to –'

'I'm very interested, Mr Baker. Your editorial budget is fifteen million dollars. Your daily circulation is eight hundred and sixteen thousand, four hundred and seventy-four, and one million, one hundred and forty thousand, four hundred and ninety-eight on Sunday, and your advertising is sixty-eight point two.'

Matt looked at her and blinked.

'With the ownership of all your newspapers, your daily circulation is over two million, with two million four Sunday circulation. Of course, that's not the largest paper in the world, is it, Mr Baker? Two of the largest newspapers in the world are printed in London. The *Sun* is the biggest, with a circulation of four million daily. The *Daily Mirror* sells over three million.'

He took a deep breath. 'I'm sorry. I didn't realize you –'

'In Japan, there are over two hundred dailies, including *Asahi Shimbun, Mainchi Shimbun,* and *Yomiuri Shimbun.* Do you follow me?'

'Yes. I apologize if I seemed patronizing.'

'Accepted, Mr Baker. Let's go back to Mrs Portman's office.'

The next morning, Leslie was in the executive conference room of the *Washington Tribune,* facing Mrs Portman and half a dozen attorneys.

'Let's talk about price,' Leslie said. The discussion lasted four hours, and when it was over, Leslie Stewart Chambers was the owner of Washington Tribune Enterprises.

It was more expensive than Leslie had anticipated. It did not matter.

There was something more important.

The day the deal was finalized, Leslie sent for Matt Baker. 'What are your plans?' Leslie asked.

'I'm leaving.'

She looked at him curiously. 'Why?'

'You have quite a reputation. People don't like working for you. I think the word they use most is "ruthless." I don't need that. This is a good newspaper, and I hate to leave it, but I have more job offers than I can handle.'

'How long have you worked here?'

'Fifteen years.'

'And you're going to just throw that away?'

'I'm not throwing anything away, I'm –'

She looked him in the eye. 'Listen to me. I think the *Tribune* is a good newspaper, too, but I want it to be a great newspaper. I want you to help me.'

'No. I don't –'

'Six months. Try it for six months. We'll start by doubling your salary.'

He studied her for a long moment. Young and beautiful and intelligent. And yet . . . He had an uneasy feeling about her.

'Who will be in charge here?'

She smiled. 'You're the editor in chief of Washington Tribune Enterprises. You will be.'

And he believed her.

Twelve

It had been six months since Dana's Land Rover had been blown up. She escaped with nothing worse than a concussion, a cracked rib, a broken wrist, and painful bruises. Jovan suffered a fractured leg and scrapes and bruises. Matt Baker had telephoned Dana that night and ordered her to return to Washington, but the incident had made Dana more determined than ever to stay.

'These people are desperate,' Dana told him. 'I can't just walk away from this. If you order me home, then I quit.'

'Are you blackmailing me?'

'Yes.'

'That's what I thought,' Matt snapped. 'I don't let anyone blackmail me. Do you understand?'

Dana waited.

'What about a leave of absence?' he asked.

'I don't need a leave of absence.' She could hear his sigh over the phone.

'All right. Stay there. But, Dana –'

'Yes?'

'Promise me that you'll be careful.'

From outside the hotel, Dana could hear the sound of machine-gun fire. 'Right.'

The city had been under heavy attack all night. Dana had been unable to sleep. Each explosion of a mortar landing meant another building destroyed, another family homeless, or worse, dead.

Early in the morning, Dana and her crew were out on the street, ready to shoot. Benn Albertson waited for the thunder of a mortar to fade away, then nodded to Dana. 'Ten seconds.'

'Ready,' Dana said.

Benn pointed a finger, and Dana turned away from the ruins behind her and faced the television camera.

'This is a city that is slowly disappearing from the face of the earth. With its electricity cut off, its eyes have been put out . . . Its television and radio stations have been shut down, and it has no ears . . . All public transportation has come to a halt, so it has lost its legs . . .'

The camera panned to show a deserted, bombed-out playground, with the rusty skeletons of swings and slides.

'In another life, children played here, and the sound of their laughter filled the air.'

Mortar fire could be heard again in the near distance. An air raid alarm suddenly sounded. The people walking the streets behind Dana continued as though they had heard nothing.

'The sound you're hearing is another air raid alarm. It's the signal for people to run and hide. But the citizens of Sarajevo have found that there is no place to hide, so they walk on in their own silence. Those who can, flee the country, and give up their apartments and all their possessions. Too many who stay, die. It's a cruel choice. There are rumors of peace. Too many rumors, too little peace. Will it come? And when? Will the children come out of their cellars and use this playground again one day? Nobody knows. They can only hope. This is Dana Evans reporting from Sarajevo for WTE.'

The red light on the camera blinked off. 'Let's get out of here,' Benn said.

Andy Casarez, the new cameraman, hurriedly started to pack up his gear.

A young boy was standing on the sidewalk, watching Dana. He was a street urchin, dressed in filthy, ragged clothes and torn shoes. Intense brown eyes flashed out of a face streaked with dirt. His right arm was missing.

Dana watched the boy studying her. Dana smiled. 'Hello.'

There was no reply. Dana shrugged and turned to Benn.

'Let's go.'

A few minutes later, they were on their way back to the Holiday Inn.

The Holiday Inn was filled with newspaper, radio, and

television reporters, and they formed a disparate family. They were rivals, but because of the dangerous circumstances they found themselves in, they were always ready to help one another. They covered breaking stories together:

There was a riot in Montenegro . . .

There was a bombing in Vukovar . . .

A hospital had been shelled in Petrovo Selo . . .

Jean Paul Hubert was gone. He had been given another assignment, and Dana missed him terribly.

As Dana was leaving the hotel one morning, the little boy she had seen on the street was standing in the alley.

Jovan opened the door of the replacement Land Rover for Dana. 'Good morning, madam.'

'Good morning.' The boy stood there, staring at Dana. She walked over to him. 'Good morning.'

There was no reply. Dana said to Jovan, 'How do you say "good morning" in Slovene?'

The little boy answered, '*Dobro jutro.*'

Dana turned to him. 'So you understand English.'

'Maybe.'

'What's your name?'

'Kemal.'

'How old are you, Kemal?'

He turned and walked away.

'He's frightened of strangers,' Jovan said.

Dana looked after the boy. 'I don't blame him. So am I.'

Four hours later, when the Land Rover returned to the alley in back of the Holiday Inn, Kemal was waiting near the entrance.

As Dana got out of the car, Kemal said, 'Twelve.'

'What?' Then Dana remembered. 'Oh.' He was small for his age. She looked at his empty right shirtsleeve and started to ask him a question, then stopped herself. 'Where do you live, Kemal? Can we take you home?' She watched him turn and walk away.

Jovan said, 'He has no manners.'

Dana said quietly, 'Maybe he lost them when he lost his arm.'

That evening in the hotel dining room, the reporters were talking about the new rumors of an imminent peace. 'The UN has finally gotten involved,' Gabriella Orsi declared.

'It's about time.'

'If you ask me, it's too late.'

'It's never too late,' Dana said quietly.

The following morning, two news stories came over the wires. The first one was about a peace agreement brokered by the United States and the United Nations. The second story was that *Oslobodjenje*, Sarajevo's newspaper, had been bombed out of existence.

'Our Washington bureaus are covering the peace agreement,' Dana told Benn. 'Let's do a story on *Oslobodjenje*.'

Dana was standing in front of the demolished building that had once housed *Oslobodjenje*. The camera's red light was on.

'People die here every day,' Dana said into the lens, 'and buildings are destroyed. But this building was murdered. It housed the only free newspaper in Sarajevo, *Oslobodjenje*. It was a newspaper that dared to tell the truth. When it was bombed out of its headquarters, it was moved into the basement, to keep the presses alive. When there were no more newsstands to sell the papers from, its reporters went out on the streets to peddle them themselves. They were selling more than newspapers. They were selling freedom. With the death of *Oslobodjenje*, another piece of freedom has died here.'

In his office, Matt Baker was watching the news broadcast. 'Dammit, she's good!' He turned to his assistant. 'I want her to have her own satellite truck. Move on it.'

'Yes, sir.'

When Dana returned to her room, there was a visitor waiting for her. Colonel Gordan Divjak was lounging in a chair when Dana walked in.

She stopped, startled. 'They didn't tell me I had a visitor.'

'This is not a social visit.' His beady black eyes focused on her. 'I watched your broadcast about *Oslobodjenje*.'

Dana studied him warily. 'Yes?'

'You were permitted to come into our country to report, not to make judgments.'

'I didn't make any –'

'Do not interrupt me. Your idea of freedom is not necessarily our idea of freedom. Do you understand me?'

'No. I'm afraid I –'

'Then let me explain it to you, Miss Evans. You are a guest in my country. Perhaps you are a spy for your government.'

'I am not a –'

'Do not interrupt me. I warned you at the airport. We are not playing games. We are at war. Anyone involved in espionage will be executed.' His words were all the more chilling because they were spoken softly.

He got to his feet. 'This is your last warning.'

Dana watched him leave. *I'm not going to let him frighten me*, she thought defiantly.

She was frightened.

A care package arrived from Matt Baker. It was an enormous box filled with candy, granola bars, canned foods, and a dozen other nonperishable items. Dana took

171

it into the lobby to share it with the other reporters. They were delighted.

'Now, that's what I call a boss,' Satomi Asaka said.

'How do I get a job with the *Washington Tribune?*' Juan Santos joked.

Kemal was waiting in the alley again. The frayed, thin jacket he had on looked as though it was about to fall apart.

'Good morning, Kemal.'

He stood there, silent, watching her from under half-closed lids.

'I'm going shopping. Would you like to go with me?'

No answer.

'Let me put it another way,' Dana said, exasperated. She opened the back door of the vehicle. 'Get in the car. Now!'

The boy stood there a moment, shocked, then slowly moved toward the car.

Dana and Jovan watched him climb into the backseat.

Dana said to Jovan, 'Can you find a department store or clothing shop that's open?'

'I know one.'

'Let's go there.'

They rode in silence for the first few minutes.

'Do you have a mother or father, Kemal?'

He shook his head.

'Where do you live?'

He shrugged.

Dana felt him move closer to her as though to absorb the warmth of her body.

The clothing store was in the Bascarsija, the old market of Sarajevo. The front had been bombed out, but the store was open. Dana took Kemal's left hand and led him into the store.

A clerk said, 'Can I help you?'

'Yes. I want to buy a jacket for a friend of mine.' She looked at Kemal. 'He's about his size.'

'This way, please.'

In the boy's section there was a rack of jackets. Dana turned to Kemal. 'Which one do you like?'

Kemal stood there, saying nothing.

Dana said to the clerk, 'We'll take the brown one.' She looked at Kemal's trousers. 'And I think we need a pair of trousers and some new shoes.'

When they left the store half an hour later, Kemal was dressed in his new outfit. He slid into the backseat of the car without a word.

'Don't you know how to say thank you?' Jovan demanded angrily.

Kemal burst into tears. Dana put her arms around him. 'It's all right,' she said. 'It's all right.'

What kind of a world does this to children?

* * *

When they returned to the hotel, Dana watched Kemal turn and walk away without a word.

'Where does someone like that live?' Dana asked Jovan.

'On the streets, madam. There are hundreds of orphans in Sarajevo like him. They have no homes, no families . . .'

'How do they survive?'

He shrugged. 'I do not know.'

The next day, when Dana walked out of the hotel, Kemal was waiting for her, dressed in his new outfit. He had washed his face.

The big news at the luncheon table was the peace treaty and whether it would work. Dana decided to go back to visit Professor Mladic Staka and ask what he thought about it.

He looked even more frail than the last time she had seen him.

'I am happy to see you, Miss Evans. I hear you are doing wonderful broadcasts, but –' He shrugged. 'Unfortunately, I have no electricity for my television set. What can I do for you?'

'I wanted to get your opinion of the new peace treaty, Professor.'

He leaned back in his chair and said thoughtfully, 'It is interesting to me that in Dayton, Ohio, they made a decision about what is going to happen to the future of Sarajevo.'

'They've agreed to a troika, a three-person presidency, composed of a Muslim, a Croat, and a Serb. Do you think it can work, Professor?'

'Only if you believe in miracles.' He frowned. 'There will be eighteen national legislative bodies and another hundred and nine different local governments. It is a Tower of political Babel. It is what you Americans call a "shotgun marriage." None of them wants to give up their autonomy. They insist on having their own flags, their own license plates, their own currency.' He shook his head. 'It is a morning peace. Beware of the night.'

Dana Evans had gone beyond being a mere reporter and was becoming an international legend. What came through in her television broadcasts was an intelligent human being filled with passion. And because Dana cared, her viewers cared, and shared her feelings.

Matt Baker began getting calls from other news outlets saying that they wanted to syndicate Dana Evans's broadcasts. He was delighted for her. *She went over there to do good*, he thought, *and she's going to wind up doing well.*

With her own new satellite truck, Dana was busier than ever. She was no longer at the mercy of the Yugoslav satellite company. She and Benn decided what stories they wanted to do, and Dana would write them and broadcast them. Some of the stories were broadcast live, and others were taped. Dana and Benn and Andy would go out on the streets and photograph whatever background was needed, then Dana would tape her commentary in an editing room and send it back on the line to Washington.

At lunchtime, in the hotel dining room, large platters of sandwiches were placed in the center of the table. Journalists were busily helping themselves. Roderick Munn, from the BBC, walked into the room with an AP clipping in his hand.

'Listen to this, everybody.' He read the clipping aloud. '"Dana Evans, a foreign correspondent for WTE, is now being syndicated by a dozen news stations. Miss Evans has been nominated for the coveted Peabody Award . . ."' The story went on from there.

'Aren't we lucky to be associated with somebody so famous?' one of the reporters said sarcastically.

At that moment, Dana walked into the dining room. 'Hi, everybody. I don't have time for lunch today. I'm going to take some sandwiches with me.' She scooped up several sandwiches and covered them with paper napkins. 'See you later.' They watched in silence as she left.

When Dana got outside, Kemal was there, waiting.

'Good afternoon, Kemal.'

No response.

'Get into the car.'

Kemal slid into the backseat. Dana handed him a sandwich and sat there, watching him silently wolf it down. She handed him another sandwich, and he started to eat it.

'Slowly,' Dana said.

'Where to?' Jovan asked.

Dana turned to Kemal. 'Where to?' He looked at her uncomprehendingly. 'We're taking you home, Kemal. Where do you live?'

He shook his head.

'I need to know. Where do you live?'

Twenty minutes later, the car stopped in front of a large vacant lot near the banks of the Miljacka. Dozens of big cardboard boxes were scattered around, and the lot was littered with debris of all kinds.

Dana got out of the car and turned to Kemal. 'Is this where you live?'

He reluctantly nodded.

'And other boys live here, too?'

He nodded again.

'I want to do a story about this, Kemal.'

He shook his head. 'No.'

'Why not?'

'The police will come and take us away. Don't.'

Dana studied him a moment. 'All right. I promise.'

*　　*　　*

The next morning, Dana moved out of her room at the Holiday Inn. When she did not appear at breakfast, Gabriella Orsi from the Altre Station in Italy asked, 'Where's Dana?'

Roderick Munn replied, 'She's gone. She's rented a farmhouse to live in. She said she wanted to be by herself.'

Nikolai Petrovich, the Russian from Gorizont 22, said, 'We would all like to be by ourselves. So we are not good enough for her?'

There was a general feeling of disapproval.

The following afternoon, another large care package arrived for Dana.

Nikolai Petrovich said, 'Since she is not here, we might as well enjoy it, eh?'

The hotel clerk said, 'I'm sorry. Miss Evans is having it picked up.'

A few minutes later, Kemal arrived. The reporters watched him take the package and leave.

'She doesn't even share with us anymore,' Juan Santos grumbled. 'I think her publicity has gone to her head.'

During the next week, Dana filed her stories, but she did not appear at the hotel again. The resentment against her was growing.

Dana and her ego were becoming the main topic of

conversation. A few days later, when another huge care package was delivered to the hotel, Nikolai Petrovich went to the hotel clerk. 'Is Miss Evans having this package picked up?'

'Yes, sir.'

The Russian hurried back into the dining room. 'There is another package,' he said. 'Someone is going to pick it up. Why don't we follow him and tell Miss Evans our opinion of reporters who think they're too good for everyone else?'

There was a chorus of approval.

When Kemal arrived to pick up the package, Nikolai said to him, 'Are you taking that to Miss Evans?'

Kemal nodded.

'She asked to see us. We'll go along with you.'

Kemal looked at him a moment, then shrugged.

'We'll take you in one of our cars,' Nikolai Petrovich said. 'You tell us where to go.'

Ten minutes later, a caravan of cars was making its way along deserted side streets. On the outskirts of the city, Kemal pointed to an old bombed-out farmhouse. The cars came to a stop.

'You go ahead and bring her the package,' Nikolai said. 'We're going to surprise her.'

They watched Kemal walk into the farmhouse. They waited a moment, then moved toward the farmhouse and burst in through the front door. They stopped, in shock. The room was filled with children of all ages, sizes, and colors. Most of them were crippled. A dozen army cots had been set up along the walls. Dana was parceling out the contents of the care package to the children when the door flew open. She looked up in astonishment as the group charged in.

'What – what are you doing here?'

Roderick Munn looked around, embarrassed. 'I'm sorry, Dana. We made a – a mistake. We thought –'

Dana turned to face the group. 'I see. They're orphans. They have nowhere to go and no one to take care of them. Most of them were in a hospital when it was bombed. If the police find them, they'll be put in what passes for an orphanage, and they'll die there. If they stay here, they'll die. I've been trying to figure out a way to get them out of the country, but so far, nothing has worked.' She looked at the group pleadingly. 'Do you have any ideas?'

Roderick Munn said slowly, 'I think I have. There's a Red Cross plane leaving for Paris tonight. The pilot is a friend of mine.'

Dana asked hopefully, 'Would you talk to him?'

Munn nodded. 'Yes.'

Nikolai Petrovich said, 'Wait! We can't get involved in anything like that. They'll throw us all out of the country.'

'You don't have to be involved,' Munn told him. 'We'll handle it.'

'I'm against it,' Nikolai said stubbornly. 'It will place us all in danger.'

'What about the children?' Dana asked. 'We're talking about their lives.'

*   *   *

Late in the afternoon, Roderick Munn came to see Dana. 'I talked to my friend. He said he would be happy to take the children to Paris, where they'll be safe. He has two boys of his own.'

Dana was thrilled. 'That's wonderful. Thank you so much.'

Munn looked at her. 'It is we who should thank you.'

At eight o'clock that evening, a van with the Red Cross insignia on its sides pulled up in front of the farmhouse. The driver blinked the lights, and under the cover of darkness, Dana and the children hurried into the van.

Fifteen minutes later, it was rolling toward Butmir Airport. The airport had been temporarily closed except to the Red Cross planes that delivered supplies and took away the seriously wounded. The drive was the longest ride of Dana's life. It seemed to take forever. When she saw the lights of the airport ahead, she said to the children, 'We're almost there.' Kemal was squeezing her hand.

'You'll be fine,' Dana assured him. 'All of you will be taken care of.' And she thought, *I'm going to miss you.*

At the airport, a guard waved the van through, and it drove up to a waiting cargo plane with the Red Cross markings painted on the fuselage. The pilot was standing next to the plane.

He hurried up to Dana. 'For God's sake, you're late! Get them aboard, fast. We were due to take off twenty minutes ago.'

Dana herded the children up the ramp into the plane. Kemal was the last.

He turned to Dana, his lips trembling. 'Will I see you again?'

'You bet you will,' Dana said. She hugged him and held him close for a moment, saying a silent prayer. 'Get aboard now.'

Moments later, the door closed. There was a roar of the engines, and the plane began to taxi down the runway.

Dana and Munn stood there, watching. At the end of the runway, the plane soared into the air and speared into the eastern sky, banking north toward Paris.

'That was a wonderful thing you did,' the driver said. 'I want you to know –'

A car screeched to a stop behind them, and they turned. Colonel Gordan Divjak jumped out of the car and glared up at the sky where the plane was disappearing. At his side was Nikolai Petrovich, the Russian journalist.

Colonel Divjak turned to Dana. 'You are under arrest. I warned you that the punishment for espionage is death.'

Dana took a deep breath. 'Colonel, if you're going to put me on trial for espionage –'

He looked into Dana's eyes and said softly, 'Who said anything about a trial?'

Thirteen

The inaugural celebrations, the parades, and the swearing-in ceremonies were over, and Oliver was eager to begin his presidency. Washington, D.C., was probably the only city anywhere completely devoted to and obsessed with politics. It was the power hub of the world, and Oliver Russell was the center of that hub. It seemed that everyone was connected in one way or another to the federal government. In the metropolitan area of Washington, there were fifteen thousand lobbyists and more than five thousand journalists, all of them nursing at the mother's milk of government. Oliver Russell remembered John Kennedy's sly put-down: 'Washington, D.C., is a city of southern efficiency and northern charm.'

On the first day of his presidency, Oliver wandered around the White House with Jan. They were familiar with its statistics: 132 rooms, 32 bathrooms, 29 fireplaces, 3 elevators, a swimming pool, putting green, tennis court, jogging track, exercise room, horseshoe pit, bowling alley, and movie theater, and eighteen acres of beautifully tended grounds. But actually living in it, being a part of it, was overwhelming.

'It's like a dream, isn't it?' Jan sighed.

Oliver took her hand. 'I'm glad we're sharing it, darling.' And he meant it. Jan had become a wonderful companion. She was always there for him, supportive and caring. More and more, he found that he enjoyed being with her.

When Oliver returned to the Oval Office, Peter Tager was waiting to see him. Oliver's first appointment had been to make Tager his chief of staff.

Oliver said, 'I still can't believe this, Peter.'

Peter Tager smiled. 'The people believe it. They voted you in, Mr President.'

Oliver looked up at him. 'It's still Oliver.'

'All right. When we're alone. But you have to realize that from this moment on, anything you do can affect the entire world. Anything you say could shake up the economy or have an impact on a hundred other countries around the globe. You have more power than any other person in the world.'

The intercom buzzed. 'Mr President, Senator Davis is here.'

'Send him in, Heather.'

Tager sighed. 'I'd better get started. My desk looks like a paper mountain.'

The door opened and Todd Davis walked in. 'Peter . . .'

'Senator . . .' The two men shook hands.

Tager said, 'I'll see you later, Mr President.'

Senator Davis walked over to Oliver's desk and nodded. 'That desk fits you just fine, Oliver. I can't tell you what a real thrill it is for me to see you sitting there.'

'Thank you, Todd. I'm still trying to get used to it. I mean – Adams sat here . . . and Lincoln . . . and Roosevelt . . .'

Senator Davis laughed. 'Don't let that scare you. Before they became legends, they were men just like you, sitting there trying to do the right thing. Putting their asses in that chair terrified them all, in the beginning. I just left Jan. She's in seventh heaven. She's going to make a great First Lady.'

'I know she is.'

'By the way, I have a little list here I'd like to discuss with you, Mr President.' The emphasis on 'Mr President' was jovial.

'Of course, Todd.'

Senator Davis slid the list across the desk.

'What is this?'

'Just a few suggestions I have for your cabinet.'

'Oh. Well, I've already decided –'

'I thought you might want to look these over.'

'But there's no point in –'

'Look them over, Oliver.' The senator's voice had cooled.

Oliver's eyes narrowed. 'Todd . . .'

Senator Davis held up a hand. 'Oliver, I don't want you to think for one minute that I'm trying to impose my will or my wishes on you. You would be wrong. I put together that list because I think they're the best men who can help you serve your country. I'm a patriot, Oliver, and I'm not ashamed of it. This country means everything to me.' There was a catch in his voice. 'Everything. If you think I helped put you in this office just because you're my son-in-law, you're gravely mistaken. I fought to make sure you got here because I firmly believe you're the man best suited for the job. That's what I care most about.' He tapped a finger on the piece of paper. 'And these men can help you do that job.'

Oliver sat there, silent.

'I've been in this town for a lot of years, Oliver. And do you know what I've learned? That there's nothing sadder than a one-term president. And do you know why? Because during the first four years, he's just beginning to get an idea of what he can do to make this country better. He has all those dreams to fulfill. And just when he's ready to do that – just when he's ready to really make a difference' – he glanced around the office – 'someone else moves in here, and those dreams just vanish. Sad to think about, isn't it? All those men with grand dreams who serve only one term. Did you know that since McKinley took office in 1897, more than half the presidents who followed him were one-term presidents? But you, Oliver – I'm going to see to it that you're a two-term president. I want you to be able to fulfill all your dreams. I'm going to see to it that you're reelected.'

Senator Davis looked at his watch and rose. 'I have to go. We have a quorum call at the Senate. I'll see you at dinner tonight.' He walked out the door.

Oliver looked after him for a long time. Then he reached down and picked up the list Senator Todd Davis had left.

In his dream, Miriam Friedland awakened and sat up in bed. A policeman was at her bedside. He looked down at her and said, 'Now you can tell us who did this to you.'

'Yes.'

He woke up, soaked in perspiration.

Early the following morning, Oliver telephoned the hospital where Miriam was.

'I'm afraid there's no change, Mr President,' the chief of staff told him. 'Frankly, it doesn't look good.'

Oliver said hesitantly, 'She has no family. If you don't think she's going to make it, would it be more humane to take her off the life-support systems?'

'I think we should wait a little while longer and see what happens,' the doctor said. 'Sometimes there's a miracle.'

Jay Perkins, chief of protocol, was briefing the president.

'There are one hundred and forty-seven diplomatic missions in Washington, Mr President. The blue book – the Diplomatic List – lists the name of every representative of a foreign government and spouse. The green book – the Social List – names the top diplomats, Washington residents, and members of Congress.'

He handed Oliver several sheets of paper. 'This is a list of the potential foreign ambassadors you will receive.'

Oliver looked down the list and found the Italian ambassador and his wife: Atilio Picone and Sylva. *Sylva.* Oliver asked innocently, 'Will they bring their wives with them?'

'No. The wives will be introduced later. I would suggest that you begin seeing the candidates as quickly as possible.'

'Fine.'

Perkins said, 'I'll try to arrange it so that by next Saturday, all the foreign ambassadors will be accredited. You might want to consider having a White House dinner to honor them.'

'Good idea.' Oliver glanced again at the list on his desk. Atilio and Sylva Picone.

Saturday evening, the State Dining Room was decorated with flags from the various countries represented by the foreign ambassadors. Oliver had spoken with Atilio Picone two days earlier when he had presented his credence papers.

'How is Mrs Picone?' Oliver had asked.

There was a small pause. 'My wife is fine. Thank you, Mr President.'

The dinner was going beautifully. Oliver went from table to table, chatting with his guests and charming them all. Some of the most important people in the world were gathered in that room.

Oliver Russell approached three ladies who were socially prominent and married to important men. But they were movers and shakers in their own right. 'Leonore . . . Delores . . . Carol . . .'

As Oliver was making his way across the room, Sylva Picone went up to him and held out her hand. 'This is a moment I've been looking forward to.' Her eyes were sparkling.

'I, too,' Oliver murmured.

'I knew you were going to be elected.' It was almost a whisper.

'Can we talk later?'

There was no hesitation. 'Of course.'

After dinner, there was dancing in the grand ballroom to the music of the Marine Band. Oliver watched Jan dancing, and he thought: *What a beautiful woman. What a great body.*

The evening was a huge success.

* * *

The following week, on the front page of the *Washington Tribune*, the headline blazed out: PRESIDENT ACCUSED OF CAMPAIGN FRAUD.

Oliver stared at it in disbelief. It was the worst timing possible. How could this have happened? And then he suddenly realized how it had happened. The answer was in front of him on the masthead of the newspaper: 'Publisher, Leslie Stewart.'

The following week, a front-page item in the *Washington Tribune* read: PRESIDENT TO BE QUESTIONED ABOUT FALSIFIED KENTUCKY STATE INCOME TAX RETURNS.

Two weeks later, another story appeared on the front page of the *Tribune*: FORMER ASSISTANT TO PRESI-DENT RUSSELL PLANS TO FILE LAWSUIT CHARGING SEXUAL HARASSMENT.

The door to the Oval Office flew open and Jan walked in. 'Have you seen the morning paper?'

'Yes, I –'

'How could you do this to us, Oliver? You –'

'Wait a minute! Don't you see what's happening, Jan? Leslie Stewart is behind it. I'm sure she bribed that woman to do this. She's trying to get her revenge because I jilted her for you. All right. She got it. It's over.'

Senator Davis was on the telephone. 'Oliver. I would like to see you in one hour.'

'I'll be here, Todd.'

Oliver was in the small library when Todd Davis

arrived. Oliver rose to greet him. 'Good morning.'

'Like hell it's a good morning.' Senator Davis's voice was filled with fury. 'That woman is going to destroy us.'

'No, she's not. She just –'

'Everyone reads that damned gossip rag, and people believe what they read.'

'Todd, this is going to blow over and –'

'It's not going to blow over. Did you hear the editorial on WTE this morning? It was about who our next president is going to be. You were at the bottom of the list. Leslie Stewart is out to get you. You must stop her. What's the line – "hell hath no fury . . ."?'

'There's another adage, Todd, about freedom of the press. There's nothing we can do about this.'

Senator Davis looked at Oliver speculatively. 'But there is.'

'What are you talking about?'

'Sit down.' The two men sat. 'The woman is obviously still in love with you, Oliver. This is her way of punishing you for what you did to her. Never argue with someone who buys ink by the ton. My advice is to make peace.'

'How do I do that?'

Senator Davis looked at Oliver's groin. 'Use your head.'

'Wait a minute, Todd! Are you suggesting that I –?'

'What I'm suggesting is that you cool her down. Let her know that you're sorry. I'm telling you she still loves you. If she didn't, she wouldn't be doing this.'

'What exactly do you expect me to do?'

'Charm her, my boy. You did it once, you can do it

again. You've got to win her over. You're having a State Department dinner here Friday evening. Invite her. You must persuade her to stop what she's doing.'

'I don't know how I can —'

'I don't care how you do it. Perhaps you could take her away somewhere, where you can have a quiet chat. I have a country house in Virginia. It's very private. I'm going to Florida for the weekend, and I've arranged for Jan to go with me.' He took out a slip of paper and some keys and handed them to Oliver. 'Here are the directions and the keys to the house.'

Oliver was staring at him. 'Jesus! You had this all planned? What if Leslie won't — what if she's not interested? If she refuses to go?'

Senator Davis rose. 'She's interested. She'll go. I'll see you Monday, Oliver. Good luck.'

Oliver sat there for a long time. And he thought: *No. I can't do this to her again. I won't.*

That evening as they were getting dressed for dinner, Jan said, 'Oliver, Father asked me to go to Florida with him for the weekend. He's getting some kind of award, and I think he wants to show off the president's wife. Would you mind very much if I went? I know there's a State Department dinner here Friday, so if you want me to stay . . .'

'No, no. You go ahead. I'll miss you.' *And I am going to miss her*, he thought. *As soon as I solve this problem with*

Leslie, I'm going to start spending more time with Jan.

Leslie was on the telephone when her secretary came hurrying in. 'Miss Stewart –'

'Can't you see I'm –'

'President Russell is on line three.'

Leslie looked at her a moment, then smiled. 'Right.' She said into the phone, 'I'll call you back.'

She pressed the button on line three. 'Hello.'

'Leslie?'

'Hello, Oliver. Or should I call you Mr President?'

'You can call me anything you like.' He added lightly, 'And have.' There was a silence. 'Leslie, I want to see you.'

'Are you sure this is a good idea?'

'I'm very sure.'

'You're the president. I can't say no to you, can I?'

'Not if you're a patriotic American. There's a State Department dinner at the White House Friday night. Please come.'

'What time?'

'Eight o'clock.'

'All right. I'll be there.'

She looked stunning in a long, clinging black knit Mandarin-necked St John gown fastened in front with buttons over-coated in twenty-two-karat gold. There was a revealing fourteen-inch slit on the left side of the dress.

The instant Oliver looked at her, memories came flooding back. 'Leslie . . .'

'Mr President.'

He took her hand, and it was moist. *It's a sign,* Oliver thought. *But of what? Nervousness? Anger? Old memories?*

'I'm so glad you came, Leslie.'

'Yes. I am, too.'

'We'll talk later.'

Her smile warmed him. 'Yes.'

Two tables away from where Oliver was seated was a group of Arab diplomats. One of them, a swarthy man with sharply etched features and dark eyes, seemed to be staring intently at Oliver.

Oliver leaned over to Peter Tager and nodded toward the Arab. 'Who's that?'

Tager took a quick look. 'Ali al-Fulani. He's the secretary at one of the United Arab Emirates. Why do you ask?'

'No reason.' Oliver looked again. The man's eyes were still focused on him.

Oliver spent the evening working the room, making his guests feel comfortable. Sylva was at one table, Leslie at another. It was not until the evening was almost over that

Oliver managed to get Leslie alone for a moment.

'We need to talk. I have a lot to tell you. Can we meet somewhere?'

There was the faintest hesitation in her voice. 'Oliver, perhaps it would be better if we didn't –'

'I have a house in Manassas, Virginia, about an hour out of Washington. Will you meet me there?'

She looked into his eyes. This time there was no hesitation. 'If you want me to.'

Oliver described the location of the house. 'Tomorrow night at eight?'

Leslie's voice was husky. 'I'll be there.'

At a National Security Council meeting the following morning, Director of Central Intelligence James Frisch dropped a bomb-shell.

'Mr President, we received word this morning that Libya is buying a variety of atomic weapons from Iran and China. There's a strong rumor that they're going to be used to attack Israel. It will take a day or two to get a confirmation.'

Lou Werner, the secretary of state, said, 'I don't think we should wait. Let's protest now, in the strongest possible terms.'

Oliver said to Werner, 'See what additional information you can get.'

The meeting lasted all morning. From time to time, Oliver found himself thinking about the rendezvous with

Leslie. *'Charm her, my boy . . . You've got to win her over.'*

On Saturday evening, Oliver was in one of the White House staff cars, driven by a trusted Secret Service agent, heading for Manassas, Virginia. He was strongly tempted to cancel the rendezvous, but it was too late. *I'm worrying for no reason. She probably won't even show up.*

At eight o'clock, Oliver looked out the window and saw Leslie's car pull into the driveway of the senator's house. He watched her get out of the car and move toward the entrance. Oliver opened the front door. The two of them stood there, silently staring at each other, and time disappeared and somehow it was as though they had never been apart.

Oliver was the first to find his voice. 'My God! Last night when I saw you . . . I had almost forgotten how beautiful you are.' Oliver took Leslie's hand, and they walked into the living room. 'What would you like to drink?'

'I don't need anything. Thank you.'

Oliver sat down next to her on the couch. 'I have to ask you something, Leslie. Do you hate me?'

She shook her head slowly. 'No. I thought I hated you.' She smiled wryly. 'In a way, I suppose that's the reason for my success.'

'I don't understand.'

'I wanted to get back at you, Oliver. I bought newspapers and television stations so that I could attack you. You're the only man I've ever loved. And when you – when you deserted me, I – I didn't think I could stand it.' She was fighting back tears.

Oliver put his arm around her. 'Leslie –' And then his lips were on hers, and they were kissing passionately.

'Oh, my God,' she said. 'I didn't expect this to happen.' And they were in a fierce embrace, and he took her hand and led her into the bedroom. They began undressing each other.

'Hurry, my darling,' Leslie said. 'Hurry . . .'

And they were in bed, holding each other, their bodies touching, remembering. Their lovemaking was gentle and fierce, as it had been in the beginning. And this was a new beginning. The two of them lay there, happy, spent.

'It's so funny,' Leslie said.

'What?'

'All those terrible things I published about you. I did it to get your attention.' She snuggled closer. 'And I did, didn't I?'

He grinned. 'I'll say.'

Leslie sat up and looked at him. 'I'm so proud of you, Oliver. The President of the United States.'

'I'm trying to be a damn good one. That's what's really important to me. I want to make a difference.' Oliver looked at his watch. 'I'm afraid I have to get back.'

'Of course. I'll let you leave first.'

'When am I going to see you again, Leslie?'

'Anytime you want to.'

'We're going to have to be careful.'

'I know. We will be.'

Leslie lay there, dreamily watching Oliver as he dressed.

When Oliver was ready to leave, he leaned over and said, 'You're my miracle.'

'And you're mine. You always have been.'

He kissed her. 'I'll call you tomorrow.'

Oliver hurried out to the car and was driven back to Washington. *The more things change, the more they stay the same*, Oliver thought. *I have to be careful never to hurt her again.* He picked up the car telephone and dialed the number in Florida that Senator Davis had given him.

The senator answered the phone himself. 'Hello.'

'It's Oliver.'

'Where are you?'

'On my way back to Washington. I just called to tell you some good news. We don't have to worry about that problem anymore. Everything is under control.'

'I can't tell you how glad I am to hear that.' There was a note of deep relief in Senator Davis's voice.

'I knew you would be, Todd.'

The following morning, as Oliver was getting dressed, he picked up a copy of the *Washington Tribune*. On the front page was a photograph of Senator Davis's country home in Manassas. The caption under it read: PRESIDENT RUSSELL'S SECRET LOVE NEST.

Fourteen

Oliver stared at the paper unbelievingly. How could she have done that? He thought about how passionate she had been in bed. And he had completely misread it. It was a passion filled with hate, not love. *There's no way I can ever stop her*, Oliver thought despairingly.

Senator Todd Davis looked at the front-page story and was aghast. He understood the power of the press, and he knew how much this vendetta could cost him. *I'll have to stop her myself*, Senator Davis decided.

When he got to his Senate office, he telephoned Leslie. 'It's been a long time,' Senator Davis said warmly. 'Too long. I think about you a lot, Miss Stewart.'

'I think about you, too, Senator Davis. In a way, everything I have I owe to you.'

He chuckled. 'Not at all. When you had a problem, I was happy to be able to assist you.'

'Is there something I can do for you, Senator?'

'No, Miss Stewart. But there's something I'd like to do

for you. I'm one of your faithful readers, you know, and I think the *Tribune* is a truly fine paper. I just realized that we haven't been doing any advertising in it, and I want to correct that. I'm involved in several large companies, and they do a lot of advertising. I mean a *lot* of advertising. I think that a good portion of that should go to a fine paper like the *Tribune*.'

'I'm delighted to hear that, Senator. We can always use more advertising. Whom shall I have my advertising manager talk to?'

'Well, before he talks to anyone, I think you and I should settle a little problem between us.'

'What's that?' Leslie asked.

'It concerns President Russell.'

'Yes?'

'This is a rather delicate matter, Miss Stewart. You said a few moments ago that you owed everything you have to me. Now I'm asking you to do me a little favor.'

'I'll be happy to, if I can.'

'In my own small way, I helped the president get elected to office.'

'I know.'

'And he's doing a fine job. Of course, it makes it more difficult for him when he's attacked by a powerful newspaper like the *Tribune* every time he turns around.'

'What are you asking me to do, Senator?'

'Well, I would greatly appreciate it if those attacks would stop.'

'And in exchange for that, I can count on getting advertising from some of your companies.'

'A great deal of advertising, Miss Stewart.'

'Thank you, Senator. Why don't you call me back when you have something more to offer?'

And the line went dead.

In his office at the *Washington Tribune*, Matt Baker was reading the story about President Russell's secret love nest.

'Who the hell authorized this?' he snapped at his assistant.

'It came from the White Tower.'

'Goddammit. She's not running this paper, I am.' *Why the hell do I put up with her?* he wondered, not for the first time. *Three hundred and fifty thousand dollars a year plus bonuses and stock options*, he told himself wryly. Every time he was ready to quit, she seduced him with more money and more power. Besides, he had to admit to himself that it was fascinating working for one of the most powerful women in the world. There were things about her that he would never understand.

When she had first bought the *Tribune*, Leslie had said to Matt, 'There's an astrologer I want you to hire. His name is Zoltaire.'

'He's syndicated by our competition.'

'I don't care. Hire him.'

Later that day, Matt Baker told her, 'I checked on

Zoltaire. It would be too expensive to buy out his contract.'

'Buy it.'

The following week, Zoltaire, whose real name Matt learned was David Hayworth, came to work for the *Washington Tribune*. He was in his fifties, small and dark and intense.

Matt was puzzled. Leslie did not seem like the kind of woman who would have any interest in astrology. As far as he could see, there was no contact between Leslie and David Hayworth.

What he did not know was that Hayworth went to visit Leslie at her home whenever she had an important decision to make.

On the first day, Matt had had Leslie's name put on the masthead: 'Leslie Chambers, Publisher.' She had glanced at it and said, 'Change it. It's Leslie Stewart.'

The lady is on an ego trip, Matt had thought. But he was wrong. Leslie had decided to revert to her maiden name because she wanted Oliver Russell to know exactly who was responsible for what was going to happen to him.

The day after Leslie took over the newspaper, she said, 'We're going to buy a health magazine.'

Matt looked at her curiously. 'Why?'

'Because the health field is exploding.'

She had proved to be right. The magazine was an instant success.

'We're going to start expanding,' Leslie told Baker. 'Let's get some people looking for publications overseas.'

'All right.'

'And there's too much fat around here. Get rid of the reporters who aren't pulling their weight.'

'Leslie –'

'I want young reporters who are hungry.'

When an executive position became open, Leslie insisted on being there for the interview. She would listen to the applicant, and then would ask one question: 'What's your golf score?' The job would often depend on the answer.

'What the hell kind of question is that?' Matt Baker asked the first time he heard it. 'What difference does a golf score make?'

'I don't want people here who are dedicated to golf. If they work here, they're going to be dedicated to the *Washington Tribune*.'

Leslie Stewart's private life was a subject of endless discussions at the *Tribune*. She was a beautiful woman, unattached, and as far as anyone knew, she was not involved with any man and had no personal life. She was one of the capital's preeminent hostesses, and important people vied for an invitation to her dinner parties. But people speculated about what she did when all the guests had left and she was alone. There were rumors that she was an insomniac who spent the nights working, planning new projects for the Stewart empire.

There were other rumors, more titillating, but there was no way of proving them.

Leslie involved herself in everything: editorials, news stories, advertising. One day, she said to the head of the advertising department, 'Why aren't we getting any ads from Gleason's?' – an upscale store in Georgetown.

'I've tried, but –'

'I know the owner. I'll give him a call.'

She called him and said, 'Allan, you're not giving the *Tribune* any ads. Why?'

He had laughed and said, 'Leslie, your readers are our shoplifters.'

Before Leslie went into a conference, she read up on everyone who would be there. She knew everyone's weaknesses and strengths, and she was a tough negotiator.

'Sometimes you can be too tough,' Matt Baker warned her. 'You have to leave them something, Leslie.'

'Forget it. I believe in the scorched-earth policy.'

*　　　*　　　*

In the course of the next year, Washington Tribune Enterprises acquired a newspaper and radio station in Australia, a television station in Denver, and a newspaper in Hammond, Indiana. Whenever there was a new acquisition, its employees were terrified of what was coming. Leslie's reputation for being ruthless was growing.

Leslie Stewart was intensely jealous of Katharine Graham.

'She's just lucky,' Leslie said. 'And she has the reputation of being a bitch.'

Matt Baker was tempted to ask Leslie what she thought her own reputation was, but he decided not to.

One morning when Leslie arrived at her office, she found that someone had placed a small wooden block with two brass balls on her desk.

Matt Baker was upset. 'I'm sorry,' he said. 'I'll take –'

'No. Leave it.'

'But –'

'Leave it.'

Matt Baker was having a conference in his office when Leslie's voice came on over the intercom. 'Matt, come up here.'

No 'please,' no 'good morning.' *It's going to be a bad-hair day*, Matt Baker thought grimly. The Ice Princess was in one of her moods.

'That's it for now,' Matt said.

He left his office and walked through the corridors, where hundreds of employees were busily at work. He took the elevator up to the White Tower and entered the sumptuous publisher's office. Half a dozen editors were already gathered in the room.

Behind an enormous desk sat Leslie Stewart. She looked up as Matt Baker entered. 'Let's get started.'

She had called an editorial meeting. Matt Baker remembered her saying, 'You'll be running the newspaper. I'll keep my hands off.' He should have known better. She had no business calling meetings like this. That was his job. On the other hand, she was the publisher and owner of the *Washington Tribune*, and she could damn well do anything she pleased.

Matt Baker said, 'I want to talk to you about the story about President Russell's love nest in Virginia.'

'There's nothing to talk about,' Leslie said. She held up a copy of *The Washington Post*, their rival. 'Have you seen this?'

Matt had seen it. 'Yes, it's just –'

'In the old days it was called a scoop, Matt. Where were you and your reporters when the *Post* was getting the news?'

The headline in *The Washington Post* read: SECOND LOBBYIST TO BE INDICTED FOR GIVING ILLEGAL GIFTS TO SECRETARY OF DEFENSE.

'Why didn't we get that story?'

'Because it isn't official yet. I checked on it. It's just –'

'I don't like being scooped.'

Matt Baker sighed and sat back in his chair. It was going to be a stormy session.

'We're number one, or we're nothing,' Leslie Stewart announced to the group. 'And if we're nothing, there won't be any jobs here for anyone, will there?'

Leslie turned to Arnie Cohn, the editor of the Sunday magazine section. 'When people wake up Sunday morning, we want them to read the magazine section. We don't want to put our readers back to sleep. The stories we ran last Sunday were boring.'

He was thinking, *If you were a man, I'd* – 'Sorry,' he mumbled. 'I'll try to do better next time.'

Leslie turned to Jeff Connors, the sports editor. Connors was a good-looking man in his mid-thirties, tall, with an athletic build, blond hair, intelligent gray eyes. He had the easy manner of someone who knew that he was good at what he did. Matt had heard that Leslie had made a play for him, and he had turned her down.

'You wrote that Fielding was going to be traded to the Pirates.'

'I was told –'

'You were told wrong! The *Tribune* is guilty of printing a story that never happened.'

'I got it from his manager,' Jeff Connors said, unperturbed. 'He told me that –'

'Next time check out your stories, and then check them out again.'

Leslie turned and pointed to a framed, yellowed newspaper article hanging on the wall. It was the front page of the *Chicago Tribune*, dated November 3, 1948. The banner headline read: DEWEY DEFEATS TRUMAN.

'The worst thing a newspaper can do,' Leslie said, 'is to get the facts wrong. We're in a business where you always have to get it right.'

She glanced at her watch. 'That's it for now. I'll expect you all to do a lot better.' As they rose to leave, Leslie said to Matt Baker, 'I want you to stay.'

'Right.' He sank back into his chair and watched the others depart.

'Was I rough on them?' she asked.

'You got what you wanted. They're all suicidal.'

'We're not here to make friends, we're here to put out a newspaper.' She looked up again at the framed front page on the wall. 'Can you imagine what the publisher of that paper must have felt after that story hit the streets and Truman was president? I never want to have that feeling, Matt. Never.'

'Speaking of getting it wrong,' Matt said, 'that story on page one about President Russell was more suitable for a cheap tabloid publication. Why do you keep riding him? Give him a chance.'

Leslie said enigmatically, 'I gave him his chance.' She stood up and began to pace. 'I got a tip that Russell is going to veto the new communications bill. That means we'll have to call off the deal for the San Diego station and the Omaha station.'

'There's nothing we can do about that.'

'Oh, yes, there is. I want him out of office, Matt. We'll help put someone else in the White House, someone who knows what he's doing.'

Matt had no intention of getting into another argument with Leslie Stewart about the president. She was fanatic on the subject.

'He's not fit to be in that office, and I'm going to do everything I can to make sure that he's defeated in the next election.'

Philip Cole, chief of correspondents for WTE, hurried into Matt Baker's office as Matt was ready to leave. There was a worried expression on his face. 'We have a problem, Matt.'

'Can it wait until tomorrow? I'm late for a –'

'It's about Dana Evans.'

Matt said sharply, 'What about her?'

'She's been arrested.'

'Arrested?' Matt asked incredulously. 'What for?'

'Espionage. Do you want me to –?'

'No. I'll handle this.'

Matt Baker hurried back to his desk and dialed the State Department.

Fifteen

She was being dragged, naked, out of her cell into a cold, dark courtyard. She struggled wildly against the two men holding her, but she was no match for them. There were six soldiers with rifles outside, waiting for her as she was carried, screaming, to a wooden post hammered into the ground. Colonel Gordan Divjak watched his men tie her to the post.

'You can't do this to me! I'm not a spy!' she yelled. But she could not make her voice heard above the sounds of mortar fire in the near distance.

Colonel Divjak stepped away from her and nodded toward the firing squad. 'Ready, aim –'

'Stop that screaming!'

Rough hands were shaking her. Dana opened her eyes, her heart pounding. She was lying on the cot in her small, dark cell. Colonel Divjak was standing over her.

Dana sat up, panicky, trying to blink away the nightmare. 'What – what are you going to do to me?'

Colonel Divjak said coldly, 'If there were justice, you would be shot. Unfortunately, I have been given orders to release you.'

Dana's heart skipped a beat.

'You will be put on the first plane out of here.' Colonel Divjak looked into her eyes and said, 'Don't ever come back.'

It had taken all the pressure that the State Department and the president could muster to get Dana Evans released. When Peter Tager heard about the arrest, he had gone in to see the president.

'I just got a call from the State Department. Dana Evans has been arrested on charges of espionage. They're threatening to execute her.'

'Jesus! That's terrible. We can't let that happen.'

'Right. I'd like permission to use your name.'

'You've got it. Do whatever has to be done.'

'I'll work with the State Department. If we can pull this off, maybe the *Tribune* will go a little easier on you.'

Oliver shook his head. 'I wouldn't count on it. Let's just get her the hell out of there.'

Dozens of frantic telephone calls later, with pressure from the Oval Office, the secretary of state, and the secretary-general of the United Nations, Dana's captors reluctantly agreed to release her.

When the news came, Peter Tager hurried in to tell Oliver. 'She's free. She's on her way home.'

'Great.'

* * *

He thought about Dana Evans on his way to a meeting that morning. *I'm glad we were able to save her.*

He had no idea that that action was going to cost him his life.

When Dana's plane landed at Dulles International Airport, Matt Baker and two dozen reporters from newspapers and television and radio stations were waiting to greet her.

Dana looked at the crowd in disbelief. 'What's –?'

'This way, Dana. Smile!'

'How were you treated? Was there any brutality?'

'How does it feel to be back home?'

'Let's have a picture.'

'Do you have any plans to go back?'

They were all talking at once. Dana stood there, overwhelmed.

Matt Baker hustled Dana into a waiting limousine, and they sped away.

'What's – what's going on?' Dana asked.

'You're a celebrity.'

She shook her head. 'I don't need this, Matt.' She closed her eyes for a moment. 'Thanks for getting me out.'

'You can thank the president and Peter Tager. They pushed all the buttons. You also have Leslie Stewart to thank.'

When Matt told Leslie the news, she had said, 'Those bastards! They can't do that to the *Tribune*. I want you to see that they free her. Pull every string you can and get her out of there.'

Dana looked out the window of the limousine. People were walking along the street, talking and laughing. There was no sound of gunfire or mortar shells. It was eerie.

'Our real estate editor found an apartment for you. I'm taking you there now. I want you to have some time off – as much as you like. When you're ready, we'll put you back to work.' He took a closer look at Dana. 'Are you feeling all right? If you want to see a doctor, I'll arrange –'

'I'm fine. Our bureau took me to a doctor in Paris.'

The apartment was on Calvert Street, an attractively furnished place with one bedroom, living room, kitchen, bath, and small study.

'Will this do?' Matt asked.

'This is perfect. Thank you, Matt.'

'I've had the refrigerator stocked for you. You'll probably want to go shopping for clothes tomorrow, after you get some rest. Charge everything to the paper.'

'Thanks, Matt. Thank you for everything.'

'You're going to be debriefed later. I'll set it up for you.'

She was on a bridge, listening to the gunfire and watching bloated bodies float by, and she woke up, sobbing. It had been so real. It was a dream, but it was happening. At that moment, innocent victims – men, women, and children – were being senselessly and brutally slaughtered. She thought of Professor Staka's words. *'This war in Bosnia and Herzegovina is beyond understanding.'* What was incredible to her was that the rest of the world didn't seem to care. She was afraid to go back to sleep, afraid of the nightmares that filled her brain. She got up and walked over to the window and looked out at the city. It was quiet – no guns, no people running down the street, screaming. It seemed unnatural. She wondered how Kemal was, and whether she would ever see him again. *He's probably forgotten me by now.*

Dana spent part of the morning shopping for clothes. Wherever she went, people stopped to stare at her. She heard whispers: 'That's Dana Evans!' The sales clerks all recognized her. She was famous. She hated it.

Dana had had no breakfast and no lunch. She was hungry, but she was unable to eat. She was too tense. It was as though she were waiting for some disaster to strike. When she walked down the street, she avoided the eyes of strangers. She was suspicious of everyone. She kept listening for the sound of gunfire. *I can't go on like this,* Dana thought.

At noon, she walked into Matt Baker's office.

'What are you doing here? You're supposed to be on vacation.'

'I need to go back to work, Matt.'

He looked at her and thought about the young girl who had come to him a few years earlier. *'I'm here for a job. Of course, I already have a job here. It's more like a transfer, isn't it? . . . I can start right away . . .'* And she had more than fulfilled her promise. *If I ever had a daughter . . .*

'Your boss wants to meet you,' Matt told Dana.

They headed for Leslie Stewart's office.

The two women stood there appraising each other. 'Welcome back, Dana.'

'Thank you.'

'Sit down.' Dana and Matt took chairs opposite Leslie's desk.

'I want to thank you for getting me out of there,' Dana said.

'It must have been hell. I'm sorry.' Leslie looked at Matt. 'What are we going to do with her now, Matt?'

He looked at Dana. 'We're about to reassign our White House correspondent. Would you like the job?' It was one of the most prestigious television assignments in the country.

Dana's face lit up. 'Yes. I would.'

Leslie nodded. 'You've got it.'

Dana rose. 'Well – thank you, again.'

'Good luck.'

Dana and Matt left the office. 'Let's get you settled,' Matt said. He walked her over to the television building, where the whole staff was waiting to greet her. It took Dana fifteen minutes to work her way through the crowd of well-wishers.

'Meet your new White House correspondent,' Matt said to Philip Cole.

'That's great. I'll show you to your office.'

'Have you had lunch yet?' Matt asked Dana.

'No, I –'

'Why don't we get a bite to eat?'

The executive dining room was on the fifth floor, a spacious, airy room with two dozen tables. Matt led Dana to a table in the corner, and they sat down.

'Miss Stewart seemed very nice,' Dana said.

Matt started to say something. 'Yeah. Let's order.'

'I'm not hungry.'

'You haven't had lunch?'

'No.'

'Did you have breakfast?'

'No.'

'Dana – when did you eat last?'

She shook her head. 'I don't remember. It's not important.'

'Wrong. I can't have our new White House correspondent starving herself to death.'

The waiter came over to the table. 'Are you ready to order, Mr Baker?'

'Yes.' He scanned the menu. 'We'll start you off light. Miss Evans will have a bacon, lettuce, and tomato sandwich.' He looked over at Dana. 'Pastry or ice cream?'

'Noth –'

'Pie à la mode. And I'll have a roast beef sandwich.'

'Yes, sir.'

Dana looked around. 'All this seems so unreal. Life is what's happening over there, Matt. It's horrible. No one here cares.'

'Don't say that. Of course we care. But we can't run the world, and we can't control it. We do the best we can.'

'It's not good enough,' Dana said fiercely.

'Dana . . .' He stopped. She was far away, listening to distant sounds that he could not hear, seeing grisly sights that he could not see. They sat in silence until the waiter arrived with their food.

'Here we are.'

'Matt, I'm not really hung –'

'You're going to eat,' Matt commanded.

Jeff Connors was making his way over to the table. 'Hi, Matt.'

'Jeff.'

Jeff Connors looked at Dana. 'Hello.'

Matt said, 'Dana, this is Jeff Connors. He's the *Tribune*'s sports editor.'

Dana nodded.

'I'm a big fan of yours, Miss Evans. I'm glad you got out safely.'

Dana nodded again.

Matt said, 'Would you like to join us, Jeff?'

'Love to.' He took a chair and said to Dana, 'I tried never to miss any of your broadcasts. I thought they were brilliant.'

Dana mumbled, 'Thank you.'

'Jeff here is one of our great athletes. He's in the Baseball Hall of Fame.'

Another small nod.

'If you happen to be free,' Jeff said, 'on Friday, the Orioles are playing the Yankees in Baltimore. It's –'

Dana turned to look at him for the first time. 'That sounds really exciting. The object of the game is to hit the ball and then run around the field while the other side tries to stop you?'

He looked at her warily. 'Well –'

Dana got to her feet, her voice trembling. 'I've seen people running around a field – but they were running for their lives because someone was shooting at them and killing them!' She was near hysteria. 'It wasn't a game, and it – it wasn't about a stupid baseball.'

The other people in the room were turning to stare at her.

'You can go to hell,' Dana sobbed. And she fled from the room.

Jeff turned to Matt. 'I'm terribly sorry. I didn't mean to –'

'It wasn't your fault. She hasn't come home yet. And God knows she's entitled to a bad case of nerves.'

Dana hurried into her office and slammed the door. She went to her desk and sat down, fighting hysteria. *Oh, God. I've made a complete fool of myself. They'll fire me, and I deserve it. Why did I attack that man? How could I have done anything so awful? I don't belong here. I don't belong anywhere anymore.* She sat there with her head on the desk, sobbing.

A few minutes later, the door opened and someone came in. Dana looked up. It was Jeff Connors, carrying a tray with a bacon, lettuce, and tomato sandwich and a slice of pie à la mode.

'You forgot your lunch,' Jeff said mildly.

Dana wiped away her tears, mortified. 'I – I want to apologize. I'm so sorry. I had no right to –'

'You had every right,' he said quietly. 'Anyway, who needs to watch a dumb old baseball game?' Jeff put the tray on the desk. 'May I join you for lunch?' He sat down.

'I'm not hungry. Thank you.'

He sighed. 'You're putting me in a very difficult position, Miss Evans. Matt says you have to eat. You don't want to get me fired, do you?'

Dana managed a smile. 'No.' She picked up half of the sandwich and took a small bite.

'Bigger.'

Dana took another small bite.

'Bigger.'

She looked up at him. 'You're really going to make me eat this, aren't you?'

'You bet I am.' He watched her take a larger bite of the sandwich. 'That's better. By the way, if you're not doing anything Friday night, I don't know if I mentioned it, but there's a game between the Orioles and the Yankees. Would you like to go?'

She looked at him and nodded. 'Yes.'

At three o'clock that afternoon, when Dana walked into the White House entrance, the guard said, 'Mr Tager would like to see you, Miss Evans. I'll have someone take you to his office.'

A few minutes later, one of the guides led Dana down a long corridor to Peter Tager's office. He was waiting for her.

'Mr Tager . . .'

'I didn't expect to see you so soon, Miss Evans. Won't your station give you any time off?'

'I didn't want any,' Dana said. 'I – I need to work.'

'Please sit down.' She sat across from him. 'Can I offer you anything?'

'No, thanks. I just had lunch.' She smiled to herself at the recollection of Jeff Connors. 'Mr Tager, I want to thank you and President Russell so much for rescuing me.' She hesitated. 'I know the *Tribune* hasn't been too kind to the president, and I –'

Peter Tager raised a hand. 'This was something above politics. There was no chance that the president was going to let them get away with this. You know the story of Helen of Troy?'

'Yes.'

He smiled. 'Well, we might have started a war over you. You're a very important person.'

'I don't feel very important.'

'I want you to know how pleased both the president and I are that you've been assigned to cover the White House.'

'Thank you.'

He paused for a moment. 'It's unfortunate that the *Tribune* doesn't like President Russell, and there's nothing you can do about it. But in spite of that, on a very personal level, if there's anything the president or I can do to help . . . we both have an enormous regard for you.'

'Thank you. I appreciate that.'

The door opened and Oliver walked in. Dana and Peter Tager stood up.

'Sit down,' Oliver said. He walked over to Dana. 'Welcome home.'

'Thank you, Mr President,' Dana said. 'And I do mean – thank you.'

Oliver smiled. 'If you can't save someone's life, what's the point of being president? I want to be frank with you, Miss Evans. None of us here is a fan of your newspaper. All of us are your fans.'

'Thank you.'

'Peter is going to give you a tour of the White House. If you have any problems, we're here to help you.'

'You're very kind.'

'If you don't mind, I want you to meet with Mr Werner, the secretary of state. I'd like to have him get a firsthand briefing from you on the situation in Herzegovina.'

'I'd be happy to do that,' Dana said.

There were a dozen men seated in the secretary of state's private conference room, listening to Dana describe her experiences.

'Most of the buildings in Sarajevo have been damaged or destroyed . . . There's no electricity, and the people there who still have cars unhook the car batteries at night to run their television sets . . .

'The streets of the city are obstructed by the wreckage of bombed automobiles, carts, and bicycles. The main form of transportation is walking . . .

'When there's a storm, people catch the water from the street gutters and put it into buckets . . .

'There's no respect for the Red Cross or for the journalists there. More than forty correspondents have been killed covering the Bosnian war, and dozens have been wounded . . . Whether the present revolt against Slobodan Milosevic is successful or not, the feeling is that because of the popular uprising, his regime has been badly damaged . . .'

The meeting went on for two hours. For Dana it was both traumatic and cathartic, because as she described what happened, she found herself living the terrible scenes all over again; and at the same time, she found it a relief to be able to talk about it. When she was finished, she felt drained.

The secretary of state said, 'I want to thank you, Miss Evans. This has been very informative.' He smiled. 'I'm glad you got back here safely.'

'So am I, Mr Secretary.'

Friday night, Dana was seated next to Jeff Connors in the press box at Camden Yards, watching the baseball game. And for the first time since she had returned, she was able to think about something other than the war. As Dana watched the players on the field, she listened to the announcer reporting the game.

'. . . it's the top of the sixth inning and Nelson is pitching. Alomar hits a line drive down the left-field line for a double. Palmeiro is approaching the plate. The count is two and one. Nelson throws a fastball down the middle and Palmeiro is going for it. What a hit! It looks like it's going to clear the right-field wall. It's over! Palmeiro is rounding the bases with a two-run homer that puts the Orioles in the lead . . .'

At the seventh-inning stretch, Jeff stood up and looked at Dana. 'Are you enjoying yourself?'

Dana looked at him and nodded. 'Yes.'

*　　*　　*

Back in D.C. after the game, they had supper at Bistro Twenty Fifteen.

'I want to apologize again for the way I behaved the other day,' Dana said. 'It's just that I've been living in a world where –' She stopped, not sure how to phrase it. 'Where everything is a matter of life and death. Everything. It's awful. Because unless someone stops the war, those people have no hope.'

Jeff said gently, 'Dana, you can't put your life on hold because of what's happening over there. You have to begin living again. Here.'

'I know. It's just . . . not easy.'

'Of course it isn't. I'd like to help you. Would you let me?'

Dana looked at him for a long time. 'Please.'

The next day, Dana had a luncheon date with Jeff Connors.

'Can you pick me up?' he asked. He gave her the address.

'Right.' Dana wondered what Jeff was doing there. It was in a very troubled inner-city neighborhood. When Dana arrived, she found the answer.

Jeff was surrounded by two teams of baseball players, ranging in age from nine to thirteen, dressed in a creative variety of baseball uniforms. Dana parked at the curb to watch.

'And remember,' Jeff was saying, 'don't rush. When the

pitcher throws the ball, imagine that it's coming at you very slowly, so that you have plenty of time to hit it. Feel your bat smacking the ball. Let your mind help guide your hands so –'

Jeff looked over and saw Dana. He waved. 'All right, fellows. That's it for now.'

One of the boys asked, 'Is that your girl, Jeff?'

'Only if I'm lucky.' Jeff smiled. 'See you later.' He walked over to Dana's car.

'That's quite a ball club,' Dana said.

'They're good boys. I coach them once a week.'

She smiled. 'I like that.' And she wondered how Kemal was and what he was doing.

As the days went on, Dana found herself coming to like Jeff Connors more and more. He was sensitive, intelligent, and amusing. She enjoyed being with him. Slowly, the horrible memories of Sarajevo were beginning to fade. The morning came when she woke up without having had nightmares.

When she told Jeff about it, he took her hand and said, 'That's my girl.'

And Dana wondered whether she should read a deeper meaning into it.

There was a hand-printed letter waiting for Dana at the office. It read: 'miss evans, don't worry about me. i'm happy. i am not lonely. i don't miss anybody. and i am going to send you back the clothes you bought me because i don't need them. i have my own clothes. goodbye.' It was signed 'kemal.'

The letter was postmarked Paris, and the letterhead read 'Xavier's Home for Boys.' Dana read the letter twice and then picked up the phone. It took her four hours to reach Kemal.

She heard his voice, a tentative 'Hello . . .'

'Kemal, this is Dana Evans.' There was no response. 'I got your letter.' Silence. 'I just wanted to tell you that I'm glad you're so happy, and that you're having such a good time.' She waited a moment, then went on, 'I wish I were as happy as you are. Do you know why I'm not? Because I miss you. I think about you a lot.'

'No, you don't,' Kemal said. 'You don't care about me.'

'You're wrong. How would you like to come to Washington and live with me?'

There was a long silence. 'Do you – do you mean that?'

'You bet I do. Would you like that?'

'I –' He began to cry.

'Would you, Kemal?'

'Yes – yes, ma'am.'

'I'll make the arrangements.'

'Miss Evans?'

'Yes?'

'I love you.'

* * *

Dana and Jeff Connors were walking in West Potomac Park. 'I think I'm going to have a roommate,' Dana said. 'He should be here in the next few weeks.'

Jeff looked at her in surprise. 'He?'

Dana found herself pleased at his reaction. 'Yes. His name is Kemal. He's twelve years old.' She told him the story.

'He sounds like a great kid.'

'He is. He's been through hell, Jeff. I want to help him forget.'

He looked at Dana and said, 'I'd like to help, too.'

That night they made love for the first time.

Sixteen

There are two Washington, D.C.'s. One is a city of inordinate beauty: imposing architecture, world-class museums, statues, monuments to the giants of the past: Lincoln, Jefferson, Washington ... a city of verdant parks, cherry blossoms, and velvet air.

The other Washington, D.C., is a citadel of the homeless, a city with one of the highest crime rates in the nation, a labyrinth of muggings and murders.

The Monroe Arms is an elegant boutique hotel discreetly tucked away not far from the corner of 27th and K streets. It does no advertising and caters mainly to its regular clientele. The hotel was built a number of years ago by an enterprising young real estate entrepreneur named Lara Cameron.

Jeremy Robinson, the hotel's general manager, had just arrived on his evening shift and was studying the guest register with a perplexed expression on his face. He checked the names of the occupants of the elite Terrace

Suites once again to make certain someone had not made a mistake.

In Suite 325, a faded actress was rehearsing for a play opening at the National Theater. According to a story in *The Washington Post*, she was hoping to make a comeback.

In 425, the suite above hers, was a well-known arms dealer who visited Washington regularly. The name on the guest register was J. L. Smith, but his looks suggested one of the Middle East countries. Mr Smith was an extraordinarily generous tipper.

Suite 525 was registered to William Quint, a congressman who headed the powerful drug oversight committee.

Above, Suite 625 was occupied by a computer software salesman who visited Washington once a month.

Registered in Suite 725 was Pat Murphy, an international lobbyist.

So far, so good, Jeremy Robinson thought. The guests were all well known to him. It was Suite 825, the Imperial Suite on the top floor, that was the enigma. It was the most elegant suite in the hotel, and it was always held in reserve for the most important VIPs. It occupied the entire floor and was exquisitely decorated with valuable paintings and antiques. It had its own private elevator leading to the basement garage, so that its guests who wished to be anonymous could arrive and depart in privacy.

What puzzled Jeremy Robinson was the name on the

hotel register: Eugene Gant. Was there actually a person by that name, or had someone who enjoyed reading Thomas Wolfe selected it as an alias?

Carl Gorman, the day clerk who had registered the eponymous Mr Gant, had left on his vacation a few hours earlier, and was unreachable. Robinson hated mysteries. Who was Eugene Gant and why had he been given the Imperial Suite?

In Suite 325, on the third floor, Dame Gisella Barrett was rehearsing for a play. She was a distinguished-looking woman in her late sixties, an actress who had once mesmerized audiences and critics from London's West End to Manhattan's Broadway. There were still faint traces of beauty in her face, but they were overlaid with bitterness.

She had read the article in *The Washington Post* that said she had come to Washington to make a comeback. *A comeback!* Dame Barrett thought indignantly. *How dare they! I've never been away.*

True, it had been more than twenty years since she had last appeared onstage, but that was only because a great actress needed a great part, a brilliant director, and an understanding producer. The directors today were too young to cope with the grandeur of real Theater, and the great English producers – H. M. Tenant, Binkie Beaumont, C. B. Cochran – were all gone. Even the reasonably competent American producers, Helburn, Belasco, and Golden, were no longer around. There was no question about it: The current theater was controlled by know-nothing parvenus with no background. The old days had been so wonderful. There were playwrights back then whose pens were dipped in lightning. Dame Barrett had starred in the part of Ellie Dunn in Shaw's *Heartbreak House*.

How the critics raved about me. Poor George. He hated to be called George. He preferred Bernard. People thought of him as acerbic and bitter, but underneath it all, he was really a romantic Irishman. He used to send me red roses. I think he was too shy to go beyond that. Perhaps he was afraid I would reject him.

She was about to make her return in one of the most powerful roles ever written – Lady Macbeth. It was the perfect choice for her.

Dame Barrett placed a chair in front of a blank wall, so that she would not be distracted by the view outside. She sat down, took a deep breath, and began to get into the character Shakespeare had created.

> '*Come, you spirits*
> *That tend on mortal thoughts! Unsex me here,*
> *And fill me from the crown to the toe top-full*
> *Of direst cruelty; make thick my blood,*
> *Stop up the access and passage to remorse,*
> *That no compunctious visitings of nature*
> *Shake my fell purpose, nor keep peace between*
> *The effect and it!*'

'. . . For God's sake, how can they be so stupid? After

all the years I have been staying in this hotel, you would think that . . .'

The voice was booming through the open window, from the suite above.

In Suite 425, J.L. Smith, the arms dealer, was loudly berating a waiter from room service. '. . . they would know by now that I order only Beluga caviar. Beluga!' He pointed to a plate of caviar on the room-service table. 'That is a dish fit for peasants!'

'I'm so sorry, Mr Smith. I'll go down to the kitchen and –'

'Never mind.' J.L. Smith looked at his diamond-studded Rolex. 'I have no time. I have an important appointment.' He rose and started toward the door. He was due at his attorney's office. A day earlier, a federal grand jury had indicted him on fifteen counts of giving illegal gifts to the secretary of defense. If found guilty, he was facing three years in prison and a million-dollar fine.

In Suite 525, Congressman William Quint, a member of a prominent third-generation Washington family, was in conference with three members of his investigating staff.

'The drug problem in this city is getting completely out of hand,' Quint said. 'We have to get it back under control.' He turned to Dalton Isaak. 'What's your take on it?'

'It's the street gangs. The Brentwood Crew is under-cutting the Fourteenth Street Crew and the Simple City Crew. That's led to four killings in the last month.'

'We can't let this go on,' Quint said. 'It's bad for business. I've been getting calls from the DEA and the chief of police asking what we're planning to do about it.'

'What did you tell them?'

'The usual. That we're investigating.' He turned to his assistant. 'Set up a meeting with the Brentwood Crew. Tell them if they want protection from us, they're going to have to get their prices in line with the others.' He turned to another of his assistants. 'How much did we take in last month?'

'Ten million here, ten million offshore.'

'Let's bump that up. This city is getting too damned expensive.'

In 625, the suite above, Norman Haff lay naked in the dark in bed, watching a porno film on the hotel's closed-circuit channel. He was a pale-skinned man with an enormous beer belly and a flabby body. He reached over and stroked the breast of his bedmate.

'Look what they're doing, Irma.' His voice was a strangled whisper. 'Would you like me to do that to you?' He circled his fingers around her belly, his eyes fastened to the screen where a woman was making passionate love to a man. 'Does that excite you, baby? It sure gets me hot.'

He slipped two fingers between Irma's legs. 'I'm ready,' he groaned. He grabbed the inflated doll, rolled over, and pushed himself into her. The vagina of the battery-operated doll opened and closed on him, squeezing him tighter and tighter.

'Oh, my God!' he exclaimed. He gave a satisfied groan. 'Yes! Yes!'

He switched off the battery and lay there panting. He felt wonderful. He would use Irma again in the morning before he deflated her and put her in a suitcase.

Norman was a salesman, and he was on the road most of the time in strange towns where he had no companionship. He had discovered Irma years ago, and she was all the female company he needed. His stupid salesmen friends traveled around the country picking up sluts and professional whores, but Norman had the last laugh.

Irma would never give him a disease.

On the floor above, in Suite 725, Pat Murphy's family had just come back from dinner. Tim Murphy, twelve, was standing on the balcony overlooking the park. 'Tomorrow can we climb up to the top of the monument, Daddy?' he begged. 'Please?'

His younger brother said, 'No. I want to go to the Smithsonian Institute.'

'Institution,' his father corrected him.

'Whatever. I want to go.'

It was the first time the children had been in the nation's capital, although their father spent more than half of every year there. Pat Murphy was a successful lobbyist and had access to some of the most important people in Washington.

His father had been the mayor of a small town in Ohio, and Pat had grown up fascinated by politics. His best friend had been a boy named Joey. They had gone through school together, had gone to the same summer camps, and had shared everything. They were best friends in the truest sense of the phrase. That had all changed one holiday when Joey's parents were away and Joey was staying with the Murphys. In the middle of the night, Joey had come to Pat's room and climbed into his bed.

'Pat,' he whispered. 'Wake up.'

Pat's eyes had flown open. 'What? What's the matter?'

'I'm lonely,' Joey whispered. 'I need you.'

Pat Murphy was confused. 'What for?'

'Don't you understand? I love you. I want you.' And he had kissed Pat on the lips.

And the horrible realization had dawned that Joey was a homosexual. Pat was sickened by it. He refused ever to speak to Joey again.

Pat Murphy loathed homosexuals. They were freaks, faggots, fairies, cursed by God, trying to seduce innocent children. He turned his hatred and disgust into a lifelong campaign, voting for antihomosexual candidates and lecturing about the evils and dangers of homosexuality.

In the past, he had always come to Washington alone, but this time his wife had stubbornly insisted that he bring her and the children.

'We want to see what your life here is like,' she said. And Pat had finally given in.

He looked at his wife and children now and thought, *It's one of the last times I'll ever see them. How could I have ever made such a stupid mistake? Well, it's almost over now.* His family had such grand plans for tomorrow. But there would be no tomorrow. In the morning, before they were awake, he would be on his way to Brazil.

Alan was waiting for him.

In Suite 825, the Imperial Suite, there was total silence. *Breathe*, he told himself. *You must breathe . . . slower, slower . . .* He was at the edge of panic. He looked at the slim, naked body of the young girl on the floor and thought, *It wasn't my fault. She slipped.*

Her head had split open where she had fallen against the sharp edge of the wrought-iron table, and blood was oozing from her forehead. He had felt her wrist. There was no pulse. It was incredible. One moment she had been so alive, and the next moment . . .

I've got to get out of here. Now! He turned away from the body and hurriedly began to dress. This would not be just another scandal. This would be a scandal that rocked the world. *They must never trace me to this suite.*

When he finished dressing, he went into the bathroom, moistened a towel, and began polishing the surfaces of every place he might have touched.

When he was finally sure he had left no fingerprints to mark his presence, he took one last look around. Her purse! He picked up the girl's purse from the couch, and walked to the far end of the apartment, where the private elevator waited.

He stepped inside, trying hard to control his breathing. He pressed G, and a few seconds later, the elevator door opened and he was in the garage. It was deserted. He started toward his car, then, suddenly remembering, hurried back to the elevator. He took out his handkerchief and wiped his fingerprints from the elevator buttons. He stood in the shadows, looking around again to make sure he was still alone. Finally satisfied, he walked over to his car, opened the door, and sat behind the wheel. After a moment, he turned on the ignition and drove out of the garage.

It was a Filipina maid who found the dead girl's body sprawled on the floor.

'O Dios ko, kawawa naman iyong babae!' She made the sign of the cross and hurried out of the room, screaming for help.

Three minutes later, Jeremy Robinson and Thom Peters, the hotel's head of security, were in the Imperial Suite staring down at the naked body of the girl.

'Jesus,' Thom said. 'She can't be more than sixteen or seventeen years old.' He turned to the manager. 'We'd better call the police.'

'Wait!' *Police. Newspapers. Publicity.* For one wild moment, Robinson wondered whether it would be possible to spirit the girl's body out of the hotel. 'I suppose so,' he finally said reluctantly.

Thom Peters took a handkerchief from his pocket and used it to pick up the telephone.

'What are you doing?' Robinson demanded. 'This isn't a crime scene. It was an accident.'

'We don't know that yet, do we?' Peters said.

He dialed a number and waited. 'Homicide.'

Detective Nick Reese looked like the paperback version of a street-smart cop. He was tall and brawny, with a broken nose that was a memento from an early boxing career. He had paid his dues by starting as an officer in Washington's Metropolitan Police Department and had slowly worked his way through the ranks: Master Patrol Officer, Sergeant, Lieutenant. He had been promoted from Detective D2 to Detective D1, and in the past ten years had solved more cases than anyone else in the department.

Detective Reese stood there quietly studying the scene. In the suite with him were half a dozen men. 'Has anyone touched her?'

Robinson shuddered. 'No.'

'Who is she?'

'I don't know.'

Reese turned to look at the hotel manager. 'A young girl is found dead in your Imperial Suite, and you don't have any idea who she is? Doesn't this hotel have a guest register?'

'Of course, Detective, but in this case –' He hesitated.

'In this case . . . ?'

'The suite is registered to a Eugene Gant.'

'Who's Eugene Gant?'

'I have no idea.'

Detective Reese was getting impatient. 'Look. If someone booked this suite, he had to have paid for it . . . cash, credit card – sheep – whatever. Whoever checked this Gant in must have gotten a look at him. Who checked him in?'

'Our day clerk, Gorman.'

'I want to talk to him.'

'I – I'm afraid that's impossible.'

'Oh? Why?'

'He left on his vacation today.'

'Call him.'

Robinson sighed. 'He didn't say where he was going.'

'When will he be back?'

'In two weeks.'

'I'll let you in on a little secret. I'm not planning to wait two weeks. I want some information now. Somebody must have seen someone entering or leaving this suite.'

'Not necessarily,' Robinson said apologetically. 'Besides the regular exit, this suite has a private elevator that goes

239

directly to the basement garage ... I don't know what the fuss is all about. It – it was obviously an accident. She was probably on drugs and took an overdose and tripped and fell.'

Another detective approached Detective Reese. 'I checked the closets. Her dress is from the Gap, shoes from the Wild Pair. No help there.'

'There's nothing to identify her at all?'

'No. If she had a purse, it's gone.'

Detective Reese studied the body again. He turned to a police officer standing there. 'Get me some soap. Wet it.'

The police officer was staring at him. 'I'm sorry?'

'Wet soap.'

'Yes, sir.' He hurried off.

Detective Reese knelt down beside the body of the girl and studied the ring on her finger. 'It looks like a school ring.'

A minute later, the police officer returned and handed Reese a bar of wet soap.

Reese gently rubbed the soap along the girl's finger and carefully removed the ring. He turned it from side to side, examining it. 'It's a class ring from Denver High. There are initials on it, P.Y.' He turned to his partner. 'Check it out. Call the school and find out who she is. Let's get an ID on her as fast as we can.'

Detective Ed Nelson, one of the fingerprint men, came up to Detective Reese. 'Something damned weird is going on, Nick. We're picking up prints all over the place, and yet someone took the trouble to wipe the fingerprints off all the doorknobs.'

'So someone was here with her when she died. Why didn't he call a doctor? Why did he bother wiping out his fingerprints? And what the hell is a young kid doing in an expensive suite like this?'

He turned to Robinson. 'How was this suite paid for?'

'Our records show that it was paid for in cash. A messenger delivered the envelope. The reservation was made over the phone.'

The coroner spoke up. 'Can we move the body now, Nick?'

'Just hold it a minute. Did you find any marks of violence?'

'Only the trauma to the forehead. But of course we'll do an autopsy.'

'Any track marks?'

'No. Her arms and legs are clean.'

'Does it look like she's been raped?'

'We'll have to check that out.'

Detective Reese sighed. 'So what we have here is a school-girl from Denver who comes to Washington and gets herself killed in one of the most expensive hotels in the city. Someone wipes out his fingerprints and disappears. The whole thing stinks. I want to know who rented this suite.'

He turned to the coroner. 'You can take her out now.' He looked at Detective Nelson. 'Did you check the fingerprints in the private elevator?'

'Yes. The elevator goes from this suite directly to the basement. There are only two buttons. Both buttons have been wiped clean.'

'You checked the garage?'

'Right. Nothing unusual down there.'

'Whoever did this went to a hell of a lot of trouble to cover his tracks. He's either someone with a record, or a VIP who's been playing games out of school.' He turned to Robinson. 'Who usually rents this suite?'

Robinson said reluctantly, 'It's reserved for our most important guests. Kings, prime ministers . . .' He hesitated. '. . . Presidents.'

'Have any telephone calls been placed from this phone in the last twenty-four hours?'

'I don't know.'

Detective Reese was getting irritated. 'But you would have a record if there was?'

'Of course.'

Detective Reese picked up the telephone. 'Operator, this is Detective Nick Reese. I want to know if any calls were made from the Imperial Suite within the last twenty-four hours . . . I'll wait.'

He watched as the white-coated coroner's men covered the naked girl with a sheet and placed her on a gurney. *Jesus Christ*, Reese thought. *She hadn't even begun to live yet.*

He heard the operator's voice. 'Detective Reese?'

'Yes.'

'There was one call placed from the suite yesterday. It was a local call.'

Reese took out a notepad and pencil. 'What was the number? . . . Four-five-six-seven-zero-four-one? . . .' Reese started to write the numbers down, then suddenly stopped. He was staring at the notepad. 'Oh, shit!'

'What's the matter?' Detective Nelson asked.

Reese looked up. 'That's the number of the White House.'

Seventeen

The next morning at breakfast, Jan asked, 'Where were you last night, Oliver?'

Oliver's heart skipped a beat. But she could not possibly have known what happened. No one could. No one. 'I was meeting with –'

Jan cut him short. 'The meeting was called off. But you didn't get home until three o'clock in the morning. I tried to reach you. Where were you?'

'Well, something came up. Why? Did you need –? Was something wrong?'

'It doesn't matter now,' Jan said wearily. 'Oliver, you're not just hurting me, you're hurting yourself. You've come so far. I don't want to see you lose it all because – because you can't –' Her eyes filled with tears.

Oliver stood up and walked over to her. He put his arms around her. 'It's all right, Jan. Everything's fine. I love you very much.'

And I do, Oliver thought, *in my own way. What happened last night wasn't my fault. She was the one who called. I never should have gone to meet her.* He had taken every possible precaution not to be seen. *I'm in the clear*, Oliver decided.

Peter Tager was worried about Oliver. He had learned that it was impossible to control Oliver Russell's libido, and he had finally worked out an arrangement with him. On certain nights, Peter Tager set up fictitious meetings for the president to attend, away from the White House, and arranged for the Secret Service escort to disappear for a few hours.

When Peter Tager had gone to Senator Davis to complain about what was happening, the senator had said calmly, 'Well, after all, Oliver is a very hot-blooded man, Peter. Sometimes it's impossible to control passions like that. I deeply admire your morals, Peter. I know how much your family means to you, and how distasteful the president's behavior must seem to you. But let's not be too judgmental. You just keep on seeing that everything is handled as discreetly as possible.'

Detective Nick Reese hated going into the forbidding, whitewalled autopsy room. It smelled of formaldehyde and death. When he walked in the door, the coroner, Helen Chuan, a petite, attractive woman, was waiting for him.

'Morning,' Reese said. 'Have you finished with the autopsy?'

'I have a preliminary report for you, Nick. Jane Doe didn't die from her head injury. Her heart stopped before she hit the table. She died of an overdose of methylenedioxymethamphetamine.'

He sighed. 'Don't do this to me, Helen.'

'Sorry. On the streets, it's called Ecstasy.' She handed him a coroner's report 'Here's what we have so far.'

AUTOPSY PROTOCOL
NAME OF DECEDENT: JANE DOE FILE NO: C-L96I

ANATOMIC SUMMARY
I. DILATED AND HYPERTROPHIC CARDIOMYOPATHY
  A. CARDIOMEGALY (750 GM)
  B. LEFT VENTRICULAR HYPERTROPHY, HEART (2.3 CM)
  C. CONGESTIVE HEPATOMEGALY (2750 gm)
  D. CONGESTIVE SPLENOMEGALY (350 mg)
II. ACUTE OPIATE INTOXICATION
  A. ACUTE PASSIVE CONGESTION, ALL VISCERA
III. TOXICOLOGY (SEE SEPARATE REPORT)
IV. BRAIN HEMORRHAGE (SEE SEPARATE REPORT)
CONCLUSION: (CAUSE OF DEATH)

DILATED AND HYPERTROPHIC CARDIO-
MYOPATHY
ACUTE OPIATE INTOXICATION

Nick Reese looked up. 'So if you translated this into English, she died of a drug overdose of Ecstasy?'

'Yes.'

'Was she sexually assaulted?'

Helen Chuan hesitated. 'Her hymen had been broken, and there were traces of semen and a little blood along her thighs.'

'So she was raped.'

'I don't think so.'

'What do you mean – you don't think so?' Reese frowned.

'There were no signs of violence.'

Detective Reese was looking at her, puzzled. 'What are you saying?'

'I think that Jane Doe was a virgin. This was her first sexual experience.'

Detective Reese stood there, digesting the information. Someone had been able to persuade a virgin to go up to the Imperial Suite and have sex with him. It would have had to be someone she knew. Or someone famous or powerful.

The telephone rang. Helen Chuan picked it up. 'Coroner's office.' She listened a moment, then handed the phone to the detective. 'It's for you.'

Nick Reese took the phone. 'Reese.' His face brightened.

'Oh, yes, Mrs Holbrook. Thanks for returning my call. It's a class ring from your school with the initials P.Y. on it. Do you have a female student with those initials? . . . I'd appreciate it. Thank you. I'll wait.'

He looked up at the coroner. 'You're sure she couldn't have been raped?'

'I found no signs of violence. None.'

'Could she have been penetrated after she died?'

'I would say no.'

Mrs Holbrook's voice came back on the phone. 'Detective Reese?'

'Yes.'

'According to our computer, we do have a female student with the initials P.Y. Her name is Pauline Young.'

'Could you describe her for me, Mrs Holbrook?'

'Why, yes. Pauline is eighteen. She's short and stocky, with dark hair . . .'

'I see.' *Wrong girl.* 'And that's the only one?'

'The only female, yes.'

He picked up on it. 'You mean you have a male with those initials?

'Yes. Paul Yerby. He's a senior. As a matter of fact, Paul happens to be in Washington, D.C., right now.'

Detective Reese's heart began to beat faster. 'He's here?'

'Yes. A class of students from Denver High is on a trip to Washington to visit the White House and Congress and –'

'And they're all in the city now?'

'That's right.'

248

'Do you happen to know where they're staying?'

'At the Hotel Lombardy. They gave us a group rate there. I talked with several of the other hotels, but they wouldn't –'

'Thank you very much, Mrs Holbrook. I appreciate it.'

Nick Reese replaced the receiver and turned to the coroner. 'Let me know when the autopsy is complete, will you, Helen?'

'Of course. Good luck, Nick.'

He nodded. 'I think I've just had it.'

The Hotel Lombardy is located on Pennsylvania Avenue, two blocks from Washington Circle and within walking distance of the White House, some monuments, and a subway station. Detective Reese walked into the old-fashioned lobby and approached the clerk behind the desk. 'Do you have a Paul Yerby registered here?'

'I'm sorry. We don't give out –'

Reese flashed his badge. 'I'm in a big hurry, friend.'

'Yes, sir.' The clerk looked through his guest register. 'There's a Mr Yerby in Room 315. Shall I –?'

'No, I'll surprise him. Stay away from the phone.'

Reese took the elevator, got off on the third floor, and walked down the corridor. He stopped before Room 315. He could hear voices inside. He unfastened the button of his jacket and knocked on the door. It was opened by a boy in his late teens.

'Hello.'

'Paul Yerby?'

'No.' The boy turned to someone in the room. 'Paul, someone for you.'

Nick Reese pushed his way into the room. A slim, tousle-haired boy in jeans and a sweater was coming out of the bathroom.

'Paul Yerby?'

'Yes. Who are you?'

Reese pulled out his badge. 'Detective Nick Reese. Homicide.'

The boy's complexion turned pale. 'I – what can I do for you?'

Nick Reese could smell the fear. He took the dead girl's ring from his pocket and held it out. 'Have you ever seen this ring before, Paul?'

'No,' Yerby said quickly. 'I –'

'It has your initials on it.'

'It has? Oh. Yeah.' He hesitated. 'I guess it could be mine. I must have lost it somewhere.'

'Or given it to someone?'

The boy licked his lips, 'Uh, yeah. I might have.'

'Let's go downtown, Paul.'

The boy looked at him nervously. 'Am I under arrest?'

'What for?' Detective Reese asked. 'Have you committed a crime?'

'Of course not. I . . .' The words trailed off.

'Then why would I arrest you?'

'I – I don't know. I don't know why you want me to go downtown.'

He was eyeing the open door. Detective Reese reached out and took a grip on Paul's arm. 'Let's go quietly.'

The roommate said, 'Do you want me to call your mother or anybody, Paul?'

Paul Yerby shook his head, miserable. 'No. Don't call anyone.' His voice was a whisper.

The Henry I. Daly Building at 300 Indiana Avenue, NW, in downtown Washington is an unprepossessing six-story gray brick building that serves as police headquarters for the district. The Homicide Branch office is on the third floor. While Paul Yerby was being photographed and fingerprinted, Detective Reese went to see Captain Otto Miller.

'I think we got a break in the Monroe Arms case.'

Miller leaned back in his chair. 'Go on.'

'I picked up the girl's boyfriend. The kid's scared out of his wits. We're going to question him now. Do you want to sit in?'

Captain Miller nodded toward a pile of papers heaped on his desk. 'I'm busy for the next few months. Give me a report.'

'Right.' Detective Reese started toward the door.

'Nick – be sure to read him his rights.'

Paul Yerby was brought into an interrogation room. It was small, nine by twelve, with a battered desk, four chairs, and a video camera. There was a one-way mirror so that officers could watch the interrogation from the next room.

Paul Yerby was facing Nick Reese and two other detectives, Doug Hogan and Edgar Bernstein.

'You're aware that we're videotaping this conversation?' – Detective Reese

'Yes, sir.'

'You have the right to an attorney. If you cannot afford an attorney, one will be appointed to represent you.'

'Would you like to have a lawyer present?' – Detective Bernstein

'I don't need a lawyer.'

'All right. You have a right to remain silent. If you waive that right, anything you say here can and will be used against you in a court of law. Is that clear?'

'Yes, sir.'

'What's your legal name?'

'Paul Yerby.'

'Your address?'

'Three-twenty Marion Street, Denver, Colorado. Look, I haven't done anything wrong. I –'

'No one says you have. We're just trying to get some information, Paul. You'd like to help us, wouldn't you?'

'Sure, but I – I don't know what it's all about.'

'Don't you have any idea?'

'No, sir.'

'Do you have any girlfriends, Paul?'

'Well, you know . . .'

'No, we don't know. Why don't you tell us?'

'Well, sure. I see girls . . .'

'You mean you date girls? You take girls out?'

'Yeah.'

'Do you date any one particular girl?'

There was a silence.

'Do you have a girlfriend, Paul?'

'Yes.'

'What's her name?' – Detective Bernstein

'Chloe.'

'Chloe what?' – Detective Reese

'Chloe Houston.'

Reese made a note. 'What's her address, Paul?'

'Six-oh-two Oak Street, Denver.'

'What are her parents' names?'

'She lives with her mother.'

'And her name?'

'Jackie Houston. She's the governor of Colorado.'

The detectives looked at one another. *Shit! That's all we need!*

Reese held up a ring. 'Is this your ring, Paul?'

He studied it a moment, then said reluctantly, 'Yeah.'

'Did you give Chloe this ring?'

He swallowed nervously. 'I – I guess I did.'

'You're not sure?'

'I remember now. Yes, I did.'

'You came to Washington with some classmates, right? Kind of a school group?'

'That's right.'

'Was Chloe part of that group?'

'Yes, sir.'

'Where's Chloe now, Paul?' – Detective Bernstein

'I – I don't know.'

'When did you last see her?' – Detective Hogan

'I guess a couple of days ago.'

'Two days ago?' – Detective Reese

'Yeah.'

'And where was that?' – Detective Bernstein

'In the White House.'

The detectives looked at one another in surprise. 'She was in the White House?' Reese asked.

'Yes, sir. We were all on a private tour. Chloe's mother arranged it.'

'And Chloe was with you?' – Detective Hogan

'Yes.'

'Did anything unusual happen on the tour?' – Detective Bernstein

'What do you mean?'

'Did you meet or talk to anyone on the tour?' – Detective Bernstein

'Well, sure, the guide.'

'And that's all?' – Detective Reese

'That's right.'

'Was Chloe with the group all the time?' – Detective Hogan

'Yes –' Yerby hesitated. 'No. She slipped away to go to the ladies' room. She was gone about fifteen minutes. When she came back, she –' He stopped.

'She what?' Reese asked.

'Nothing. She just came back.'

The boy was obviously lying.

'Son,' Detective Reese asked, 'do you know that Chloe Houston is dead?'

They were watching him closely. 'No! My God! How?' The surprised look on his face could have been feigned.

'Don't you know?' – Detective Bernstein

'No! I – I can't believe it.'

'You had nothing to do with her death?' – Detective Hogan

'Of course not! I love . . . I loved Chloe.'

'Did you ever go to bed with her?' – Detective Bernstein

'No. We – we were waiting. We were going to get married.'

'But sometimes you did drugs together?' – Detective Reese

'No! We never did drugs.'

The door opened and a burly detective, Harry Carter, came into the room. He walked over to Reese and whispered something in his ear. Reese nodded. He sat there staring at Paul Yerby.

'When was the last time you saw Chloe Houston?'

'I told you, in the White House.' He shifted uncomfortably in his chair.

Detective Reese leaned forward. 'You're in a lot of

trouble, Paul. Your fingerprints are all over the Imperial Suite at the Monroe Arms Hotel. How did they get there?'

Paul Yerby sat there, pale-faced.

'You can quit lying now. We've got you nailed.'

'I – I didn't do anything.'

'Did you book the suite at the Monroe Arms?' – Detective Bernstein

'No, I didn't.' The emphasis was on the 'I.'

Detective Reese pounced on it. 'But you know who did?'

'No.' The answer came too quickly.

'You admit you were in the suite?' – Detective Hogan

'Yes, but – but Chloe was alive when I left.'

'Why did you leave?' – Detective Hogan

'She asked me to. She – she was expecting someone.'

'Come on, Paul. We know you killed her.' – Detective Bernstein

'No!' He was trembling. 'I swear I had nothing to do with it. I – I just went up to the suite with her. I only stayed a little while.'

'Because she was expecting someone?' – Detective Reese

'Yes. She – she was kind of excited.'

'Did she tell you who she was going to meet?' – Detective Hogan

He was licking his lips. 'No.'

'You're lying. She did tell you.'

'You said she was excited. What about?' – Detective Reese

Paul licked his lips again. 'About – about the man she was going to meet there for dinner.'

'Who was the man, Paul?' – Detective Bernstein

'I can't tell you.'

'Why not?' – Detective Hogan

'I promised Chloe I would never tell anyone.'

'Chloe is dead.'

Paul Yerby's eyes filled with tears. 'I just can't believe it.'

'Give us the man's name.' – Detective Reese

'I can't do that. I promised.'

'Here's what's going to happen to you: You're going to spend tonight in jail. In the morning, if you give us the name of the man she was going to meet, we'll let you go. Otherwise, we're going to book you for murder one.' – Detective Reese

They waited for him to speak.

Silence.

Nick Reese nodded to Bernstein. 'Take him away.'

Detective Reese returned to Captain Miller's office.

'I have bad news and I have worse news.'

'I haven't time for this, Nick.'

'The bad news is that I'm not sure it was the boy who gave her the drug. The worse news is that the girl's mother is the governor of Colorado.'

'Oh, God! The papers will love this.' Captain Miller took a deep breath. 'Why don't you think the boy's guilty?'

'He admits he was in the girl's suite, but he said she told him to leave because she was expecting someone. I think the kid's too smart to come up with a story that stupid. What I do believe is that he knows who Chloe Houston was expecting. He won't say who it was.'

'Do you have any idea?'

'It was her first time in Washington, and they were on a tour of the White House. She didn't know anyone here. She said she was going to the ladies' room. There is no public rest room in the White House. She would have had to go outside to the Visitor's Pavilion on the Ellipse at 15th and E streets or to the White House Visitor Center. She was gone about fifteen minutes. What I think happened is that while trying to find a ladies' room, she ran into someone in the White House, someone she might have recognized. Maybe someone she saw on TV. Anyway, it must have been somebody important. He led her to a private washroom and impressed her enough that she agreed to meet him at the Monroe Arms.'

Captain Miller was thoughtful. 'I'd better call the White House. They asked to be kept up-to-date on this. Don't let up on the kid. I want that name.'

'Right.'

As Detective Reese walked out the door, Captain Miller reached for the telephone and dialed a number. A few minutes later, he was saying, 'Yes, sir. We have a material witness in custody. He's in a holding cell at the Indiana Avenue police station . . . We won't, sir. I think the boy will give us the man's name tomorrow . . . Yes, sir. I understand.' The line went dead.

Captain Miller sighed and went back to the pile of papers on his desk.

At eight o'clock the following morning, when Detective Nick Reese went to Paul Yerby's cell, Yerby's body was hanging from one of the top bars.

Eighteen

Dead 16-year-old identified as daugh-ter of Colorado governor

Boyfriend in police custody hangs himself

Police hunt mystery witness

He stared at the headlines and felt suddenly faint. Sixteen years old. She had looked older than that. What was he guilty of? Murder? Manslaughter, maybe. Plus statutory rape.

He had watched her come out of the bathroom of the suite, wearing only a shy smile. *'I've never done this before.'*

And he had put his arms around her and stroked her. *'I'm glad the first time is with me, honey.'* Earlier, he had shared a glass of liquid Ecstasy with her. *'Drink this. It will make you feel good.'* They had made love, and afterward she had complained about not feeling well. She had gotten out of bed, stumbled, and hit her head against the table. An accident. Of course, the police would not see it that way. *But there's nothing to connect me with her. Nothing.*

The whole episode had an air of unreality, a nightmare that had happened to someone else. Somehow, seeing it in print made it real.

Through the walls of the office, he could hear the sound of traffic on Pennsylvania Avenue, outside the White House, and he became aware again of his surroundings. A cabinet meeting was scheduled to begin in a few minutes. He took a deep breath. *Pull yourself together.*

In the Oval Office were gathered Vice President Melvin Wicks, Sime Lombardo, and Peter Tager.

Oliver walked in and sat behind his desk. 'Good morning, gentlemen.'

There were general greetings.

Peter Tager said, 'Have you seen the *Tribune*, Mr President?'

'No.'

'They've identified the girl who died at the Monroe Arms Hotel. I'm afraid it's bad news.'

Oliver unconsciously stiffened in his chair. 'Yes?'

'Her name is Chloe Houston. She's the daughter of Jackie Houston.'

'Oh, my God!' The words barely escaped the president's lips.

They were staring at him, surprised at his reaction. He

recovered quickly. 'I – I knew Jackie Houston . . . a long time ago. This – this is terrible news. Terrible.'

Sime Lombardo said, 'Even though Washington crime is not our responsibility, the *Tribune* is going to hammer us on this.'

Melvin Wicks spoke up. 'Is there any way we can shut Leslie Stewart up?'

Oliver thought of the passionate evening he had spent with her. 'No,' Oliver said. 'Freedom of the press, gentlemen.'

Peter Tager turned to the president. 'About the governor . . . ?'

'I'll handle it.' He flicked down an intercom key. 'Get me Governor Houston in Denver.'

'We've got to start some damage control,' Peter Tager was saying. 'I'll get together statistics on how much crime has gone down in this country, you've asked Congress for more money for our police departments, et cetera.' The words sounded hollow even to his own ears.

'This is terrible timing,' Melvin Wicks said.

The intercom buzzed. Oliver picked up the telephone. 'Yes?' He listened a moment, then replaced the receiver. 'The governor is on her way to Washington.' He looked at Peter Tager. 'Find out what plane she's on, Peter. Meet her and bring her here.'

'Right. There's an editorial in the *Tribune*. It's pretty rough.' Peter Tager handed Oliver the editorial page of the newspaper. PRESIDENT UNABLE TO CONTROL CRIME IN THE CAPITAL. 'It goes on from there.'

'Leslie Stewart is a bitch,' Sime Lombardo said quietly. 'Someone should have a little talk with her.'

In his office at the *Washington Tribune*, Matt Baker was re-reading the editorial attacking the president for being soft on crime when Frank Lonergan walked in. Lonergan was in his early forties, a bright, street-smart journalist who had at one time worked on the police force. He was one of the best investigative journalists in the business.

'You wrote this editorial, Frank?'

'Yes,' he said.

'This paragraph about crime going down twenty-five percent in Minnesota, that's still bothering me. Why did you just talk about Minnesota?'

Lonergan said, 'It was a suggestion from the Ice Princess.'

'That's ridiculous,' Matt Baker snapped. 'I'll talk to her.'

Leslie Stewart was on the telephone when Matt Baker walked into her office.

'I'll leave it to you to arrange the details, but I want us to raise as much money for him as we can. As a matter of fact, Senator Embry of Minnesota is stopping by for lunch today, and I'll get a list of names from him. Thank you.' She replaced the receiver. 'Matt.'

Matt Baker walked over to her desk. 'I want to talk to you about this editorial.'

'It's good, isn't it?'

'It stinks, Leslie. It's propaganda. The president's not responsible for controlling crime in Washington, D.C. We have a mayor who's supposed to do that, and a police force. And what's this crap about crime going down twenty-five percent in Minnesota? Where did you come up with those statistics?'

Leslie Stewart leaned back and said calmly, 'Matt, this is my paper. I'll say anything I want to say. Oliver Russell is a lousy president, and Gregory Embry would make a great one. We're going to help him get into the White House.'

She saw the expression on Matt's face and softened. 'Come on, Matt. The *Tribune* is going to be on the side of the winner. Embry will be good for us. He's on his way here now. Would you like to join us for lunch?'

'No. I don't like people who eat with their hands out.' He turned and left the office.

In the corridor outside, Matt Baker ran into Senator Embry. The senator was in his fifties, a self-important politician.

'Oh, Senator! Congratulations.'

Senator Embry looked at him, puzzled, 'Thank you. Er – for what?'

'For bringing crime down twenty-five percent in your state.' And Matt Baker walked away, leaving the senator looking after him with a blank expression on his face.

*　　*　　*

Lunch was in Leslie Stewart's antique-furnished dining room. A chef was working in the kitchen preparing lunch as Leslie and Senator Embry walked in. The captain hurried up to greet them.

'Luncheon is ready whenever you wish, Miss Stewart. Would you care for a drink?'

'Not for me,' Leslie said. 'Senator?'

'Well, I don't usually drink during the day, but I'll have a martini.'

Leslie Stewart was aware that Senator Embry drank a lot during the day. She had a complete file on him. He had a wife and five children and kept a Japanese mistress. His hobby was secretly funding a paramilitary group in his home state. None of this was important to Leslie. What mattered was that Gregory Embry was a man who believed in letting big business alone – and Washington Tribune Enterprises was big business. Leslie intended to make it bigger, and when Embry was president, he was going to help her.

They were seated at the dining table. Senator Embry took a sip of his second martini. 'I want to thank you for the fundraiser, Leslie. That's a nice gesture.'

She smiled warmly. 'It's my pleasure. I'll do everything I can to help you beat Oliver Russell.'

'Well, I think I stand a pretty good chance.'

'I think so, too. The people are getting tired of him and his scandals. My guess is that if there's one more scandal between now and election, they'll throw him out.'

Senator Embry studied her a moment. 'Do you think there will be?'

Leslie nodded and said softly, 'I wouldn't be surprised.'

The lunch was delicious.

The call came from Antonio Valdez, an assistant in the coroner's office. 'Miss Stewart, you said you wanted me to keep you informed about the Chloe Houston case?'

'Yes . . .'

'The cops asked us to keep a lid on it, but since you've been such a good friend, I thought –'

'Don't worry. You'll be taken care of. Tell me about the autopsy.'

'Yes, ma'am. The cause of death was a drug called Ecstasy.'

'What?'

'Ecstasy. She took it in liquid form.'

I have a little surprise for you that I want you to try . . . This is liquid Ecstasy . . . A friend of mine gave me this . . .'

And the woman who had been found in the Kentucky River had died of an overdose of liquid Ecstasy.

Leslie sat there motionless, her heart pounding.

There is a God.

Leslie sent for Frank Lonergan. 'I want you to follow up on the death of Chloe Houston. I think the president is involved.'

Frank Lonergan was staring at her incredulously. 'The president?'

'There's a cover-up going on. I'm convinced of it. That boy they arrested, who conveniently committed suicide ... dig into that. And I want you to check on the president's movements the afternoon and evening of her death. I want this to be a private investigation. Very private. You'll report only to me.'

Frank Lonergan took a deep breath. 'You know what this could mean?'

'Get started. And Frank?'

'Yes?'

'Check the Internet for a drug called Ecstasy. And look for a connection with Oliver Russell.'

In a medical Internet site devoted to the hazards of the drug, Lonergan found the story of Miriam Friedland, the former secretary to Oliver Russell. She was in a hospital in Frankfort, Kentucky. Lonergan telephoned to inquire about her. A doctor said, 'Miss Friedland passed away two days ago. She never recovered from her coma.'

Frank Lonergan put in a telephone call to the office of Governor Houston.

'I'm sorry,' her secretary told him, 'Governor Houston is on her way to Washington.'

Ten minutes later, Frank Lonergan was on his way to National Airport. He was too late.

As the passengers descended from the plane, Lonergan saw Peter Tager approach an attractive blonde in her forties and greet her. The two of them talked for a moment, and then Tager led her to a waiting limousine.

Watching in the distance, Lonergan thought, *I've got to talk to that lady.* He headed back toward town and began making calls on his car phone. On the third call, he learned that Governor Houston was expected at the Four Seasons Hotel.

When Jackie Houston was ushered into the private study next to the Oval Office, Oliver Russell was waiting for her.

He took her hands in his and said, 'I'm so terribly sorry, Jackie. There are no words.'

It had been almost seventeen years since he had last seen her. They had met at a lawyers' convention in Chicago. She had just gotten out of law school. She was young and attractive and eager, and they had had a brief, torrid affair.

Seventeen years ago.

And Chloe was sixteen years old.

He dared not ask Jackie the question in his mind. *I don't want to know.* They looked at each other in silence, and for a moment Oliver thought she was going to speak of the past. He looked away.

Jackie Houston said, 'The police think Paul Yerby had something to do with Chloe's death.'

'That's right.'

'No.'

'No?'

'Paul was in love with Chloe. He never would have harmed her.' Her voice broke. 'They – they were going to get married one day.'

'According to my information, Jackie, they found the boy's fingerprints in the hotel room where she was killed.'

Jackie Houston said, 'The newspapers said that it . . . that it happened in the Imperial Suite at the Monroe Arms.'

'Yes.'

'Oliver, Chloe was on a small allowance. Paul's father was a retired clerk. Where did Chloe get the money for the Imperial Suite?'

'I – I don't know.'

'Someone has to find out. I won't leave until I know who is responsible for the death of my daughter.' She frowned. 'Chloe had an appointment to see you that afternoon. Did you see her?'

There was a brief hesitation. 'No. I wish I had. Unfortunately, an emergency came up, and I had to cancel our appointment.'

*   *   *

In an apartment at the other end of town, lying in bed, their naked bodies spooned together, he could feel the tension in her.

'Are you okay, JoAnn?'

'I'm fine, Alex.'

'You seem far away, baby. What are you thinking about?'

'Nothing,' JoAnn McGrath said.

'Nothing?'

'Well, to tell the truth, I was thinking about that poor little girl who was murdered at the hotel.'

'Yeah, I read about it. She was some governor's daughter.'

'Yes.'

'Do the police know who she was with?'

'No. They were all over the hotel questioning everybody.'

'You, too?'

'Yeah. All I could tell them was about the telephone call.'

'What telephone call?'

'The one someone in that suite made to the White House.'

He was suddenly still. He said casually, 'That doesn't mean anything. Everybody gets a kick out of calling the White House. Do that to me again, baby. Got any more maple syrup?'

* * *

Frank Lonergan had just returned to his office from the airport when the phone rang. 'Lonergan.'

'Hello, Mr Lonergan. This is Shallow Throat.' Alex Cooper, a small-time parasite who fancied himself a Watergate-class tipster. It was his idea of a joke. 'Are you still paying for hot tips?'

'Depends on how hot.'

'This one will burn your ass. I want five thousand dollars for it.'

'Goodbye.'

'Wait a minute. Don't hang up. It's about that girl who was murdered at the Monroe Arms.'

Frank Lonergan was suddenly interested. 'What about her?'

'Can you and me meet somewhere?'

'I'll see you at Ricco's in half an hour.'

At two o'clock, Frank Lonergan and Alex Cooper were in a booth at Ricco's. Alex Cooper was a thin weasel of a man, and Lonergan hated doing business with him. Lonergan wasn't sure where Cooper got his information, but he had been very helpful in the past.

'I hope you're not wasting my time,' Lonergan said.

'Oh, I don't think it's a waste of time. How would you feel if I told you there's a White House connection to the girl's murder?' There was a smug smile on his face.

Frank Lonergan managed to conceal his excitement. 'Go on.'

271

'Five thousand dollars?'

'One thousand.'

'Two.'

'You have a deal. Talk.'

'My girlfriend's a telephone operator at the Monroe Arms.'

'What's her name?'

'JoAnn McGrath.'

Lonergan made a note. 'So?'

'Someone in the Imperial Suite made a telephone call to the White House during the time the girl was there.'

I think the president is involved,' Leslie Stewart had said. 'Are you sure about this?'

'Horse's mouth.'

'I'll check it out. If it's true, you'll get your money. Have you mentioned this to anyone else?'

'Nope.'

'Good. Don't.' Lonergan rose. 'We'll keep in touch.'

'There's one more thing,' Cooper said.

Lonergan stopped. 'Yes?'

'You've got to keep me out of this. I don't want JoAnn to know that I talked to anyone about it.'

'No problem.'

And Alex Cooper was alone, thinking about how he was going to spend the two thousand dollars without JoAnn's knowing about it.

The Monroe Arms switchboard was in a cubicle behind

the lobby reception desk. When Lonergan walked in carrying a clipboard, JoAnn McGrath was on duty. She was saying into the mouthpiece, 'I'm ringing for you.'

She connected a call and turned to Lonergan. 'Can I help you?'

'Telephone Company,' Lonergan said. He flashed some identification. 'We have a problem here.'

JoAnn McGrath looked at him, surprised. 'What kind of problem?'

'Someone reported that they're being charged for calls they didn't make.' He pretended to consult the clipboard. 'October fifteenth. They were charged for a call to Germany, and they don't even know anyone in Germany. They're pretty teed off.'

'Well, I don't know anything about that,' JoAnn said indignantly. 'I don't even remember placing any calls to Germany in the last month.'

'Do you have a record of the fifteenth?'

'Of course.'

'I'd like to see it.'

'Very well.' She found a folder under a pile of papers and handed it to him. The switchboard was buzzing. While she attended to the calls, Lonergan quickly went through the folder. October 12th ... 13th ... 14th ... 16th ...

The page for the fifteenth was missing.

Frank Lonergan was waiting in the lobby of the Four

Seasons when Jackie Houston returned from the White House.

'Governor Houston?'

She turned. 'Yes?'

'Frank Lonergan. I'm with the *Washington Tribune*. I want to tell you how sorry all of us are, Governor.'

'Thank you.'

'I wonder if I could talk to you for a minute?'

'I'm really not in the –'

'I might be able to be helpful.' He nodded toward the lounge off the main lobby. 'Could we go in there for a moment?'

She took a deep breath. 'All right.'

They walked into the lounge and sat down.

'I understand that your daughter went on a tour of the White House the day she . . .' He couldn't bring himself to finish the sentence.

'Yes. She – she was on a tour with her school friends. She was very excited about meeting the president.'

Lonergan kept his voice casual. 'She was going to see President Russell?'

'Yes. I arranged it. We're old friends.'

'And did she see him, Governor Houston?'

'No. He wasn't able to see her.' Her voice was choked. 'There's one thing I'm sure of.'

'Yes, ma'am.'

'Paul Yerby didn't kill her. They were in love with each other.'

'But the police said –'

'I don't care what they said. They arrested an innocent boy, and he – he was so upset that he hanged himself. It's awful.'

Frank Lonergan studied her for a moment. 'If Paul Yerby didn't kill your daughter, do you have any idea who might have? I mean, did she say anything about meeting anyone in Washington?'

'No. She didn't know a soul here. She was so looking forward to . . . to . . .' Her eyes brimmed with tears. 'I'm sorry. You'll have to excuse me.'

'Of course. Thanks for your time, Governor Houston.'

Lonergan's next stop was at the morgue. Helen Chuan was just coming out of the autopsy room.

'Well, look who's here.'

'Hi, Doc.'

'What brings you down here, Frank?'

'I wanted to talk to you about Paul Yerby.'

Helen Chuan sighed. 'It's a damn shame. Those kids were both so young.'

'Why would a boy like that commit suicide?'

Helen Chuan shrugged. 'Who knows?'

'I mean – are you sure he committed suicide?'

'If he didn't, he gave a great imitation. His belt was wrapped around his neck so tightly that they had to cut it in half to bring him down.'

'There were no other marks or anything on his body that might have suggested foul play?'

She looked at him, curious. 'No.'

Lonergan nodded. 'Okay. Thanks. You don't want to keep your patients waiting.'

'Very funny.'

There was a phone booth in the outside corridor. From the Denver information operator, Lonergan got the number of Paul Yerby's parents. Mrs Yerby answered the phone. Her voice sounded weary. 'Hello.'

'Mrs Yerby?'

'Yes.'

'I'm sorry to bother you. This is Frank Lonergan. I'm with the *Washington Tribune*. I wanted to –'

'I can't . . .'

A moment later, Mr Yerby was on the line. 'I'm sorry. My wife is . . . Newspapers have been bothering us all morning. We don't want to –'

'This will only take a minute, Mr Yerby. There are some people in Washington who don't believe your son killed Chloe Houston.'

'Of course he didn't!' His voice suddenly became stronger. 'Paul could never, never have done anything like that.'

'Did Paul have any friends in Washington, Mr Yerby?'

'No. He didn't know anyone there.'

'I see. Well, if there's anything I can do . . .'

'There is something you can do for us, Mr Lonergan. We've arranged to have Paul's body shipped back here, but I'm not sure how to get his possessions. We'd like to have whatever he ... If you could tell me who to talk to ...'

'I can handle that for you.'

'We'd appreciate it. Thank you.'

In the Homicide Branch office, the sergeant on duty was opening a carton containing Paul Yerby's personal effects. 'There's not much in it,' he said. 'Just the kid's clothes and a camera.'

Lonergan reached into the box and picked up a black leather belt.

It was uncut.

When Frank Lonergan walked into the office of President Russell's appointments secretary, Deborah Kanner, she was getting ready to leave for lunch.

'What can I do for you, Frank?'

'I've got a problem, Deborah.'

'What else is new?'

Frank Lonergan pretended to look at some notes. 'I have information that on October fifteenth the president had a secret meeting here with an emissary from China to talk about Tibet.'

'I don't know of any such meeting.'

'Could you just check it out for me?'

'What did you say the date was?'

'October fifteenth.' Lonergan watched as Deborah pulled an appointment book from a drawer and skimmed through it.

'October fifteenth? What time was this meeting supposed to be?'

'Ten P.M., here in the Oval Office.'

She shook her head. 'Nope. At ten o'clock that night the president was in a meeting with General Whitman.'

Lonergan frowned. 'That's not what I heard. Could I have a look at that book?'

'Sorry. It's confidential, Frank.'

'Maybe I got a bum steer. Thanks, Deborah.' He left.

Thirty minutes later, Frank Lonergan was talking to General Steve Whitman.

'General, the *Tribune* would like to do some coverage on the meeting you had with the president on October fifteenth. I understand some important points were discussed.'

The general shook his head. 'I don't know where you get your information, Mr Lonergan. That meeting was called off. The president had another appointment.'

'Are you sure?'

'Yes. We're going to reschedule it.'

'Thank you, General.'

* * *

Frank Lonergan returned to the White House. He walked into Deborah Kanner's office again.

'What is it this time, Frank?'

'Same thing,' Lonergan said ruefully. 'My informant swears that at ten o'clock on the night of October fifteenth the president was here in a meeting with a Chinese emissary to discuss Tibet.'

She looked at him, exasperated. 'How many times do I have to tell you that there was no such meeting?'

Lonergan sighed. 'Frankly, I don't know what to do. My boss really wants to run that story. It's big news. I guess we'll just have to go with it.' He started toward the door.

'Wait a minute!'

He turned. 'Yes?'

'You can't run that story. It's not true. The president will be furious.'

'It's not my decision.'

Deborah hesitated. 'If I can prove to you that he was meeting with General Whitman, will you forget about it?'

'Sure. I don't want to cause any problems.' Lonergan watched Deborah pull the appointment book out again and flip the pages. 'Here's a list of the president's appointments for that date. Look. October fifteenth.' There were two pages of listings. Deborah pointed to a 10:00 P.M. entry. 'There it is, in black and white.'

'You're right,' Lonergan said. He was busy scanning the page. There was an entry at three o'clock.

Chloe Houston.

Nineteen

The hastily called meeting in the Oval Office had been going on for only a few minutes and the air was already crackling with dissension.

The secretary of defense was saying, 'If we delay any longer, the situation is going to get completely out of control. It will be too late to stop it.'

'We can't rush into this.' General Stephen Gossard turned to the head of the CIA. 'How hard is your information?'

'It's difficult to say. We're fairly certain that Libya is buying a variety of weapons from Iran and China.'

Oliver turned to the secretary of state. 'Libya denies it?'

'Of course. So do China and Iran.'

Oliver asked, 'What about the other Arab states?'

The CIA chief responded. 'From the information I have, Mr President, if a serious attack is launched on Israel, I think it's going to be the excuse that all the other Arab states have been waiting for. They'll join in to wipe Israel out.'

They were all looking at Oliver expectantly. 'Do you have reliable assets in Libya?' he asked.

'Yes, sir.'

'I want an update. Keep me informed. If there are signs of an attack, we have no choice but to move.'

The meeting was adjourned.

Oliver's secretary's voice came over the intercom. 'Mr Tager would like to see you, Mr President.'

'Have him come in.'

'How did the meeting go?' Peter Tager asked.

'Oh, it was just your average meeting,' Oliver said bitterly, 'about whether I want to start a war now or later.'

Tager said sympathetically, 'It goes with the territory.'

'Right.'

'Something of interest has come up.'

'Sit down.'

Peter Tager took a seat. 'What do you know about the United Arab Emirates?'

'Not a lot,' Oliver said. 'Five or six Arab states got together twenty years ago or so and formed a coalition.'

'Seven of them. They joined together in 1971. Abu Dhabi, Fujaira, Dubai, Sharjah, Ras al-Khaimah, Umm al-Qaiwan, and Ajman. When they started out, they weren't very strong, but the Emirates have been incredibly well run. Today they have one of the world's highest standards of living. Their gross domestic product last year was over thirty-nine billion dollars.'

Oliver said impatiently, 'I assume there's a point to this, Peter?'

'Yes, sir. The head of the council of the United Arab Emirates wants to meet with you.'

'All right. I'll have the secretary of defense –'

'Today. In private.'

'Are you serious? I couldn't possibly –'

'Oliver, the Majlis – their council – is one of the most important Arab influences in the world. It has the respect of every other Arab nation. This could be an important breakthrough. I know this is unorthodox, but I think you should meet with them.'

'State would have a fit if I –'

'I'll make the arrangements.'

There was a long silence. 'Where do they want to meet?'

'They have a yacht anchored in Chesapeake Bay, near Annapolis. I can get you there quietly.'

Oliver sat there, studying the ceiling. Finally, he leaned forward and pressed down the intercom switch. 'Cancel my appointments for this afternoon.'

The yacht, a 212-foot Feadship, was moored at the dock. They were waiting for him. All the crew members were Arabs.

'Welcome, Mr President.' It was Ali al-Fulani, the secretary at one of the United Arab Emirates. 'Please come aboard.'

Oliver stepped aboard and Ali al-Fulani signaled to one of the men. A few moments later, the yacht was underway.

'Shall we go below?'

Right. Where I can be killed or kidnapped. This is the stupidest thing I have ever done, Oliver decided. *Maybe they brought me here so they can begin their attack on Israel, and I won't be able to give orders to retaliate. Why the hell did I let Tager talk me into this?*

Oliver followed Ali al-Fulani downstairs into the sumptuous main saloon, which was decorated in Middle Eastern style. There were four muscular Arabs standing on guard in the saloon. An imposing-looking man seated on the couch rose as Oliver came in.

Ali al-Fulani said, 'Mr President, His Majesty King Hamad of Ajman.'

The two men shook hands. 'Your Majesty.'

'Thank you for coming, Mr President. Would you care for some tea?'

'No, thank you.'

'I believe you will find this visit well worth your while.' King Hamad began to pace. 'Mr President, over the centuries, it has been difficult, if not impossible, to bridge the problems that divide us – philosophical, linguistic, religious, cultural. Those are the reasons there have been so many wars in our part of the world. If Jews confiscate the land of Palestinians, no one in Omaha or Kansas is affected. Their lives go on the same. If a synagogue in Jerusalem is bombed, the Italians in Rome and Venice pay no attention.'

Oliver wondered where this was heading. Was it a warning of a coming war?

'There is only one part of the world that suffers from all the wars and bloodshed in the Middle East. And that is the Middle East.'

He sat down across from Oliver. 'It is time for us to put a stop to this madness.'

Here it comes, Oliver thought.

'The heads of the Arab states and the Majlis have authorized me to make you an offer.'

'What kind of an offer?'

'An offer of peace.'

Oliver blinked. 'Peace?'

'We want to make peace with your ally, Israel. Your embargoes against Iran and other Arab countries have cost us untold billions of dollars. We want to put an end to that. If the United States will act as a sponsor, the Arab countries – including Iran, Libya, and Syria – have agreed to sit down and negotiate a permanent peace treaty with Israel.'

Oliver was stunned. When he found his voice, he said, 'You're doing this because –'

'I assure you it is not out of love for the Israelis or for the Americans. It is in our own interests. Too many of our sons have been killed in this madness. We want it to end. It is enough. We want to be free to sell all our oil to the world again. We are prepared to go to war if necessary, but we would prefer peace.'

Oliver took a deep breath. 'I think I would like some tea.'

* * *

'I wish you had been there,' Oliver said to Peter Tager. 'It was incredible. They're ready to go to war, but they don't want to. They're pragmatists. They want to sell their oil to the world, so they want peace.'

'That's fantastic,' Tager said enthusiastically. 'When this gets out, you're going to be a hero.'

'And I can do this on my own,' Oliver told him. 'It doesn't have to go through Congress. I'll have a talk with the Prime Minister of Israel. We'll help him make a deal with the Arab countries.' He looked at Tager and said ruefully, 'For a few minutes there, I thought I was going to be kidnapped.'

'No chance,' Peter Tager assured him. 'I had a boat and a helicopter following you.'

'Senator Davis is here to see you, Mr President. He has no appointment, but he says it's urgent.'

'Hold up my next appointment and send the senator in.'

The door opened and Todd Davis walked into the Oval Office.

'This is a nice surprise, Todd. Is everything all right?'

Senator Davis took a seat. 'Fine, Oliver. I just thought you and I should have a little chat.'

Oliver smiled. 'I have a pretty full schedule today, but for you –'

'This will take only a few minutes. I ran into Peter Tager. He told me about your meeting with the Arabs.'

Oliver grinned. 'Isn't that wonderful? It looks like we're finally going to have peace in the Middle East.' He slammed a fist on the desk. 'After all these decades! That's what my administration is going to be remembered for, Todd.'

Senator Davis asked quietly, 'Have you thought this through, Oliver?'

Oliver frowned. 'What? What do you mean?'

'Peace is a simple word, but it has a lot of ramifications. Peace doesn't have any financial benefits. When there's a war, countries buy billions of dollars' worth of armaments that are made here in the United States. In peacetime, they don't need any. Because Iran can't sell its oil, oil prices are up, and the United States gets the benefit of that.'

Oliver was listening to him unbelievingly. 'Todd – this is the opportunity of a lifetime!'

'Don't be naive, Oliver. If we had really wanted to make peace between Israel and the Arab countries, we could have done it long ago. Israel is a tiny country. Any one of the last half-dozen presidents could have forced them to make a deal with the Arabs, but they preferred to keep things as they were. Don't misunderstand me. Jews are fine people. I work with some of them in the Senate.'

'I don't believe that you can –'

'Believe what you like, Oliver. A peace treaty now

would not be in the best interest of this country. I don't want you to go ahead with it.'

'I have to go ahead with it.'

'Don't tell me what you have to do, Oliver.' Senator Davis leaned forward. 'I'll tell you. Don't forget who put you in that chair.'

Oliver said quietly, 'Todd, you may not respect me, but you must respect this office. Regardless of who put me here, I'm the president.'

Senator Davis got to his feet. 'The president? You're a fucking blow-up toy! You're my dummy, Oliver. You take orders, you don't give them.'

Oliver looked at him for a long moment. 'How many oil fields do you and your friends own, Todd?'

'That's none of your goddam business. If you go through with this, you're finished. Do you hear me? I'm giving you twenty-four hours to come to your senses.'

At dinner that evening, Jan said, 'Father asked me to talk to you, Oliver. He's very upset.'

He looked across the table at his wife and thought, *I'm going to have to fight you, too.*

'He told me what was happening.'

'Did he?'

'Yes.' She leaned across the table. 'And I think what you're going to do is wonderful.'

It took a moment for Oliver to understand. 'But your father's against it.'

'I know. And he's wrong. If they're willing to make peace – you have to help.'

Oliver sat there listening to Jan's words, studying her. He thought about how well she had handled herself as the First Lady. She had become involved in important charities and had been an advocate for a half-dozen major causes. She was lovely and intelligent and caring and – it was as though Oliver were seeing her for the first time. *Why have I been running around? Oliver thought. I have everything I need right here.*

'Will it be a long meeting tonight?'

'No,' Oliver said slowly. 'I'm going to cancel it. I'm staying home.'

That evening, Oliver made love to Jan for the first time in weeks, and it was wonderful. And in the morning, he thought, *I'm going to have Peter get rid of the apartment.*

The note was on his desk the next morning.

> *I want you to know that I am a real fan of yours, and I would not do anything to harm you. I was in the garage of the Monroe Arms on the 15th, and I was very surprised to see you there. The next day when I read about the murder of that young girl, I knew why you went back to wipe your fingerprints off the elevator buttons. I'm sure that all the newspapers would be interested in my*

*story and would pay me a lot of money. But like
I said, I'm a fan of yours. I certainly would not
want to do anything to hurt you. I could use some
financial help, and if you are interested, this will be
just between us. I will get in touch with you in a few
days while you think about it.*

*Sincerely,
A friend*

'Jesus,' Sime Lombardo said softly. 'This is incredible.
How was it delivered?'

'It was mailed,' Peter Tager told him. 'Addressed to the
president, "Personal."'

Sime Lombardo said, 'It could be some nut who's just
trying to –'

'We can't take a chance, Sime. I don't believe for
a minute that it's true, but if even a whisper of this
gets out, it would destroy the president. We must protect him.'

'How do we do that?'

'First, we have to find out who sent this.'

Peter Tager was at the Federal Bureau of Investigation
headquarters at 10th Street and Pennsylvania Avenue,
talking to Special Agent Clay Jacobs.

'You said it was urgent, Peter?'

'Yes.' Peter Tager opened a briefcase and took out a

single sheet of paper. He slid it across the desk. Clay Jacobs picked it up and read it aloud:

'"I want you to know that I'm a real fan of yours . . . I will get in touch with you in a few days while you think about it."'

Everything in between had been whited out.

Jacobs looked up. 'What is this?'

'It involves the highest security,' Peter Tager said. 'The president asked me to try to find out who sent it. He would like you to check it for fingerprints.'

Clay Jacobs studied the paper again, frowning. 'This is highly unusual, Peter.'

'Why?'

'It just smells wrong.'

'All the president wants is for you to give him the name of the individual who wrote it.'

'Assuming his fingerprints are on it.'

Peter Tager nodded. 'Assuming his fingerprints are on it.'

'Wait here.' Jacobs rose and left the office.

Peter Tager sat there looking out the window, thinking about the letter and its possible terrible consequences.

Exactly seven minutes later, Clay Jacobs returned.

'You're in luck,' he said.

Peter Tager's heart began to race. 'You found something?'

'Yes.' Jacobs handed Tager a slip of paper. 'The man you're looking for was involved in a traffic accident about a year ago. His name is Carl Gorman. He works as a clerk at the Monroe Arms.' He stood there a moment, studying Tager. 'Is there anything else you'd like to tell me about this?'

'No,' Peter Tager said sincerely. 'There isn't.'

'Frank Lonergan is on line three, Miss Stewart. He says it's urgent.'

'I'll take it.' Leslie picked up the telephone and pressed a button. 'Frank?'

'Are you alone?'

'Yes.'

She heard him take a deep breath. 'Okay. Here we go.' He spoke for the next ten minutes without interruption.

Leslie Stewart hurried into Matt Baker's office. 'We have to talk, Matt.' She sat down across from his desk. 'What if I told you that Oliver Russell is involved in the murder of Chloe Houston?'

'For openers, I'd say you are paranoid and that you've gone over the edge.'

'Frank Lonergan just phoned in. He talked to Governor Houston, who doesn't believe that Paul Yerby killed her daughter. He talked to Paul Yerby's parents. They don't believe it either.'

'I wouldn't expect them to,' Matt Baker said. 'If that's the only –'

'That's just the beginning. Frank went down to the

morgue and spoke to the coroner. She told him that the kid's belt was so tight that they had to cut it away from his throat.'

He was listening more intently now. 'And –?'

'Frank went down to pick up Yerby's belongings. His belt was there. Intact.'

Matt Baker drew a deep breath. 'You're telling me that he was murdered in prison and that there was a cover-up?'

'I'm not telling you anything. I'm just reporting the facts. Oliver Russell tried to get me to use Ecstasy once. When he was running for governor, a woman who was a legal secretary died from Ecstasy. While he was governor, his secretary was found in a park in an Ecstasy-induced coma. Lonergan learned that Oliver called the hospital and suggested they take her off life-support systems.' Leslie leaned forward. 'There was a telephone call from the Imperial Suite to the White House the night Chloe Houston was murdered. Frank checked the hotel telephone records. The page for the fifteenth was missing. The president's appointments secretary told Lonergan that the president had a meeting with General Whitman that night. There was no meeting. Frank spoke to Governor Houston, and she said that Chloe was on a tour of the White House and that she had arranged for her daughter to meet the president.'

There was a long silence. 'Where's Frank Lonergan now?' Matt Baker asked.

'He's tracking down Carl Gorman, the hotel clerk who booked the Imperial Suite.'

＊　　＊　　＊

Jeremy Robinson was saying, 'I'm sorry. We don't give out personal information about our employees.'

Frank Lonergan said, 'All I'm asking for is his home address so I can –'

'It wouldn't do you any good. Mr Gorman is on vacation.'

Lonergan sighed. 'That's too bad. I was hoping he could fill in a few blank spots.'

'Blank spots?'

'Yes. We're doing a big story on the death of Governor Houston's daughter in your hotel. Well, I'll just have to piece it together without Gorman.' He took out a pad and a pen. 'How long has this hotel been here? I want to know all about its background, its clientele, its –'

Jeremy Robinson frowned. 'Wait a minute! Surely that's not necessary. I mean – she could have died anywhere.'

Frank Lonergan said sympathetically, 'I know, but it happened here. Your hotel is going to become as famous as Watergate.'

'Mr –?'

'Lonergan.'

'Mr Lonergan, I would appreciate it if you could – I mean this kind of publicity is very bad. Isn't there some way –?'

Lonergan was thoughtful for a moment. 'Well, if I

spoke to Mr Gorman, I suppose I could find a different angle.'

'I would really appreciate that. Let me get you his address.'

Frank Lonergan was becoming nervous. As the outline of events began to take shape, it became clear that there was a murder conspiracy and a cover-up at the highest level. Before he went to see the hotel clerk, he decided to stop at his apartment house. His wife, Rita, was in the kitchen preparing dinner. She was a petite redhead with sparkling green eyes and a fair complexion. She turned in surprise as her husband walked in.

'Frank, what are you doing home in the middle of the day?'

'Just thought I'd drop in and say hello.'

She looked at his face. 'No. There's something going on. What is it?'

He hesitated. 'How long has it been since you've seen your mother?'

'I saw her last week. Why?'

'Why don't you go visit her again, honey?'

'Is anything wrong?'

He grinned. 'Wrong?' He walked over to the mantel. 'You'd better start dusting this off. We're going to put a Pulitzer Prize here and a Peabody Award here.'

'What are you talking about?'

'I'm on to something that's going to blow everybody

away – and I mean people in high places. It's the most exciting story I've ever been involved in.'

'Why do you want me to go see my mother?'

He shrugged. 'There's just an outside chance that this could get to be a little dangerous. There are some people who don't want this story to get out. I'd feel better if you were away for a few days, just until this breaks.'

'But if you're in danger –'

'I'm not in any danger.'

'You're sure nothing's going to happen to you?'

'Positive. Pack a few things, and I'll call you tonight.'

'All right,' Rita said reluctantly.

Lonergan looked at his watch. 'I'll drive you to the train station.'

One hour later, Lonergan stopped in front of a modest brick house in the Wheaton area. He got out of the car, walked to the front door, and rang the bell. There was no answer. He rang again and waited. The door suddenly swung open and a heavyset middle-aged woman stood in the doorway, regarding him suspiciously.

'Yes?'

'I'm with the Internal Revenue Service,' Lonergan said. He flashed a piece of identification. 'I want to see Carl Gorman.'

'My brother's not here.'

'Do you know where he is?'

'No.' Too fast.

Lonergan nodded. 'That's a shame. Well, you might as well start packing up his things. I'll have the department send over the vans.' Lonergan started back down the driveway toward his car.

'Wait a minute! What vans? What are you talking about?'

Lonergan stopped and turned. 'Didn't your brother tell you?'

'Tell me what?'

Lonergan took a few steps back toward the house. 'He's in trouble.'

She looked at him anxiously. 'What kind of trouble?'

'I'm afraid I'm not at liberty to discuss it.' He shook his head. 'He seems like a nice guy, too.'

'He is,' she said fervently. 'Carl is a wonderful person.'

Lonergan nodded. 'That was my feeling when we were questioning him down at the bureau.'

She was panicky. 'Questioning him about what?'

'Cheating on his income tax. It's too bad. I wanted to tell him about a loophole that could have helped him out, but –' He shrugged. 'If he's not here . . .' He turned to go again.

'Wait! He's – he's at a fishing lodge. I – I'm not supposed to tell anybody.'

He shrugged. 'That's okay with me.'

'No . . . but this is different. It's the Sunshine Fishing Lodge on the lake in Richmond, Virginia.'

'Fine. I'll contact him there.'

'That would be wonderful. You're sure he'll be all right?'

'Absolutely,' Lonergan said. 'I'll see that he's taken care of.'

Lonergan took I-95, heading south. Richmond was a little over a hundred miles away. On a vacation, years ago, Lonergan had fished the lake, and he had been lucky.

He hoped he would be as lucky this time.

It was drizzling, but Carl Gorman did not mind. That's when the fish were supposed to bite. He was fishing for striped bass, using large minnows on slip bobbers, far out behind the rowboat. The waves lapped against the small boat in the middle of the lake, and the bait drifted behind the boat, untouched. The fish were in no hurry. It did not matter. Neither was he. He had never been happier. He was going to be rich beyond his wildest dreams. It had been sheer luck. *You have to be at the right place at the right time.* He had returned to the Monroe Arms to pick up a jacket he had forgotten and was about to leave the garage when the private elevator door opened. When he saw who got out, he had sat in his car, stunned. He had watched the man return, wipe off his fingerprints, then drive away.

It was not until he read about the murder the following day that he had put it all together. In a way, he felt sorry for the man. *I really am a fan of his. The trouble is, when you're that famous, you can never hide. Wherever you go, the world knows you. He'll pay me to be quiet. He has no choice. I'll start with a hundred thousand. Once he pays that, he'll have to keep paying. Maybe I'll buy a chateau in France or a chalet in Switzerland.*

He felt a tug at the end of his line and snapped the rod toward him. He could feel the fish trying to get away. *You're not going anywhere. I've got you hooked.*

In the distance, he heard a large speedboat approaching. *They shouldn't allow power boats on the lake. They'll scare all the fish away.* The speedboat was bearing down on him.

'Don't get too close,' Carl shouted.

The speedboat seemed to be heading right toward him.

'Hey! Be careful. Watch where you're going. For God's sake —'

The speedboat plowed into the rowboat, cutting it in half, the water sucking Gorman under.

Damn drunken fool! He was gasping for air. He managed to get his head above water. The speedboat had circled and was heading straight for him again. And the last thing Carl Gorman felt before the boat smashed into his skull was the tug of the fish on his line.

When Frank Lonergan arrived, the area was crowded with police cars, a fire engine, and an ambulance. The ambulance was just pulling away.

Frank Lonergan got out of his car and said to a bystander, 'What's all the excitement?'

'Some poor guy was in an accident on the lake. There's not much left of him.'

And Lonergan knew.

At midnight, Frank Lonergan was working at his computer, alone in his apartment, writing the story that was going to destroy the President of the United States. It was a story that would earn him a Pulitzer Prize. There was no doubt about it in his mind. This was going to make him more famous than Woodward and Bernstein. It was the story of the century.

He was interrupted by the sound of the doorbell. He got up and walked over to the front door.

'Who is it?'

'A package from Leslie Stewart.'

She's found some new information. He opened the door. There was a glint of metal, and an unbearable pain tore his chest apart.

Then nothing.

Twenty

Frank Lonergan's living room looked as if it had been struck by a miniature hurricane. All the drawers and cabinets had been pulled open and their contents had been scattered over the floor.

Nick Reese watched Frank Lonergan's body being removed. He turned to Detective Steve Brown. 'Any sign of the murder weapon?'

'No.'

'Have you talked to the neighbors?'

'Yeah. The apartment building is a zoo, full of monkeys. See no evil, hear no evil, speak no evil. *Nada.* Mrs Lonergan is on her way back here. She heard the news on the radio. There have been a couple other robberies here in the last six months, and –'

'I'm not so sure this was a robbery.'

'What do you mean?'

'Lonergan was down at headquarters the other day to check on Paul Yerby's things. I'd like to know what story Lonergan was working on. No papers in the drawers?'

'Nope.'

'No notes?'

'Nothing.'

'So either he was very neat, or someone took the trouble to clean everything out.' Reese walked over to the work table. There was a cable dangling off the table, connected to nothing. Reese held it up. 'What's this?'

Detective Brown walked over. 'It's a power cable for a computer. There must have been one here. That means there could be backups somewhere.'

'They may have taken the computer, but Lonergan might have saved copies of his files. Let's check it out.'

They found the backup disk in a briefcase in Lonergan's automobile. Reese handed it to Brown.

'I want you to take this down to headquarters. There's probably a password to get into it. Have Chris Colby look at it. He's an expert.'

The front door of the apartment opened and Rita Lonergan walked in. She looked pale and distraught. She stopped when she saw the men.

'Mrs Lonergan?'

'Who are –?'

'Detective Nick Reese, Homicide. This is Detective Brown.'

Rita Lonergan looked around. 'Where is –?'

'We had your husband's body taken away, Mrs Lonergan.

I'm terribly sorry. I know it's a bad time, but I'd like to ask you a few questions.'

She looked at him, and her eyes suddenly filled with fear. The last reaction Reese had expected. What was she afraid of?

'Your husband was working on a story, wasn't he?'

His voice echoed in her mind. *'I'm on to something that's going to blow everybody away – and I mean people in high places. It's the most exciting story I've ever been involved in.'*

'Mrs Lonergan?'

'I – I don't know anything.'

'You don't know what assignment he was working on?'

'No. Frank never discussed his work with me.'

She was obviously lying.

'You have no idea who might have killed him?'

She looked around at the open drawers and cabinets. 'It – it must have been a burglar.'

Detective Reese and Detective Brown looked at each other.

'If you don't mind, I'd – I'd like to be alone. This has been a terrible shock.'

'Of course. Is there anything we can do for you?'

'No. Just . . . just leave.'

'We'll be back,' Nick Reese promised.

When Detective Reese returned to police headquarters,

he telephoned Matt Baker. 'I'm investigating the Frank Lonergan murder,' Reese said. 'Can you tell me what he was working on?'

'Yes. Frank was investigating the Chloe Houston killing.'

'I see. Did he file a story?'

'No. We were waiting for it, when —' He stopped.

'Right. Thank you, Mr Baker.'

'If you get any information, will you let me know?'

'You'll be the first,' Reese assured him.

The following morning, Dana Evans went into Tom Hawkins's office. 'I want to do a story on Frank's death. I'd like to go see his widow.'

'Good idea. I'll arrange for a camera crew.'

Late that afternoon, Dana and her camera crew pulled up in front of Frank Lonergan's apartment building. With the crew following her, Dana approached Lonergan's apartment door and rang the bell. This was the kind of interview Dana dreaded. It was bad enough to show on television the victims of horrible crimes, but to intrude on the grief of the stricken families seemed even worse to her.

The door opened and Rita Lonergan stood there. 'What do you —?'

'I'm sorry to bother you, Mrs Lonergan. I'm Dana

Evans, with WTE. We'd like to get your reaction to –'

Rita Lonergan froze for a moment, and then screamed, 'You murderers!' She turned and ran inside the apartment.

Dana looked at the cameraman, shocked. 'Wait here.' She went inside and found Rita Lonergan in the bedroom. 'Mrs Lonergan –'

'Get out! You killed my husband!'

Dana was puzzled. 'What are you talking about?'

'Your people gave him an assignment so dangerous that he made me leave town because he . . . he was afraid for my life.'

Dana looked at her, appalled. 'What – what story was he working on?'

'Frank wouldn't tell me.' She was fighting hysteria. 'He said it was too – too dangerous. It was something big. He talked about the Pulitzer Prize and the –' She started to cry.

Dana went over to her and put her arms around her. 'I'm so sorry. Did he say anything else?'

'No. He said I should get out, and he drove me to the train station. He was on his way to see some – some hotel clerk.'

'Where?'

'At the Monroe Arms.'

'I don't know why you're here, Miss Evans,' Jeremy Robinson protested. 'Lonergan promised me that if I

304

cooperated, there would be no bad publicity about the hotel.'

'Mr Robinson, Mr Lonergan is dead. All I want is some information.'

Jeremy Robinson shook his head. 'I don't know anything.'

'What did you tell Mr Lonergan?'

Robinson sighed. 'He asked for the address of Carl Gorman, my hotel clerk. I gave it to him.'

'Did Mr Lonergan go to see him?'

'I have no idea.'

'I'd like to have that address.'

Jeremy looked at her a moment and sighed again. 'Very well. He lives with his sister.'

A few minutes later, Dana had the address in her hands. Robinson watched her leave the hotel, and then he picked up the phone and dialed the White House.

He wondered why they were so interested in the case.

Chris Colby, the department's computer expert, walked into Detective Reese's office holding a floppy disk. He was almost trembling with excitement.

'What did you get?' Detective Reese asked.

Chris Colby took a deep breath. 'This is going to blow your mind. Here's a printout of what's on this disk.'

Detective Reese started to read it and an incredulous

305

expression came over his face. 'Mother of God,' he said. 'I've got to show this to Captain Miller.'

When Captain Otto Miller finished reading the printout, he looked up at Detective Reese. 'I – I've never seen anything like this.'

'There's never been anything like this,' Detective Reese said. 'What the hell do we do with it?'

Captain Miller said slowly, 'I think we have to turn it over to the U.S. attorney general.'

They were gathered in the office of Attorney General Barbara Gatlin. With her in the room were Scott Brandon, director of the FBI; Dean Bergstrom, the Washington chief of police; James Frisch, director of Central Intelligence, and Edgar Graves, Chief Justice of the Supreme Court.

Barbara Gatlin said, 'I asked you gentlemen here because I need your advice. Frankly, I don't know how to proceed. We have a situation that's unique. Frank Lonergan was a reporter for the *Washington Tribune*. When he was killed, he was in the middle of an investigation into the murder of Chloe Houston. I'm going to read you a transcript of what the police found on a disk in Lonergan's car.' She looked at the printout in her hand and started to read aloud:

'"I have reason to believe that the President of the

United States has committed at least one murder and is involved in four more –"'

'What?' Scott Brandon exclaimed.

'Let me go on.' She started to read again.

'"I obtained the following information from various sources. Leslie Stewart, the owner and publisher of the *Washington Tribune*, is willing to swear that at one time, Oliver Russell tried to persuade her to take an illegal drug called liquid Ecstasy.

'"When Oliver Russell was running for governor of Kentucky, Lisa Burnette, a legal secretary who worked in the state capitol building, threatened to sue him for sexual harassment. Russell told a colleague that he would have a talk with her. The next day, Lisa Burnette's body was found in the Kentucky River. She had died of an overdose of liquid Ecstasy.

'"Then-Governor Oliver Russell's secretary, Miriam Friedland, was found unconscious on a park bench late at night. She was in a coma induced by liquid Ecstasy. The police were waiting for her to come out of it so that they could find out who had given it to her. Oliver Russell telephoned the hospital and suggested they take her off life support. Miriam Friedland passed away without coming out of the coma.

'"Chloe Houston was killed by an overdose of liquid Ecstasy. I learned that on the night of her death, there was a phone call from the hotel suite to the White House. When I looked at the hotel telephone records to check it, the page for that day was missing.

'"I was told that the president was at a meeting that night, but I discovered that the meeting had been canceled. No one knows the president's whereabouts that night.

'"Paul Yerby was detained as a suspect in Chloe Houston's murder. Captain Otto Miller told the White House where Yerby was being held. The following morning Yerby was found hanging in his cell. He was supposed to have hanged himself with his belt, but when I looked through his effects at the police station, his belt was there, intact.

'"Through a friend at the FBI, I learned that a blackmail letter had been sent to the White House. President Russell asked the FBI to check it for fingerprints. Most of the letter had been whited out, but with the aid of an infrascope, the FBI was able to decipher it.

'"The fingerprints on the letter were identified as belonging to Carl Gorman, a clerk at the Monroe Arms Hotel, probably the only one who might have known the identity of the person who booked the suite where the girl was killed. He was away at a fishing camp, but his name had been revealed to the White House. When I arrived at the camp, Gorman had been killed in what appeared to be an accident.

'"There are too many connections for these killings to be a coincidence. I am going ahead with the investigation, but frankly, I'm frightened. At least I have this on the record, in case anything should happen to me. More later."'

'My God,' James Frisch exclaimed. 'This is . . . horrible.'

'I can't believe it.'

Attorney General Gatlin said, 'Lonergan believed it, and he was probably killed to stop this information from getting out.'

'What do we do now?' Chief Justice Graves asked. 'How do you ask the President of the United States if he's killed half a dozen people?'

'That's a good question. Impeach him? Arrest him? Throw him in jail?'

'Before we do anything,' Attorney General Gatlin said, 'I think we have to present this transcript to the president himself and give him an opportunity to comment.'

There were murmurs of agreement.

'In the meantime, I'll have a warrant for his arrest drawn up. Just in case it's necessary.'

One of the men in the room was thinking, *I've got to inform Peter Tager.*

Peter Tager put the telephone down and sat there for a long time, thinking about what he had just been told. He rose and walked down the corridor to Deborah Kanner's office.

'I have to see the president.'

'He's in a meeting. If you can –'

'I have to see him now, Deborah. It's urgent.'

She saw the look on his face. 'Just a moment.' She

picked up the telephone and pressed a button. 'I'm sorry to interrupt you, Mr President. Mr Tager is here, and he said he must see you.' She listened a moment. 'Thank you.' She replaced the receiver and turned to Tager. 'Five minutes.'

Five minutes later, Peter Tager was alone in the Oval Office with President Russell.

'What's so important, Peter?'

Tager took a deep breath. 'The Attorney General and the FBI think you're involved in six murders.'

Oliver smiled. 'This is some kind of joke . . .'

'Is it? They're on their way here now. They believe you killed Chloe Houston and –'

Oliver had gone pale. 'What?'

'I know – it's crazy. From what I was told, all the evidence is circumstantial. I'm sure you can explain where you were the night the girl died.'

Oliver was silent.

Peter Tager was waiting. 'Oliver, you can explain, can't you?'

Oliver swallowed. 'No. I can't.'

'You have to!'

Oliver said heavily, 'Peter, I need to be alone.'

Peter Tager went to see Senator Davis in the Capitol.

'What is it that's so urgent, Peter?'

'It's – it's about the president.'

'Yes?'

'The attorney general and the FBI think that Oliver is a murderer.'

Senator Davis sat there staring at Tager. 'What the hell are you talking about?'

'They're convinced Oliver's committed several murders. I got a tip from a friend at the FBI.'

Tager told Senator Davis about the evidence.

When Tager was through, Senator Davis said slowly, 'That dumb son of a bitch! Do you know what this means?'

'Yes, sir. It means that Oliver –'

'Fuck Oliver. I've spent years putting him where I want him. I don't care what happens to him. I'm in control now, Peter. I have the power. I'm not going to let Oliver's stupidity take it away from me. I'm not going to let anyone take it away from me!'

'I don't see what you can –'

'You said the evidence was all circumstantial?'

'That's right. I was told they have no hard proof. But he has no alibi.'

'Where is the president now?'

'In the Oval Office.'

'I've got some good news for him,' Senator Todd Davis said.

Senator Davis was facing Oliver in the Oval Office. 'I've

been hearing some very disturbing things, Oliver. It's insane, of course. I don't know how anyone could possibly think you –'

'I don't, either. I haven't done anything wrong, Todd.'

'I'm sure you haven't. But if word got out that you were even suspected of horrible crimes like these – well, you can see how this would affect the office, can't you?'

'Of course, but –'

'You're too important to let anything like this happen to you. This office controls the world, Oliver. You don't want to give this up.'

'Todd – I'm not guilty of anything.'

'But they think you are. I'm told you have no alibi for the evening of Chloe Houston's murder?'

There was a momentary silence. 'No.'

Senator Davis smiled. 'What happened to your memory, son? You were with me that evening. We spent the whole evening together.'

Oliver was looking at him, confused. 'What?'

'That's right. I'm your alibi. No one's going to question my word. No one. I'm going to save you, Oliver.'

There was a long silence. Oliver said, 'What do you want in return, Todd?'

Senator Davis nodded. 'We'll start with the Middle Eastern peace conference. You'll call that off. After that, we'll talk. I have great plans for us. We're not going to let anything spoil them.'

Oliver said, 'I'm going ahead with the peace conference.'

Senator Davis's eyes narrowed. 'What did you say?'

'I've decided to go ahead with it. You see, what's important is not how long a president stays in this office, Todd, but what he does when he's in it.'

Senator Davis's face was turning red. 'Do you know what you're doing?'

'Yes.'

The senator leaned across the desk. 'I don't think you do. They're on their way here to accuse you of murder, Oliver. Where are you going to make your goddam deals from – the penitentiary? You've just thrown your whole life away, you stupid –'

A voice came over the intercom. 'Mr President, there are some people here to see you. Attorney General Gatlin, Mr Brandon from the FBI, Chief Justice Graves, and –'

'Send them in.'

Senator Davis said savagely, 'It looks like I should stick to judging horseflesh. I made a big mistake with you, Oliver. But you just made the biggest mistake of your life. I'm going to destroy you.'

The door opened and Attorney General Gatlin entered, followed by Brandon, Justice Graves, and Bergstrom.

Justice Graves said, 'Senator Davis . . .'

Todd Davis nodded curtly and strode out of the room. Barbara Gatlin closed the door behind him. She walked up to the desk.

'Mr President, this is highly embarrassing, but I hope you will understand. We have to ask you some questions.'

313

Oliver faced them. 'I've been told why you're here. Of course, I had nothing to do with any of those deaths.'

'I'm sure we're all relieved to hear that, Mr President,' Scott Brandon said, 'and I assure you that none of us really believes that you could be involved. But an accusation has been made, and we have no choice but to pursue it.'

'I understand.'

'Mr President, have you ever taken the drug Ecstasy?'

'No.'

The group looked at one another.

'Mr President, if you could tell us where you were on October fifteenth, the evening of Chloe Houston's death . . .'

There was a silence.

'Mr President?'

'I'm sorry. I can't.'

'But surely you can remember where you were, or what you were doing on that evening?'

Silence.

'Mr President?'

'I – I can't think right now. I'd like you to come back later.'

'How much later?' Bergstrom asked.

'Eight o'clock.'

Oliver watched them leave. He got up and slowly walked into the small sitting room where Jan was working at a desk. She looked up as Oliver entered.

314

He took a deep breath and said, 'Jan, I – I have a confession to make.'

Senator Davis was in an icy rage. *How could I have been so stupid? I picked the wrong man. He's trying to destroy everything I've worked for. I'll teach him what happens to people who try to double-cross me.* The Senator sat at his desk for a long time, deciding what he was going to do. Then he picked up a telephone and dialed.

'Miss Stewart, you told me to call you when I had something more for you.'

'Yes, Senator?'

'Let me tell you what I want. From now on, I'll expect the full support of the *Tribune* – campaign contributions, glowing editorials, the works.'

'And what do I get in exchange for all this?' Leslie asked.

'The President of the United States. The attorney general has just sworn out a warrant for his arrest for a series of murders.'

There was a sharp intake of breath. 'Keep talking.'

Leslie Stewart was speaking so fast that Matt Baker could not understand a word. 'For God's sake, calm down,' he said. 'What are you trying to say?'

'The president! We've got him, Matt! I just talked to Senator Todd Davis. The chief justice of the Supreme

Court, the chief of police, the director of the FBI, and the U.S. attorney general are in the president's office now with a warrant for his arrest on charges of murder. There's a pile of evidence against him, Matt, and he has no alibi. It's the story of the goddam century!'

'You can't print it.'

She looked at him in surprise. 'What do you mean?'

'Leslie, a story like this is too big to just – I mean the facts have to be checked and rechecked –'

'And rechecked again until it becomes a headline in *The Washington Post*? No, thank you. I'm not going to lose this one.'

'You can't accuse the President of the United States of murder without –'

Leslie smiled. 'I'm not going to, Matt. All we have to do is print the fact that there is a warrant for his arrest. That's enough to destroy him.'

'Senator Davis –'

'– is turning in his own son-in-law. He believes the president is guilty. He told me so.'

'That's not enough. We'll verify it first, and –'

'With whom – Katharine Graham? Are you out of your mind? We run this right now, or we lose it.'

'I can't let you do this, not without verifying everything that –'

'Who do you think you're talking to? This is my paper, and I'll do anything I like with it.'

Matt Baker rose. 'This is irresponsible. I won't let any of my people write this story.'

'They don't have to. I'll write it myself.'

'Leslie, if you do this, I'm leaving. For good.'

'No, you're not, Matt. You and I are going to share a Pulitzer Prize.' She watched him turn and walk out of the office. 'You'll be back.'

Leslie pressed down the intercom button. 'Have Zoltaire come in here.'

She looked at him and said, 'I want to know my horoscope for the next twenty-four hours.'

'Yes, Miss Stewart. I'll be happy to do that.' From his pocket, Zoltaire took a small ephemeris, the astrological bible, and opened it. He studied the positions of the stars and the planets for a moment, and his eyes widened.

'What is it?'

Zoltaire looked up. 'I – something very important seems to be happening.' He pointed to the ephemeris. 'Look. Transiting Mars is going over your ninth house Pluto for three days, setting off a square to your –'

'Never mind that,' Leslie said impatiently. 'Cut to the chase.'

He blinked. 'The chase? Ah, yes.' He looked at the book again. 'There is some kind of major event happening. You are in the middle of it. You're going to be even more famous than you are now, Miss Stewart. The whole world is going to know your name.'

Leslie was filled with a feeling of intense euphoria. The whole world was going to know her name. She was at the awards ceremonies and the speaker was saying, 'And now, the recipient of this year's Pulitzer Prize for the most important story in newspaper history. I give you Miss Leslie Stewart.' There was a standing ovation, and the roar was deafening.

'Miss Stewart . . .'

Leslie shook away the dream.

'Will there be anything else?'

'No,' Leslie said. 'Thank you, Zoltaire. That's enough.'

At seven o'clock that evening, Leslie was looking at a proof of the story she had written. The headline read: MURDER WARRANT SERVED ON PRESIDENT RUSSELL. PRESIDENT ALSO TO BE QUESTIONED IN INVESTIGATION OF SIX DEATHS.

Leslie skimmed her story under it and turned to Lyle Bannister, her managing editor. 'Run it,' she said. 'Put it out as an extra. I want it to hit the streets in an hour, and WTE can broadcast the story at the same time.'

Lyle Bannister hesitated. 'You don't think Matt Baker should take a look at —?'

'This isn't his paper, it's mine. Run it. Now.'

'Yes, ma'am.' He reached for the telephone on Leslie's desk and dialed a number. 'We're going with it.'

*　　*　　*

318

At seven-thirty that evening, Barbara Gatlin and the others in the group were preparing to return to the White House. Barbara Gatlin said heavily, 'I hope to God it isn't going to be necessary to use it, but just to be prepared, I'm bringing the warrant for the president's arrest.'

Thirty minutes later, Oliver's secretary said, 'Attorney General Gatlin and the others are here.'

'Send them in.'

Oliver watched, pale-faced, as they walked into the Oval Office. Jan was at his side, holding his hand tightly.

Barbara Gatlin said, 'Are you prepared to answer our questions now, Mr President?'

Oliver nodded. 'I am.'

'Mr President, did Chloe Houston have an appointment to see you on October fifteenth?'

'She did.'

'And did you see her?'

'No. I had to cancel.'

The call had come in just before three o'clock. *'Darling, it's me. I'm lonely for you. I'm at the lodge in Maryland. I'm sitting by the pool, naked.'*

'We'll have to do something about that.'

'When can you get away?'

'I'll be there in an hour.'

Oliver turned to face the group. 'If what I'm about to tell you should ever leave this office, it would do irreparable damage to the presidency and to our relations

319

with another country. I'm doing this with the greatest reluctance, but you leave me no choice.'

As the group watched in wonder, Oliver walked over to a side door leading to a den and opened it. Sylva Picone stepped into the room.

'This is Sylva Picone, the wife of the Italian ambassador. On the fifteenth, Mrs Picone and I were together at her lodge in Maryland from four o'clock in the afternoon until two o'clock in the morning. I know absolutely nothing about the murder of Chloe Houston, or any of the other deaths.'

Twenty-One

Dana walked into Tom Hawkins's office. 'Tom, I'm on to something interesting. Before Frank Lonergan was murdered, he went to the home of Carl Gorman, a clerk who worked at the Monroe Arms. Gorman was killed in a supposed boating accident. He lived with his sister. I'd like to take a crew over there to do a taped segment for the ten o'clock news tonight.'

'You don't think it was a boating accident?'

'No. Too many coincidences.'

Tom Hawkins was thoughtful for a moment. 'Okay. I'll set it up.'

'Thanks. Here's the address. I'll meet the camera crew there. I'm going home to change.'

When Dana walked into her apartment, she had a sudden feeling that something was wrong. It was a sense she had developed in Sarajevo, a warning of danger. Somebody had been here. She walked through the apartment slowly, warily checking the closets. Nothing was amiss.

It's my imagination, Dana told herself. But she did not believe it.

When Dana arrived at the house that Carl Gorman's sister lived in, the electronic news-gathering vehicle had arrived and was parked down the street. The ENG was an enormous van with a large antenna on the roof and sophisticated electronic equipment inside. Waiting for Dana were Andrew Wright, the soundman, and Vernon Mills, the cameraman.

'Where are we doing the interview?' Mills asked.

'I want to do it inside the house. I'll call you when we're ready.'

'Right.'

Dana went up to the front door and knocked. Marianne Gorman opened the door. 'Yes?'

'I'm –'

'Oh! I know who you are. I've seen you on television.'

'Right,' Dana said. 'Could we talk for a minute?'

Marianne Gorman hesitated. 'Yes. Come in.' Dana followed her into the living room.

Marianne Gorman offered Dana a chair. 'It's about my brother, isn't it? He was murdered. I know it.'

'Who killed him?'

Marianne Gorman looked away. 'I don't know.'

'Did Frank Lonergan come here to see you?'

The woman's eyes narrowed. 'He tricked me. I told

322

him where he could find my brother and –' Her eyes filled with tears. 'Now Carl is dead.'

'What did Lonergan want to talk to your brother about?'

'He said he was from the IRS.'

Dana sat there watching her. 'Would you mind if I did a brief television interview with you? You can just say a few words about your brother's murder and how you feel about the crime in this city.'

Marianne Gorman nodded. 'I guess that will be all right.'

'Thank you.' Dana went to the front door, opened it, and waved to Vernon Mills. He picked up his camera equipment and started toward the house, followed by Andrew Wright.

'I've never done this kind of thing before,' Marianne said.

'There's nothing to be nervous about. It will only take a few minutes.'

Vernon entered the living room with the camera. 'Where do you want to shoot this?'

'We'll do it here, in the living room.' She nodded toward a corner. 'You can put the camera there.'

Vernon placed the camera, then walked back to Dana. He pinned a lavaliere microphone on each woman's jacket. 'You can turn it on whenever you're ready.' He set it down on a table.

Marianne Gorman said, 'No! Wait a minute! I'm sorry. I – I can't do this.'

'Why?' Dana asked.

'It's . . . it's dangerous. Could – could I talk to you alone?'

'Yes.' Dana looked at Vernon and Wright. 'Leave the camera where it is. I'll call you.'

Vernon nodded, 'We'll be in the van.'

Dana turned to Marianne Gorman. 'Why is it dangerous for you to be on television?'

Marianne said reluctantly, 'I don't want them to see me.'

'You don't want who to see you?'

Marianne swallowed. 'Carl did something he . . . he shouldn't have done. He was killed because of it. And the men who killed him will try to kill me.' She was trembling.

'What did Carl do?'

'Oh, my God,' Marianne moaned. 'I begged him not to.'

'Not to what?' Dana persisted.

'He – he wrote a blackmail letter.'

Dana looked at her in surprise. 'A blackmail letter?'

'Yes. Believe me, Carl was a good man. It's just that he liked – he had expensive tastes, and on his salary, he couldn't afford to live the way he wanted to. I couldn't stop him. He was murdered because of that letter. I know it. They found him, and now they know where I am. I'm going to be killed.' She was sobbing. 'I – I don't know what to do.'

'Tell me about the letter.'

Marianne Gorman took a deep breath. 'My brother was going away on a vacation. He had forgotten a jacket that he wanted to take with him, and he went back to the hotel. He got his jacket and was back in his car in the garage when the private elevator door to the Imperial Suite opened. Carl told me he saw a man get out. He was surprised to see him there. He was even more surprised when the man walked back to the elevator and wiped off his fingerprints. Carl couldn't figure out what was going on. Then the – the next day, he read about that poor girl's murder, and he knew that this man had killed her.' She hesitated. 'That's when he sent the letter to the White House.'

Dana said slowly, 'The White House?'

'Yes.'

'Who did he send the letter to?'

'The man he saw in the garage. You know – the one with the eye patch. Peter Tager.'

Twenty-Two

Through the walls of the office, he could hear the sound of traffic on Pennsylvania Avenue, outside the White House, and he became aware again of his surroundings. He reviewed everything that was happening, and he was satisfied that he was safe. Oliver Russell was going to be arrested for murders he hadn't committed, and Melvin Wicks, the vice president, would become president. Senator Davis would have no problem controlling Vice President Wicks. *And there's nothing to link me to any of the deaths*, Tager thought.

There was a prayer meeting that evening, and Peter Tager was looking forward to it. The group enjoyed hearing him talk about religion and power. Peter Tager had become interested in girls when he was fourteen. God had given him an extraordinarily strong libido, and Peter had thought that the loss of his eye would make him unattractive to the opposite sex. Instead, girls found his eye patch intriguing. In addition, God had given Peter the gift of persuasion, and he was able to charm diffident young girls into the backseats of cars, into barns, and into beds. Unfortunately, he had gotten one of them pregnant and had been forced to marry her. She bore him two children. His family could have become an onerous burden, tying him down. But it turned out to be a marvelous cover for his extracurricular activities. He had seriously thought of going into the ministry, but then he had met Senator Todd Davis, and his life had changed. He had found a new and bigger forum. Politics.

In the beginning, there had been no problems with his secret relationships. Then a friend had given him a drug called Ecstasy, and Peter had shared it with Lisa Burnette, a fellow church member in Frankfort. Something had gone wrong, and she had died. They found her body in the Kentucky River.

The next unfortunate incident had occurred when Miriam Friedland, Oliver Russell's secretary, had had a bad reaction and lapsed into a coma. *Not my fault*, Peter Tager thought. It had not harmed him. Miriam had obviously been on too many other drugs.

Then, of course, there was poor Chloe Houston. He had run into her in a corridor of the White House where she was looking for a rest room.

She had recognized him instantly and was impressed. 'You're Peter Tager! I see you on television all the time.'

'Well, I'm delighted. Can I help you with something?'

'I was looking for a ladies' room.' She was young and very pretty.

'There are no public rest rooms in the White House, miss.'

'Oh, dear.'

He said conspiratorially, 'I think I can help you out. Come with me.' He had led her upstairs to a private bathroom and waited outside for her. When she came out, he asked, 'Are you just visiting Washington?'

'Yes.'

'Why don't you let me show you the real Washington? Would you like that?' He could feel that she was attracted to him.

'I – I certainly would – if it isn't too much trouble.'

'For someone as pretty as you? No trouble at all. We'll start with dinner tonight.'

She smiled. 'That sounds exciting.'

'I promise you it will be. Now, you mustn't tell anyone we're meeting. It's our secret.'

'I won't. I promise.'

'I have a high-level meeting with the Russian government at the Monroe Arms Hotel tonight.' He could see that she was impressed. 'We can have dinner at the Imperial Suite there, afterward. Why don't you meet me there about seven o'clock?'

She looked at him and nodded excitedly. 'All right.'

He had explained to her what she had to do to get inside the suite. 'There won't be any problem. Just call me to let me know you're there.'

And she had.

* * *

In the beginning, Chloe Houston had been reluctant. When Peter took her in his arms, she said, 'Don't. I – I'm a virgin.'

That made him all the more excited. 'I don't want you to do anything you don't want to do,' he assured her. 'We'll just sit and talk.'

'Are you disappointed?'

He squeezed her hand. 'Not at all, my dear.'

He took out a bottle of liquid Ecstasy and poured some into two glasses.

'What is that?' Chloe asked.

'It's an energy booster. Cheers.' He raised his glass in a toast and watched as she finished the liquid in her glass.

'It's good,' Chloe said.

They had spent the next half hour talking, and Peter had waited as the drug began to work. Finally, he moved next to Chloe and put his arms around her, and this time there was no resistance.

'Get undressed,' he said.

'Yes.'

Peter's eyes followed her into the bathroom, and he began to undress. Chloe came out a few minutes later, naked, and he became excited at the sight of her young, nubile body. She was beautiful. Chloe got into bed beside him, and they made love. She was inexperienced, but the fact that she was a virgin gave Peter the extra excitement that he needed.

In the middle of a sentence, Chloe had sat up in bed, suddenly dizzy.

'Are you all right, my dear?'

'I – I'm fine. I just feel a little –' She held on to the side of the bed for a moment. 'I'll be right back.'

She got up. And as Peter watched, Chloe stumbled, fell, and smashed her head against the sharp corner of the iron table.

'Chloe!' He leaped out of bed and hurried to her side. 'Chloe!'

He could feel no pulse. *Oh, God,* he thought. *How could you do this to me? It wasn't my fault. She slipped.*

He looked around. *They mustn't trace me to this suite.* He had quickly gotten dressed, gone into the bathroom, moistened a towel, and begun polishing the surfaces of every place he might have touched. He picked up Chloe's purse, looked around to make sure there were no signs that he had been there, and took the elevator down to the garage. The last thing he had done was to wipe his fingerprints off the elevator buttons. When Paul Yerby had surfaced as a threat, Tager had used his connections to dispose of him. There was no way anyone could connect Tager to Chloe's death.

And then the blackmail letter had come. Carl Gorman, the hotel clerk, had seen him. Peter had sent Sime to get rid of Gorman, telling him that it was to protect the president.

That should have been the end of the problem.

But Frank Lonergan had started asking questions, and

it had been necessary to dispose of him, too. Now there was another nosy reporter to deal with.

So there were only two threats left: Marianne Gorman and Dana Evans.

And Sime was on his way to kill them both.

Twenty-Three

Marianne Gorman repeated, 'You know – the one with the eye patch. Peter Tager.'

Dana was stunned. 'Are you sure?'

'Well, it's hard not to recognize someone who looks like that, isn't it?'

'I need to use your phone.' Dana hurried over to the telephone and dialed Matt Baker's number. His secretary answered.

'Mr Baker's office.'

'It's Dana. I have to talk to him. It's urgent.'

'Hold on, please.'

A moment later, Matt Baker was on the line. 'Dana – is anything wrong?'

She took a deep breath. 'Matt, I just found out who was with Chloe Houston when she died.'

'We know who it was. It was –'

'Peter Tager.'

'What?' It was a shout.

'I'm with the sister of Carl Gorman, the hotel clerk who was murdered. Carl Gorman saw Tager wiping his fingerprints off the elevator in the hotel garage the night Chloe Houston died. Gorman sent Tager a blackmail letter, and I think Tager had him murdered. I have a camera crew here. Do you want me to go on the air with this?'

'Don't do anything right now!' Matt ordered. 'I'll handle it. Call me back in ten minutes.'

He slammed down the receiver and headed for the White Tower. Leslie was in her office.

'Leslie, you can't print –'

She turned and held up the mock-up of the head-line: MURDER WARRANT SERVED ON PRESIDENT RUSSELL.

'Look at this, Matt.' Her voice was filled with exaltation.

'Leslie – I have news for you. There's –'

'This is all the news I need.' She nodded smugly. 'I told you you'd come back. You couldn't stay away, could you? This was just too big to walk away from, wasn't it, Matt? You need me. You'll always need me.'

He stood there, looking at her, wondering: *What happened to turn her into this kind of woman? It's still not too late to save her.* 'Leslie –'

'Don't be embarrassed because you made a mistake,' Leslie said complacently. 'What did you want to say?'

Matt Baker looked at her for a long time. 'I wanted to say goodbye, Leslie.'

She watched him turn and walk out the door.

Twenty-Four

'What's going to happen to me?' Marianne Gorman asked.

'Don't worry,' Dana told her. 'You'll be protected.' She made a quick decision. 'Marianne, we're going to do a live interview, and I'll turn the tape of it over to the FBI. As soon as we finish the interview, I'll get you away from here.'

Outside, there was the sound of a car screaming to a stop.

Marianne hurried over to the window. 'Oh, my God!'

Dana moved to her side. 'What is it?'

Sime Lombardo was getting out of the car. He looked at the house, then headed toward the door.

Marianne stammered, 'That's the – the – other man who was here asking about Carl, the day Carl was killed. I'm sure he had something to do with his murder.'

Dana picked up the phone and hastily dialed a number.

'Mr Hawkins's office.'

'Nadine, I have to talk to him right away.'

'He's not in. He should be back in about –'

'Let me talk to Nate Erickson.'

Nate Erickson, Hawkins's assistant, came on the phone. 'Dana?'

'Nate – I need help fast. I have a breaking news story. I want you to put me on live, immediately.'

'I can't do that,' Erickson protested. 'Tom would have to authorize it.'

'There's no time for that,' Dana exploded.

Outside the window, Dana saw Sime Lombardo moving toward the front door.

In the news van, Vernon Mills looked at his watch. 'Are we going to do this interview or not? I have a date.'

Inside the house, Dana was saying, 'It's a matter of life and death, Nate. You've got to put me on live. For God's sake, do it now!' She slammed the receiver down, stepped over to the television set, and turned it on Channel Six.

A soap opera was in progress. An older man was talking to a young woman.

'You never really understood me, did you, Kristen?'

'The truth is that I understand you too well. That's why I want a divorce, George.'

'Is there someone else?'

Dana hurried into the bedroom and turned on the set there.

Sime Lombardo was at the front door. He knocked.

'Don't open it,' Dana warned Marianne. Dana checked to make sure that her microphone was live. The knocking at the door became louder.

'Let's get out of here,' Marianne whispered. 'The back –'

At that moment, the front door splintered open and Sime charged into the room. He closed the door behind him and looked at the two women. 'Ladies. I see that I have both of you.'

Desperately, Dana glanced toward the television set.

'If there is someone else, it's your fault, George.'

'Perhaps I am at fault, Kristen.'

Sime Lombardo took a .22 caliber semiautomatic pistol out of his pocket and started screwing a silencer onto the barrel.

'No!' Dana said. 'You can't –'

Sime raised the gun. 'Shut up. Into the bedroom – go on.'

Marianne mumbled, 'Oh, my God!'

'Listen . . .' Dana said. 'We can –'

'I told you to shut up. Now move.'

Dana looked at the television set.

'I've always believed in second chances, Kristen. I don't want to lose what we had – what we could have again.'

The same voices echoed from the television set in the bedroom.

Sime commanded, 'I told you two to move! Let's get this over with.'

. As the two panicky women took a tentative step toward the bedroom, the red light on the camera in the corner suddenly turned on. The images of Kristen and George faded from the screen and an announcer's voice said, 'We interrupt this program to take you now live to a breaking story in the Wheaton area.'

As the soap opera faded, the Gorman living room suddenly appeared on the screen. Dana and Marianne were in the foreground, Sime in the background. Sime stopped, confused, as he saw himself on the television set.

'What – what the hell is this?'

In the van, the technicians watched the new image flash on the screen. 'My God,' Vernon Mills said. 'We're live!'

Dana glanced at the screen and breathed a silent prayer. She turned to face the camera. 'This is Dana Evans coming to you live from the home of Carl Gorman, who was murdered a few days ago. We're interviewing a man who has some information about his murder.' She turned to face him. 'So – would you like to tell us exactly what happened?'

Lombardo stood there, paralyzed, watching himself on the screen, licking his lips. 'Hey!'

From the television set, he heard himself say, 'Hey!' and he saw his image move, as he swung toward Dana. 'What – what the hell are you doing? What kind of trick is this?'

'It's not a trick. We're on the air, live. There are two million people watching us.'

Lombardo saw his image on the screen and hastily put the gun back into his pocket.

Dana glanced at Marianne Gorman, then looked Sime Lombardo square in the eye. 'Peter Tager is behind the murder of Carl Gorman, isn't he?'

In the Daly Building, Nick Reese was in his office when an assistant rushed in. 'Quick! Take a look at this! They're at Gorman's house.' He turned the television set to Channel Six, and the picture flashed on the screen.

'Did Peter Tager tell you to kill Carl Gorman?'

'I don't know what you're talking about. Turn that damned television set off before I –'

'Before you what? Are you going to kill us in front of two million people?'

'Jesus!' Nick Reese shouted. 'Get some patrol cars out there, fast!'

In the Blue Room in the White House, Oliver and Jan' were watching station WTE, stunned.

'*Peter?*' Oliver said slowly. 'I can't believe it!'

Peter Tager's secretary hurried into his office. 'Mr Tager, I think you had better turn on Channel Six.' She gave him a nervous look and hurried out again. Peter Tager looked after her, puzzled. He picked up the remote and pressed a button, and the television set came to life.

Dana was saying, '. . . and was Peter Tager also responsible for the death of Chloe Houston?'

'I don't know anything about that. You'll have to ask Tager.'

Peter Tager looked at the television set unbelievingly. *This can't be happening! God wouldn't do this to me!* He sprang to his feet and hurried toward the door. *I'm not going to let them get me. I'll hide!* And then he stopped. *Where? Where can I hide?* He walked slowly back to his desk and sank into a chair. Waiting.

In her office, Leslie Stewart was watching the interview, in shock.

Peter Tager? No! No! No! Leslie snatched up the phone and pressed a number. 'Lyle, stop that story! It must not go out! Do you hear me? It –'

Over the phone she heard him say, 'Miss Stewart, the papers hit the streets half an hour ago. You said . . .'

Slowly, Leslie replaced the receiver. She looked at the headline of the *Washington Tribune*: MURDER WARRANT SERVED ON PRESIDENT RUSSELL.

Then she looked up at the framed front page on the wall: DEWEY DEFEATS TRUMAN.

'*You're going to be even more famous than you are now, Miss Stewart. The whole world is going to know your name.*'

Tomorrow she would be the laughingstock of the world.

At the Gorman home, Sime Lombardo took one last, frantic look at himself on the television screen and said, 'I'm getting out of here.'

He hurried to the front door and opened it. Half a dozen squad cars were screaming to a stop outside.

Twenty-Five

Jeff Connors was at Dulles International Airport with Dana, waiting for Kemal's plane to arrive.

'He's been through hell,' Dana explained nervously. 'He – he's not like other little boys. I mean – don't be surprised if he doesn't show any emotion.' She desperately wanted Jeff to like Kemal.

Jeff sensed her anxiety. 'Don't worry, darling. I'm sure he's a wonderful boy.'

'Here it comes!'

They looked up and watched the small speck in the sky grow larger and larger until it became a shining 747.

Dana squeezed Jeff's hand tightly. 'He's here.'

The passengers were deplaning. Dana watched anxiously as they exited one by one. 'Where's –?'

And there he was. He was dressed in the outfit that Dana had bought him in Sarajevo, and his face was freshly washed. He came down the ramp slowly, and when he saw Dana, he stopped. The two of them stood there, motionless, staring at each other. And then they were running toward each other, and Dana was holding him, and his good arm was squeezing her tightly, and they were both crying.

When Dana found her voice, she said, 'Welcome to America, Kemal.'

He nodded. He could not speak.

'Kemal, I want you to meet my friend. This is Jeff Connors.'

Jeff leaned down. 'Hello, Kemal. I've been hearing a lot about you.'

Kemal clung to Dana fiercely.

'You'll be coming to live with me,' Dana said. 'Would you like that?'

Kemal nodded. He would not let go of her.

Dana looked at her watch. 'We have to leave. I'm covering a speech at the White House.'

It was a perfect day. The sky was a deep, clear blue, and a cooling breeze was blowing in from the Potomac River.

They stood in the Rose Garden, with three dozen other television and newspaper reporters. Dana's camera was focused on the president, who stood on a podium with Jan at his side.

President Oliver Russell was saying, 'I have an important announcement to make. At this moment, there is a meeting of the heads of state of the United Arab Emirates, Libya, Iran, and Syria, to discuss a lasting peace treaty with Israel. I received word this morning that the meeting is going extremely well and that the treaty should be signed within the next day or two. It is of the utmost importance that the Congress of the United States solidly support us in helping this vital effort.' Oliver turned to the man standing next to him. 'Senator Todd Davis.'

Senator Davis stepped up to the microphone, wearing his trademark white suit and white, broad-brimmed leghorn hat, beaming at the crowd. 'This is truly a historic moment in the history of our great country. For many years, as you know, I have been striving to bring about peace between Israel and the Arab countries. It has been a long and difficult task, but now, at last, with the help and guidance of our wonderful president, I am happy to say that our efforts are finally coming to fruition.' He turned to Oliver. 'We should all congratulate our great president on the magnificent part he has played in helping us to bring this about . . .'

Dana was thinking, *One war is coming to an end. Perhaps this is a beginning. Maybe one day we'll have a world where adults learn to settle their problems with love instead of hate, a world where children can grow up without ever hearing the obscene sounds of bombs and machine-gun fire, without fear of their limbs being torn apart by faceless strangers.* She turned to look at Kemal, who was excitedly whispering to Jeff. Dana smiled. Jeff had proposed to her. Kemal would have a father. They were going to be a family. *How did I get so lucky?* Dana wondered. The speeches were winding down.

The cameraman swung the camera away from the podium and moved into a close-up of Dana. She looked into the lens.

'This is Dana Evans, reporting for WTE, Washington, D.C.'